Novels by James Thayer

The Gold Swan
Force 12
Terminal Event
Man of the Century
Five Past Midnight
White Star
S-Day: A Memoir of the Invasion of England
Ringer
Pursuit
The Earhart Betrayal
The Stettin Secret
The Hess Cross

James Thayer

The Gold Swan

A Novel

Simon & Schuster
New York   London   Toronto
Sydney   Singapore

SIMON & SCHUSTER
Rockefeller Center
1230 Avenue of the Americas
New York, NY 10020

SIMON & SCHUSTER and colophon are registered trademarks
of Simon & Schuster, Inc.

For information regarding special discounts for bulk purchases,
please contact Simon & Schuster Special Sales at
1-800-456-6798 or business@simonandschuster.com

Designed by Jeanette Olender
Manufactured in the United States of America

10 9 8 7 6 5 4 3 2 1

Library of Congress Cataloging-in-Publication Data
Thayer, James Stewart.
The gold swan : a novel / James Thayer.
p. cm.
1. Architects—Fiction. 2. Skyscrapers—Fiction.
3. Hong Kong (China)—Fiction. I. Title.
PS3570.H347 G65 2002
813'.54—dc21   2002021753
ISBN 0-684-86286-7

My heartfelt thanks to

John D. Reagh III, Peggy Williams,
Stephen N. Roberts, Dr. K. Rainer Massarsch,
to my editor, Michael Korda,
and to my wonderful wife, Patricia W. Thayer.

For my brother, Jay McMillan Thayer,
and his wife, Laurie Dinnison Thayer, and their sons,
Joseph Greenough Thayer and Ulysses Jay Thayer.

Part One

We shape our buildings: thereafter they shape us.

WINSTON CHURCHILL

1

I had just become an orphan, just that moment. Made an orphan in a terrible way, though I didn't know it yet, walking along Hollywood Road, passing a shop that sold gilt birdcages and dozen-armed Buddhas, and making my way toward my apartment in the Mid-Levels. So I had a few more minutes of peace.

"You are thinking of moving back to the States?" my friend Jay Lee asked, stepping along beside me on the sidewalk.

"I was only hired for the Swan's construction," I replied. "And I don't have any plans here after it's done."

"Maybe we can hire you," he suggested. "We've got a great need for your skills. You could stay here."

"Nah. I'm sick of kimchi. I can't even stand the smell. I've got to get away from it."

"Kimchi is Korean food, not Chinese. Get it right, will you?"

Lee was a head shorter than me. His hair was in a military cut, and so black it was blue in the gray light. His nose was flat against his face, and his eyes were slanted. Of course, almost all eyes in Hong Kong are slanted. Lee was wearing a dove-gray suit and a red and blue club tie. The suit was well tailored and didn't show the holster under his left shoulder. He was chief of the Hong Kong Police Force's Organized Crime and Triad Bureau. His name was Lee Yik-kee, but he asked that his *gweilo* friends call him Jay.

"Besides, now that your police department reports to Beijing, I'd never get a job with you. They don't like me in the Forbidden City."

I was sticking him, and he knew it. Still, he couldn't help himself.

"Our force does not—I repeat, does not—report to Beijing. How many times do I have to tell you that?"

I started to breathe heavily as we walked up the hill. All around us, buildings rose in even formation. Hong Kong is known for daring architecture, but not here, partway up Victoria Peak, where apartment buildings, dozens upon dozens of them, looked as if they had rolled out of a factory on a conveyor belt. Young Filipino women passed us as they walked downhill toward the Star Ferry. They worked as nannies in the Mid-Levels. The sun was behind the hills, and day was quickly fading to darkness.

Faint echoes from a siren came from all directions. I turned to look downhill, using it as an excuse for a breather. My back was already damp. I had been in Hong Kong ten years. Most of that time I was either sweating from the heat and humidity or shivering from the over air-conditioned offices and shops. That and the smells. I had never become accustomed to Hong Kong's ripeness, and still, after a decade here, a scent will rise up from some hole in the ground or reach out some window and fairly grab me by the head and turn me around. I'm from Medford, Oregon. Nothing smells bad in Medford.

"Here he comes again," Jay Lee said. "Where does he get the stamina, I wonder?"

I followed Lee's gaze. The shrill sound of a siren echoed off the buildings, seeming to come from everywhere. I spotted the flashing lights, several banks of them, coming our way.

Lee laughed. "He's got motorcycles trailing his car this time, not just in front. It looks like the arrival of the German general staff."

Every fifth car in Hong Kong was a Mercedes, but few were like this. The black sedan was stretched to a car-and-a-half and had medallions on the front bumper and two small pennants mounted above the front fenders. Lee laughed again.

I asked, "Where does he find time to do his work?"

"He's got a staff of a hundred, I heard. Maybe they do all the work. Maybe he uses a pencil to scratch out something on a napkin and then passes it to them."

The procession worked its way up the hill, the motorcycles flashing red and blue, other cars and pedestrians not in a particular hurry to get out of the way. Lee and I crossed the street at an intersection. The Mercedes caught up with us and pulled into the curved drive in front of the building on the opposite side of the street. Several photographers were waiting, and a TV camera crew.

"I wonder who he is visiting tonight," I said. "Who lives in that building?"

Lee replied, "Wu Jintau, one of the East Asia Shipping Wus. And Quin Jemin, who owns the forty Quick Copy shops here and in Macau. Those're the only ones I know offhand."

"Must be nice, never having to buy your own meals," I said.

"There's Wu Jintau and his wife, coming out from under the portico to greet him."

The policemen left their motorcycles to form a loose cordon on the entrance walkway. The Mercedes driver emerged from the car and rushed to a rear door to open it. The policemen left their motorcycles to escort John Llewellyn as he rose from the car, his silver hair like a beacon in the failing light. Llewellyn was slender, with narrow shoulders and a long neck. He was wearing a blue suit, and he stepped quickly toward Wu, his hand extended. Cameras flashed. A reporter called out a question, and Llewellyn appeared to ask his host for permission to pause for a moment to meet the press. When passersby began to gather, the policemen gently held them back.

"He's like Ben Franklin in Paris," I said. "Crowds gather everywhere he goes."

"Who is Ben Franklin?" Lee asked.

I glanced at him. "Are you asking that just to kill me dead?"

After pausing a moment for the photographers, and carefully including the Wus in most of the poses, John Llewellyn allowed Wu and his wife to escort him under the overhanging roof and into the building. The onlookers began to go their own ways.

Lee said, "After what Llewellyn has accomplished, he deserves the acclaim. Let him have his crowds and press conferences and motor-

cades. He has earned them. Every single person in Hong Kong believes that, and you do, too."

"You like the thing?" I asked. We resumed our walk up the sidewalk.

"Now *you* are trying to kill *me* dead, Clay."

"I mean, you've never mentioned if you even like the damned
thing, you're always talking about police work. You like it?"

"It's the loveliest and most dramatic man-made structure on earth.
Pure and simple, no arguments. You bet I like it."

Lee deliberately larded his English with Americanisms when speak-
ing with me. Had he been conversing with my Australian counterpart,
Lee would have said, "Too right I like it." When he talked with the
Aussie and me at the same time, it was an entertaining performance.

"Well, I haven't made up my mind about it," I said. "It's just not
very Hong Kong, is all."

"The trouble with you, Clay, is that your image of Hong Kong is of
junks and coolie hats."

We reached the level of the next intersection, then turned for a view
toward the harbor. Pedestrians flowed around us.

The tower was framed between the buildings, and again, for the
thousandth time, it astonished me. At 2,500 feet high, the Fifth Millennium China Tower was the tallest man-made structure on earth,
two-and-a-half times higher than the Eiffel Tower, more than two
Statues of Liberty taller than any other man-made structure in the
world. It rose from an island in Victoria Bay north of the Hong Kong
Convention and Exhibition Center, far enough out into the bay so
that it would remain an island once the reclaimed land projects off the
Wan Chai coastline were completed. The tower's island was man-
made.

Few folks in Hong Kong called it the Fifth Millennium China
Tower, a phrase that Jay Lee had said was as much a mouthful in Cantonese as in English. The tower was known in Hong Kong and around
the world as the Gold Swan, and for good reason. It resembled no
other structure in the world. It wasn't a needle, like the CN Tower
in Toronto, nor was it an obelisk, like the Washington Monument.

Rather, the tower was in the form of the moon in its first quarter, a grand swoop. The structure's midpoint, which was 1,250 feet above grade, was fully 500 feet off of the vertical alignment between top and bottom.

The tower had razor-sharp convex and concave edges. Like the Seagram Building in New York City, it was clad in bronze from top to bottom. The structure resembled a dragon's neck, or the Communist sickle, or an Arabian scimitar, and these nicknames were traded back and forth in the press during much of the tower's construction.

With viewing platforms and restaurants on top of the giant curve, and with the bronze glowing in the sun, a consensus developed that the tower most closely resembled a long and graceful gold swan's neck and head. So while the official name of the tower is still the Fifth Millennium China Tower, Hong Kong citizens took to calling it the Gold Swan. It had been under construction four years, and it was scheduled to open to the public in one month. Hong Kong and all of China were preparing for the event, which organizers promised would rival an Olympics opening ceremony.

"Come on, admit it," Lee said, standing at my shoulder. "It's breathtaking."

"I heard John Llewellyn and his firm generated ten thousand architectural drawings for the tower."

"And five thousand people have worked on it for four years," Lee said. "Those are big numbers."

"They going to finish it on time?" I asked. "It looks like it's going to be close."

"Beijing will make it happen. They are betting heavily on the Gold Swan and its inaugural week."

Two construction derricks were still attached to the viewing deck's roof, and a number of the bronze plates near the top had yet to be put into place. The temporary elevator, used to take workers and smaller supplies up the tower, was still in place, and it was also curved, following the flow of the swan's neck, an ingenious design in its own right. The construction elevator was scheduled to come down within two weeks.

John Llewellyn had insisted that the man-made island on which the tower sat be as free of "disastrous eye clutter"—his term—as possible. So the only other permanent structure on the concrete pad at the tower's base was a one-story terminal, where sightseers from Hong Kong and Kowloon would disembark from the ferries. The terminal was deliberately plain, as close to invisible as architecture could make it, and it was a hundred yards from the tower. Also on the island, but to be removed prior to the opening celebrations, were ten construction shacks, forklifts, construction supplies, portable lavatories, Dumpsters for waste, and piles of this and that. A temporary wooden dock that had been used for early arrivals of crew and material via construction launches and barges was being dismantled. A floating crane, two barges, and a tug were near the wooden dock.

I asked, "How long will it be before a freighter loses its way in a fog and plows into the island, do you think?"

"Every port has similar inconveniences."

"When did you become such a defender of the thing?"

Lee gazed at the tower. "It took me a while, but now I'm a convert. The Gold Swan has become China's new icon, just as it was meant to be. It has already replaced the Great Wall as the symbol of China. The tower is our Sydney Opera House and our Eiffel Tower and our Brandenburg Gate."

"I didn't think the Great Wall needed to be replaced," I said. I wondered why I sounded so sour.

"The Great Wall looks backward in time," Lee replied. "The Gold Swan looks forward. The twentieth century was America's. The twenty-first will be China's."

"You believe that?"

"The people in Beijing who commissioned the Gold Swan believe it," Lee said, "and that tower is their announcement of it to the world."

I studied the tower for a moment. John Llewellyn had created a monument that was filled with contradictions. It was the tallest structure ever created by man, and made of steel and bronze, those metals that are the very embodiment of solidity, and it was a massive thing.

Yet it was also slender, with delicate edges, and was one long, elegant curve that some architecture critics were calling feminine. It was solid and inert, planted out there in the middle of the harbor, yet it was also soaring, more than seven hundred feet higher than the Peak, reaching skyward in a fluid, rounded motion, touching the clouds. And it was a chameleon, its bronze casing throwing back the gold of the sun, and also reflecting images of passing clouds and the restless water of the harbor, endlessly changing as the day unfolded.

"It seems alive, doesn't it?" Lee asked.

I nodded. "Maybe that's it. I can't get a fix on the tower, as if it's alive, moving out ahead of judgments I might make about it."

The peal of another siren worked its way between the buildings. After a moment an ambulance rounded a corner below us and came up the hill. It was a white van with a broad red stripe along the body.

We started up the sidewalk again. The ambulance passed us.

"That's the trouble with you Americans," Lee announced. "You don't think big enough."

"Yeah?"

He said, "You've only got the Empire State Building and the Gateway Arch and—what?—the Space Needle. Midgets, all of them."

I lived on Kennedy Road near the Junior School, in an apartment tower called the New Horizon. The building is undistinguished in every respect except that I can afford it. My apartment has one bedroom, a small kitchen, a living room and a bathroom, and I can give anyone a tour of the apartment by just having them turn a circle. San Francisco, which I've always viewed as densely populated, has thirty thousand people per square mile. By comparison, some parts of Hong Kong have five-hundred thousand. It's a crowded place, and I don't complain about my small quarters.

"What are you doing with your old man tonight?" Lee asked.

"Going out for Chinese food, like we do every night. Luckily this city has a lot of it. My dad loves the stuff."

"It irks me when *gweilos* call our cuisine *Chinese food*. There's Chiuchow, Sichuan, Pekingese, Yangzhou, and a dozen others."

"Then why can't I tell the difference?"

Lee smiled. "It's a deliberate act of maintaining ignorance on your part."

"I don't like to argue with a fellow carrying a pistol."

"I suspect you take your father to the first noodle bar you come to and eat the same thing every night. Noodle this and rice that, night after night. Am I right?"

My father had visited me four times a year in Hong Kong since I arrived here. Three days in advance, he would call and tell me when he was going to show up. His name is Alan Williams, and he is a retired orchardist, who owned seven thousand acres of trees—mostly pears, but some other fruit, too—near Medford, Oregon. His orchard was a huge spread, an operation employing forty people year-round and another four-hundred during the harvest. My father had built it up, acquiring smaller orchards one after another all his life, sometimes taking big risks with the bankers. I believe it broke his heart when I decided I didn't want to be a farmer, though he never let on. I just never took to standing out among rows of fruit trees. He sold the farm a few years ago to Harry & David, the Medford-based fruit-packer and gift-box–shipper, which already owned thousands of acres of producing trees. My father was suddenly a wealthy retiree, and he realized that he had been almost nowhere in his life, and I mean I don't think he had left Oregon more than two or three times before he retired, except for his time in the navy; so when he visited me the first time in Hong Kong, the fact that there was some world beyond the Medford Valley hit him with the force of revelation. He has been coming back since, and I try to show him a good time. He won't let me pay for anything during his visits.

My mother died when I was twelve, is why I haven't mentioned her. Liver cancer got her, and quickly. She was there and then she was gone. That was the first thing to break my father's heart. My not wanting to grow pears was another. I wish I had more memories of my mother.

"I tell you what," Jay Lee said. "Tonight let me take you and your father to a place I know. You and he will get some real Hong Kong food, not this touristy stuff I'm sure you are feeding your dad."

"I was going to take him to an American-style steakhouse tonight. Give us a break from soy sauce."

"My cousin owns a small restaurant near the Man Mo Temple. He'll treat us like emperors." Lee had met my father several times.

"Tell him that as a matter of principle I don't eat eyeballs, tentacle suckers, or hair from any species. And an American would say 'treat us like kings,' not 'treat us like emperors.' It's a subtle thing, but you need to know it."

I was teasing him, but he worked on his American English so diligently that I could see concentration on his face as he registered my correction, tucking it away to use later. He would never make the mistake again.

Three pajama-clad amahs passed us, chatting gaily, sounding like caged birds at a tea house. One of them had blazing gold front teeth.

I asked, "Did your cousin come here doing the breast stroke, two strokes ahead of the sharks, like you?"

"We weren't swimming. We had a raft made of tied-together inner tubes. How many times do I have to tell you? At least, we weren't swimming when we started out. And no, his family came over five years later."

During the Cultural Revolution, Jay Lee's parents had paddled to Hong Kong across Mirs Bay, bringing their three children with them. Five of their six inner tubes leaked—they had been manufactured by the Red Star People's Tire Plant in Canton, so little more could have been expected, Lee's father would say later—and by the time the family reached Hong Kong's shore, both parents and the oldest children were in the water, clinging to the last inner tube, on which sat the baby. Almost as soon as his clothes were dry, Lee's father opened a *dai pai dong*—a market stand, which was a two-foot-square folding table—that sold deep-fried pig's intestines. He quickly determined that more profit could be made from selling pirated Rolling Stones cassettes. After a few years passed, he rented three parking spots from a chemical company in Sham Shui on the Kowloon side and began selling used cars—some stolen, some not. Then he rented eight parking spots. When the chemical company moved to the New Territories, Lee's father purchased its warehouse and parking lot, and inveigled the Bavarian Motor Works to grant him a distributorship, BMW hoping to find the same Hong Kong reception that its archrival Mercedes-Benz had received.

By the time Jay Lee was eighteen, his father could send him to the prestigious Hong Kong University, and then to the University of Michigan for a master's degree in police science. I had asked Lee once if he had ever thought about going into his father's car business, and he replied that he had given it "about as much thought as you gave to growing pears."

Lee's father was now a member of the Hong Kong Jockey Club—that singular mark of having arrived in Hong Kong society—and owned a home—a compound, really, with two houses and water gardens—just off Peak Road. He had retired, but Lee's two brothers ran the BMW business, and the Ferrari and Jaguar dealerships the father had picked up along the way.

Lee's place was two streets west, and we often walked home together. The exterior of my apartment building is concrete made to resemble sandstone. Each unit has a balcony, so the sides of the building look like waffle irons. Chinese architecture traditionally avoids the stiff and the rectilinear, but in the Mid-Levels this tradition could not compete with the demands of efficiency caused by limited space. My building was one big block. From my deck on the twentieth floor I have a view of the decks of a similar building across the street. I once counted the buildings that would have to be removed for me to be able to look at the harbor, and it came to six. The top two floors of my building have harbor views, and cost four times more than I pay for the same square footage.

I have never believed in premonitions, which assume the ability to know the future or to communicate by telepathy. Such nonsense was at odds with the mental rigor of my police training. But as Lee and I crossed Caine Road, I saw the ambulance's flashing lights splashing against the sandstone wall of my building and I was abruptly invaded by a sense of fear, as if a cold brand had been applied to my back.

"Jay?" I said, more a gasp.

He looked at me. "Yeah?" After a moment he added, "You okay?"

"That ambulance." I pointed, as if he might not see it otherwise. I discovered that I had stopped on the sidewalk. Lee had pulled up next to me. The ambulance that was parked next to my apartment building was frightening me, for no good reason. That's what I mean by a premonition. Two police cars were parked a few yards down the street, their rotating bubble lights sending out blue and red beams.

"Something is wrong," I said dully.

"That's usually the case when an ambulance shows up," he said lightly.

I started toward the ambulance. Attendants were pulling a collapsible litter from its cargo bay. I sidestepped a palm planter and walked under a wrought-iron arbor along which bougainvillea grew, then passed between two concrete benches. Jay Lee followed me.

Three policemen were standing around a body, which was splayed out near the base of the building. The body's legs were bent at unnatural angles. The concrete patio and the benches and policemen and the body were washed repeatedly in red and yellow lights from the ambulance. The ambulance attendants rolled the litter up to the body.

I stepped nearer. The ugly premonition wouldn't go away. A policeman walked in my direction to turn me away, but Lee showed him his badge and he allowed us to approach the body.

I knelt near the fractured corpse. The skull had cracked open on impact, and gray brains were visible under strands of white hair.

Jay Lee put his hand on my shoulder. It was my father.

2

Police headquarters are in Caine House on Arsenal Street in Wan Chai. Jay Lee and I were shown into the commissioner's office. The commissioner rose from behind his massive mahogany desk to shake my hand. I had met Kwok Kan-yan several times, always on business. I held him in high regard, as did most everyone in his force. He gestured toward a chair in front of his desk. He nodded at his subordinate, Jay Lee, who took the chair next to mine. The desk rested on a thick blue rug adorned with impressions of the Hong Kong police seal.

When I glanced at a large table globe next to his desk, the commissioner asked, "Can you tell me when this globe was manufactured?"

"A long while ago," I ventured. Metal time dials were on both the north and south poles. The twenty-inch orb was mounted on a basswood stand.

He turned the globe several degrees and pointed at the United States. "The Colorado Territory in your country is not labeled here. The territory was organized in 1861." He spoke English with a clipped British accent. He turned the globe and pointed again. "But the town of Nicholaievsk in Russia, just north of Manchuria, is on the globe. Nicholaievsk was founded in 1851. So, this globe was manufactured sometime in that ten-year period."

"Detective work." I smiled at him. "Once again you live up to your reputation, Commissioner."

He returned the grin. "A hollow globe, a hollow compliment. A fine symmetry. Hong Kong is teaching you well."

I might not have gotten this far into the commissioner of police's office without Jay Lee's help. Lee was rising quickly in the force, and had Kwok's eye, I had heard.

Commissioner Kwok had a smooth, usually expressionless face, except for an occasional lift of the corners of his mouth that passed for his smile. His forehead was high and unlined. He was in his sixties but looked two decades younger, and his eyes were lively, reflecting his energy. He was wearing a suit and tie, not a uniform. His office was paneled in oak, and heavy red curtains framed the windows. A computer monitor was on the cabinet behind him.

He said, "You have come to inquire about the investigation into your father's death."

"It's been a week. If you could give me an update . . ."

"We have completed the investigation." Kwok spread his palms on his desk, as if flattening a manuscript. "It was a simple matter, really."

"Simple because you have concluded it was suicide?"

"We have found no evidence your father's death was anything but suicide."

I bit down, trying not to angrily blurt out something I would regret. After a few seconds I managed, "My father would never commit suicide."

Jay Lee nodded in agreement. He had some courage, siding against his superior.

The commissioner pressed a button on an intercom box on his desk and said something in Cantonese. A uniformed sergeant immediately entered the room from a side door and handed Kwok an expandable file folder. As the sergeant returned through the door, the commissioner stood to lean over the desk to hand me the file.

I was startled. The results of investigations were usually pried from a police force only by subpoena, yet I had just been given the file. On it in English was my father's name, Alan Williams, and then Chinese script, presumably his name in Cantonese.

"Mr. Williams, look through the file. Take your time. You will find that because of your reputation, and the regard which the Hong Kong

Police Force holds you in, our investigation of your father's death was particularly thorough."

I opened the file, averting my eyes from the first items, large photographs of my father's shattered body. I found the Preliminary Scene Assessment and read through it. Then I found the Scene Walkthrough, the Initial Documentation, and the Scene Security Report. The documents were in English and Cantonese.

"Note that we fingerprinted every surface in your apartment," Kwok said.

I nodded. "You left some dust behind."

"You must have no friends," the commissioner said, not unkindly. "We found only your and your father's fingerprints."

I lifted the fingerprint file out of the accordion file to leaf through it.

The commissioner said: "Whenever something comes in contact with another item, it either takes or leaves a portion of itself or picks up a portion of the other, as you know. So we flew in Shin Wing-kai from Singapore to look for footprints on your rug."

I wasn't in the mood to be impressed, but I was. I knew of Shin, and I also knew how difficult footwear impressions were to obtain from a carpet. Most investigations wouldn't have bothered.

"Your apartment was secured by the first officer on the scene, so there wasn't a lot of unaccounted traffic through your rooms before Shin arrived. He spent an entire day in your place, using an electrostatic dust lifter and lifting film. He found shoe imprints, but they appear to be yours and your father's, though we can't be absolutely certain of this. Lifting prints from carpets isn't an accurate science. You have big feet, and so did your father."

He may have been trying to lighten my mood, or he may have been telling me that it was unlikely a person of Chinese descent—with smaller shoes, most likely—had been in my apartment to murder my father.

When I lifted a folder labeled "Elimination Sample," Jay Lee said, "Your father forgot to flush the toilet."

"Perpetrators often use the bathroom at the scene of their crime," Kwok explained unnecessarily. "The urine we found was your father's, however."

Kwok and Lee said nothing while I spent five more minutes with the file. Evidence collection had been thorough.

Then the commissioner said: "Investigators have spoken with sixteen residents of your apartment building who live on your floor. No one saw a stranger on your floor anytime near your father's death. The doormen and two maintenance men have also been interviewed, as have the woman who owns the flower stall near the building's front door and the taxi drivers who frequent the stand half a block west of your building. Nothing unusual was discovered."

"Commissioner, I appreciate your department's attention to this." My anger had abated.

Police often give slight attention to suicides, not when there are perpetrators to catch in other crimes, but Commissioner Kwok had seen that a thorough investigation had been undertaken.

Still, I said, "But my father would never kill himself. I will never be convinced otherwise."

"You have overlooked two items in the file, Mr. Williams," Kwok said. "Small but significant facts."

"Look closely at the clothing inventory, the clothes your father was wearing when he died."

I dug around in the file and pulled it out.

"Do you see anything unusual?" Kwok asked.

"Afraid I don't."

"Your father's spectacles were in his pants pocket."

It took a moment for the information to register, and then I felt as if I were being made smaller by it. Ah, hell.

"As you know, Mr. Williams, suicides usually do not commit their final act while wearing their eyeglasses. They almost always put them into a pocket. As he lay there on the sidewalk under your balcony, his glasses were in his pocket."

"Well . . ." I had nothing to say.

"And please, Mr. Williams, examine the inventory of items found in your father's shaving kit."

I had glanced at it, without paying it much attention. I pulled it out of the folder again.

The commissioner said, "Among the items found in the kit was a prescription bottle containing Effexor."

I shook my head. I'd never heard of it.

"It's a brand name for venlafaxine, a medicine that corrects an imbalance of neurotransmitters."

"What's the medicine used for?"

"Clinical depression."

I hesitated. "My father wasn't depressed."

The commissioner didn't say anything.

"I mean, he wasn't."

Kwok puckered his mouth slightly.

"I was his son, his only family. I would've known."

Lee said, "We've taken enough of the commissioner's time, Clay."

"I mean, I would've known if my father was depressed." Wouldn't I?

The commissioner rose from his chair, stepped around the desk, and guided me toward the door. Jay Lee followed us.

"The file is still open," Kwok said. "If we turn up anything, you'll be informed immediately."

Which meant that the investigation was already history, and the file would soon be forgotten, stored at the police annex on Jaffe Road for five years, and then it would be microfilmed, with the originals destroyed, and placed even deeper in the annex. I thanked the commissioner for his time and his efforts, said goodbye to Lee, who returned to his office in the building, and then I crossed into Harcourt Garden. I had much to think about. And I had my sorrow, which I wasn't handling well.

* * *

I am senior security consultant for the Fifth Millennium China Tower, a title I share with an Australian and a German. We are all retired agents from our countries' national police services. Our task is to work with the Hong Kong police and China's Ministry of State Security to prevent a terrorist attack on the tower or its workers. The authorities in Beijing and Hong Kong knew how easy it would be to gain access to and to damage such a structure. Because of the World Trade Center disaster, our team had been given broad powers.

I sat on a bench in the park, near a bauhinia tree, with its pink and white orchidlike blossoms, each of them raised up to the sun. Longtail magpies picked at the grass near a bank of bamboo. The bamboo stems clicked together in the soft wind. It was still early in the morning, and two dozen people were nearby, going through their tai chi forms. They moved slowly, and in unison, flowing from one ancient form—snake, tiger, mantis—to another, seeking harmony in body and spirit. Visible behind them was the triangular, ultramodern, seventy-two-story Bank of China Tower. Maybe a third of the people crossing the park had cell phones to their ears.

I had been working hard. All of the security consultants had. I say this somewhat defensively because, truth be told, we hadn't turned up one scintilla of evidence that any organization from anywhere was planning an attack on the tower. The Australian, Jack Rainey, says the terrorists are fully aware that we—heavy-hitting police specialists—are on the job, and that's why there are no impending attacks, though he can't get it out without chuckling.

Prior to this job I had the same title at Hong Kong's new Chek Lap Kok airport. And before that I spent twenty years in the FBI, ending my career as deputy assistant director (DAD) in the Counterterrorism Division. I was thinking of retiring from the FBI after those two decades, tired of it, and wondering what I might do, maybe teaching police science at some university, or maybe working at Boeing in Seattle, in their security office, when the Chek Lap Kok Construction Security Agency contacted me. My first instinct was that I had no interest in working for the Hong Kong authorities, especially after the 1997 handover. But the CLKCSA recruiting officer (pronounced *click-sa;* the Chinese police are as addicted to acronyms as are United States police forces) told me, "We are extremely serious about security at the new airport." I asked, "How serious?" And he named a figure that was precisely twice my highest FBI salary, and said a living allowance would also be included. I thought about it for five seconds, then accepted.

I was married once. At the time, I was a special agent in the San Francisco office. When I was promoted to special agent in charge of the Wichita Falls, Texas, office—big title, little office—my wife chose San Francisco. There was more to it than that, but I am entirely done examining that failed relationship. She has since remarried, to a cardiologist, and she and I exchange newsy Christmas cards, the amount of news diminishing as the years pass. She has three children now, the oldest in high school. I'm at an age, mid-forties, when I'm beginning to wish I had children. I mentioned this to my father two weeks ago, and he advised that I first find a wife. Now I can't mention anything to my father.

I had to work to unclench my fists. I knew, sitting there on that park bench, that my father did not commit suicide. I didn't care about his eyeglasses being found in his pocket and a prescription antidepressant in his shaving kit. Suicide was counter to everything I knew about him, and to his own vigorously held religious beliefs. For most of his adult life he had been a deacon at the Medford First Presbyterian Church. Committing suicide was out of the question. It was forbidden by God. And he was a man in love with his retirement, in love with the idea of coming over to Hong Kong as often as he could to pal around with his son. Alan J. Williams would never do it, never jump from a twenty-story balcony.

Several elderly ladies paused at the corner of the park, where a wayside shrine had been erected, a small concrete structure not larger than a birdbath. The ladies burned joss sticks, arranging their thoughts and deeds to the spiritual force that courses through all the environment, which Cantonese call *hey* and Mandarins call *qi*. Thin strands of smoke rose from the shrine.

I never took to my father's churchgoing, by the way. Once I got to be fifteen, he became tired of wrestling me to Sunday school, so he would go off in his late-model Oldsmobile by himself every Sunday. He was good enough not to hector me about it, and he said God speaks to people in different ways. So I'm a backsliding Presbyterian, which makes me a Methodist by default, maybe. I still don't go to church. I might start someday, though.

The Hong Kong police weren't the only ones investigating my father's death. I had made dozens of telephone calls to the States. It made sense that if someone threw my father from the twentieth-floor deck, my father must have had an enemy. I had to relay the news of his death to many old friends in Oregon, but I also quizzed them about my father. Were there aspects about him I didn't know, any dark secrets, maybe a shadow life he was living, as improbable as that was? Could he have picked up a mortal enemy along the way? My notion that my father might have an enemy who would kill him was scoffed at by those who knew him back in Medford, as I suspected it would be, and the idea he might have committed suicide was also heartily ridiculed.

Three young ladies passed the bench, all talking boisterously at once. Cantonese is the only language that cannot be spoken in a whisper, it is said.

So I had been presented a ghastly puzzle. A man who would never kill himself and would never be murdered was nevertheless dead from a two-hundred-foot fall from a balcony that had a high rail around it. Hong Kong police investigators were at a dead end, and so was I.

"Mr. Williams?" A voice to my left, startling me.

I turned to a young man, maybe twenty years old, who was wearing slacks and a tan and green Nordstrom shirt. He had a shy grin and was nodding, as if that might prompt me to identify myself.

"May I please ask, are you Mr. Clay Williams?" His English was American, with long syllables, not the clipped, language-school British English so common in Hong Kong. His dark hair was closely cropped, and his eyes were alert. He maintained a smile.

"I am. Who are you?"

An elderly man carrying a black mynah bird in a cage passed us, the mynah whistling and clacking, then raking the cage's bars with its beak, sounding like a playing card flicked by bicycle spokes.

"My uncle would like to speak with you. He doesn't know English, and he has asked that I interpret. May I introduce you to him?"

"Who are you, and who is your uncle?"

The young man half turned toward the west and nodded. I followed his gaze but didn't see anybody who stood out from the steady stream of folks walking through the park to their jobs.

"My name is Zhu Jintau." He tentatively extended his hand toward mine, and I shook it.

"You're a professional interpreter?" I asked.

He shook his head. "Only when called upon by my uncle. Here he is."

I looked west again, and didn't see anybody coming toward me, but Zhu made a slight motion with his hand toward police headquarters, and I turned that way to see that an elderly gentleman was four steps away from the bench and closing. His head was almost bald, with only a few strands of white hair floating above it, hovering like insects. His spectacles flashed on and off in the light. Behind the eyeglasses his eyes were small and bright with intelligence and cunning. He had a fixed half-grin. White hair grew from his ears. An old scar, a wound poorly knitted together, paralleled his jawbone on his right cheek.

"I would like to introduce my uncle. Mr. Clay Williams, this is Mr. Wen Quichin."

Only by an act of will did I not leap up from the bench. There were probably thirty thousand Wens in Hong Kong. And Quichin wasn't too uncommon. But still, Wen Quichin?

I took a quick breath, then managed, "Pardon me?"

"This is Wen Quichin," the interpreter said again. The second name sounded like a cash register closing.

I stood to shake Wen's hand, and I studied his face closely, wondering if this was the fabled man who carried that name.

Then the young man tipped me off by saying, "You may have heard of him."

Yes, I had, as had every policeman in Asia. How many *gweilos* had ever seen this face? How many police officials? Only two photographs of Wen Quichin were known to exist, and they were from his much younger days, and were both grainy, as Wen had been moving quickly when they were taken. He had always moved quickly.

"Mr. Wen, I'm. . . ." I was about to say *honored*. But should I be honored to be meeting a man with a hundred deaths on his hands? Maybe two hundred? No one really knew the number, except Wen, if he bothered to count. "How do you do, sir?" I shouldn't have added *sir*, either, I suppose.

I scooted along the bench so that Zhu Jintau and the old man could sit down. Zhu placed himself in the middle. Wen was wearing a pair of loose cotton slacks held up by suspenders and an old-fashioned collarless white shirt with black buttons. Heavy brown brogans were on his feet. He sat quickly, with more energy than his slight, aged appearance would suggest.

He stared at me. I wondered how many men had seen this face as their last earthly sight. Then he spoke, in a quiet, oddly gargling voice, as if his vocal cords had taken on most of the burden of age.

His words stopped after a few seconds, and his nephew translated, speaking in the first person, as if the words came directly from the old man. " 'My grandson has disappeared. I cannot find him.' "

Wen Quichin apparently didn't subscribe to the Chinese custom of investing time in building *quanxi*—a relationship—between people, rather than immediately bringing up the topic. Hong Kong police estimated that four thousand people reported to Wen Quichin, working a vast enterprise in Hong Kong and Kowloon and the New Territories. Perhaps he didn't have the time to develop *quanxi*.

"I'm sorry your grandson is missing," I replied. "I am unclear how I might help you."

He spoke again, rapidly and in a soft voice, words not meant for passersby. Cantonese consists of sounds that I find hard to believe the human mouth can manufacture. I've been in Hong Kong for a decade, and I haven't been able to pick up much of it. Wen Quichin was a small man, five feet two is my guess, and slender. Other than wearing a Patek Philippe wristwatch, he offered no evidence of his reputed vast wealth. His hands were long-boned and delicate, not hands easy to imagine savagely wielding an ax, which they did expertly, if you believed the stories.

But he offered sure evidence of himself, by sitting here with me on a park bench. I had often discussed Wen with Jay Lee—Lee being head of the police's Organized Crime and Triad Bureau—and Lee had speculated that Wen Quichin might be a myth. Turncoats were few in Wen's organization, but those few informants available to Lee had never seen the old man. Orders the informants had received from the organization were filtered through many layers. Lee said that many Hong Kong citizens thought that Wen may never have existed, or might be long-dead, and the organization used his name and reputation to keep its own members and competitors in line. The Hong Kong police knew otherwise, that Wen was alive and prospering. And here he sat, talking to me as if at tea. I spotted a heavily built man standing near the bamboo grove who studied pedestrians passing the bench, undoubtedly a bodyguard. There would be others in the park. Wen had spent a lifetime making blood enemies.

The nephew translated. " 'We can help each other, Mr. Williams.' "

"What do you have in mind, Mr. Wen?"

Wen Quichin was the leader of 88K, a Hong Kong–based triad that was the largest criminal organization in Asia. The triad specialized in extortion, murder, kidnapping, illegal gambling, prostitution, blackmail, arson, loan sharking, drug trafficking, and human smuggling. If it was illegal, 88K was good at it. When he was fifteen years old, Wen became an 88K recruit; recruits are called blue lanterns. He progressed up the ranks, moving from white paper fan (administrator) to red pole (enforcer) to straw sandal (recruiter), and finally to dragon head, the leader, a position he had held for twenty years. The Hong Kong Police Force's profile of Wen was filled with rumor, contradictions, undoubtedly planted information, and perhaps much truth. It was said that his nickname was Concrete because of his manner of collecting his loan-sharking accounts early in his career, which was to toss the delinquent customer into an empty concrete mixing truck, and roll the drum around and around until the customer called for mercy.

Of the estimated sixty triads in Hong Kong, only about a third are engaged in criminal endeavors. The word *triad* comes from the societies' sacred symbol, a triangle of which each side represents an elemental power: earth, man, and heaven.

All triads—criminal and otherwise—are social clubs with elaborate rituals and long traditions. The Hong Kong police believe 88K was formed in the year 1674 to overthrow the Manchurians and restore the Ming Dynasty. Over the years, the triad's ambitions have become considerably less noble.

Lately, finding less profit in gambling and its other businesses, 88K had become a smuggler of people from China to North America, usually sealed inside steel cargo containers, maybe twenty people locked inside with no plumbing and no ventilation on a journey across the ocean that might take fourteen days. The fatality rate was unknown, but the Royal Canadian Mounted Police have estimated that one in ten Chinese died during the crossing.

"'Do you have children, Mr. Williams?'" Wen asked through the interpreter.

I shook my head. "I've never had the good fortune." What did the dragon head want?

The nephew interpreted. "'Yes, they are good fortune.'"

An unexpected encounter with a notorious criminal would set off alarms in any policeman. A man who made his living entombing people in a shipping container, certain death awaiting some of them, would be up to no good. Perhaps an attempted bribe, perhaps blackmail. I would never willingly meet with Wen or anyone like him without wearing a wire, without heavy surveillance, and without armed backup. Yet here I was, on my own, chatting away with a notorious gangster.

"'It has been a week since your father died,'" the young man said, relaying Wen's words.

I was astonished Wen would know anything about my father. How would the dragon head of 88K, one of the most fearsome criminal entities in the world, be aware of a retired Medford pear-grower? I remained silent.

The nephew continued, "'It is unlikely your father jumped to his death.'"

But now I had to ask, "How do you know about my father, and the manner of his death?"

After the translation and response, the nephew answered, "'We made inquiries about your father.'"

I felt fear beginning to rise in me. "What business do you have asking around about my father? And how do you know whether he was murdered or committed suicide?"

After the quick rendering to Chinese, Wen held up his hand in a placatory gesture. Zhu Jintau translated, "'You and I are linked by events that evening, Mr. Williams.'"

"I'm only aware of one event that night, my father dying from a twenty-story fall. What does it have to do with you?"

"'We Cantonese favor large families with many sons,'" the gangster's nephew interpreted. "'Perhaps you know that about our culture.'"

I didn't say anything. When I looked off to my right, toward the United Centre and Queensway, I saw another man I thought to be a bodyguard, sitting on a nearby bench. He was carrying a rolled-up newspaper in one hand and a hiker's two-way radio in the other. He smiled pleasantly at me.

The translator continued, "'My two sons were killed nine years ago. I have one daughter. She has one son. I am the subject of some ridicule among my enemies for lack of'"—the nephew hesitated, searching for the word, then added—"'progeny.'"

I sat there listening, not even nodding as he spoke, unwilling to commit to anything with even the smallest movement.

"'My grandson is fifteen years old,'" the nephew translated. "'He is the only direct male heir that I have. I hope that he follows in my path, though he has shown an unfortunate bent for education, and may attend a university.'"

This may have been the gangster's idea of a joke, though he didn't smile when he said it.

The nephew translated. "'My grandson disappeared the same night your father fell to his death, perhaps within the same ten minutes.'"

"Missing from where?"

The nephew might have been able to answer the question on his own, but he dutifully rendered it into Cantonese, listened for a moment, then said, "'My grandson lives with his parents in your building, on the twentieth floor, the same floor as you.'"

"You think his disappearance and my father's death are related?" I asked.

The old man spoke with the first emotion I had seen, clenching a hand and chopping the air with his chin. "'I do not believe in coincidences such as this, Mr. Williams. Yes, something happened that night that killed your father and took my grandson.'"

"Is there any chance your grandson ran away from home?"

Zhu translated my question, and Wen spoke to him angrily, which his nephew didn't render into English. A few more words were exchanged between them.

Zhu nodded meekly, then turned back to me. "'Hong Kong children are not like American children. My grandson would never run away, and the suggestion is silly. He was kidnapped.'"

"How is it possible my father's death has anything to do with your missing grandson?"

The 88K's dragon head didn't answer my question directly. "'All my life I have worked in the alleys and back streets, in the docklands, and in the factories and mills.'"

He meant, of course, that people in the alleys and back streets and the other places paid him protection money, not that he actually had been, say, a laborer in a metal-stamping plant.

"'If a diamond merchant on Nathan Road closes his shop thirty minutes early to visit his mistress, I learn about it before the merchant later gets home to his wife.'" Wen's voice was rising, and he was now speaking through clenched teeth. "'If a bettor at Happy Valley has his pocket picked, I learn about it almost before the bettor does. If an old woman in Kowloon Park falls and breaks her hip, I know about it before she reaches the hospital, and . . .' "

The nephew carefully put a hand on Wen's arm, and this gesture was apparently so unusual and startling that Wen immediately stopped speaking. He breathed deeply, and the struggle to compose himself was evident on his face.

He began again, and Zhu translated, " 'I have many, many people here who are anxious to do me services, and who are eager to give me information.' "

An elderly woman using a walker neared the bench, scooting along slowly. Her gray hair was pulled back into a tight bun. She pulled crumbs from a pocket, and sprinkled them on the walkway, and was quickly surrounded by pigeons.

" 'And yet I have been unable to find out anything about my grandson's disappearance. Not one thing, not a grain of evidence about it.' "

I tried again. "How could my father and your grandson be somehow connected?"

The nephew translated my question and then Wen's response: " 'That's what you and I will discover. You have many contacts, many, many contacts in places I cannot reach into. So we will discover the connection, you and I.' "

"You and I?" I blurted. "You are proposing a partnership, you and me?"

After translation the gangster waved away my suggestion, smiling. " 'I never take on partners. I have no use for them. They are nothing but trouble.' "

"Then what?" I asked.

Still smiling, Wen held out his little hand, and his nephew translated. " 'Welcome to the 88K.' "

3

My father taught me justice. Alan Williams was a big man in the Medford Valley, though I didn't know it when I was a kid. I began to suspect as much when one day he and I were driving along a dirt road alongside a sixty-acre pear orchard we called the Porcupine Place. All Dad's orchards had names, such as Larry's Twenty and Old Well Valley. Some of them were five acres, some a hundred, in a patchwork west of Medford, around Jacksonville. This was during the harvest, and the orchards were filled with pickers, mostly Mexicans who followed the harvests, beginning in May in Texas and California, and ending up in British Columbia in October. Local high school and college students also worked the pear trees.

My father was driving his pickup, and I was sitting next to him, bouncing along the rutted road. I was twelve years old, and he was hoping I would absorb some of the orchard business. My father was six and a half feet tall, with enormous arms and hands, made even larger by my memories. I never saw him outside without a straw cowboy hat. His face was tanned to the color of beef jerky. He had quit Copenhagen a year or two before, and he sucked on Pep-O-Mint Lifesavers morning to night, so he always smelled of mint.

We came to the crossroads at the county road, and Dad asked, "What's going on, you think?"

I peered through the windshield. A woman and two children, maybe five and three years old, were standing at the intersection. The woman was bent over a fourth person, a man who was hunched over the drainage ditch, his hands on his knees. Their old, rusted-out Buick was parked alongside the dirt road. The three-year-old, a little girl in a tattered dress, was crying and hugging her mother's leg. The man sank down to the road, and held his head in his hands. Late summer heat lay over the orchards, without a trace of a breeze, and yellow dust that had been kicked up by passing trucks was suspended in thick curtains over the dirt road.

Dad pulled the pickup over, then yanked back on the parking brake. I followed him out of the cab. He spoke Spanish, not well, but enough to get by with the picking crews. He knelt down next to the man and asked him a few questions in Spanish. The man at first shook his head, not wanting to tell what happened, but Dad persisted. The man's forehead was purple and green, and knobby with swollen skin, and his nose was bleeding. His cheek was split open, and blood ran down his chin onto his blue denim shirt.

My father spoke a few words to the man, who repeatedly shook his head, so then Dad talked with the man's wife. She spoke quickly. Dad nodded his understanding. He told me to get the canvas water bag from the truck. The bag was hung from the hood latch and was suspended over the grille so that it was cooled by the radiator fan. I lugged it over to Dad, who pulled a handkerchief from his pocket, poured water over it, then passed it to the woman, who dabbed it at her husband's face, trying to clean him up. Then Dad held the bag for the Mexican while he took several huge pulls of water.

Then Dad led me back to the truck. We got in, and he turned the engine over and we pulled away. Dad's mouth was set in a grim, uncompromising line. He said, "That lady says Danny Barger was short-weighting them. When he complained to Barger, Barger's two sons beat the hell out of him."

Danny Barger owned a small orchard west of my father's fields. Barger had a short temper and a cussed disposition, and spent his life looking for reasons to get angry. Barger was "too stupid to pour piss from a boot," as my father liked to say.

We drove to one of Dad's weighing stations. Workers were paid by weight, and a line of four or five pickers was in front of the big scale, each worker carrying a gunny sack of pears hung from his shoulders by a sling. Dad's scale man was weighing the sacks and making notes on a pad. Dad lifted a fifty-pound lead weight—certified by the Oregon Agricultural Commission as being precisely fifty pounds—from a rack next to the scale, and he told me to get another one and follow him. I wrestled with it and managed to lug it over to the truck and roll it onto the bed. The weights were used twice a day to calibrate the scale.

Then we drove over to Danny Barger's spread. Barger was at the scale, making notes on a clipboard. Three pickers were there, waiting to weigh their loads, and so were Barger's two sons, whose idea of work was to hang out by the soda cooler. Pear trees were all around, their heavy, fruit-laden boughs held up by wood poles. Without a word, my father lifted both fifty-pound weights from the truck, one in each hand, walked over to Barger—who was about to bark out something, but saw the look on my father's face, and wisely remained silent—and placed the weights on Barger's scale. The red indicator rose to eighty-five pounds.

Dad turned to Barger. "You've been short-weighting your pickers."

"The hell you talking about?" Barger was a squat man, with no neck and a pinched, angry face.

His two sons—they were in their early twenties—ambled over, their thumbs hooked onto their jeans pockets. Both were wearing grimy white T-shirts.

Dad turned to them. "You two idiots stay out of this, or I'll slap you both silly and dump you into the irrigation canal. You understand me?"

The Barger boys stopped cold, and the bullying scowls vanished from their faces.

My father said, "Barger, you owe Arturo Mendez—who I just found out by my westerly orchard—another thirty dollars. That's what I figure you short-weighting him all week adds up to. Thirty dollars. Give me the money. I'll see that he gets it."

Barger puffed himself up and was about to let loose with a string of invective, but my father stepped close, and he locked his gaze on Barger, and he balled his fists, and Barger knew it was pay up or get mostly killed, so he reached for his wallet.

My father took the bills, then announced in Spanish that Barger had his thumb on the scales, but that Williams Farms was shy of hands, and that he had work for anybody who wanted it. Dad waited while the pickers cashed out for their load. Barger scowled mightily but was afraid to object. His sons stood on the dirt, welded to the spot by Dad's threat. Barger's pickers climbed into the back of Dad's truck.

We drove the crew to our mess hall, as it was lunchtime, and on the way we picked up Arturo Mendez and his family, my father handing him the thirty dollars and giving his children a handful of Pep-O-Mints. During lunch Dad telephoned the Jackson County sheriff, who arrested Barger's sons later that day. They served two months in jail for assault and battery.

So my father had started out that day intending to give me a lesson on pear farming but instead instructed me on justice. My father was a man of integrity, I learned then, and I learned again and again as he guided me from being a boy to being a man.

My father deserved justice, and I was going to see that he received it. I didn't care how long it took or what I had to do. I was going to find his killer and deal with him.

* * *

My office was in a construction trailer on Heroes of the Revolution Island, the man-made island in Victoria Harbor that is the platform for the Gold Swan. Citizens of Hong Kong howled when Beijing announced the island's name, but there was nothing to be done.

Because I share the office with the others on the security team, the place is cramped, and I'm always glad to leave it, even if it means stepping out into Hong Kong's thick, humid air, which for those of us from northern climates has the feel of magma. I walked out into the sunshine and once again was astonished at the structure standing before me.

I had never become accustomed to it. The thing jolted me every

time, and did so again. There it was, the western edge with the sharp
angle of a ship's prow, filling my vision. I lifted my head back so I could
look up at the golden, curving tower, which was so large it created its
own vertical horizon, often giving me a brief touch of vertigo. In the
bright light, the curved gold shaft was iridescent, reflecting the light
like water, throwing darts of rippling color across the flat platform. I
gazed at it, stupefied again by the brazenness of the thing. After I
could finally break my gaze, I walked across the island toward the cafeteria trailers.

Once a week I had lunch with the architecture project manager,
Anne Iverson, who reported to John Llewellyn. Our first meeting had
been a routine introduction, exchanging information about our jobs,
but then she called me a week later to suggest lunch again, and since
then we had been meeting once a week for lunch, seldom talking
about business. I might've asked her for dinner at some point, had I
not known that she was involved with John Llewellyn, something few
people were aware of. As a security consultant, I heard things. She
didn't hide the relationship from me, occasionally laughing and saying
she was "girlfriend number twenty-four," or saying Llewellyn was old
enough to be her father's older brother. She and Llewellyn kept it out
of the papers.

I walked between two spools of wire rope. Heroes of the Revolution Island still resembled a construction site. Some of the finish work
remained to be completed on the tower, and electrical and plumbing
installations continued. The ferry terminal on the island's east side
was behind schedule. Klieg lights had been set up around it so that
work could be carried on into the night. So now, only a few weeks before the inauguration, much equipment remained on the island.

Though I did not know it, half a mile away, a young man had just
begun paddling toward the island on an inner tube. His short journey
would have a profound consequence for me. He sailed in perilous waters, filled with shipping, and he and his tube were lost among the
whitecaps. He paddled steadily with his hands, fighting the current,
aiming for the island, and for me.

I worked my way between construction equipment toward the cafeteria. Temporary vehicle lanes had been painted on the island's concrete surface, which was a flat expanse that resembled an aircraft carrier's deck. The island itself—apart from the tower—was a masterwork of engineering and construction. At one time the largest dredging fleet in the world was assembled here, including cutter suction dredgers, trailing suction hopper dredgers, and dozens of barges. First, the marine mud on the bay floor was removed, then a circular rock seawall was built—some of the boulders weighing three tons—and then the area inside the wall was filled with marine fill and rock fill, 35 million cubic yards in all. Then a forty-foot cap of concrete, reinforcing steel, and tensioning cables was laid over the fill and the seawall. The island—that part of it that ranged out from the tower's base, more than a hundred yards in all directions—was an unusual Hong Kong item: open space. It was purposely left flat and unobstructed to further dramatize the tower that rose from its center. Marine-green tile was being laid over some of the platform, in a pattern I hadn't figured out yet. The tile contractor was also behind in its work, and had crews on-site around the clock.

I passed the vehicle yard, containing mostly forklifts and flatbed trucks, which were behind a chain-link fence. That morning I had reported to the FBI Wen Quichin's approach to me. Though the agency no longer employed me, it would have been foolish not to have informed them, to leave myself exposed to blackmail. I went to the FBI's office in the New Asia Bank Building on Hennessy Road, rather than emailing or phoning the agent there, because my office's phone conversations and email and faxes were almost surely fed through the Security Service in Beijing. And I made sure I wasn't followed on my way there.

The agent in the office, Fred Allison, had worked with me in Washington, D.C. He was suitably astonished at the dragon head's appearing in front of me at the park, and agreed with me that Wen's quip, "Welcome to 88K," was an attempt at humor. No *gweilo* ever joined a triad. Still, the offer from Wen to work together was real enough, it seemed. My doing so was quickly cleared with Washington. The Hong Kong police were not to be told.

I entered one of the seven cafeteria trailers on the island. This one served western food, and most of the folks inside were from the United States, Australia, and Canada, with a few New Zealanders thrown in. Most were contractor crews, suppliers' representatives, project managers, and engineers. I picked up a sub sandwich and a bottle of water at the counter, and walked to the corner table where Anne Iverson was eating a salad and waiting for me.

"How're you doing?" she asked, tapping the table by way of an invitation to sit, as she always did.

"Better."

"Any luck figuring it out?"

I told her the few things I knew, those pieces of information revealed by the Hong Kong police, including the antidepressant medications my father was taking, and that his eyeglasses were in his pants pocket when he fell. I also said I was still convinced my father would never kill himself.

She reached over and gave my hand a gentle squeeze. "I'm sorry for you, Clay."

Anne Iverson's eyes were a peculiar blue, so light as to be almost gray. I mentioned to her once, by way of being witty, that many sled dogs, such as the Siberian husky and the Alaskan malamute, have her color eyes, and I think she was pleased with the comparison. Her hair had been lighter, almost flax white, when she was a child, she had said, but had darkened over the years, and now was gold, with darker caramel streaks through it. She kept it fairly short, down to her shoulders, and often wore a ponytail, as she was doing today. She was slender and fine-boned. Her nose was small, and there were a few light freckles across the bridge. Her lips were full, and she had a wide smile, one that hung from her cheekbones, an irresistible invitation to return a grin. Her chin was a touch outsized, but only a touch. It lent her face a pleasingly willful cast.

She apparently detested small talk, as I had never heard any of it from her. Being the son of a farmer, I like to open most any conversation with comments about the weather, but Anne wouldn't have anything to do with it. And I had begun to think that she had a topic selected for each of our lunch meetings, sometimes American politics, sometimes the curious nature of Hong Kong, sometimes the tower's upcoming inauguration. Today's topic was apparently me.

"You never mention your wife," Anne said. "Why is that?"

"She's my ex-wife, and that's the main reason."

She smiled. "She ditch you?"

"It's been a long time. I hardly remember her. Nice day outside. A little warm for me, though."

She laughed lightly. "What's her name?"

I lifted the top slice of bread to check the contents of my sandwich. I didn't say anything.

Anne asked, "You won't even say her name?"

"Her name was Olivia. I should've known. It's a troublemaker's name."

She laughed again. "What was her trouble?"

"I appreciate your interest, Anne, but I don't want to talk about my ex-marriage with my ex-wife."

"Sure you do. You've been dying to unburden yourself."

Anne had an architecture degree from UCLA, and a master's degree in project management from the same school. Earlier in the project she had helped to develop conceptual studies and flow diagrams, and then had been a coordinator of teams preparing the construction documents, including plans, details, sections, and schedules. Her tasks had evolved as the tower was designed and built, and now she coordinated all the engineering consultants' work and monitored progress to maintain schedules, budgets, and compliance with contracts. At this stage of construction, she was acting more as a project manager than as an architect. She called herself the bridge between the architectural and engineering sides.

I said, "Olivia was a good businesswoman, it turns out. She had a hobby, and she made a fortune with it."

"What hobby?" Anne speared an artichoke heart with her fork.

"When I was assigned to the FBI office in San Francisco, she opened a small florist shop on Sansome Street. She always liked flowers and floral arranging. It was a hobby, really."

"What a wonderful way to make a living," Anne said. "Arranging flowers and never having to squint at a CAD design."

"Olivia's storefront business was a money-loser from day one. Then, two years into it, she had the notion that people could order bouquets of flowers from the computer, via the Internet. This was back before Amazon and FTD Online. She promised customers in San Francisco that she would have the flowers to the recipient within two hours."

"Did her plan work?"

"Within two years she was employing three hundred people in the Bay Area, and after yet another two years, she sold her business to FTD Online for eighteen million dollars." I bit into my sandwich.

"Then what happened?"

After a moment I replied: "I was transferred away from San Francisco. Olivia had her money, and had become an arts patron. She bought her way into San Francisco society, and enjoyed it too much to leave."

"You sound bitter."

"Not in the slightest."

She asked, "Why is your jaw clenched?"

"I don't like talking about my ex-wife, is why." If I took a large, mouth-filling bite of my sandwich, maybe Anne wouldn't ask any more questions.

"You feel you were financially and socially left behind?"

I chewed for a while, then said, "I loved my wife. She ditched me."

"Well . . ."

"She didn't even have the courtesy of dumping me for another man. It was for a city, San Francisco."

"There's probably more to it than that, isn't there?"

I bit off another huge hunk of the sandwich. I stared out the small window, across Victoria Bay, where a rack of office buildings was being built around Kowloon Bay. Building height restrictions had been eased in neighborhoods around the bay now that the old airport had closed.

After a moment of my silence, Anne said, "I didn't mean to pry, Clay. Sorry."

"Yes, you did." I chewed, then added, "I don't mind, really. I'll just ignore questions I don't want to answer."

"Well, if you ever want to bend my ear about it, I'll listen."

I nodded. My view was of the Hong Kong side. I didn't see the boy coming, paddling along on his inner tube.

"So." Anne indicated the remains of my sandwich with her finger. The sandwich was loaded with pepperoni, ham, three kinds of cheese, and half a cup of mayonnaise. "You've quit your diet?"

"Only for today," I said. "Only for this lunch."

"You don't need to lose weight." With a vaudevillian's timing she paused a beat, then added, "Not much, anyway."

No, not much. I'm at an age when things are settling. I've had to add a notch to my belts, but only one notch. I don't have the extra fabric in the seats of my pants anymore. But I'm no longer the thirty pounds overweight that I was when I was at the FBI's Wichita Falls office, the trouble being my genetic predisposition against turning aside Mexican food. A Chihuahua Express was next door to the FBI office, and sometimes I would eat there twice a day. But I've lost most of those extra pounds.

The skin under my eyes has loosened, and I think my nose is getting bigger, a peculiar aspect of aging I hadn't known about. Still, I work out at least four times a week and can run five miles in under eight minutes a mile. I like to run before dawn, which comes late in Hong Kong, not until seven in the morning or so. I wind around Hong Kong's dark streets, running by elderly women squatting over open braziers preparing breakfast, and groups of men wearing hardhats gathering for their walk to work, and passing hundreds of street vendors pushing their carts, moving their merchandise to their spots for the day. Sometimes in the dark I'll become lost in Hong Kong's alleys and dead ends, jogging along, turning whatever direction strikes me at the moment. It's disorienting and exhilarating. When I'm tired of it, I head higher up the slope, which always offers views so I can get my bearings, and then I head back home. I used to do five hundred sit-ups a day. Now I manage only forty, and accompany myself with undignified grunts. I used to do two hundred push-ups a day. Now I don't bother.

My hair is dark, not quite black, more of a walnut color, and it's curly, so much so that I was called Brillo in junior high school. My forehead is higher than it used to be. My wife—my ex-wife—used to say my green eyes had a merry, un-FBI cant to them, as if I were always amused. My face is rather narrow and long, and my ears are tight against my head, which Olivia once said was my best feature, them and my elbows, and these comments should've told me something, I suppose. I'm not always amused, despite my eyes, by the way.

Anne broke open the roll on her plate. She spread butter on it. Butter is scarce in Hong Kong because the Cantonese don't eat it. Llewellyn made sure his employees had lunches to their liking.

She was direct, so I could be direct. "How are you and John Llewellyn doing?"

She glanced over my shoulder. "Why don't you ask him yourself?"

I followed her gaze. The great architect had just entered the cafeteria. All eyes snapped to him as if "Eyes right" had been barked by a drill instructor. He moved by tables slowly, shaking hands and chatting briefly with a dozen people, smiling widely and patting backs. He was wearing a light gray suit and a red club tie.

I said, "He's like a politician. He's working the crowd."

"I detect a touch of dislike," Anne replied.

"I don't know Llewellyn well enough to like or dislike him. I've only met him a couple of times."

But I knew a lot about him. Most everyone did by then. Llewellyn had just that week appeared on the cover of *Time* and *Newsweek* and the *Economist*, was granting interviews to anyone who asked, and had become inescapable at the newsstand and on television.

Educated at St. Albans and Harvard, John Llewellyn had once been the premier architect-intellectual in America. He was slender, urbane, and ironic, and many of the writers who profiled him were clearly charmed by him. They appreciated that he avoided the Byzantine extravagance of architect-speak but could refer easily to Lutyens and De Stijl. His clients found him charming with just the right amount of deference.

Early in his career, Llewellyn adopted Flatiron Building–designer Daniel Burnham's motto: "Make no small plans. They lack the power to move men's hearts." But Llewellyn's career had a slow start: in his first six years as an architect his only commissions were a remodel of his uncle's home and a new house for his parents. Then in 1973, when he was twenty-eight years old, he published *Form and Function in Architecture.* The book was an instant sensation, wittily scoffing at the long rows of Bauhaus glass cubes that lined city streets and calling for a return to "messy vitality." Llewellyn's treatise embraced the distorted rather than the straightforward and the inconsistent rather than the logical. It gave the nod to playful ornamentation and color. Llewellyn's book was the most important architectural manifesto since Le Corbusier's in 1923.

The box people were in full flight. Suddenly the influences of Gropius and Mies van der Rohe were broken. Postmodernism was born. Overnight, John Llewellyn became the most influential architect in America.

Big commissions rolled in, and within a few years Llewellyn had a staff of a hundred. He had rejected the International style, and he also rejected the concept of architectural teamwork as practiced by Gropius and other Modernist architects. He designed all structures his office handled, even if his involvement was only a few charcoal slashes on a piece of paper. His employees were acolytes, paid little, overworked, underappreciated, but nevertheless delighted to sit at Llewellyn's feet, to be associated with that glittering name.

Llewellyn designed the enormous eighty-thousand-seat Sports Palace in Paris, the ninety-story General Motors Building in Detroit, the new terminal at the Sydney airport, and dozens of other buildings, all bearing his irreverent and unmistakable stamp. His designs were copied around the world. Classical motifs were mixed with bizarre alterations. Many different materials appeared on the same building, and many colors. Showy fillips became the norm. Whether praising or panning Llewellyn, critics agreed he had a seminal influence on world architecture.

But all this was ten years ago. A new generation of architects had appeared in the last decade, and they treated Llewellyn's work as passé. Their manifesto was that less is, in fact, more. Postmodernism faded. Ornamentation was out. The downtown cube made a comeback.

Commissions no longer streamed into Llewellyn's office. He laid off much of his staff. Llewellyn knew he was passing into history. He was only sixty years old. He was desperate. The *New York Times* reported that at one point he was discovered in his New York home, unconscious from an overdose of sleeping pills, which Llewellyn later claimed was somehow an accident.

But Frank Lloyd Wright's practice was in decline for fifteen years, and was instantly resuscitated by his master stroke, Fallingwater. So maybe there was hope. If only Llewellyn knew where. China's president showed him the way.

Carrying a salad on a tray, Llewellyn finally worked his way over to our table. I wasn't sure he would remember my name, so I said it aloud as he shook my hand. He had small hands, and they were soft. He smiled at me. I was confident he had no memory of what my job was here. He slipped into the empty chair. I enjoyed these thirty-minute sessions with Anne Iverson, and I begrudged the famous architect's appearance at our table.

But he turned to me and said, "I'm sorry about your father. A terrible thing. How are you doing?"

I told him I was fine, stretching the truth. I was surprised he knew anything about my father's death, or would bother to mention it. Llewellyn quickly rose in my estimation. His silver hair was perfectly in place. He had finely planed cheekbones and a narrow nose. A delicate notch was on his chin. His eyelashes were long and were also silver. His blue eyes were widely spaced and seemed candid. I could see something of his mother in his face.

"Your reputation must precede you, Clay." He smiled with his small, even teeth. "We've had no suggestion of any terrorist activity, nothing that will disrupt the opening ceremonies, not even protestors."

"It makes my job easy," I replied. Llewellyn had remembered what my job was. I was flattered.

"Are you receiving the cooperation you were promised?" he asked.

"I believe so."

"We have let your presence be known in certain circles," Llewellyn said. "You are a deterrent. So you are performing an extremely valuable service, even if it might not seem so day to day."

I nodded my thanks. He was going out of his way to make me seem important to the project, a kindness. Maybe I liked this fellow after all. Llewellyn didn't often mingle with us laborers, so most eyes in the trailer were on him. For a short while, the world had been puzzled how John Llewellyn had landed this job, designing the Fifth Millennium China Tower, which was, although the century was new, instantly labeled by architects the commission of the century.

The Chinese government hired John Llewellyn and his firm. China's president, Chen Langing, asked Llewellyn to design a giant, instantly recognizable edifice that would deliver several messages. Located in Hong Kong, the structure would be a reminder to all world citizens that Hong Kong was now fully Chinese, as much a part of the country as was Beijing and Shanghai. Chen wanted Llewellyn to devise a structure that would also make an irrefutable statement to the United States and Japan and Taiwan that China was now modern and powerful, and no longer to be fooled with. Chen demanded that Llewellyn's design be a grand and soaring symbol of China's emergence as a premier—soon *the* premier—world power.

John Llewellyn delivered. The official Chinese press was rhapsodic. The country's big-city newspapers regularly devoted pages to the project. Beijing television crews were in the city full-time, filing daily reports on the tower's progress. President Chen had visited the site four times. On each occasion he was photographed beaming, an uncharacteristic expression for a man known to be dour and intense.

Sure indications of the weight the Chinese government was giving to the tower's debut were the changes taking place in Hong Kong, small and large, as the city was prepared to host the event. Many of Hong Kong's skyscrapers were being draped with exterior neon signs, some of them sixty and seventy stories tall. The Bank of China Tower, Central Plaza, Lee Gardens, the Cosco Tower, the Hopewell Center, and other buildings would display green dragons and gold lions and red chrysanthemums, all in neon, to the half-million visitors expected to attend. The new convention center would be rimmed with neon.

Public works projects had been under way for several years, preparing Hong Kong for the big day. Twenty miles of Hong Kong and Kowloon streets had been dug up, so that new sidewalks could be laid and the sewage and water lines replaced. Two massive new sewage treatment plants had been built, one on each side of the bay, and old Hong Kong hands said the city no longer had that famous brown smell. The few remaining buildings that spoke of the city's history— the domed Supreme Court Building (now where the legislative council met), St. John's Cathedral, the red-brick French mission on the hill above Queen's Road—were being retiled and cleaned. Hong Kong Park, Victoria Park, the Zoological and Botanical Gardens, the Kowloon Tsai Park, and other parks were being renovated, hundreds of gardeners working long shifts. Eight hotels, including the Grand Hyatt, the Ritz-Carlton, and the Kowloon Shangri-la, were rushing to complete new towers.

A temporary barracks town was being constructed near Sha Tin in the New Territories where, it was rumored, the beggars and addicts and prostitutes would be deposited after massive police sweeps just before opening week. Hong Kong has relatively little street crime, but the police were also rounding up known pickpockets and cutpurses and muggers.

The Star ferries—*Celestial Star, Morning Star, Solar Star,* and the others—had been refitted and now gleamed, and four new ferries had just been built and delivered, one of them named *Red Star,* to the consternation of the city's braver newspapers. A second funicular tram to the peak had been built.

Hong Kong and Macau-based lighters, junks, and fishing trawlers had been ordered to install chemical toilets, a regulation that was being vigorously enforced through surprise police inspections. Thousands of teenagers, all wearing green T-shirts while on the job, were being employed by the new Hong Kong Beach Authority to patrol the formerly litter-strewn beaches between Tsuen Wan and Tuen Mun, Silvermine Bay, and other beaches twice daily to pick up litter, much of which was white Styrofoam packing material. Virtually every portable grandstand in Asia and Australia and New Zealand had been rented, hauled to Hong Kong, and would be installed on the shores facing the tower. The fireworks show marking the Handover was the largest in history, and the city promised twice the explosive poundage for the tower opening.

John Llewellyn knew how to engage you, I'll give him that. As we ate lunch, he asked several questions about my work, and I tried to make it sound more interesting than it was. He looked me in the eye the entire time, nodding his understanding, and asking pertinent questions. Not once did he glance over my shoulder, as if hoping someone else would arrive. His questions revealed he was listening closely to what I said, and understanding it. He picked gently at his salad all the while. After a few moments he deftly switched the conversation to Anne, and he said several things that made us laugh. She put up with more small talk from him than from me. His cuff links occasionally tapped the table.

Then Llewellyn said, "So I've searched you out, Anne, to say I need to alter our plans for the weekend. I've been invited to New Delhi for an interview."

"The government there?" she asked. "They are interviewing you for a commission?"

He laughed lightly. "You don't understand the dynamics of it, now that the Fifth Millennium China Tower is nearly completed. I'm interviewing them. And they are paying me a significant appearance fee for the interview."

He looked at me, his eyes glittering. "Times have changed for me, thanks to the tower. People are again returning my phone calls."

I smiled. "I'm glad."

He rose from the table. I thought for a moment he might lean over to give Anne a smooch, but he settled for gripping her hand before turning to go. I was on the verge of saying something inappropriate to her about dating the boss when my cell phone jiggled in my pocket. I excused myself and pulled the phone out as I crossed the cafeteria to the door, following the architect.

The Australian, Jack Rainey, told me a kid had just paddled up to the island on an inner tube, had been captured by the Hong Kong police who patrol the island's perimeter, and was asking to speak to me. The police had brought him to our trailer.

So I said goodbye to Anne, then retraced my steps across the island. Outside my trailer were two Hong Kong police officers. I showed them my ID, then entered the trailer. Jack Rainey was sitting at his desk and was passing a bag of potato chips to a young man—fifteen or sixteen years old—who was still wet from crossing the bay.

The youngster was wearing jeans and a T-shirt that advertised Ted Nugent's CD *Full Bluntal Nugity*. Dried saltwater was on the lenses of his rimless spectacles. He was wearing orthodontic braces. He stood up when I approached the cubicle.

Rainey said, "He'll only talk to you, he says." Rainey was tall, and so slender he seemed made of nothing but bones. "I'll give you some privacy." He gathered himself up from the chair and left us.

The young man squeezed the package of chips. He glanced at my face, then looked at his shoes. He was nervous. Water dripped onto the floor.

I sat in my chair and smiled at him. "May I help you?"

"Are you Mr. Clay Williams?"

I said I was.

"And you live in the New Horizon apartment building?" His English was as good as mine.

"That's right."

He brought his gaze up. "I know what happened to your father."

4

"Are you packing?" the boy asked. His name was Soong Chan.

"What do you mean?"

"Are you carrying heat?"

"The FBI doesn't use those terms," I said.

"Really?"

"Not since Eliot Ness."

This troubled him, I could tell. He was a student of American cinema, like many Hong Kong teenagers.

He asked, "What do they call it, then?"

"Carrying a weapon, I suppose. The manual doesn't specify what we should call it."

"Well, I don't want to go up there without you carrying a weapon."

Soong Chan and I were outside my apartment building, staring up at my balcony.

"I go up there every day," I said. "It's perfectly safe."

"It wasn't safe for your father or my friend."

I nodded. "You've got a point. But I'm with you, and I'm big and tough. And you look pretty tough yourself."

He pulled at an ear lobe. "I don't know . . ."

"I can get a couple of policemen to go up with us, if you'd like."

He vigorously shook his head. "No policemen. The people who took Shui-ban might've been cops. Do you use the word *cops*?"

"Yes, for city policemen. FBI agents are called *feds*." I smiled at him. "But I don't have time to stand out here on the sidewalk teaching you American slang."

He laughed, sort of. The boy was still nervous. His arms were crossed in front of him. He had cleaned the saltwater smears from his glasses. His clothes had dried quickly. We had stopped at the Central Ferry Pier, and he had pulled an expandable, cloth-sided briefcase from a rental locker there. It was expanded to its full extent, and it was heavy, and he had labored under its burden as we had walked, carrying it in one hand for half a block, then switching it to his other hand. When I asked him about the contents of the briefcase, he said they belonged to the 20th Floor Physics Club, but wouldn't elaborate, saying he would show me when the time had come.

"So you don't live in the building?" I asked.

"My parents and I live up the street." He waved toward the Peak.

"You are being vague," I said.

"I don't know who to trust, not after seeing what happened to my friend Shui-ban."

"Why did you come to me?"

"Because your father was involved, and you are a policeman."

"I'm not a policeman anymore, not really," I said.

Much of my job consisted of reviewing intelligence reports. The United States had a vested interest in the region's stability, and so the CIA and the FBI had cleared me to receive intelligence regarding known terrorist movements, even though I was working for the Chinese. And so I was funneled reports from those two organizations, and from the National Security Agency, the Bureau of Alcohol, Tobacco, and Firearms, the U.S. Army's Military Intelligence Brigade, the Air Force's National Air Intelligence Center, and the 497th Intelligence Group. I was in frequent contact with the United States' Office of Homeland Security, founded after the attack on the World Trade Center.

Many countries believed the Chinese proclamation that this was the Chinese century and were currying favor with Beijing, so my security group in the trailer also received information from Australia's Federal Police, Germany's Bundeskriminalamt, and the Republic of Georgia's Internal Forces, which had inherited many of the KGB's files. The Greek Internal Security Agency and the South African Police Service shared information with us, as did Scotland Yard and the Police Service of Northern Ireland. Asian intelligence organizations also contributed, including the National Police Agency of Japan, Philippine National Police, and of course the Hong Kong police's Criminal Intelligence Division. Interpol gave us access to their Automated Search Facility, a database containing files on 230,000 potential suspects.

The countries that contributed intelligence asked that we notify them of anything that might affect their security, which we did. Our group, sitting in our trailer, had become a clearinghouse for worldwide terrorism intelligence, the contributing nations finding that we were an acceptable medium for sharing information. Suggestions had been made that we continue in some capacity after the tower's completion.

But, as I mentioned, though we had worked hard, sorting through vast amounts of information, and though we had forwarded to contributing nations intelligence they found useful, we had discovered nothing to suggest the tower was in jeopardy. No terrorists were headed our way, as best we could tell.

I had used my foreign security service connections to inquire about my father's death. The investigators at the NSA, Scotland Yard, the Bundeskriminalamt, and the others might have been amused that I would ask them if their organizations knew anything about my father, a Medford, Oregon pear-grower, and whether he might have done something that had led to his death. Did he have a past of which I was unaware, some intrigue, some foreign connection? The contacts at the security services all knew that my father had recently perished, and they humored me by giving me reports. They could find not one scintilla of evidence that he had been anything but a fruit farmer.

"Are you staying with your parents?" I asked the boy.

He shook his head.

"Your mom and dad know where you are?"

"I'm staying with my uncle, in Hoi Ha, in the New Territories, out near Ocean Point. My parents drove me out there. They are afraid for me, too. I'm not even going to school because those people might find me there."

"Who are 'those people,' you figure?"

"I don't know," he replied.

"Come on," I said. "We don't need to be carrying heat. They are long gone."

He followed me as I walked under the portico. The doorman smiled at me. The doors opened automatically and we entered the building. The floor was sea-green marble. A few red leather chairs and sofas were in a greeting room to the right of the lobby. We entered the elevator, and the boy pushed the button for the twentieth floor.

"This is just what I did," he said. "I rode up the elevator, like I do every Tuesday and Thursday. That's when our club would meet." Out of deference to me being an American, the boy used *elevator*, rather than *lift*, the term used by most Hong Kong English-speakers.

The elevator rose quickly.

I asked, "How many guys in your club?"

He said with fragile dignity, "Two."

"Two?"

"Me and Hsu Shui-ban."

I said, "Maybe clubs are smaller in Hong Kong."

"We call ourselves the 20th Floor Physics Club."

"How long have you been in the club, you and your friend Shui-ban?"

"Since we were ten," Soong Chan said. "Our first project was a leaf collection." He grinned at me. "And then we put together an insect collection, and then when we were twelve, we made our Rock 'n' Rats projects, where we tested white lab rats to see how rock and roll affected their appetites."

"How does it?"

"The louder it gets, the less the rats eat."

"Same with me."

He said, "Our projects are more complicated these days."

The elevator stopped at the twentieth floor. The door opened and we stepped out and turned to the right.

"This is where I was," the boy said. "I'd just gotten off the elevator."

"And what did you see?"

"Two men were coming out of Shui-ban's apartment door."

"Where is it? Which door?"

"It's number twelve."

The boy had stopped just outside the elevator and displayed no interest in going farther down the hall.

"Number twelve? That's the Hsus' apartment, isn't it?"

He replied, "My friend is Hsu Shui-ban."

I still hadn't figured out which Hong Kong names were first names and which were surnames—not by their sound, anyway. Shui-ban was the first name, I had just learned. Hsu was the last name. I knew the Hsus. That is, I knew them well enough to say hello when I passed them in the hall. And I knew they had a teenage son, had seen him in the hallway, carrying a backpack on his way to school. I didn't know anything about the family, though. Only at that moment did I make the connection between my neighbors, the Hsus, and this young man, Soong Chan.

I said, "So tell me what happened."

"The two men were moving quickly, not quite running, but walking fast. Shui-ban was fighting them, but each of the men held one of his arms, and they tugged him along."

"Did you recognize the men?"

He shook his head. "I had never seen them before."

"What did they look like? What were they wearing?"

"Both wore coats and jackets and ties. They looked like business-people. Or they could have been police detectives. I didn't know. But I knew they were dragging Shui-ban down the hall against his will. And one of the men's coats flapped open, and I could see he was wearing a pistol holster on his belt. So I was afraid of them."

I asked again, "And you didn't know either of the men?"

"I'd never seen them before."

"Did they see you?"

"I don't think so. I ducked back into the elevator before the door closed, and I held the door open, my head peeking out. I guess I was sort of hoping to be able to help Shui-ban maybe." He hesitated, but then his chin came up. "But I was afraid."

"I would've been scared, too. So what happened next?"

"Your father opened your apartment door."

"Why did he do that?"

"I don't know, sir. He might have heard them scuffling with Shui-ban, or he might have just stepped outside to maybe go for a walk. I don't know."

"Did my father say anything?"

"He did, but I couldn't hear the words clearly, and then he held up a hand as if to stop the men."

I asked, "And did the men say anything to him?"

"Not that I heard."

We were still standing at the elevator, but then Soong Chan stepped along the hall, with small and careful steps, looking over his shoulder to make sure I was with him. He only came up to my shoulders. He was slender, with a bookish look to him.

He said, "And then—this isn't nice and you won't like it—your father stepped in front of the men, and one of them hit him."

"Hit him? With what, a fist?"

"With his fist, right on your father's face."

The autopsy would not have shown evidence of my father being struck because of the damage caused by landing on the concrete.

"And then the man grabbed your father and pushed him into your apartment, and closed the door. The other man held Shui-ban, his hand across Shui-ban's mouth."

"How long was the man in my apartment?"

"I don't know. I was really afraid, and I put my head back into the elevator and pressed the DOWN button."

"So you didn't see the men again?"

"I ran away. I didn't see where they went with Shui-ban."

I asked, "Why didn't you go to the police?"

"I thought those two men probably were the police. They were dressed in nice clothes, and one of them had a pistol, maybe both of them. They looked like police to me. I thought they were arresting Shui-ban. And I thought they might try to arrest me, too."

"Why would they arrest Shui-ban?"

Soong Chan didn't say anything for a moment. "He has a biography of Marconi that he hasn't returned to the library. It's been overdue for weeks. But I don't think he'd be arrested for that. Do you?"

"Probably not."

"I'm afraid, Mr. Williams. Those policemen—or whoever they are —are looking for me. They've come to my parents' home four times, and they have visited my school, and they've gone to my grandparents' apartment over in Mong Kok."

Mong Kok was a neighborhood on the Kowloon side, around Argyle Street.

"And my father has told my uncle—where I'm hiding—that he has seen men who look like policemen, even though they are in regular clothes—watching our building from across the street."

"If they are looking for you, why haven't they visited your uncle in the New Territories village?"

"He's not my real uncle." He swung the briefcase from his right hand to his left hand. "He was a close friend of my grandfather, and our whole family honors him by calling him *uncle*. The police probably haven't made the connection, and so they don't know where I am."

"Do you know anything about your friend Hsu Shui-ban's family?" I asked.

"His father works for Cathay Pacific, in their offices. He's an executive. His mother stays at home."

"I mean, do you know about his grandfather?"

"You know about his grandfather?" the boy countered. "I didn't think foreigners knew anything about . . . about that."

I grinned at him. "His grandfather is the 88K's dragon head."

"Yes, I know that. Everyone knows that, except round-eyes, I thought. No offense."

"Is it possible that Hsu Shui-ban was kidnapped by a triad, maybe one of 88K's enemies?"

"Maybe. But those two guys who grabbed Shui-ban didn't look like triad members to me."

"They have a look?"

Soong Chan replied, "They do not wear suits much, not that I've seen."

I asked, "Do you have any other connection with Hsu Shui-ban, other than being in the 20th Floor Physics Club with him?"

"We attend the same school."

"Other than that?" I asked. "Anything in common other than your school and your club?"

"No."

"Hsu's grandfather is 88K's dragon head," I said. "I need to ask you this: is your family involved in the triads? Maybe your family has made enemies."

He said with starched dignity, "My father is a senior vice president at the Hong Kong & Shanghai Bank. My family has never had anything to do with the triads."

I asked, "What was the 20th Floor Physics Club doing?"

"I'll show you."

He led me along the hallway. We passed my door and knocked on the Hsu family's door. Soong spoke at some length to the woman who opened the door. Her expression reflected her doubt. Finally, she tried a smile, nodded at us, and stepped aside so we could enter her apartment.

Mrs. Hsu's expression was carefully deadpan. Her dark hair was tied in a bun behind her head. Her face was small, with tiny, precise features. She was as tall as Soong Chan's shoulders, and Soong Chan was only as tall as my shoulders. Mrs. Hsu was wearing western clothes—a skirt to her knees and a blue blouse. She clasped her hands in front of her and wouldn't look directly at me. Despite her careful appearance, Mrs. Hsu's face was haggard with worry and fear, with purple-green crescents under her eyes. I tried smiling reassuringly at her, but she refused to look at me. Soong Chan made the introductions, and if Soong mentioned Mrs. Hsu's first name, I didn't catch it.

She led us into the living room. The Cantonese of Hong Kong, which is to say 95 percent of the residents, rarely entertain at home, and seldom does someone who isn't a member of the family enter their home. I'm sure this was an extraordinary event for Mrs. Hsu, admitting a stranger—a *gweilo* at that—into her family's apartment.

Soong Chan translated. Mrs. Hsu had offered condolences about my father. She asked, "'Do you think you can help find my son, Mr. Williams?'"

"I'm not sure. I have some contacts."

This apartment had a considerably better view than mine, and we could see past the edge of the building across the street, the building that entirely blocked my view of the harbor. A large aquarium dominated the front room. My friend Jay Lee had told me that many Hong Kong residents install aquariums in their homes because fish deflect evil. On the walls of the front room were several ornately framed mirrors. Each mirror was octagonal, consisting of eight trigrams. Lee had said that mirrors also deflect evil. On a display table was an intricately painted, circular feng shui board, about a foot across, which displayed eight trigrams. *Feng shui* means *wind and water*, and is the ancient Taoist art of proper placement. Along one wall was a four-part folding screen with paper hinges. The screen was decorated with paintings of willow branches, some of the design in gold leaf. Along another wall was a display cabinet that held several dozen small jade pieces. Low-voltage lights were built into the cabinet, and the jade—ranging in color from olive green to lima-bean green—threw off reflected light. Other than these items, everything else in the room was western and modern, including a burgundy leather couch and a glass and stainless-steel coffee table. In one corner was a beanbag chair in front of a TV set, with a Nintendo box and a stack of games. This would have been Mrs. Hsu's son's corner.

Soong apparently asked her if we could step out onto the deck. She nodded and opened the latch. I followed him outside. The only thing on the deck was a fan palm, sitting in a ceramic pot in a corner. Soong Chan pulled a tripod from his briefcase. He set it up quickly, placing the legs precisely on three red markings on the deck, dime-sized circles of red paint. Then he pulled out a piece of equipment. I didn't recognize it.

"Is that a camcorder?" I asked.

He laughed, a good-natured note of victory that this fellow could possibly think the 20th Floor Physics Club would toy with a camcorder. "It's a laser range finder. We built it ourselves."

"I'm impressed."

He mounted it on the tripod. "We searched all over for parts, looking everywhere."

"In America, the word is *scrounging*."

"That's just what we did. We bought the silicon avalanche photodiode on eBay." He leaned over to secure the mounting nut. "We bought the input capacitor from Waterloo Road Electrical Supply over in Kowloon."

Mrs. Hsu watched us from her living room. The building across the street blocked the view straight ahead, but sizable views were to our right: the Wan Chai neighborhood, including a view of the Convention and Exhibition Center and the Fifth Millennium China Tower, at least the top half of the tower, the bottom being hidden behind buildings.

Soong Chan said, "We couldn't find a diode driver, at least for an amount we could afford to pay. So Shui-ban mentioned it to his grandfather, and two days later a driver was delivered here by Federal Express. It's a good one, and it allows for trimpot adjustment of amplitude, pulse width, and pulse repetition rate."

"Did Hsu Shui-ban's grandfather send it to you and Shui-ban, do you think?"

He fiddled with the range finder. "Hsu and I knew better than to ask him."

"Does Hsu know about his grandfather? What Wen Quichin does for a living?"

He looked at me as if I were a toddler. "There is no one in the city who doesn't. Of course he knows."

"Where do you think the driver came from?" I asked.

"From the Red Army."

"How do you know?"

"ARMY OF THE PEOPLE'S REPUBLIC OF CHINA was stamped on the metal case." He smiled. "I don't know how Hsu's grandfather arranged for the driver's liberation from the army."

He unrolled a power cord and plugged one end into the range finder and the other into an outlet near the palm.

"The digital readout is from a Casio calculator," Soong Chan said. "This thing mounted on top is a monocular that has crosshairs, so we can sight the beam. It's adjustable, using these three wing nuts you see here. We built the monocular mount from scratch because we couldn't scrounge up a rifle telescope mount."

The mechanism's housing was a utilitarian gray metal cube that might once have contained an electric meter. The lens—or whatever it was, the business end of it—stuck out from the front of the box, looking like a small telescope.

"How'd you learn to build this?" I asked.

He flicked his hand, indicating it was nothing. "On the Internet. It's easy to find plans to build anything. First we were going to build a fifteen-foot rocket and shoot it off from the Peak, but we decided it wouldn't be too safe."

"Probably a good decision," I said.

"Then we started to build a parabolic listening device."

"You only started?"

He smiled. "We decided there wasn't anybody we really wanted to listen to. So we built this. It took us four months to gather all the parts. We had to teach ourselves soldering."

Soong Chen switched on the device. The switch was an old-fashioned stainless-steel toggle knob, something found in the cockpit of a forty-year-old airplane.

I asked, "What do you do with your range finder?"

He hesitated, then looked at me. "We find ranges."

I nodded. "That makes sense. What ranges?"

"Anything and everything. Do you know how a laser range finder works?"

"I've got a political science degree. How would I know that?"

"It measures the range by precisely timing the interval between sending and receiving electromagnetic waves. It's like radar, except that it uses light instead of radio waves. Let me show you."

He adjusted the tripod's head lock and table lock so that the range finder was aimed across the street. He pointed with his hand. "Do you see the satellite dish on the building there?"

"Sure." The building was our building's harborside neighbor.

He bent down to look at the LCD readout. "The satellite dish's mount—that piece of metal that holds it in place—is 90.223 meters away."

"Not bad."

He adjusted the tripod to point the range finder in another direction. After looking through the spotting scope, he made smaller adjustments. "That stop sign down there on the corner is 156.442 meters away."

"I thought you needed a mirror to bounce the laser light back," I said.

"Not for closer distances." He looked at me. "The American army's tanks have laser range finders so their guns can be accurately aimed, but nobody from the tank has to crawl forward and place a mirror on the pillbox."

"I hadn't thought about that."

"For long-range measurements, a mirror is used," Soong Chan said. "A mirror was left on the moon by the astronauts so accurate measurements could be made."

"How did the astronauts know exactly how to place the mirror, so the light would be sent back to earth exactly where it came from?"

"They used a cube corner mirror."

I waited for him to explain.

He turned the tripod mount, aiming the range finder in another direction, then glanced down to make sure he hadn't knocked the tripod's legs off the red marks on the deck.

He said, "A cube corner mirror is a cube that has been cut in half, and a rounded mirror—half a globe—is put inside it. Doesn't matter what direction the beam comes from, the cube corner mirror sends it back the way it came. We use a cube mirror sometimes."

"Where'd you get it?" I asked.

"We tried making one, but couldn't figure it out," he said. "So we bought one from a survey supply store here. They aren't very expensive."

"What do you do with the mirror?"

"One of us—either Shui-ban or me—will go up to the Peak with the range finder and a Motorola walkie-talkie, and the other will walk around in the streets below, putting out our cube mirror, and we'll take measurements. We've taken probably three thousand different measurements in the past two months, since we finished building the range finder. A mirror gives us more accurate measurements at longer distances than just bouncing the laser beam off the target, such as a building."

I asked, "Why are you and Hsu Shui-ban taking all these measurements?"

"For fun. And we've started writing all of them down so we can use them for our science project due at the end of the term. We don't know how we'll use them in our science project, but we will. Maybe we will present a precise map of the Central District. We don't know yet."

"So you have a notebook with all your measurements? Or do you keep track of them in a computer?"

"We have a notebook," Soong Chan said. "It's at my uncle's."

"Mind if I look at it?"

"It's just a bunch of measurements, pages and pages of them." But he nodded. "Sure, you can look."

"If the only thing you and Hsu Shui-ban have in common is your school and your physics club, is it possible the men who kidnapped Hsu were looking for this rangefinder?"

"I don't know. Anybody can buy a range finder. We built ours because we didn't want to spend money to buy one that is this accurate. It would have been very expensive."

I asked, "Could the kidnappers have been looking for your book of measurements?"

"Why would they do that?" He adjusted the tripod, changing the direction of the laser beam. "Anyone can take measurements like we did. All you need is a range finder. Those distances are no big secret or anything."

I stood there, rubbing my jaw, stumped.

"This is our best shot," Soong Chan said, bent down to the spotting scope. "We were amazed when we got it."

"You've aimed the laser at the Gold Swan?"

He grinned. "Right near the top of it. There's a piece of metal or glass there that reflects like a mirror." He looked down at the LCD. "That point on the tower, which is just below the first restaurant level, is 3622.44 meters away."

He stepped aside so I could view that point through the scope, then look at the readout. I said, "Science projects have come a long way since I was a kid."

Soong Chan packed up the range finder, then folded the tripod and put it into the bookcase. From inside her apartment, Mrs. Hsu had been watching us. When Soong Chan and I left the deck to enter the living room, she stepped forward. Her hands were clasped tightly in front of her.

She spoke in Cantonese, and Soong Chan translated. "Mrs. Hsu wants to know if you will help find her son."

"I'm going to find the men who killed my father. I'll try to find your son, too."

She walked us to the door. Soong opened it. With Soong translating, I told her that I would let her know of any progress I made.

She held out her hand, so I held out mine, palm up. She placed in it a small jade carving. I held it up for a better look. It was a jade dog, rather emaciated, as I could see the animal's ribs. The dog was curled up and sleeping, its muzzle near its tail. The piece of jade was no larger than an inch long. I knew nothing about jade, but even so I could tell this was a finely wrought piece of art. I could see the dog's eyelashes, and the hairs on its back, all rendered delicately in stone. It was cool to the touch.

Mrs. Hsu spoke and Soong Chan translated, "'This is a charm from the Ch'ing Dynasty. It is over two hundred fifty years old, and made of jadeite. It is for you.'"

I looked up at her.

Just before she closed her door, she said, "'It will bring you good luck as you search for my son.'"

5

The prize was five feet tall, and manufactured by Waterford in Ireland. It was a slender crystal obelisk, having the precise design of the Obelisk of Luxor at the Place de la Concorde in Paris. The obelisk was atop a one-foot-square slab of crystal, and was displayed next to the podium under hanging low-voltage lights, so the crystal's facets reflected shafts of light. The prize weighed almost a hundred pounds.

The Frank Lloyd Wright Prize was the most prestigious award in architecture. The prize was given to an architect not for a distinguished career, as were other architecture awards such as the Pritzker, but for a single structure. Philip Johnson had won it for the AT&T Building (today the Sony Building) in New York. I. M. Pei had been awarded the prize for his Pyramide at the Louvre in Paris. Frank Gehry won for the Guggenheim Museum in Bilbao, Spain. The prize was an annual award, but it was not given out some years, and architects worldwide believed the committee—comprised of noted academics and critics—received much snooty satisfaction in periodically passing over an entire year's worth of the profession's offerings.

This year John Llewellyn was the recipient. The committee's press release noted that the tower was not quite completed but that "such a singular and compelling vision and such a significant and vital contribution to world architecture as represented by the Fifth Millennium China Tower argues against delay in making the award." Normally the recipient of the Frank Lloyd Wright Prize traveled to Chicago to receive the award, but so many committee members wanted to see the

Gold Swan with their own eyes that the presentation was being made in Hong Kong.

I was wearing a tuxedo, with a standing collar and a white tie. A thousand other tuxedos were in the room, as were evening gowns of all varieties. This event was a tough ticket, and the Mandarin Oriental Hotel's ballroom was filled to the corners. The only folks not wearing evening clothes were members of the delegation from Beijing, and the press, who roamed the room with their cameras and recorders. Xinua, China's official news agency, had at least twenty people covering the event. Scores of Hong Kong print and TV reporters were there, as were writers from news magazines and trade magazines from around the world.

The tower management had been invited to the award ceremony, is how I had gotten in the door. Chinese security officers were everywhere because sharing the table of honor with John Llewellyn was Chen Langing, China's president, who had flown in from Beijing that afternoon. Their elevated table was brightly lit for the benefit of the television cameras around the room. Llewellyn and Chen looked like negative images of each other, Llewellyn with his silver hair, pale skin, and white dinner jacket, and Chen with his black hair, tawny skin, and dark business suit. Their heads were bent toward each other, they were deep in conversation, and it looked as if they were purposely excluding the dozen aides flanked around them that each man had brought to the ceremony.

The dinner had already been served that evening, the speeches made, and the prize awarded. Guests were beginning to leave the ballroom. I smiled at Anne Iverson when she broke away from a group of tuxedoed celebrants and walked up to me. A wineglass was in her hand.

She asked, "Did you have a lot of trouble, the way you thought you would?"

A few seconds passed before I understood her. Then I replied, "Less paperwork than I had feared."

"Where did you send them?" she asked.

She was referring to my father's ashes. His body had been cremated earlier in the week, after it had been discharged from the medical examiner's custody.

"To one of my father's friends who lives near Medford. Next time I return to Oregon, I'll spread the ashes in one of Dad's old orchards."

She sipped her wine. She was wearing an ankle-length black sheath dress with no sleeves. Three thin silver bracelets were on her left wrist, and diamond studs were in her ears. Her streaked, honey-blond hair fell in loose waves to her shoulders.

She studied me with her peculiar gray-blue eyes. "What did you find out from the boy who rafted across the bay to your office?"

"Not much."

She renewed her smile. "You are dodging my question."

"I'll tell you all I know when I have something solid," I replied. "All I have now is a kid's story." I glanced at John Llewellyn and Chen Langing. "They don't need an interpreter, looks like."

China's president and the tower's architect were still huddled together, excluding everyone else—aides, event organizers, anyone—who might try to intrude. Neither man was smiling, a contrast to the jovial face each presented when publicly discussing the Fifth Millennium China Tower.

Anne said, "Chen Langing speaks English as well as you and I."

"I guess I didn't know that."

"Chen never speaks English when being interviewed or whenever else he is on camera. He doesn't want to give sanction to the English language."

"Chen learned it at Harvard, I suppose."

"At Harvard in general, and from John Llewellyn in particular. They were friends there."

I nodded. The entire world knew that Chen and Llewellyn first met at Harvard. It was mentioned in everything written about the tower.

Anne said: "John told me that he and Chen were closer than the Chinese government wants to let on these days. They met in their freshman year. Chen was at Harvard because at the time Chen's father ran China's interest section in Washington, D.C. Chen appeared at Harvard that fall, with two Mao jackets and only a few words of English. John said that one day that fall, when Chen was sitting alone in their dining hall, John took his meal over to Chen's table and plopped himself down across from him."

"They got along, I take it."

"As John tells it, they each saw potential in the other that very same day, sitting across from each other. Potential for what, they might not have known back then. But potential, nevertheless."

The FBI had taught me never to have a beer or a glass of wine or a highball in my hand at a gathering that included the press, a habit I hadn't been able to shake, and my evening clothes didn't have useful pockets anywhere on them, so I stood there, my arms hanging at my sides with nothing to do.

"They started spending time together," Anne went on. "John introduced Chen to Cambridge pubs and to beer, and to just hanging out. He showed him how to play pinball and throw the Frisbee, and took him to Red Sox games."

Standing near the wall, wearing his usual half-smile, was Darrel Reese, who was the United States' vice-consul, with an office on Garden Road on the Hong Kong side. Reese's assistant at the office performed Reese's consulate functions, leaving Reese time for his actual job, which was an intelligence agent for the CIA. Beijing knew his real job, Reese had told me, and Beijing knew he knew they knew. Still, he carried on, saying that being followed whenever he left his apartment was part of the job. Reese caught me looking at him, dipped his chin, and raised a finger, indicating he wanted to speak with me.

Anne said: "John Llewellyn came to view himself as Chen's protector and guide, helping Chen get a new room when Chen's roommate wouldn't tolerate his cigarette smoking, taking Chen to the student clinic when he broke his finger, that sort of thing. Then, in their junior year, John got Chen into the Rose and Thorn Dinner Club. Chen was the first Asian admitted."

Three Mitsubishi fifteen-by-twenty-foot flat panel screens were on the walls near the podium, installed for the occasion. They displayed views of the tower. One video had been taken from a helicopter as it slowly circled the tower. The construction equipment still remaining on the platform had been digitally removed, so the tower in the video appeared as it would in a month. Another view was from a stationary time-lapse camera, which in the course of sixty seconds showed the tower as it looked throughout a clear and sunny day, the sweeping bronze column changing colors as the sun passed through the sky. The third Mitsubishi screen showed another time-lapse sequence, the camera on Victoria Peak, a shot taken each day over the past four years, the opening seconds of the video showing a portion of the empty harbor, nothing but seawater and the Kowloon skyline in the background, and the last shot showing the nearly completed tower, with the platform and the tower miraculously rising from the sea over the sixty-second video. It was mesmerizing.

Anne said, "Llewellyn took Chen home over several Christmases, and the two of them went up to Quebec for a spring break."

"What did Llewellyn get in return?"

"What do you mean?"

I replied, "John Llewellyn doesn't strike me as someone who does anything without an eventual payback in mind."

"Why would you say that?" Her voice was noticeably cooler.

I shrugged. "Just my impression. He's a chit-collector." Then I tried to lessen the offense by adding, "We all are, I suppose."

She sipped her wine, a tiny sip, as if the glass were a prop. "And as I said, John told me that even back in college he and Chen both knew the other would go far."

John Llewellyn could spot them, it turns out. Chen Langing began his career as a production manager for a radio factory in Changchun. After several years he joined the Communist Party and was quickly given more and more authority, including three years as minister of the electronics industry, and then for four years he was mayor of Shanghai. He was made a member of the Politburo in 1992, and general secretary of the Communist Party soon after that. He was picked by Deng Xiaoping to be president because of his loyalty to Deng and because Chen had shown himself to be a subtle, ruthless, and capable administrator as mayor of Shanghai.

"John and Chen kept in touch all through the years," Anne said, gently shaking her head at a waiter, turning aside another glass of wine.

"And Llewellyn finally collected the chit," I said. "The Fifth Millennium China Tower commission, the most important architectural commission in a hundred years."

She flicked her hand, as if discarding a useless part of the conversation. "Maybe the two of them are friends. Maybe it's as simple as that: a loyal friend giving business to another."

I nodded toward the head table. "They don't look any too friendly right now."

John Llewellyn and Chen Langing were still speaking with each other, and if I hadn't just heard Anne's comments about the loyalty and friendship between them, I would have said they were arguing. Both held their hands over their mouths to avoid lip-readers. A finger of Chen's other hand was wiggling near Llewellyn's jaw, as if he were scolding. Llewellyn's head ducked left and right, small motions, but oddly pugilistic, as if he were avoiding blows. Then suddenly Chen smiled, turned back to the audience, beaming, the picture of avuncular, satisfied authority. He put his hand on Llewellyn's arm. When Llewellyn dropped his hand, he was smiling, too, but it was a narrow, forced grin, it looked to me.

I asked abruptly, "Did Llewellyn make it up to you after he abandoned you for New Delhi?"

A grin slid across her face. "My, we are nosy, aren't we?"

"My FBI training at work."

"When he returned from New Dehli, I found a red jeweler's box on my desk. It contained a silver necklace on which hung a ruby the size of a fingernail. I instantly sent it back to him."

"You are a saint."

"I'm his employee. I'm not going to accept gifts from him." A glower worked under her brows. "I've worked too hard and too long to have coworkers think I got here that way."

"Is that why you keep your relationship a secret?" I asked.

Her expression shifted. "It's not exactly a secret. You know about it, for one."

"For a man who spends half of his life facing press photographers, Llewellyn has done a remarkable job keeping your romance out of the papers."

"He has connections," she laughed, nodding at Chen, who was still standing just behind the head table.

Llewellyn and Chen were now surrounded by photographers and reporters. Chen's bodyguards had moved closer. Llewellyn was holding forth, gesturing expansively and smiling winningly. An interpreter stood nearby to render his words into Cantonese or Mandarin for the Asian press.

Darrel Reese was approaching, chatting with one person and another, but getting closer all the while. He was drinking something that might've been a gin and tonic or a 7Up. Reese had once told me that Beijing put the word out that no mention of John Llewellyn's romances was to appear in Hong Kong newspapers. Hong Kong media were not as independent as they once were.

"Plus, I don't like the world knowing my business," Anne added. "I'm happy he and I aren't the subject of gossip columns and tabloid photographs."

"Then you aren't going to like this week's *People* magazine."

"Why not?"

"There's a big photo of you and him holding hands as you emerge from a restaurant."

She drew herself up stiffly. "*People*? How did they get a photo of us?"

"A friend back home sent me an email with a hotlink to the magazine's Web site, is how I know."

"I mean, are they snooping around?"

"Probably purchased the photo from a paparazzo."

"That's dreadful," she said, more to herself.

"It gets worse. They identify you as 'Anne Iverson, Llewellyn's voluptuous and lively chief assistant.'"

"Oh, for Pete's sake." She closed her eyes. "Is *People* sold in Hong Kong?"

"Only at about four hundred outlets."

"What about my hard work and professionalism, and what about the beauty and dignity of the Fifth Millennium China Tower? Did the article mention any of this?"

"Not a word. The article says that John Llewellyn averages three girlfriends a year."

"Ugh." She made a face. "How am I going to show up at work tomorrow? How am I going to look my coworkers in the eyes?"

With the air of one who has suffered much, Anne drifted away from me, stepping between groups of people and disappearing into the crowd. I'm not sure she knew where she was going. Maybe she wanted to chew on this bad news by herself.

Darrel Reese finally made his way over to me. He was grinning with the benevolence of superior knowledge.

He asked, "Want to trade some information?"

"Why don't CIA guys ever give away information?" I asked. "It's always a deal, a bargain, some scheme to gain more than you give. Nothing is ever a gift. Why is that?"

He laughed. In his youth Reese's hair had been red, but it had darkened and grayed over the years, and was now the color of rust. His chin was large and square, with a perfectly flat bottom, as if designed by an engineer. His eyes were bright blue, and set well back in his head. He was a small man, and nippy, filled with barely contained energy. He constantly rose and fell on his toes, and he always appeared about to dart off, even when he had just arrived. He was wearing a tuxedo.

"Clay, all you have to do is confirm or deny," Reese said. "And it has nothing to do with your work or mine."

"What then?"

"It has to do with your history."

My mouth turned down. "Here we go again."

"It's the separation of myth from fact," Reese said. He was goading me. "That's what the CIA is all about. I'm trained to do it."

"Can't you let it rest?" I asked. "It was a long time ago."

"Either it was a terrific piece of vigilantism or it was an accident." Reese rose on his toes like an orchestra conductor, then settled back down. "I've always wanted to know. You tell me, and I'll give you my information."

I pulled at my earlobe. Reese was referring to the death of one of my early partners, Bill Adamson. When it happened, Adamson was a five-year veteran of the FBI and I was in my first year. We were in Seattle and were called to assist in the apprehension of a bank robber, the bank being on Fourth Avenue. Bank robbers in downtown Seattle almost always flee toward the Pike Street Market, the large open-air produce, fish, and crafts bazaar on a steep slope that overlooks Elliot Bay. I suppose they figure they can get lost in the crowd there. Over the radio, Bill and I were given the suspect's description and were ordered to the Pike Street Market. Two minutes after we arrived, as we were on a stairwell between the second and third floors, we spotted him and he spotted us. From the folds of his jacket, he brought up a pistol and fired. The suspect had fired wildly, but it was a lucky shot, taking off much of Bill Adamson's head. Then the suspect frantically turned to run down the next flight of stairs, but he tripped over his feet and fell down eight stairs before his head caught in a banister rail while his body continued down the stairs. His neck was broken, and he was dead within seconds.

That's how it happened. I said so then, and I say so now. I did not murder Bill Adamson's killer by throwing him down those steps, or by sticking his neck between two banisters and wrenching down on him hard, furious that he had shot my partner. A few days later the FBI administered a lie-detector test to me. I passed it. Then I swore an oath to a medical examiner's jury. They believed me. The suspect's mother brought an action for wrongful death against me. It was laughed out of court on summary judgment.

Yet I had gained an unwanted tag at the FBI. I had passed the lie-detector test, and the jury and judge had believed me. But in my fellow agents' minds there was a chance that I had done FBI agents nation-wide a service by tossing the murderer of one of their colleagues down the stairs and was somehow able to beat the interrogations. For the rest of my FBI career, whenever I met an FBI agent I hadn't known before, I detected a knowing twinkle in his or her eye, and an extra second on the handshake, in silent thanks for my good deed. So I carried a reputation I didn't deserve and didn't want.

Darrel Reese prompted, "So?"

I sighed aloud, something I don't like doing. "I had nothing to do with that fellow falling down the stairs that day."

"I work for the CIA." Reese smiled with his thin, bloodless lips. "Nine out of ten things I hear are lies or exaggerations."

"My statement to you is the tenth."

When a waiter came by, Reese deposited his empty glass on the tray. Anne Iverson had apparently recovered and was chatting with several men near the ballroom's main door. Three massive crystal chandeliers lined the room's ceiling. John Llewellyn and Chen Langing were being escorted to the door by a sizable crowd. Several men guarded the crystal obelisk, which would later be transported to Llewellyn's apartment.

Reese laughed. "I'm getting the bad end of my information exchange."

"So what do you have?"

He rose on his toes. He was beaming with his impending victory. He hesitated, savoring the moment, enjoying the vast difference in our level of knowledge.

Then he said, "That boy, the gangster's grandson who disappeared the day your father died?" He paused again, eyeing me. "We've found him."

* * *

I had been puzzled by the invitation. A dinner with Anne Iverson and John Llewellyn? Anne had called, inviting me, apologizing that it was spur-of-the-moment, but Llewellyn has so few free evenings, and she never knew when another one might come along, and why don't I meet them that evening for dinner at John's place? The three of us? It sounded peculiar.

Llewellyn's apartment was just off Victoria Park Road in Causeway Bay, as close to the harbor as could be got. Anne had given me the code for the elevator reserved for the four penthouse apartments, and I left the elevator, walked along a short hall, and pressed on the bell button.

John Llewellyn opened the door, greeted me with a puckish smile, and whispered, "Don't blame me. I had nothing to do with it."

I glanced at him, but his face gave nothing away. I moved along a wide hallway toward the bank of windows overlooking the harbor. Anne Iverson rose from a chair and stepped toward me. She was wearing a sugary expression.

Then she slid to one side to make way for someone else. A woman stepped into view.

Anne said, "Clay, I'd like you to meet Beth Fowler, a coworker of mine."

I'm confident my expression resembled a stunned trout. Was this a blind date? I'm a professional in my forties, a fellow of some reserve and decorum, and rather shy to boot. I do not go on blind dates. I have not had a blind date since I was fifteen, and it was an education, the young lady fleeing me at the first opportunity, going for a Coke at the movie theater's refreshment counter and leaving the movie theater entirely. Not that I remember it.

Anne said, "I've wanted you two to meet for some time now."

Only the fiercest application of willpower kept me from groaning aloud. This was worse than a blind date. It was an ambush blind date. I had just been ambushed.

My date's smile faltered, and her eyes flicked questioningly to Anne. She had been surprised, too, it looked like. So she was going to have to put up with some stranger, too. It was a double-ambush blind date. As I removed my jacket, I glared at Anne. She ignored it entirely, passing my jacket to a maid who had appeared for that purpose.

Beth Fowler smiled gamely, then she rolled her eyes for my benefit. "I'm surprised at this development."

"So am I," I replied. "But I'm happy to meet you anyway."

Beth Fowler had an overfeatured face, with large brown eyes and a prominent nose. She was wearing black slacks and a blue silk blouse. Her mouth was wide and finely sculpted, and her smile was quick in coming, and she looked at me, then at Anne, still grinning. She was going to treat this surprise date as a lark. If she could smile, so would I. She would bring this up later with Anne, I'm sure, and so would I.

John Llewellyn escorted us into the living room, which had three separate seating areas, each with a slightly different décor. The room was overly air-conditioned, and he guided us toward a fireplace, which was fueled by gas, but had remarkably realistic logs made of metal. Most of the furniture in this corner was of black leather and stainless steel. The room was two stories tall, with a modern stainless-steel winding stairway up to the second floor, and with a balcony along the upper floor where hallways led off to other rooms. Windows were everywhere, and Hong Kong's harbor was displayed before us, lit gaily at night. John Llewellyn's tower was also before us, rising from the water like a giant golden scythe, lit at night by powerful spotlights sunk into the pad. Surrounded by black water and black sky, the tower was spectral, seeming to float in the air without support. The Frank Lloyd Wright Prize was in a corner of the room, spotlighted from above. A five-foot-high bronze sculpture near the north window had been crafted—I would learn later—by Jacques Lipchitz in 1926. A young woman—either one of the caterers or Llewellyn's maid—approached to ask what I would like to drink, and I asked for a beer.

Llewellyn took a chair next to Anne. He held a martini glass. He continued where he had left off when I rang the bell, apparently, as if I hadn't interrupted the conversation. "So for most of history we were limited to four- and five-story buildings, the greatest height a landlord could expect a tenant to climb to an office or apartment."

I glanced out the window. I could see a hanging lantern on a passing junk, and a cruise ship with an enormous X on its stack that was pulling into a slip across the bay.

"The more-or-less simultaneous invention of the elevator—first powered by steam, then by hydraulics, and later by electricity—and the fireproof, wind-braced steel frame let us reach higher. And, I should add, the invention of the caisson foundation."

Anne Iverson occasionally shot me a glance. She was still smiling. She thought herself clever, I suppose, getting Beth Fowler and me here together. Anne wore a black skirt too tight for work, and a black, sleeveless ribbed cotton sweater. Her legs were crossed, and she was bouncing her foot up and down, I think for my benefit, teasing me. She was mighty pleased with herself, trapping me like this, it looked like.

Llewellyn sipped his martini. "So the Woolworth Building in New York, built in 1910, used all these technologies, and is considered the first skyscraper. And it was the tallest building in the world for many years."

"What about the Eiffel Tower?" I asked. "It was built—when?—in 1889, and it's almost a thousand feet high."

"You point to Beijing's problem," Llewellyn said, delighted with the turn in the conversation. "They wanted the highest, but the highest what? The Eiffel Tower is a tower, not a building, and it is a distinction that is argued and argued."

"Why?" I asked.

"If I were to show you scale drawings of Chicago's Sears Tower and Kuala Lumpur's twin Petronas Towers, and ask you which is the tallest, you would probably say the Sears Tower."

The maid returned with a chilled pilsner glass of beer for me. Then she placed a silver tray of filo-covered prawns on the table in front of the davenport where I was sitting.

"Both the Sears Tower and the Petronas Towers have what appear to be extension towers on their roofs. The Petronas Towers' extension towers just barely reach the Sears Tower roof. So clearly the Sears Tower is tallest." Llewellyn grinned with his impending revelation.

"But not so. The Sears Tower's two extension towers are considered antennas, while the Petronas Towers' extensions are considered a part of the building. So the Petronas Towers' extensions—which are considered structural—are higher than the ceiling of the highest inhabited floor of the Sears Tower, and this makes the Petronas Towers taller."

I was about to ask why this was important, and my expression must have relayed the question, because Llewellyn held up his hand at me so I wouldn't interrupt.

He said, "Over the years, four methods of measuring a structure's height have been developed: height to the structural top, height to the highest occupied floor, height to the roof, and height to the top of the antenna."

Anne was leaning back in her chair, making no effort to guide the conversation, apparently accustomed to monologues.

"So the determination of the world's tallest structure depends on how measurements are made," Llewellyn said. "The Sears Tower is the tallest, if height to the highest occupied floor and height to the top of the roof are the measure. The Petronas Towers are tallest if the height to the structural top is the measure."

I reached for a prawn, dipping it in a red sauce. Llewellyn was wearing a thin silver link bracelet.

Llewellyn said, "The World Trade Center was the highest if height to the top of the antennas is the measure, but now it's the Sears Tower. And this doesn't even count structures that aren't freestanding, such as the 2,063-foot-high KTHI television tower in North Dakota. When I say it isn't freestanding, I mean that if the support cables were severed, the antenna would collapse, as did the then-tallest-ever man-made structure, the 2,115-foot Warsaw TV tower. It fell over when its cables gave way in 1991. After it collapsed, the Poles started calling it "'the world's longest tower.'"

Across the bay, Kowloon's buildings were a curtain of light. An oceangoing tug was slowly pulling a long barge, which was carrying construction equipment of some sort—looked like cranes—but I couldn't be sure because of the darkness. The barge seemed to be heading for the Fifth Millennium China Tower. Below Llewellyn's window was the Noon Day Gun, which was fired every day at twelve o'clock. A cannon was first set off a hundred years ago to greet a Jardine & Matheson opium ship coming into the harbor. This one isn't the same cannon, though. Citizens complained the six-pounder was too loud, so it was replaced by a three-pounder in 1962.

"So on that day five years ago I met with Chen Langing and his associates in Beijing, and I had to convince them of my plan to build the 2,500-foot tower." Llewellyn interrupted himself to sip his martini. "One of the ways to do so was to outline the confusion arising when measuring buildings for the honor of being the tallest."

He paused again, this time to reach for a prawn, and I used the break to try to be sociable. "Beth, you work with Anne?"

She replied, "I'm an architect. I head the restaurant and view deck drafting team."

Llewellyn might not have heard her. "This took place at a meeting of the Central Committee of the Politburo. I had already won over Chen, of course, but he told me he needed to bring along the others on the committee."

Anne said, "Beth is from San Francisco, your old stomping grounds, Clay."

Oblivious to our attempts to chat, Llewellyn went on, "I also pointed out to the Politburo the little games played by those who want the honor of owning the tallest structure. For example, the Central Plaza building here in Wan Chai was carefully designed to be one story taller than the Bank of China Tower in Central, so it would be the tallest building in Asia."

"You were an FBI agent?" Beth asked. "Must have been an exciting career. Not like pushing pencils around on a drafting board."

"FBI agents do a lot of pushing pencils nowadays, too."

Llewellyn swept his hand left to right. "So I knew I had only one chance to win the Central Committee over, and I knew that the presentation had to be dramatic. I mean, these people's backgrounds were as soldiers and farm administrators and factory operators and bureaucrats. They wouldn't see my vision unless I presented it to them in a compelling way. So—listen to this: it's brilliant if I don't mind saying so—when the committee entered the room, they found on their meeting table scale models of London's St. Paul's Cathedral and Egypt's Pyramid of Cheops."

"Beth is also a pilot," Anne said. "She owns a Cessna 182."

"Flying is a passing fad," I said. "Nothing will come of it."

Beth laughed politely. Anne nodded, perhaps approving of my attempt at humor.

Llewellyn looked at me vaguely, as if trying to place me. "And I told the assembled men—most of them working assiduously to fill the ashtrays in front of them, some of them in Mao jackets, if you can imagine—that for much of recorded history these were the two tallest man-made structures on earth."

I noticed then that John Llewellyn was a compilation of odd little habits. He lifted his chin—a small, abrupt movement—whenever he made a point. He gestured constantly, but the hand movements never seemed in sync with what he was saying. They were a beat ahead of his words, as if his hands were faster than his mouth. He constantly interrupted his sentences with a fast and full smile, as if he had forgotten to smile when appropriate, and so needed to insert it later. And he was a winker. Every so often, he punctuated the end of a particularly snappy sentence with a wink. I don't like winks. I'm not sure why.

"And, let me tell you, these scale models were lovely. They cost me six thousand dollars each to have them made, and they were about five feet tall, and perfectly proportioned. Even these insular old Chinese bureaucrats recognized the models as being St. Paul's and the Pyramid, and undoubtedly they wondered what I was up to."

"John, maybe you'd like to give Beth and Clay a tour of your place."

Llewellyn nodded but didn't break his pace. "I told the Politburo members—speaking through one of their interpreters—that these two structures, St. Paul's and the Pyramid of Cheops, were mankind's notion of the attainable. For centuries they were the absolute limit of our imaginations. They were as high as we could go."

I glanced again out the window. The tug was getting nearer and nearer to the tower. Every day I was emailed a list of vessels that would enter Victoria Harbor, and the harbormaster informed me of any unscheduled ships. No vessel was allowed to come within a hundred yards of the tower's artificial island unless cleared by my office. The Hong Kong police moored a manned thirty-two-foot patrol boat at the island, near the ferry terminal, to chase away unscheduled vessels that were sailing too close to the island. The hundred-yard perimeter was well-marked with buoys, but the patrol boat still turned aside a dozen vessels each day, mostly fishing boats and sampans.

"And just when they were wondering what my point was, my assistants carried in a model of the Eiffel Tower, built to the same scale as the models of the Pyramid and St. Paul's." Llewellyn's gaze was on the stainless-steel pipes above the fireplace, and he was beaming with the happy memory. "My assistants placed it on the table next to the other models, and it soared above them. I explained to Chen and the other Politburo members that when the magnificent Eiffel Tower was completed in 1889, the world stopped talking about St. Paul's Cathedral and the Pyramid of Cheops and every other building in the world. In the public imagination they became little things, irrelevant and of another era. The Politburo members studied the three models, the Eiffel Tower soaring above the others, and many of them—who had up to then been entirely poker-faced—nodded. They could see how that would happen, how the Eiffel Tower would grab the world's attention."

The tug pulling the barge had been traveling at two or three knots, but now it slowed so that it was little more than drifting. The tug was near the southerly hundred-yard boundary. The perimeter buoys were large, with blinking lights on them. I could see them from Llewellyn's apartment. No doubt the tug skipper could also see them.

"And then, preparing for my masterstroke of salesmanship, my assistants cleared away the three models and brought in more models. These were of the tallest structures in the world at the time: the CN Tower in Toronto, the Petronas Towers, the Sears Tower, and the Empire State Building. And they also brought out models of Hong

Kong's highest buildings, the Central Plaza and the Bank of China. It was an impressive display, models of all these mammoth buildings." He laughed. "I let the old geezers gaze at them for a moment."

I rose in my chair for a better look at the harbor. Then I stepped toward the window. Why wasn't the patrol boat leaving its mooring to head out toward the tug? My moving toward the window didn't cause John Llewellyn to pause in the retelling of his glorious moment.

He was grinning at the memory. "All these models of the world's tallest structures made an imposing miniature skyline on the Politburo's huge oak table. And I told those old fellows that these represented the most imposing, magnificent, and stately buildings the world had to offer."

I reached for my cell phone and punched in a number. Anne Iverson looked over her shoulder at me. Binoculars were on a window ledge. I peered through them. No, I didn't recognize the tug. The name on the side of the boat was in Cantonese script.

"And then we brought out the scale model of my proposal, the Fifth Millennium China Tower. It took three of my assistants to lift it. It was placed in the middle of the other models. It was painted a bronze color, and was on an islandlike pedestal. It was to the other buildings' scale."

"This is Clay Williams," I said into the phone. "Let me talk to Lien Yang-sun. Right away. I don't care what he is doing."

Lien was my superior, the director of security for the tower. The tug crossed the buoy perimeter, drifting closer and closer to the tower. I knew of all vessels with permission to do this. I didn't know this one.

Llewellyn placed his glass on the table so he could gesture with both hands, framing the retelling of his victory. "The model of the Fifth Millennium China Tower soared above the others. It made the other structures look pedestrian. It made them look dated and dull. It made them look overly functional and charmless and square. Everybody at the table knew it. I could tell in their normally unreadable faces."

I said, "Director Lien, an unidentified tug and barge have just entered the tower's restricted area."

Llewellyn said, "The effect was so powerful, the other Politburo members simply glanced at President Chen. He didn't have to poll the committee. Not a word was spoken."

"It is?" I asked. "Since when, Director?"

Llewellyn crowed, "My tower—which would become the grandest, most provocative, the loveliest structure ever to grace the earth—was approved by unanimous, silent, overwhelming consensus. Tears rolled down my cheeks, I must admit."

The architect brushed unseen dust from his trousers and sat back down, perhaps expecting a gush of admiration that I'm sure he always received on telling of this adventure. Beth Fowler obliged, marveling at his triumph, saying just the right things. I drifted back over to the chairs.

I found it hard to participate during the rest of the evening, and Anne glanced at me reprovingly several times, perhaps beginning to think she had invited a dullard to dinner.

Director Lien had gruffly told me in his perfect English that I was not to concern myself with the tug and barge, or any other vessels that would be approaching the tower, and that if I did, my contract would be instantly terminated.

The *taipans*—merchant princes—were the first to live on the Peak, where it was cooler and the sea breezes made life tolerable. Sites for their mansions were carved out of the granite sides of the mountain, and the homes were in narrow tiers, one above the next, overlooking the harbor. Horses and carriages couldn't make it up the steep slope, so the *taipans* walked or used sedan chairs. The homes were stratified on the mountain—the higher up the Peak, the more magnificent the home, just as society was stratified. At one point in the last century, only forty-three Hong Kong residents were considered sufficiently worthy to be invited to Government House, and they all lived on the Peak. Only in the 1950s did the Chinese of Hong Kong begin to live on the slope.

I walked passed St. Joseph's Church, then up Garden Road, and wound around to May Road, then onto Tregunter Path, where benches were placed every so often for the weary walker. By then I was sweating freely, as it was all uphill. No homes fronted the path, but rather steep steps led up through the foliage to higher perches. Addresses were painted on the second or third step, or on small plaques on posts near the steps. I walked along, peering up the hill, through the boughs of sweet-smelling camphor trees—known in Hong Kong as *romantic trees* because their trunks wind around each other—that were clinging to the hill. I found the address and began climbing the steps, which had moss growing on the risers. The steps were in a tunnel of foliage, mostly wild orchid and cassia trees. In the branches somewhere above me, a needletail let loose with its call, and cicadas made their metallic buzz from every direction. A security camera was on a post, its lens pointed down toward Tregunter Path.

After perhaps fifty steps the landscape along the steps began to be patterned, more of a garden with yellow and red azaleas and purple rhododendrons. I was breathing heavily by the time I arrived at the lawn, which was a narrow strip bordered by precisely trimmed rows of English boxwood. Just beyond the boxwood was all of Victoria Harbor, the tower cutting the view into two halves. A brick pathway led to the house.

A man stepped into my vision from somewhere off to the left, maybe from behind a tree. He was carrying a shotgun, its barrel pointed at the ground. He stared at me but said nothing. I moved toward the house. Another fellow appeared, this time from behind a corner of the house. I couldn't see a weapon in his hands, but I'm sure he had one somewhere. Both men were wearing white pants and white shirts, maybe informal uniforms. I could see a third bodyguard in a window on the first floor. To one side of the house was an English garden, with paths, trellises, boxwood hedges, and flower beds of foxglove, azaleas, and many other species, all precisely laid out.

Two gardeners were installing marigolds in a planting bed that ran the length of the house. Another gardener was applying lawn fertilizer with a spreader. They averted their eyes and kept to their work. The house was more a mansion, a Georgian structure that looked as if it had been brought here from the Kent countryside. It was made of gray brick, and the slate roof had three chimneys, which aren't seen much in Hong Kong. A short flight of steps led to a red Palladian door that had a heavy brass knocker in the center. The house was two stories high, and the front had ten sash windows, each with many panes. At the rear, the house was up against the hill, which rose steeply above it.

I climbed to the door, which opened as I neared it. The dragon head, Wen Quichin, stood there, a narrow smile on his face. Behind him stood Zhu Jintau, his nephew, the young interpreter.

Wen spoke, and Zhu interpreted. "'Thank you for coming. Your steep climb up my steps will be rewarded.'"

As I followed Wen and his nephew along a hallway, I peered quickly into the main room. The furniture was a mix of modern Asian furniture and English antiques, including a marble side table that had feet carved to resemble a lion's paws.

Standing on a stool was a young woman in a white wedding dress. One sleeve was missing. She smiled shyly at me. A seamstress was on her knees, a pin cushion strapped to her wrist, working on the hem.

Zhu translated Wen's words, "'My granddaughter is getting married soon. Her name is Chan Juan.'" Zhu added, "'Her name means *graceful* and *ladylike.*'"

She indeed was graceful, balanced on the stool, tall and willowy.

Wen chuckled. "'I will have no fortune left by the time she is married.'"

We entered a sitting room that had four burgundy leather chairs, and an entertainment center along one wall that contained a large television, and VCR, DVD, and stereo systems. A bookshelf along another wall held rows of leather-bound, gold-embossed ornamental books. The two windows in the room looked out on a wall of vines and boughs.

Wen sat in a chair and gestured for me to take another. His nephew remained standing. An elderly woman appeared with a tea service. She placed it on a black wood table that was topped with mother-of-pearl inlays in floral patterns. She didn't pour the tea but rather left that to the dragon head, who did so slowly and with slightly exaggerated movements. He set out only two cups. His nephew, Zhu Jintau, apparently forgotten, would do without.

The triad leader spoke and his nephew translated, "'I hope you are recovering from your terrible loss.'"

"I'm doing better. Thank you."

"'Losing a father is a terrible experience,'" Wen said. "'You have my sympathy.'"

Unsure of the ceremony, I waited until he lifted his tea, and then I imitated him. He sipped loudly. I was a bit quieter. It was green tea, with a sharp herbal flavor.

When he continued, the nephew again rendered the words into

English. "'We have formed a worthwhile partnership. Your information has proven accurate.'"

The CIA agent, Darrel Reese, had told me that a friend in the New Territories village of Sha Tin, on Shenzhen Bay near the mouth of the Pearl River, had reported that several men appeared to be holding a boy in an abandoned net storage building. I had asked Reese about the friend, and Reese hesitated, but only a moment, before telling me it was an elderly man who had been an aide to Chiang Kai-shek, and who had spent twelve years at the Wisdom in Work reeducation camp in Yenan, near the Ordos Desert in Inner Mongolia, and who had then been allowed to become a cobbler's assistant in Canton, where he had been a walk-in at the U.S. consulate there. The fellow was ready to work against Mao's regime, at great risk to himself, but unfortunately he had nothing of note to report because of his modest circumstances in Canton, far away from China's political or military centers. Still, for many years, if he saw a Red Army regiment on the move, he would dutifully send a message to the consulate, using a drop-box system the CIA had taught him.

Then five years ago he asked the consulate to help him and his family move to Hong Kong. The CIA rewarded him for his work and his risk, and quietly paid those who needed to be paid—corruption being endemic at Canton's Kwangtung Region Emigration Office—and even hired a truck and a bus to move the fellow and his family, which turned out to consist of three sons, three daughters, and twenty-eight assorted in-laws and grandchildren, to the New Territories. There the fellow, now in his mid-seventies, had set up a shop selling Nike and Reebok beach waders and Sun System hats to the fishermen.

He was done with his spying, of course. Nothing to spy on in the New Territories. But after the Handover, the Reds began making inroads into Hong Kong and Kowloon and the New Territories, little things at first, but making more and more aggressive displays of power as the years passed. So several times he had telephoned the U.S. consulate with information, once about an unmarked blue helicopter that had landed in a grain field near the ponds, another time about a Red

Army colonel who for some reason visited the fish manager's office in full uniform one day. And five days ago when the old fellow saw these two men, maybe three, who appeared to be hiding a boy in an abandoned building, he again telephoned the U.S. consulate in Hong Kong. He described the boy, and it was indeed Wen's grandson, Hsu Shui-ban.

That day on the park bench, the 88K's dragon head, Wen Quichin, had given me a phone number, and I had used it, later telling Wen of my conversation with his grandson's friend, Soong Chan, and how Soong had seen two men spirit Wen's grandson away, and I further told him where his grandson had been spotted, the information Darrel Reese had given me at the Frank Lloyd Wright Award ceremony. Through an interpreter Wen had replied with only, "'I will take care of it.'"

So now he had invited me to his house on the Peak, perhaps to update me on whether he had taken care of it, whatever that meant. He sat there behind his spectacles, a small man surrounded by a large leather chair, a man of immense power and vitality, serving me tea.

He said through his nephew, "'I did not find my grandson at the hut near the fish pond, though I believe he was there a few hours before I arrived.'"

"Your grandson is alive, then?" I asked. Zhu translated.

"'Yes. For how long, I do not know.'" Wen again sipped his tea. On the table next to the silver service was a videocassette. "'We were able to gain some information from the person we found at the hut.'"

I wondered if the gangster's language was filled with slang and poor grammar, and whether his nephew was cleaning it up for my benefit.

"'I have learned,'" Wen continued, speaking through his nephew, "'that your father died just as you said, just as my grandson's friend, little Soong Chang, said he did.'"

"How do you know?" I asked.

"'We questioned a man we found there. It turns out this fellow was one of the kidnappers of my grandson, and one of the murderers of your father.'"

"He told you this?" I asked.

"'And much more, yes.'" Wen's half-smile never varied.

"Who is he?"

"'His name is Sun Guo-ning. He said he works for the Shenzhen Security Company, a business that claims to supply security guards, portable fencing, and the like.'"

A grandfather clock chimed from somewhere in the house.

I asked, "Who was he working for? I mean, who ordered him to kidnap your grandson?"

"'We have determined that the Shenzhen Security Company is a front. For what, we don't know yet. It is a small office on Princess Margaret Road in Shenzhen. We are working on it.'"

"And what about the other guy who was there that day?" I asked.

"'We know his name, thanks to Sun Guo-ning. We are looking for him. I do not doubt we will find him.'"

"And Sun Guo-ning could tell you nothing about why he took your grandson?"

The old man shook his head sharply. "'We are confident Sun was not keeping any information from us. He and his partner had been ordered to take the boy to the fishing net hut and hold him there until told otherwise. Your father was thrown from the balcony because he came across them taking the boy, and they didn't want a witness. The boy was moved from the hut just before we got there, and Sun was cleaning the place up, removing evidence.'"

The triad leader poured us more tea. Someday, I would ask him about the scar on his cheek. Or maybe I wouldn't.

He said, "'You are looking for the men who killed your father because you are interested in justice. Is that correct?'"

I wondered if I was being asked to implicate myself. After a moment I replied, "Yes."

He spoke in Cantonese to his nephew, who lifted the video cassette from the table and inserted it into the VCR below the television set. Wen used a remote control to switch on the TV.

"'This is a videotape of Sun Guo-ning, taken yesterday,'" Wen said. He waved his hand and his nephew left the room.

There were no credits, no fade-in, and no sound. Suddenly on the screen appeared a man sitting on a straight-back wooden chair, his hands behind him, obviously bound together at the wrists.

"'Sun Guo-ning,'" 88K's dragon head repeated.

The point of view was from directly in front of the man, and the camera slowly zoomed toward him. A utility sink was visible in the background. Sun's lower lip was split, and blood had dribbled onto his chin. The skin around his left eye was swollen so much that the eye wasn't visible. His expression—that which I could make out around the bruises—was of resignation.

A hand gripping a small automatic pistol appeared at the upper left-hand corner of the video frame. The hand jerked with the pistol's recoil. Sun Guo-ning's expression didn't change in the slightest. He spilled sideways in his chair to the floor.

The camera panned back. Sun Guo-ning was still bound to his chair, but was now lying on his side on the tile floor. Blood pooled under Sun's head. The gunman had stepped out of the frame.

Only after a moment could I pull my eyes away from the television screen. The dragon head was looking at me, and he was smiling.

He said one word in English. "Justice."

*　*　*

Following Anne Iverson toward the tower's entryway, I took a second to prepare myself, then looked skyward, up the vast sweep of the tower. It was a new horizon, a rising crescent, unconnected with any reality except itself. No prior experience prepared a person for looking upon the tower, particularly from here, right under it. Nothing else in the world resembled it in size or grandeur. And it was difficult for the mind to accommodate. When I wasn't actually looking at the tower, my mind automatically returned to comfortable scales, to the restful and the pedestrian, to the mundane. Then, the next time I looked at the tower, I received another jolt. Most other folks reacted the same way, I suspect. I was shocked every time I looked at the Gold Swan. And here, up close, right under the entryway doors, with the thing rising above me, as tall as a shaft of lightning, the tower was overwhelmingly strange and otherworldly.

Anne was following my thoughts. She said, "I've never gotten used to the tower, just like you. And I don't think John Llewellyn has, either."

She had called me, saying we needed to talk. Her office was too crowded, so we had agreed to go for a walk and an elevator ride. The entranceway was under an arc cut into the bronze façade. The arc was about fifty feet high at its peak, and was filled in with glass. The glass doors, which would eventually be powered, were set in an open position. Whenever I enter a building in Hong Kong, I brace myself against the blast of chilled air, but the air conditioners were not yet operating, and it was as hot inside the main hallway as out. Twenty-five hundred feet of metal was above us.

Anne laughed. "This hall is the only serious argument President Chen had with John Llewellyn."

"How so?" I said.

"Beijing wanted to make this entrance hallway a grand statement, sort of a Hallway of the Proletariat, an enormous cavern."

"Beijing still uses words like *proletariat?*"

"At the top, they do, John tells me. Less so for public consumption. But President Chen wanted the equivalent of an indoor football field in here, with dizzyingly high ceilings and huge red banners hung from the walls."

"To make the visitor feel small compared to the power of the state," I commented. "And there's an ancient saying about Hong Kong, that it is farthest from the emperor. The tower is designed to cure that impression, too."

She nodded. "John fought him and fought him, and finally threatened to walk off the job if the entrance wasn't made in a reasonable scale. Chen and the other Central Committee members finally gave in."

The hallway was designed to handle crowds waiting for the elevators. Crowd control, however, was going to be principally done on shore, the number of ferry runs limited to the number of visitors the elevators and the viewing areas could accommodate. This would allow for a smooth visit, with only small crowds and short waits. A number of op-ed writers had said that Beijing feared crowds of any size.

The hall wasn't a long cube, but rather the walls curved, and there were a few nooks and crannies, and many small sitting areas. Eventually a number of vendors' carts and other attractions would be allowed in the hallway, insuring that it was always festive and pleasantly noisy. The ceiling was a comfortable height above us. A hundred or more artists from Hong Kong and China were working on wall mosaics, installing the tiles, as Anne and I walked toward the elevator bank. The right to display the mosaics was the result of a nationwide competition, the artists vying to be immortalized in the hallway of China's most famous landmark.

Electricians were also working in the hall, as were representatives from many other trades. Granite counters were being installed, and railings that would guide visitors this way and that. Light fixtures were being worked on. Ladders were everywhere. Canvas tarps were spread on the floor below painters. The door to the elevator control room was open, and three or four technicians were bent over a control panel that glowed with red and green lights.

The lift system was a one-off design. Elevators had never before been produced in this manner, rising 2,500 vertical feet on a curved route. The British engineering firm of Leavitt & Smith had been retained to design the Fifth Millennium China Tower's elevators. Everyone involved with the tower was wearing laurels, it seemed, and Leavitt & Smith had been awarded the Royal Academy of Engineering's MacRobert Award for engineering innovation.

Each of the four elevators would carry eighty passengers. Anne and I stepped into one, then sat on padded benches along the side. The door hissed closed. A suggestion of movement indicated the elevator was on its way.

I hadn't mentioned to Anne my visit to 88K's dragon head earlier that day, or the turmoil that it had caused me, not only from witnessing on video the killing of the kidnapper but also from the realization that I might have made a terrible error in entering into any sort of arrangement with the gangster. After watching the killing, I had protested to the dragon head that I hadn't bargained for this sort of thing, and he had looked at me as if I were a child and had asked what I had in mind when dealing with the murderers of my father. I didn't have an answer, so I quieted down, finished my tea, and fled his home as quickly as I could.

"The elevators were another argument," Anne said. "Some in the Central Committee wanted the elevators to have windows, so that riders could see Victoria Harbor fall away as they shot up the tower. But President Chen prevailed with his thinking that the Fifth Millennium China Tower wasn't an amusement park ride, but rather was a monument."

I had been up the elevator a number of times. "I can hardly tell we are moving."

She said, "That's part of it. John didn't want the ride up to be bumpy or noisy, reminders that we are moving almost thirty miles an hour. He wanted to save all of the impact for the last moment, when we step out onto the platform."

Anne was wearing black jeans and a blue denim shirt, her field clothes. My ears popped.

She said, "Notice how bright it is in here, how white the light is, and sort of harsh?"

I nodded. "Now that you mention it."

"That's so we won't squint so much when we step out into the sun. John didn't want visitors spending their first minute on the viewing platform with their eyes screwed closed, and not seeing the view."

Above the door was a built-in monitor that displayed the elevator's progress. It showed that we were quickly nearing the top, passing the communications floor, the two restaurant floors, and were approaching the viewing level, the very top. The elevator slowed, though it was hard to tell. With a whisper the doors slid open. We walked across the elevator lobby, just above the New Century Restaurant, which, when it opened, would become the highest restaurant above grade in the world. I followed Anne out into the sun.

At first, all I could see was a yellow swollen sun and a bleached blue sky, with a thin jet contrail off to the west, but as I stepped out onto the viewing platform, and walked closer to the rail, Hong Kong rose up into my view. To my left was the convention center, on its man-made peninsula, and just behind it was the Central Plaza, which rose to 1,241 feet, not quite half the size of the tower. And there was the Bank of China Tower—the crisscrossed girders were said to be inspired by bamboo—which was for three short years the tallest building in Asia, until the Central Plaza was built. The skyscrapers along the Wan Chai and Central District shoreline were an imposing phalanx, the ranks close and deep. They glittered in the sun, and they represented the work of the world's elite architects: I. M. Pei, Dennis Lau and Ng Chun Man, Hsin-Yieh, Cesar Pelli, and Norman Foster.

Yet their work was diminished from this angle, high above the structures and looking down at them. The city seemed a miniature. I was too far away to see anything in a human scale, none of the touches that made the city livable and lively, such as hanging baskets of flowers and the banners, the vendors' carts, students in their school uniforms, and the neon Chinese lettering. And I was too far away to smell the exhaust fumes, duck guano, and incense, and to hear the blasting radios, the clatter of mah-jongg tiles, and the laughter. From this distance, Hong Kong seemed bled of its vitality.

Still, it was lovely, with the Peak on my left, the hills of the New Territory to the right, and the sapphire harbor below. A blue-hulled Blue Ocean Lines container ship was rounding the head at Sai Ying Pun and entering the harbor. In the distance were the green hills of Lantau Island, with the new airport next to it. I could see Butterfly Beach, and Brothers Point and Pillar Point on the New Territories, and I could see even farther, to the mouth of the Pearl River.

I'm not afraid of heights, usually. Flying in airplanes, even small ones, doesn't bother me, and I can stand on Central Plaza's forty-fourth-floor skydeck, and not think about the distance between me and the street below, but the tower was different. The viewing platform hung out over the water, with nothing below but air because the

tower was a giant curve, with the curve behind the viewer when looking toward the Central District. I stepped cautiously toward the edge
of the platform, then gripped the rail and looked down. Far, far below
was the man-made island, and I was suspended above Hong Kong like
a balloon. I swallowed quickly.

Anne Iverson chuckled. "Your knuckles are as white as bone, Clay."

"My father took me to the Grand Coulee Dam on the Columbia
River when I was a kid. I'll never forget looking down at the cascading
water. The water pulled at me, inviting me to jump, assuring me it was
an entirely reasonable thing to do. My dad said he felt the same thing.
I get that feeling here, too."

She looked at me, an eyebrow raised.

I hastily added, "It's just a weird sensation, is all. I get it when I'm
perched high on some structure. Lots of people feel it."

She asked, "Notice the difference between this viewing platform
and others around the world, such as the top of the Empire State
Building?"

I shook my head.

"There's no grillwork and wire and glass to prevent jumpers.
There's just this railing, and the glass below the rail to cut down the
wind. This was the source of another argument between John and the
Central Committee. John thought such precautions were necessary
because the tower would be a magnet for suicides and hang-glider pi-
lots and midnight bungee jumpers and the rest."

"How did the Central Committee counter that?" I asked.

"LegCo, the Hong Kong legislature, has passed a law saying that
anyone using the tower for flying or jumping or climbing sports will
be sentenced to five years in prison. And as for the suicides, the Central Committee essentially shrugged its collective shoulders."

She turned to the view, and after a moment she said, "I was surprised by the news this morning. You?"

"I saw a tug and barge approach the island last night, and I was told
it was none of my business, but, still, I was surprised. And you were,
too? This is an architectural issue, isn't it? I thought this kind of thing
was precisely your business."

The wind tossed her honey-colored hair. She looked at me pensively. "It was. It should have been. I don't have an explanation for it, and I haven't seen John Llewellyn to ask him about it."

I looked at her. "So you and I have been shut out. Who else?"

"Most everybody. This morning I spoke with Hao Linh-nam, who is COO with East Asia Management, the construction management firm, and he said he didn't know what was going on, and he was clearly upset. And I also called Charles Bao, of Bao Contracting, who built the island's ferry terminal, and he said he wasn't asked to submit a bid, and knows nothing about it."

"How about your office?" I asked, "Have you talked to John Llewellyn's secretary, maybe? Somebody else he works with every day?"

"He works with me every day," she said. "I'd know if anybody knew."

I shifted my gaze back down to the harbor just below the tower. "Well, whoever is doing it is sure moving quickly."

A new fleet had appeared overnight in Victoria Harbor. Moored near the tower's man-made island below us were two dozen tugs, and barges that carried boring and jacking equipment, pump stations, dump trucks, crawlers, and graders. Several of the barges were specialized concrete mixers, where sand and gravel and cement and whatever else went in one side, and concrete came out the other. Other barges carried steel sheet pilings and others carried reinforcing rods. Four dump barges had grab-dredging cranes mounted on them.

Anne pointed. "More are coming."

Passing the convention center were two more tugs, both with barges in tow. On the back of one was a three-story piece of equipment I couldn't identify, and the other barge was carrying boulders the size of trucks.

"How was it kept out of the papers so long, do you think?" I asked.

She gestured despairingly. "How'd they keep it from you and me for so long, and how'd they keep it from all the others?"

The headlines in that morning's *South China Morning Post*, and all the other Hong Kong newspapers, had announced that a second ferry terminal was going to be constructed on the tower's island, this one on the west end. The first terminal, which was nearly completed, was on the east end. The article explained that when the tower opened it would instantly be the world's most popular tourist destination, and that a second terminal was needed to handle the expected crowds, that greater-than-first-anticipated tourist access dictated a second ferry terminal on the island. The new terminal would be larger than the first, and would require extensive dredging and filling, as the island would be extended eighty meters east to accommodate the new structure. Compaction of the fill at the west end would be required, to bear the weight of the new terminal. The tower's opening would not be delayed, however. It was a massive project, kept secret, and then suddenly announced.

"I thought the architects and engineers had crowd management figured out years ago," I said.

"I did, too." She caught her lower lip in her teeth. "But I guess not. And none of my team was in on the decision or design for the new ferry terminal, which is puzzling."

Anne and I stood there for a moment without speaking. Two Star ferries passed each other mid-channel. From behind us came the rattling noise of an arc welder. The sense of unreality imparted by being on a platform half a mile high was countered somewhat by the warm breeze, something familiar, reminding me of harvest winds in the Medford Valley. I enjoyed the sensation, the warm wind, with Hong Kong spread out before me like a map.

I asked, "What about Llewellyn's theory about clutter? Didn't he want the man-made island to be as barren as possible so it wouldn't detract from the sweep of the tower? Isn't another ferry terminal going to clutter up things?"

She shook her head, not knowing the answer.

"And if Llewellyn is worried about clutter, why isn't the first ferry terminal simply expanded? More mooring piers could be added, and you could double the traffic the east terminal could handle. Why isn't that being done?"

"I'm not entitled to know the reason, apparently." Her voice was dark with resentment. "This is as much a surprise to me as it is to you."

When Anne abruptly turned back toward the elevators, I followed her.

Her face lengthened. "John never mentioned a word of it to me."

A dozen workmen had arrived to complete terrazzo work in the lobby. The elevator was waiting, and Anne and I entered it. We rode down in glum silence, her eyes on the elevator floor the entire way. Crescents were bitten into the corners of her mouth. When we reached the bottom, the doors opened and we stepped out into the hallway, then walked to the entrance and out into the sun.

"All the engineering and procuring were kept from me and the other staff," she said, mostly talking to herself as she turned toward her office trailer. "Who did all the planning?"

"I don't know," I said to her back.

"And what sort of a project is done in secret?"

I didn't know the answer to that, either.

"Well, I'm really puzzled," she said, turning toward her office trailer.

She would have been even more puzzled had she known that at that moment twenty policemen were on their way to the island to make an arrest.

7

Hong Kong isn't known for riots, the citizenry priding itself on its order. There have been a few, though. In 1956 some city bureaucrat ordered Nationalist Party banners removed from buildings during a celebration of the October Revolution, and riots ensued. In 1966 during the Cultural Revolution, Communist agitators sparked riots in the city that had the whiff of a coup. In 1984 a taxi drivers' strike somehow led to destructive mobs roaming the streets. But these were considered shocking exceptions. Stability is prized in Hong Kong perhaps more than any other civic virtue. Above the entrance to the Canton-Shanghai Bank is the inscription in stone ESTO PERPETUA—Let It Be Perpetual.

So I wasn't expecting a riot at the tower, but a riot is what happened, a bit of lawlessness that I might have joined, throwing bottles and pushing and shoving, had I gotten there in time.

I was at my computer in the trailer, completing that week's security summary—trying to make the utter absence of news sound interesting—and typing away, when sudden motion outside my window caught my attention. Workers pass my window all day, but hardly ever are they running, and it was the quick movement that turned my head, and what I saw surprised me: twenty or more policemen, all carrying batons and plastic shields, were sprinting toward one of the cafeteria trailers. And these were not Hong Kong police, but police from somewhere else in China, identifiable because all big-city mainland police wear a dark blue uniform known as Style-99. I rose from my desk and crossed to the door for a better look.

Shouts of outrage were coming from a crowd that had gathered outside the trailer. I could see the kepis of several policemen who were inside the crowd and were being jostled around.

Anne Iverson emerged from her office and appeared at my elbow. She asked what was going on and I shook my head. More and more workers ran across the island to join the crowd. News of some sort had spread quickly across the island. The cafeteria trailer had three steps up to the door, and I saw two men emerge, pulling a third person behind them.

"Plainclothes cops, looks like," I said.

"Who are they after?"

"I don't know. I didn't hear anything about this."

"I thought this was your bailiwick," she said in an accusatory tone. "You are supposed to know everything about tower security. How can an arrest be made on this island and you not know anything about it?"

I didn't have an answer. The man being arrested struggled. His face popped into view, but too quickly for me to identify. The policemen roughly shoved the man to the ground, maybe to cuff him. The angry shouting increased. As they neared the crowd, the baton-carrying policemen formed a wedge, their shields on the outside, and when they reached the outskirts of the crowd, they hardly slowed. The wedge easily pushed aside the throng, which then closed behind the police formation. More and more people joined the crowd, all of them construction workers, all of them Hong Kong Chinese. Several cops used their batons, slashing out alongside their shields. Screams of pain and rage came from the group. A stone arced into the air, then another one, landing among the police.

I started running. For a second I could see the arrested man again, and blood was flowing down his forehead. His mouth was open as if he were shouting, but no sound came out. His eyes were white all around. More rocks were thrown at the police. One of the mob swung a length of rebar at a cop, but it was easily parried by the shield, and the man was felled by a billy club, sinking out of sight among all the others. The shouting and cursing and shoving and scuffling had become a deep rumble, the sound of a locomotive. Two shields parted, and the man was pushed into the center of the wedge. A whistle blew, and the formation began working its way out of the mob.

And by now it truly was a mob. Shrieks of rage came from it. Many beat on the shields with their fists. They wore hard hats and work gloves, and many had on carpenter's belts. Several tried kicking the shields aside, but the formation held, and broke free of the mob. An arc welder's canister was thrown at the policemen, and then came more bricks and other construction debris. The formation made its way toward two police launches at the terminal.

I tried to intercept the wedge. Holding up my tower ID—as if that had any weight anywhere—I planted myself in front of the wedge, and I yelled out, "Stop. Police."

It sounded foolish even as I said it. They were the police. I was a consultant. Or maybe the policemen didn't hear me, what with all the shouting and cursing going on behind them. Or—more probably—they heard and simply ignored me. The wedge came on, me standing there, ID in the air, the shields reflecting the sun, helmets visible above them.

The wedge didn't stop, didn't even slow. The front shield struck me chin to knee cap, and I bounced off, my hand still holding aloft my silly little ID card. The wedge was moving only at walking speed, and so I wasn't hurt, but before I could gather my feet under me, a shield rammed me again. This time it shoved me to one side, and I thought I heard the shield-bearer say something apologetic, though it was in Cantonese, so I couldn't be sure. I was shunted aside, shield to shield, until I was standing harmlessly to one side, my ID still in my hand. The formation passed me, the policemen's boots tramping on the concrete. I couldn't see the arrested man, who was somewhere behind all the shields.

The mob followed the police, hurling a few stones and shouting epithets. The formation reached the edge of the island, where the two police vessels were waiting. The cops began boarding the boats, keeping their shields toward the crowd. A few small stones were thrown toward the boats, but the mob had been defeated, and was quickly dissolving into small groups of workers, who gestured and talked animatedly.

I glimpsed the arrested man again. His arms were behind his back, and two policemen hurried him into the first launch, then shoved him forward into the day cabin, a cop's hand on his head to bend him down to clear the hatchway. When the last of the policemen stepped over the rail into the boats, the diesel engines roared and the vessels powered away from the island, blue lights flashing on the radar arcs. Feeling like a helpless dolt, I turned back toward Anne Iverson.

She asked, "Why would they do that? Make an arrest using all those policemen?"

Clouds crossed the sky above us. The top of the tower vanished within a cloud for a moment before reappearing. I rubbed my forearm where a shield had hit it. "I don't know."

"I mean, why put on such a display? That person could have been arrested at his home, I suppose, but they came here instead."

I said, "Usually when an arrest is made using that much force, the police are trying to make a statement."

"What statement?"

I shook my head. The workers were slowly returning to the cafeteria trailers or to their stations. "You know as much about it as I do."

"Is your arm hurt?" she asked.

I hastily removed my left hand from my right forearm. "A bump, is all."

"Let me look at it?"

"It's nothing."

She grabbed my arm and held it up. "It's just a bump."

"Like I said."

She laughed lightly. "A bump this small doesn't qualify you for being my big hero."

We walked back to the trailers. I resisted the urge to ask her what, precisely, *would* qualify me.

*   *   *

Inside the U.S. consulate in Hong Kong is a room that I was assured was bugproof. Darrel Reese sat next to me, in front of a small stack of photographs. Also in the room was Ross Shepherd, whose job hadn't been explained to me but who I assumed was with the CIA, same as Reese. On a wall was a monitor, and a remote control was in Reese's hand. The room contained a heavy oak conference table, padded chairs, and a narrow table along one wall, on which was a telephone. Light came from recessed canisters above the table and along the walls. The place smelled of Pine-Sol.

"Take a look, Clay." Reese glanced down at a photo, then used the remote to bring up an identical photograph on the monitor. "This was taken yesterday morning."

The monitor filled with an aerial view of a body of water, too much of a close-up for me to recognize the shoreline. In the center of the photo was a tugboat pulling a barge. A slight wake behind both vessels indicated they were moving toward the bottom of the photo. Several smaller boats were also visible, tucked into the shore at the top of the photograph.

"This is the Yangtze River near Wuhan. This tugboat is pulling a grab dredger. You can see the dredger's cab and machinery room aft. The boom is tied down fore and aft across the debris dump." A red arrow appeared on the monitor, controlled by Reese's remote. "And this black mechanism on the bottom of the dump is the grab. It's used for hauling up rocks and silt from the bottom of a river or bay."

Ross Shepherd wore rimless spectacles. His skin was pallid, as if he never left this room to go out into the sun, but his eyes were a hard blue, missing nothing and constantly moving. A red knit sports shirt hung loosely on his thin frame. He said, "This grab dredger was manufactured in Wuhan four years ago, and has spent its entire working life on the Three Gorges Dam, never leaving the area."

The Yangtze is the longest river in Asia. When completed, the Three Gorges Dam will be almost a mile and a half long and six hundred feet high, and will create a reservoir longer than Lake Superior, which will bury under water 19 cities and 326 villages, forcing almost two million people to resettle. The dam will generate more electricity than any other installation on earth, almost twice that of the massive Grand Coulee Dam in Washington State, more than eighteen nuclear power plants. The Chinese also believe the Three Gorges Dam will help prevent Yangtze flooding that has claimed more than 300,000 lives in the past century.

Shepherd said, "That is, until yesterday this grab dredger had never left the Three Gorges site. Suddenly the vessel is heading downstream toward the ocean. And here's another."

Up on the monitor came a second craft. A shoreline could also be seen, with several buildings and a small pier.

Reese said, "This vessel is the *Coast Argosy*, owned by Amoil Leasing of Houston, and currently leased to the China Three Gorges Project Corporation. It's a trailer suction hopper dredger, the largest-capacity dredger in the world."

Shepherd added, "The *Coast Argosy* has been in China for five years, first assigned to the Chek Lap Kok Airport project and then to the Fifth Millennium China Tower's island. For the past two years the dredger has been on the Yangtze, at the Three Gorges Dam. But yesterday it left the Three Gorges site and set sail down the Yangtze."

I asked, "Are the grab dredger and the *Coastal Argosy* headed toward Hong Kong? To join the fleet that's been assembling here for the past two days?"

"We don't know." Reese's face—normally cheery, with its canted eyes and mischievous grin—was hard with thought. A new photograph appeared on the monitor. "And here's something else. This photograph was taken about three weeks ago. It shows some work on the new Kwangtung highway, between Canton and Shaokuan, about twenty-two miles north of Canton." He moved the red arrow around on the screen, stopping here and there. "You see here four scrapers and two crawler dozers and five dump trucks."

Reese leaned forward in his chair, his elbows on the table. "And now here is a photograph of the same project yesterday. This photo is two miles farther along the highway, where you would expect that the equipment—the trucks and graders and dozers—would be working. And indeed you can see where they were working. See those tractor tracks? The dozer tracks are sharp, not worn down by rain or wind. The dozer had been on this Kwangtung highway construction site just a day or two before this photo was taken."

"But now it's gone," Shepherd concluded, "as is all the rest of the heavy equipment. The Kwangtung highway project shut down a day or two ago."

I asked, "Where has all this highway equipment gone?"

"Not far from here." Reese glanced at the remote in his hand. When he pressed a button, another photo appeared on the monitor. "This is a sand and gravel yard at Shatou, on Shenzhen Bay, just across the New Territories border. This yard was the main source of fill for Heroes of the Revolution Island. You can see here where the side of the mountain has been cut into, and you can see the jaw-crushers and the conveyor belts. And there's a lot of earth-moving equipment here, too." He moved the red arrow. "This crawler dozer here, take a look at the tread marks."

I leaned forward for a better look. "What am I trying to find?"

"Here's a closer shot." Reese clicked the remote, and a new photograph appeared, this one showing two rows of linked track prints in the dirt. "Two of the links are broken on this tractor's left side. Only half the link remains for both of them, and these links are three links from each other. Now let me backtrack in our photos."

The monitor went dark for a second, then up came the photo of the Kwangtung highway project again, this one taken before the earth-moving equipment had been taken away.

"Now, here's a photo of tracks left in the dirt at the highway site." Another scene came up, this one a closer shot. "You can see that same pattern here. Two fractured links with three links separating them have left their prints in the dirt here."

"So the bulldozer that had been working on the highway up in Kwangtung is now at the sand and gravel lot just across the New Territories border, not too far from here?"

Shepherd nodded. "We think all that road equipment was moved south to this gravel yard in the past few days."

I scratched the back of a hand. "Are you suggesting that all this equipment is going to be used in the construction of the second ferry terminal? That work on the Three Gorges Dam and the new highway has been interrupted to build a second terminal?"

Darrel Reese cracked a knuckle. He was good at it, sounding like a pistol shot. "We don't know. We want your help finding out. You are plugged in over there on Heroes of the Revolution Island. If anyone can find out, you can."

My deal with the tower management was clear on this subject: I could turn over any information I came across to my country's intelligence agencies. I wouldn't have joined the project had it been otherwise. And the Chinese knew I would do so anyway, and so the agreement allowing me to do so cleared away any need for subterfuge. And as I say, my group had become a worldwide clearinghouse for intelligence regarding terrorists, and this was due to the free flow of information.

I said, "I've recently been told that my capacity to gather information is being limited."

Reese raised an eyebrow. I told him and Ross Shepherd about my call to Lien Yang-sun, the tower's director of security, my superior, who had bluntly told me that the new fleet gathering around the tower for the ferry terminal construction was beyond my responsibilities, the first such limitation in my years at the project.

Reese chewed on his lower lip. "Well, you'll run across information about it, I'm sure."

The telephone rang, and Reese leaned back in his chair to grab the receiver. He spoke several words, then listened for a moment, his face professionally composed. He replaced the handset, then said, "That arrest yesterday on the island, where the riot squad was used? We've just learned that the person arrested was Yao Bok-kee."

I inhaled sharply through my teeth. Yao was the founder of All-Asia Geotech, the firm that did the site investigation and feasibility studies before the island was built, including initial desk studies, then seabed surveys and lab tests of soil and rock, and then design work on the island. The firm also did compaction studies as the island rose from the bay. All-Asia Geotech owned the *Jaeger*, a twenty-eight-hundred-ton vessel with a five-story drill tower amidships and which used such equipment as a seacalf seabed testing system. I had had lunch with Yao many times, finding him lively and funny.

I asked, "Why was he arrested?"

"Graft, according to the Beijing district prosecutor's office."

"That's impossible," I exclaimed. "Yao is dedicated to the tower, and completely honest." At least I assumed he was honest. "When is the trial?"

"The trial was this morning." Reese pulled a corner of his mouth down with a finger. "Yao was found guilty, and executed ninety minutes ago."

*   *   *

The head of the U.S. consulate asked if I would give the bad news to John Llewellyn. Jay Lee, who would represent the Hong Kong police, went with me. One of Llewellyn's senior executives had just been arrested and executed, and Llewellyn needed to learn about it. We were walking across Heroes of the Revolution Island, on the tower's shadow, toward Llewellyn's office trailer.

"You've never been in his office?" Jay asked.

"Never been invited."

"Can't you just bust in, you being an official security consultant, with your colorful ID card and big salary and everything?"

I tried to snort contemptuously, but it didn't sound convincing even to my ears because in truth my salary was big, at least when compared to that of a Hong Kong police officer, even someone as high-ranking as Jay Lee.

I said, "You've already made your fortune, so don't worry about it."

He laughed. "Yes, I worked hard for my wealth, as you know."

Hong Kong citizens are much more comfortable talking about money and wages than are Americans, so I had once asked Jay how he could afford to live in his Mid-Levels apartment on a police captain's salary. He replied, "What you want to know is if my wealthy BMW-dealing father gives me an allowance. No, he does not." Then how? I asked. Everyone in Hong Kong believes in luck, Jay replied. Most of us are *ting yat dai fook*, a big winner tomorrow, meaning luck will surely come our way even though it hasn't yet. One day eighteen years ago when he was still a beat policeman, luck came his way, Jay told me. Entirely by chance, he was issued an automobile license plate that had *888 888* on it. Eight is the lucky number in business. Henry Tian—who had had his own bit of luck as a young man when he invested a small amount of money in a lime-rich Pearl River delta sandbar, and rose to be one of Hong Kong's wealthiest citizens—paid Jay Lee a million and a half U.S. dollars for the license plate. Jay had invested the money wisely and was "quite comfortable," he had said. He liked police work, is why he had stayed on the beat. Hong Kong slang for a wealthy single man is *a diamond bachelor*. "You'll get lucky someday, too," he had advised.

John Llewellyn's trailer had been elegantly fitted out, we could tell from a distance. Mine was standard-issue, rented from some lot, with a loud air conditioner stuck into a window, but Llewellyn's was a double-wide, with large windows and a heavy glass door through which could be seen a receptionist. The door handle was a glass bar with stainless-steel fittings. The receptionist smiled at me, about to turn aside another request for a few minutes of Llewellyn's time, but I showed her my ID and she reluctantly waved me through.

Critics had said Llewellyn was a showman first and an architect second, or a salesman first and an architect second, but Llewellyn looked the architect first just then, as Jay and I entered his office. He was bent over a drawing table, making wide strokes on white paper, Anne Iverson at his elbow and nodding. To work for Llewellyn was to nod a lot, I had heard. The room had a dozen other tables arranged around Llewellyn's, and each place was taken by a young architect, Llewellyn's acolytes, those underpaid and eager followers who were selected to sit at the great man's feet. All eyes turned to Jay and me, rough outsiders who had somehow breached the inner sanctum. I assumed that Llewellyn's work on the tower was completed and that he and his of-

fice were remaining in Hong Kong for the opening festivities. Jack
Rainey, my Australian counterpart, had suggested that Llewellyn enjoyed the attention in Hong Kong so much that he couldn't bear to
leave. Anne said, though, that Llewellyn demanded strict obedience to
his designs, even to the smallest details, and that he remained in Hong
Kong to insure that the finishing touches—such things as the color of
the paper towel dispensers in the washrooms—were to his specifications.

Other than the architects' drafting tables, copy machines, and a few
other necessities, the office resembled a London club, with lacquered
walls, several wing chairs off to one side, and heavy oak bookcases,
though they were filled not with books but with loose-leaf code and
specifications binders. A swiveling library-style magazine rack was
near a fern stand.

Llewellyn looked up and hesitated only for a moment before smiling. Anne wore a perplexed expression at my appearance.

"What do you think, Clay?" Llewellyn swept his hand across the
table. "Like it?"

Jay and I stepped to the center table. I gazed down at the drawing,
wondering whether it was perhaps upside down.

He said, "I've been commissioned to build the new airport terminal
in Rio."

"Del Rio, Texas?" I asked.

He laughed graciously. "I've never mastered the skill of drawing,
unfortunately, but you can get a taste of what we have in mind. It's
preliminary, of course. The commission was just finalized yesterday.
How does it look?"

The drawing consisted of soaring angles and loops that seemed to
float in the air, and long shafts—could they be telephone poles?—here
and there. I couldn't make anything of it.

I said, "You've caught the Ipanema spirit, that's for sure."

He laughed again, delighted. John Llewellyn had the reputation of
one who spent too much time in front of a mirror. His appearance—
precisely fashionable clothing, manicured nails, carefully placed hair,
a keyboard of perfect teeth, surgically tightened skin around his eyes,

at least according to rumor—spoke purposely to his sophistication. Yet I noticed then, standing there with Jay Lee, that today Llewellyn had the look of one who had spent the night carousing bar to bar. He was haggard, with new bags under his eyes, and his face—always pale—had a peculiar yellow tinge to it, as if he had taken an overdose of antimalarial pills. And, against all precedent, several wisps of his silver hair were out of place, as if he had worriedly run his fingers over his scalp. Then I noticed that his right hand was trembling, shaking as if he suffered the ague. Apparently he spotted it too, because he casually slipped his left hand over to grip his right hand. Maybe Llewellyn had come down with something, one of those hothouse diseases that rake the British whenever they venture south from their island to engage in a bit of colonizing. Dengue fever, maybe. Llewellyn looked ill.

"This is Captain Lee Yik-kee of the Hong Kong police," I said. "Captain Lee is head of the Organized Crime and Triad Bureau."

Llewellyn shook his hand, and then Anne insisted on doing so also, though I could tell Jay was uncomfortable taking a female stranger's hand in his, however briefly, despite his earnest study of American culture.

Llewellyn was alert, his eyes locked on Jay Lee. Perhaps he was wary, as he bit his lower lip. And was there a touch of fear displayed in the single tic of his eyes? An involuntary glance at the door for an escape? I was reading too much into his reaction, I was sure. Jay Lee would have missed none of it, though. Confronting anyone else acting as Llewellyn was, Lee would be preparing himself to bring out his handgun and sprint after the suspect.

The architect's composure returned quickly. "I hope this isn't about those parking tickets my driver has been collecting. Commissioner Kwok promised to take care of them for me." Llewellyn chuckled, inviting us to do so also.

Anne obliged, a bit more of the sycophant than I had taken her for, but Jay Lee's face was a professional mask. For a few seconds he stared levelly at Llewellyn, as Jay always did when he met someone new, trying to elicit a spontaneous confession, standard police procedure the world around. Llewellyn dropped his eyes first, maybe for the first time in his life.

Rather than ask why I would bring a policeman to Llewellyn's office, Anne said, as if to delay bad news, "We spent the morning talking with a realtor in Los Angeles. John is opening a West Coast office."

"A small space in Century City," Llewellyn said, rallying. "It'll be a satellite office, where I'll be closer to West Coast clients."

A satellite office would be a mark of Llewellyn's renewed respect and caché in the architectural world, thanks to the success of the Fifth Millennium China Tower. His assistants scattered around the trailer, and his thirty other employees in New York, were another indication of how far he had come since the architectural world had rejected his rejection of the International style, and had cast aside his architectural ornamentation and whimsy, forcing Llewellyn to spend years on the outside. The Fifth Millennium China Tower had turned it all around. Llewellyn was now taking on two partners, Jeffrey Hong, designer of Singapore's new horse-racing facility, and Peter Rhodes, the Englishman who was chief architect of New York City's Trump Grand. Llewellyn wanted to "globalize his firm," Anne had mentioned to me.

Llewellyn was quickly acquiring other proof of his resurgence. Anne had told me he had just purchased fifty acres on Bali, where he was going to design his own compound, a series of buildings—a home, a guest house, an art gallery, a pool house, a conservatory—that would be works of art, each a statement of his vision, where every wall sconce and every slice of marble and every bamboo leaf would be the direct and exclusive result of John Llewellyn's applied genius. Llewellyn had gleefully told Anne, "My Bali retreat is going to make Philip Johnson's Glass House compound seem like a South Dakota pasture." Anne had also reported that Llewellyn had just purchased a Learjet 31A to commute between New York, Los Angeles, and Bali. My father would have said Llewellyn with his new success was acting like a blind dog in a meat house.

"What brings you to the office today, gentlemen?" Llewellyn finally asked.

"I'm sorry to have to report this," I began. "Your chief geotech engineer, Yao Bok-kee, has been arrested."

"I saw it happen and was astonished," Llewellyn said. "Why would Yao be arrested?"

"For graft." Might as well tell it all at once. "He has been tried in Beijing, and he has been executed."

Anne Iverson's hand went to her mouth, and she stared at me, her eyes pleading, as if I might be able to retract the information. Llewellyn took it harder, much harder. His face lost the little color it had, and his mouth sagged open, and he staggered against the table. He leaned involuntarily toward Anne, and she had to push against him to keep him from toppling. A soft groan escaped him.

I hurried around the table to help, taking an arm to guide him to a chair.

"I . . . I . . . I . . . ," was all Llewellyn could manage. His gaze was on the far wall, though I don't think he was seeing anything.

Anne went to the water cooler. Llewellyn brought a hand up to his head, pressing his temple. Many of the other architects in the office had risen from their chairs, but so rigidly hierarchical was Llewellyn's office that none of them dared approach the master's table.

When Anne returned with the cup of water, she said, "I can take care of this, Clay."

Which was a dismissal, so Jay and I left the office, stepping out onto the island's concrete surface. The tower's shadow had moved, acting as a sundial, and was now off a few degrees to our east.

"You'd have thought we brought news of his father's death, the way he acted, all that paralyzing grief." Then Jay quickly added. "Sorry, Clay. About the father."

I nodded. "I didn't see grief. Not from Llewellyn."

We stopped by a portable generator.

Jay looked at me. "No grief? What was that we just saw, then?"

I thought about it for a moment. "Fear. Pure fear."

8

We were back in my office, Jay Lee and me, and Jack Rainey had nicely served us coffee and then returned to his computer. I sat at my desk, and Jay pulled up a chair.

"So you think John Llewellyn's reaction was fear when we told him of the geotech's death?" Jay sipped his coffee. "Could Llewellyn be in on some racket with Yao? Maybe they were skimming off some of the construction funds."

"It's possible, but the accounting giant, Deloitte and Touche, has two dozen auditors working on the tower's finances. The Chinese don't want a trace of a scandal, and that's why they gladly pay for the huge auditing team."

Jay said, "So it'd be extremely difficult to slip anything past them?"

"And Llewellyn wouldn't have any reason to cook the books. He's getting everything he wants in life from the tower: the fame, a huge commission, and the resurgence of his career. And embezzling would be beneath him. It wouldn't fit into his vision of himself."

"So why did the news of Yao's execution make Llewellyn almost catatonic?"

I shook my head. We drank our coffee in silence for a moment. Then I asked, "Is Yao's background being looked into?"

"By our Criminal Intelligence Bureau. I spoke with them this morning. Yao is a solid citizen. There's absolutely nothing in his past that would suggest he would engage in embezzlement. And no evidence of Yao spending beyond his salary, which is almost always the case with embezzlers."

"And what about the hurry in which Yao was tried and executed?" I asked. "Don't the Chinese authorities have a thirty-day appeal period? I've never heard of them rushing the sentence like this, not since the Cultural Revolution, anyway."

Jay said, "It's my thinking that this was entirely an extrajudicial procedure. I suspect the trial was one in name only, and I'd be surprised if Yao was allowed an attorney."

My computer chimed. I had set the machine so that regular emails wouldn't announce themselves with a noise, otherwise it'd sound like an alarm clock all day. Some of my email correspondents had a priority address, and when one of those came in—and it was rare—the computer bonged.

I brought up the email program, and it showed a message from Yu Chi-yin, head of Singapore's Criminal Investigation Department.

I brought up the message. I read it, then bent forward to the screen to read it again. "Well, I'll be damned."

"What is it?" Jay asked.

I said tonelessly, "Little Harold Lethbridge has been killed."

Jack Rainey rose from his chair. "Killed? What do you mean?"

"That's all Yu sent, a two-sentence message. He says he'll send more momentarily, as soon as he can gather the facts."

Harold Lethbridge was the founder and chief executive officer of EMU, Inc., which was once called Earth Movers Unlimited. Lethbridge was an Australian whose father had owned a dump truck and called it a company. Little Harry, as the son was called even after he topped six feet six, inherited his father's dump truck, and within ten years owned forty of them, and within another ten years owned the region's largest earth-moving company, with over eight hundred employees, three hundred pieces of heavy equipment, and thirty barges, with projects in seven countries. My father had an intense liking for Australians because as a U.S. Navy sailor he had served with them in the Philippines in World War II, and he had said there's no one better in the world to have a beer with, and I could see why when I had interviewed Harold Lethbridge several times as part of my job. Lethbridge had been exuberant and friendly, and hid his cockiness behind a broad Australian accent and an ever-present smile. He was one of those folks you immediately want to be of service to. He owned a full acre on the Sydney Harbor where you could see the Opera House from most of his home's windows. Lethbridge's firm had been Heroes of the Revolution Island's principal fill contractor. Now he was dead.

I tapped the base of the keyboard, waiting for more information from Yu Chi-yin down in Singapore.

Jay Lee said, "I must talk to you about something, Clay." He had dropped his voice, and his words were meant only for me.

I turned to him.

He said, "I've been trying to understand why you would visit the 88K's dragon head, Wen Quichin, at his home on the Peak."

I leaned back in my chair. I had been caught. I felt blood rising to my cheeks. "You watch his home?"

"My department does," he replied. "It is our job. His house is under surveillance every moment of the day."

"Wen contacted me. He had some information for me, he said." That was part of it. I didn't want to lie to Lee, but I also didn't want a lecture or a warning from him.

"And did you get your information?" Jay's voice had gained an officious tone.

"The 88K found one of my father's murderers, and has dealt with him."

Jay knew what that meant, of course. "Why would a criminal organization be looking for your father's killers? Because it is somehow tied in with the disappearance of the teenager who lives on your floor, Hsu Shui-ban, the dragon head's grandson?"

I nodded. "The same people who kidnapped the boy murdered my father. Dad happened out into the hallway, and witnessed what was going on, so they silenced him."

Jay was wearing a carefully tailored light blue suit and a green tie. He also wore a look of ill usage. "Why didn't you come to me with all this?"

My computer bonged again, but I kept my attention on my friend Jay Lee. "Your boss, Commissioner Kwok, told me that my father's spectacles were found in his pocket—a sure sign of a jumper—and that he had been taking an antidepressant. You were in the commissioner's office when he informed me of these two indications of suicide. You heard him yourself."

"Yes, I did."

"At first I thought his investigators were either mistaken, or those two things—the eyeglasses and the drug—were some of the unexplainable peculiarities that are always present in a homicide investigation. There's always loose ends, things that don't fit together. I knew my father would never kill himself."

He nodded, not yet appeased.

"But when I spoke with an eyewitness—a young man named Soong Chan, who was Hsu's friend, who saw the kidnappers grab my father in the hallway—I knew that the commissioner had been lying to me about my father's eyeglasses and the drug. He, or one of his subordinates, had planted evidence tending to indicate suicide. Or maybe they just generated a report about it, not bothering to plant the evidence. Commissioner Kwok was trying to stop me from looking into it further."

Jay asked, "So you didn't reveal all this to me? Because I'm Kwok's subordinate?"

"Jay, I didn't want to put you in a bad situation, where you had information at odds with what your boss had told you was the official line, and where you would have to choose sides: me—a friend of yours—or your boss."

"You didn't trust me with the information, didn't trust my judgment on what to do with it." Both his hands were on his knees.

I didn't say anything.

"There are ways to deal with these dilemmas," he said, staring me right in the eyes. "They involve having finesse and being smart. I can handle it. You should have known that."

I hesitated. "Yes, I should have, Jay. I'm sorry."

He nodded briskly. Then he abruptly held out his hand, and I shook it. If I couldn't trust Jay Lee in Hong Kong, I was truly in trouble. I briefly told him how Hsu had been located near the fishing village, of my relaying the information to Wen, and my later visit to Wen's home, where the triad leader showed me the video of the kidnapper's execution.

Jay absorbed all this, his eyes on the middle distance, occasionally muttering "Yes," and "Good," and when I had finished, he nodded again, and said, "Let's see what else you've received from Singapore."

I brought up the message, and read aloud, "'Harold Lethbridge died at approximately 2 P.M. Singapore time after apparently resisting a mugging.'"

"A mugging in Singapore?" Jay asked. "Since when?"

"'The attack occurred on the south bank of the Singapore River, near the Boat Quay, outside Penny Black, a pub where the deceased had just eaten lunch. His three companions—all believed to be subordinates at Lethbridge's company—had already departed, and Lethbridge was waiting for his car. Attached are photos of the body, inventory of personal effects found on the body, and transcripts of preliminary interviews with the valets. More to follow.'"

"I've seen enough dead bodies in my time," I said. "I don't need to look at Harold Lethbridge's."

"Me, neither," Jay said.

I turned away from the monitor. "I don't believe in coincidences. Do you?"

"I'm a policeman," Jay replied. "Of course not."

"The Fifth Millennium China Tower has lost two senior executives in the past two days. One by arrest and execution, and the other by a mugging."

Jay asked, "So what do you think?"

"Maybe John Llewellyn has a reason to be frightened."

*   *   *

"So you think he has run away?" I asked.

Anne picked at her cottage cheese, which had been prepared in a blend of nuts and curry. "Well, maybe not. John claimed he had a meeting in Brisbane, so he left this morning."

"Had the Brisbane meeting been on his schedule a long time?"

"He doesn't consult with me regarding his schedule, but I usually know when he is about to leave Hong Kong. He didn't say a word about this." She smiled quickly. "So I had an opening, and I called you for lunch."

We had decided to take in the second-best view in Hong Kong, so we had ridden the old cogwheel tram from Central up to the Peak, then crossed the road to Café Deco.

"Did you quit your diet again?" Anne asked, glancing at my Sichuan pizza.

"Just for this meal." I cut into the pizza with a fork. It was loaded with roasted duck, chilies, bean sprouts, shiitake mushrooms, black beans, and peppers. "Do you think the meeting in Brisbane is a pretext, that Llewellyn just wanted to get out of Hong Kong?"

"Why would he?" Anne asked pointedly, as if I were suggesting she was the reason he might want to flee the city.

"When Jay Lee and I told him of Yao's execution, he seemed afraid. Really afraid."

"He and Yao were friends. It was grief and shock you saw, not fright."

I said around my pizza, "I've seen grief, and I've seen fright, and I know the difference. Suddenly, Llewellyn was scared witless. He almost toppled to the floor. You saw him."

"Well . . ."

"Why, do you think?"

"I don't know." She took another miniature bite of her salad. "He's due back here tomorrow, and if he's coming back so quickly, maybe he isn't running from something."

I shrugged.

"How can you eat so fast?" She smiled. "You're like a big Shop-Vac."

I reluctantly put down my fork, then reached for my glass of iced tea. "Have you noticed anything peculiar about John Llewellyn's behavior lately?"

She shook her head.

"He looked worn-out and fragile and timid," I said, "even before we informed him of Yao's arrest and death. His hands were shaking."

"He's tired, is all."

"When I get tired, my eyes droop and I yawn, but my hands don't shake. Something else is going on."

She slowly twirled her fork. "I think he made a major concession to Beijing, and he won't admit it's a concession, not to me and maybe not to himself."

"The new ferry terminal?"

"He was adamantly opposed to erecting anything on Heroes of the Revolution Island, except for the east ferry terminal, which was a necessity, and couldn't be designed around. Yet somehow Beijing—maybe the president himself—has impressed on John the need for a second terminal. That terminal—that big piece of clutter that is being constructed so suddenly at the west end of the island—is against all the principles I've ever heard John talk about. I never thought he would agree to such a thing."

I asked, "Did he agree?"

"He must have." She sipped her wine. "Nothing occurs on the island or the tower without his knowledge and agreement."

"Has he spoken with you about it, about the new terminal?"

"Not a word, which is another funny thing. He likes nothing better than to sit in front of his fireplace and lay out for me his architectural vision, and how it applies to the Fifth Millennium China Tower. He speaks of his reverence for beauty, the importance of the aesthetic as opposed to technical wizardry or social commentary, his contempt for the orthodox. And then he ties it all in to the tower, saying it is the perfect synthesis of all his beliefs."

"He viewed the tower and island as perfect, is what you're saying?"

She nodded. "And then, a week ago, the chairman of the tower commission, whose office is in Beijing, announced that a second ferry terminal will be built. It was the first I'd heard of it."

"They must've consulted with Llewellyn about it," I suggested.

"When I asked John about it, he said he 'had no problems with it.' Those were his words. No problems with a sudden addition to the project that flies in the face of all his beliefs?"

"Did you talk to him about it?" I asked.

"He wouldn't speak about the new terminal. He brushed aside my questions, and he was abrupt doing so." Anne squared her napkin on her lap. "It's clear he is unhappy about it, but I don't know why he won't discuss it, and I don't know why he has agreed to it."

I didn't say anything, wondering if I dared eat more of my pizza. I cut off a small portion with my knife.

"I thought John and I were . . . soul mates on this project," Anne said. "Maybe not."

When Anne had called for lunch, I suggested we have it somewhere other than the cafeteria trailer. She had seemed delighted with the idea. The restaurant was always fully booked and always crowded, and this day was no exception. About half locals and half tourists, I guessed. Anne had used her Llewellyn connections to obtain reservations for us. Now we were sitting in a corner of the restaurant, with windows on two sides that overlooked the harbor. The city was far below. The harbor was filled with launches, ferries, hovercraft, lighters, hydrofoils, sampans, garbage scows, motor yachts, police boats, walla-wallas, tourist junks, and, near the tower, all the new dredging craft. The tower precisely split my view, as if it were the spine of a coffee-table book of Hong Kong photos.

Anne was wearing a cedar-green two-button jacket over cotton pants of the same color. Small sterling silver oval hoops were in her ears, and a silver bangle bracelet was around her left wrist. Wind had been blowing at the top of the Peak, and she hadn't combed her golden hair, and it was nicely tossed. She must have been out in the sun lately, as the freckles across the bridge of her nose were a shade darker than I remembered. She was glumly staring at her plate, perhaps thinking about John Llewellyn, and where she fit into his life.

I thought I would divert her attention. "You told me once you were raised in San Diego. What'd your father do there?"

She looked up, startled, as if she had forgotten I was there. She brightened, maybe at my clumsy effort to change her mood.

"He was an orthodontist." She smiled widely. "Still is, actually."

"An orthodontist?" I wanted to say no wonder she had a dazzling, alluring smile, but I settled for, "Well, no wonder you have remarkably even teeth."

Anne laughed, and she started again on her cottage cheese. I can't imagine eating cottage cheese for lunch. Or anytime, for that matter.

"How did you become an architect?" I asked.

"It's because my father is an orthodontist that I became an architect."

A waiter refilled my tea glass.

She went on, "Ever notice how some people are so talented and they are so successful in their profession that they think they must be good at any profession?"

I nodded, and resumed eating my pizza, hoping she wouldn't again comment on the alacrity with which I consume anything on a plate in front of me.

"My father was that way," she said. "He had a big office, four patients' chairs, all of them always full, and he employed seven people full-time, and he spent ten hours a day looking into kids' mouths. So this is back when I was a college sophomore, still not knowing what to major in. Mom and Dad decided to remodel our house, a big remodel, right down to the studs."

Anne's laugh was uninhibited, from the back of her throat, and she laughed then, and her face lit up and she was forgetful of herself. "So it's a month into the remodel, and Daddy's in a huff over a missed deadline, and so he fires the architect and general contractor and decides to run the job himself."

"Big mistake?"

"A disaster. As the days passed, he started getting into his office later and later, and leaving earlier and earlier, working on the house, and when he started to fiddle with the blueprints, bad things began to happen."

"Like what?"

She said gaily: "The new fireplace sank eight inches below the floor. A window looked out onto a wall. Risers on the steps to the second floor were only four inches high, so he constantly missed his step on them. Like the bilge of an old boat, our basement started taking in three inches of water every day. One corner of the house was not forty-five degrees, but forty-six, and so the back half of the house wasn't squared. The ceiling over the living room was two inches lower on the east end. And on and on." She laughed again, her voice running up the scales.

"So what happened?" I asked.

"I was home from college for the summer, and I was lifeguarding at our neighborhood pool, but that was only a couple hours a day, so I started helping Dad, studying the blueprints, making calls to subcontractors and suppliers, doing more and more every day, talking to the foundation workers and the electricians and plumbers, getting them to do things. Dad returned to his orthodontia practice."

"And you found your career?" I bit into another slice of pizza.

"When Dad fired himself, I took over. By the time I returned to UCLA at the end of the summer, the house was mostly finished and was in good order. My dad paid me as he would have the general contractor, grinning widely as he wrote the check and thanking me profusely for bailing him out."

I ate some salad, carefully pacing myself.

She beamed. "And Dad said I was like the Roman emperor Augustus, who had found Rome a city of brick and left it a city of marble. It's the nicest thing anyone has ever said to me."

I chewed daintily.

"I had a revelation that summer," she said. "Creating things, building something from nothing, that's what I was born for. When I returned to school that fall, I started taking architecture and construction management courses."

She sipped a glass of water, then took several bites of her meal.

I was mopping my mouth with a napkin when she asked, "So are you still in love with your wife? Your ex-wife?"

So apropos of nothing was her question that my hand stopped mid-mop. I stared at her, finally lowering the napkin. "No."

"You aren't?"

"No."

"Are you being honest?"

"I'm always honest." With my fork I lifted an olive from the salad. "Unless the situation requires deception. This one doesn't."

She smoothed the napkin across her lap. "How do you not love someone you once loved?"

"I didn't know certain things about Olivia that were later revealed to me. Mainly that she was capable of throwing aside a reasonably intelligent, fairly hardworking, not-entirely-unattractive-person-when-looked-at-from-a-distance such as myself."

She smiled.

My voice rose, and I tried to stop it but couldn't. "And she did it so casually, too. It didn't seem to bother her, flicking me aside like tissue."

"Well . . ."

I took a long breath. I despise self-pity, but I was suddenly desperate to make Anne Iverson understand what had happened to me. I had never spoken with anybody about it, not even my father, so thorough was my drubbing. "It was as if Olivia's attention span was just too short, as if I had lost her attention. She no longer had interest in me, so she went on to something else, the way you would put aside one section of the Sunday paper and pick up the next."

"Clay . . ."

"After she left me, I would call her up on the phone, struggling to keep my rage and humiliation and sorrow out of my voice, and at the same time listening closely to her voice, wondering at the absence of emotion. Nothing. I couldn't hear regret, couldn't hear frustration with me, couldn't detect anger. Her voice was always as even as an answering machine's."

"So you tried to get Olivia to return to you?"

"Sure. One demeaning attempt after another." I rubbed a temple. "Olivia couldn't be bothered listening. She shooed me away."

Anne sadly shook her head.

"So, as I say, I didn't know this about Olivia when I married her. I didn't know that she was capable of such vast indifference. Had I known, I would have never fallen for her like I did. And now that I know, I have factored it into my assessment of her."

" 'Factored into my assessment'?" she asked. "You sound like a project engineer, like me."

"But that's exactly what I did. She's not the person I fell in love with. So no, I don't love her anymore."

Her lower lip came out, and her gaze dropped, as if she needed a moment to gather in this information. I was embarrassed at my own breathless candor. I quickly took another bite of pizza, lest any more verbiage spill out.

I chewed for a while, then said, "That's the second time you've asked me about my ex-wife. Why so interested?"

"I'm not interested in your ex-wife. I'm interested in . . . the emotion."

"You are trying to determine if you love John Llewellyn."

She hesitated. "Maybe."

I said flatly, "No, you don't love him."

She was startled, her chin coming up and her eyes widening. Then she laughed. "Clay, with all due respect, you don't know anything about my relationship with John."

"I can prove to you that you don't love him."

She twirled her fork as she stared at me, her eyes amused.

I asked, "Want to bet?"

"A wager? A bet you can prove I don't love John Llewellyn?"

I said, "Loser pays the lunch check."

"I'll take that bet." She smiled and leaned back in her chair. "So prove it."

I rubbed my chin in a professorial manner. "You understand that you are tapping into a vast well of experience here, both as a male and as an FBI agent."

"All you are doing now is bumping your gums together. Prove it."

"Love is a very narrow concept," I announced.

"You are stalling."

"It can be confused with many other emotions."

She made a production of tapping her fingers on the table. A busboy came by to remove our plates and silverware. Out the window, far beyond the tower, a JAL 747 made its approach to Chek Lap Kok. When the waiter approached, Anne and I declined offers of dessert, then she turned her gaze back to me.

"As best as I can tell, here are the noted aspects of John Llewellyn's personality," I said. "He has an air of authority."

Ann nodded.

"He is often imperious."

She dipped her chin again.

"He has an unquenchable thirst for success. He has an uncanny ability to please and flatter those from whom he wants something."

She wasn't nodding now, but she was sure paying attention. Her gaze pushed me back in the chair.

Intrepid, I continued, "He is a dandy, and never appears anywhere without French cuffs, Bruno Magli shoes, a Patek Philippe wristwatch, perfectly combed hair, and you could cut your hand on the creases in his pants."

Anne's smile had gained a touch of frost.

"In a group photo, he makes sure he is always in the center. He takes that place as a matter of right."

"You are being picky," she said.

"He is constitutionally incapable of passing a mirror without looking into it."

"And petty."

I said, "He never carries money. No bills, no coins. Ever noticed that? Whatever he wants, whether it's a cup of coffee or a five-course dinner, someone else buys, whoever is at hand."

She clucked her tongue.

"And have you noticed the magazines in his office? *Paris Fashion* and *Trends Magazine* and something called *Culturekiosk*. I mean, who reads that stuff?"

"What do you prefer? *Guns and Ammo*?"

"Llewellyn has his life built around props, is what I'm saying. His Rolls-Royce—who drives a Rolls-Royce anymore?—his new Learjet, all the stainless steel and glass in his apartment, and yes, I'm being picky and petty."

The waiter returned with our check.

"Are you suggesting that I'm one of his props?" Frost had turned to winter.

I remained steadfastly silent, unwilling to admit that this was precisely my thought, and unwilling to implicate myself further by the slightest sound.

But then I couldn't help myself, and I added, "And he's got a weak, wet handshake."

Her voice was brittle. "Are you through?"

I guess not. "Despite all of this, you find Llewellyn attractive."

"He is handsome, successful, witty, and wealthy." She ticked them off on her fingers.

I did my best to sound Socratic. "And so we must wonder why you find him attractive."

"I just told you why."

"The reason is that John Llewellyn has an aura. He casts this energy field around himself, and it feels good to others when they stand in it."

"That's preposterous."

"The power, the success, his energy, his reputation, his fortune. It all creates this thrilling atmosphere, this magnificent penumbra, and it makes people giddy just standing near him."

"And that's what I am? Giddy?"

Please, mouth, remain tightly closed. Not even a squeak. And don't mention the liver spots on the back of his hands.

She waited a few seconds, running her fingers across the table several times, as if brushing aside crumbs.

I said, "And he is missing the most important ingredient."

"Which is?"

"Lovability."

"Lovability?"

"He isn't the slightest bit lovable."

She threw her head back and laughed, full-throated notes that caused nearby diners to turn our way.

"You've confused love with the enjoyment you get standing in his aura," I insisted. "Go on, you can admit it."

"Here's what I'll admit." She reached across the table for the check, wadded it up into a ball, then tossed it so it bounced off my forehead. She rose from her chair, then said over her shoulder as she walked away, "I admit you just lost your wager."

*   *   *

He might not have been lovable, but John Llewellyn was a genius, a realization that was slow in coming to me. In my life, three structures have had a profound effect on me, something beyond mere admiration for the design or appreciation of the place's history or the dull thought that it was pretty. These are sites that reached out to me, that made me pause and reflect, and for which I felt a strong attachment.

The first is the Lincoln Monument, of course, because I'm an American. Langston Hughes felt the same way: "Let's go see Old Abe / Sitting in the marble and the moonlight / Sitting lonely in the marble and the moonlight . . ."

The second is the Alamo in San Antonio. The Alamo had a back door, but 184 Texans chose not to use it.

And the third—and this is inexplicable—is the Arc de Triomphe in Paris. Why I should commune with a monument that celebrates a warmonger's spread of his cruel dictatorship over most of Europe is beyond me. But I sat at an outdoor restaurant on the Champs Élysées drinking the most expensive beer of my life and fell in love with the Arc. Perhaps it was the beer, though I don't think so, as I still carry that feeling.

In the days after my father's death, I began to hesitate whenever the Fifth Millennium China Tower caught my gaze on the street or in an office or wherever I was, and I would stare at it, and I began to contemplate the thing, realizing that I enjoyed its presence, that bold stab at the sky. I would try to take in the entire curve top to bottom and try to fathom it all.

I had begun to have a relationship with the Gold Swan, an unworldly admiration for the thing. The tower was everything a person aspires to. It was elegant, slender and tall, glittering, and bold. It was courageous and defiant, watching over Hong Kong like a sentinel. Like a world's fair, the tower pointed to a gleaming future—not the one envisioned by Beijing, one of Chinese dominance in Asia and a continuation of its calcified totalitarianism—but to more world prosperity and more advances in the sciences and arts. It opened the mind and expanded the concept of the possible. The tower asked for better from anyone who gazed upon it.

If all that sounds too ennobling for a big piece of metal, I should point out that the tower was also practical in a small way: it acted as a compass. You could always tell where you were in Hong Kong by the angle of the Gold Swan's enormous curve in relationship to your point of view, whether on the Kowloon side, where the tower curved out to your left, or the Hong Kong side, where it curved out to your right. If you were, say, in Victoria Park near Causeway Bay, your view was of the tower's full half-oval sweep to the right. But if you were in Sheun Wan, at the entrance to Victoria Harbor on the Hong Kong side, the curve was much less pronounced because you were looking at it almost straight-on. The tower instantly oriented you. That I almost always knew where I was in Hong Kong anyway—geographically, it's not that big of a city—is beside the point. The tower was there to help.

Like its designer, the tower lacked lovability, but I had come to love it anyway, just like the Lincoln Memorial and the Alamo and the Arc de Triomphe. I wasn't alone. Hong Kong citizens were mad for the thing. The city was gripped by tower fever. I believe that's just what John Llewellyn had intended. He wanted devotion to his masterpiece, and had succeeded. He was a genius.

Part Two

The physician can bury his mistakes, but the architect can only advise his clients to plant vines.

FRANK LLOYD WRIGHT

9

Victoria Harbor, the body of water between Hong Kong and Kow-loon, was once more than a mile and a half wide, but landfill projects over the decades have made it narrower and narrower, and now the Star ferries hardly need to accelerate to displacement speed before ar-riving at the opposite shore. Getting to Kowloon on the ferry or the underground is easy and quick, but I seldom go there, having little business and no friends there.

I mentioned this to Anne Iverson as we strolled along Kowloon Street, and she nodded, not saying anything but pausing before the performance of a six-year-old boy who did three consecutive back handsprings on a cardboard mat before holding out his hand. Anne dropped a Hong Kong dollar into it. This was only an hour after she had bopped me with the lunch check up at the Peak. As I was leaving the restaurant, hurrying after her, my phone rang, and the caller was the translator, Wen Quichin's nephew, asking if I would meet Wen in Kowloon right away and giving me an address. The nephew also asked if I would bring the woman with whom I was having lunch. So that meant that I had been followed, or that someone in the restaurant re-ported to the 88K.

Anne was smiling by the time I had caught up with her at the tram, saying she would think about what I had said about her relationship with John Llewellyn, but that didn't mean I wasn't a horse's butt. We road down the tram, walked a few blocks, then boarded Mass Transit Railway's Tsuen Wan Line, which carried us under the harbor over to Kowloon. We got off at the Ngau Tau Kok station, which is east of the old airport. Kowloon means "nine dragons." The place was built on the back of eight dragons, and the ninth was the emperor's back.

"Why does Wen want to meet me, you think?" Anne asked in a loud voice, over the street noise. She hadn't hesitated an instant when I had relayed the gangster's invitation.

"Maybe to give you some advice on your relationship with John Llewellyn."

She laughed, then put her arm in mine as we walked along. Cars drive on the left in Hong Kong, which means an American has about a 50 percent chance of getting run over every time he steps off a curb, so I was careful. I enjoyed the light touch of Anne's hand. I had thought we might take a taxi, but all five cabs at the taxi stand had a red tag on their windshield, meaning they were off-duty. So we walked along. Many of the buildings were concrete government-built tenements, with laundry poles jutting from the windows, shirts and pants waving idly in the wind. These gray buildings housed newcomers and the soon-to-be-lucky. Colorful banners hung from streetlight poles.

"Does the 88K leader really exist?" Anne asked, stepping around a letter writer who was bent over his wood block, a Bic in one hand. "I thought Wen was a myth."

"He's flesh and blood."

"And how do you know him?"

"I get around."

She laughed again. She was acting like a student on a holiday, walking briskly, her gaze constantly shifting to take it all in, smiling widely. I began to think she didn't get out much.

I decided to impress her. "Those three fellows over there, all three in black pants? They have recently moved here from Beijing."

"You can tell?"

"By the way they walk. It's the repressed, anxious walk of a crane. It's a dead giveaway."

We passed a *dai pai dong*—a market stand—selling not Rolex but Rollex watches and not Kodak but Koduk cameras, and another selling squid on a stick and dough balls dipped in honey. A cart contained mangos, durians, papayas, oranges, mangosteens, and strawberries. An old woman was bent over the cart, intently studying a strawberry, turning it over and over. A store window displayed joints of pork and glazed ducks. Another vendor with a cart was selling pressed pig heads, the eyeballs a glutinous green. A vanilla-ball seller was ladling custard into a mold. At the direction of a customer, a fishmonger plucked a hand-sized fish from a tank, placed it on a cutting board, and skinned and gutted it quickly, pausing to show the customer the exposed and still-beating heart to prove the fish was fresh. Skinned rats, tail and all, hung from another vendor's stand. A fortune-teller sat on the curb, his caged bird ready to lift a slip of paper from a tray whenever tempted with a seed. Stall after stall sold overruns and cut-price seconds. Two Sikh policemen walked slowly along. Sikhs are employed as cops because the triads have difficulty buying them off. Children ran about. Shoppers haggled. Old friends talked loudly to one another. A river of people filled the street between the buildings. Radios blared from all directions. To deter demons, small wind chimes hung from some stalls. The smell was of cooking oil, duck feces, and old sweat.

Anne appeared dazed. "I've never seen this before."

"You've been in Hong Kong for years."

"Conferences and ceremonies and dinners and parties and work. I've never left the main streets, I guess."

Anne and I continued walking east, and we left the bazaar and entered a narrower street of tenements. Here newcomers from China slept in shifts, ten and twelve per cubicle, and here storm sewers on both sides of the street were filled with fetid brown water. Idlers are uncommon in Hong Kong, but here bantam-thin men in gray singlets leaned out windows and propped themselves up against light poles, cigarettes pinched between two fingers and held above their palms. They stared at us as we passed. *Gweilos* didn't often find this corner of Kowloon.

Anne walked more closely to me. "Do you know anything about Mr. Wen?"

I spoke about Hong Kong triads for a moment, and about Wen's control of much of the city's vice. Then I said, "Jay Lee, who is chief of the police's Organized Crime and Triad Bureau, let me read his department's file on Wen Quiching. The dragon head's empire isn't limited to Hong Kong but stretches into the sprawling new cities on the New Territories' border."

A rat popped out of a curb grate and scurried under a stack of rotted pallets in a walkway between two buildings. An old man sat on a cage of chickens. He wore a grimy T-shirt, and holes were in the knees of his pants, but around his left wrist was a thick silver bracelet.

"Wen had two sons, and both are dead. The oldest son was handling 88K's narcotics business, and he was murdered by a drug gang from the Monywa Valley in Burma, according to the OCTB. The Burmese gang was called the Holan. The gang was Wen's main source of opium."

"Why was he killed?" Anne asked.

"A drug deal gone bad, is the OCTB's guess. His body floated up on Shelter Island."

"Did Wen retaliate?" Anne asked.

"Holan forgot who they were dealing with. The opium supplier's headquarters were in the Monywa Valley, in an old English, colonial-style mansion. Six weeks after Wen's son was killed, thirty-two Holan members were found dead at and around the mansion, including the gang's chief and his main subordinates. Execution-style, all of their hands had been tied behind their backs. Holan ceased to exist, and its poppy fields and rendering plants were taken over by a neighboring gang that saw an opportunity."

"And we are going to meet this fellow?"

"We've made a deal. He's helping me and I'm helping him."

"Are you up to it?" she asked.

"I'm not in over my head, if that's what you're saying."

"You're crazy, dealing with gangsters, is what I'm saying. What happened to his other son?"

"The police don't know," I replied. "Maybe Wen doesn't know, either. He just disappeared, and the police assume he was killed. Wen told me himself that he no longer has any sons."

"So drugs and people-smuggling are Wen's principle businesses?"

"And about a dozen other criminal activities. But Jay Lee thinks 88K makes half its income now from legitimate businesses—garbage pickup and construction and freight-handling."

Five junkyard dogs—their fur dun and yellow, their ribs showing— loped by us in a pack. A boy, maybe seven years old, stepped out of a doorway, intercepted us on the street, and began a manic soft-shuffle dance, his feet tapping and spinning crazily and his arms churning like windmill blades. After thirty seconds he abruptly stopped and held out his hand. Anne pressed an HK dollar into it. He grinned at us. Then his little brother, maybe five years old, sprinted out into the street to stand before us, and did his best imitation of his older brother, flailing away with his arms and legs, dancing on the cigarette butts that littered the street.

Anne gave him a dollar, too, and said, "We'd better hurry. I'm almost out of pocket change."

"Jay Lee told me that the Holan reprisal was undoubtedly planned by Wen's red pole, a fellow named Shao Long."

"What's the red pole?" she asked as we stepped aside two fellows playing dominos, the tiles on an upside-down cardboard box.

"The 88K's enforcer. Jay told me there's a legend about Shao Long, that for every person he kills on Wen's orders, Wen gives him an emerald, and that Shao Long has them implanted in his teeth, so that he has a green smile."

"Is that one of those alligators-in-the-sewers legends that every city has?"

"Jay has never seen Shao Long, so he can't say. Jay thinks it's a rumor, but he admits that anything is possible with 88K."

After another half a block, I caught sight of a man walking along with us, a dozen feet off to our left. He slowed when we slowed and picked up the pace when we did so. He wasn't hiding from us but rather was a discreet escort. He wore black cotton pants and a white shirt with the tails out. Then I saw another one, another escort, a few steps farther behind, shadowing us in the same way. Both studied Anne and me as we moved along the street. A pale sun was overhead, silver instead of gold.

We had entered a dilapidated area of Kowloon, one that was jammed with people but which had none of the happy noise and sparkle of the bazaar. Tropical rot had stained the concrete buildings green and brown. Garbage was scattered across the street and stood in piles two-feet high at the base of some buildings. An iron railing was around an open manhole in the street, though it didn't look like anyone had been working on the site for weeks, no flags or cones, no nearby equipment.

Anne whispered, "I've never felt more foreign."

I pulled the address out of my pocket. On a doorway was 233. The next would be 235, the address I was looking for. Hong Kong Cantonese avoid the number 4 on street addresses because 4 is pronounced *shih*, a homonym for death. The building was three stories high, and unremarkable in every respect, presenting a stained wall on the street containing a door and rows of small windows. Glass from a second-story window was missing. A downspout had pulled away from the gutter at a corner of the building, and it hung out into space, held precariously by a bracket a floor below.

A man wearing a Nike workout coat met us at the door. He nodded and stepped aside, allowing us to enter, though he eyed Anne suspiciously. The room contained Formica-topped tables and mess-hall chairs. We followed him to the rear of the room, then up a narrow stairway where mold grew along the walls. We came to the second floor, then continued on up, Anne ahead of me. A pungent smell hung in the stairway, a gamy, treacly odor that thickened the air.

We stepped into a room that was in a spell of languor. About thirty people were sitting and lying on wood beds against the wall. Others were lying on straw mats on the floor. Their boneless postures—many leaning companionably against each other for support, arms and legs draped casually over the bedposts or hanging to the floor—spoke of utter contentment and a beatific malaise, accented by the curtains of smoke hanging in the room that obscured the walls and beds, then wafted aside to reveal them again. The room was lit with only one table lamp, and much of it was in gloomy half-light. Green and blue dragons—with leering visages and breathing fire—were painted on the walls. Several of the guests were smoking eighteen-inch-long wooden pipes, exhaling slow rolling clouds of gray smoke. An attendant wearing an apron and slippers walked around the room with a tray on which was a silver service, stopping in front of one person, then another, offering items from a silver tray. Moving slowly as if underwater, one of the smokers took a small black ball from the tray. The smoker tamped it into the bowl of his pipe.

Anne whispered, "My lord, our first date, and you've brought me to an opium den?"

"This is a date?"

The gangster appeared out of the smoke. He was smiling and nodding, and he gripped my hand. His old hand felt like a handful of sticks in mine. He seemed delighted to see me. His nephew, Zhu Jintau, was a right behind him, also smiling.

Wen spoke quietly, and his nephew translated, "'This is my first place of business, Mr. Williams. It is where I got my start. I still view the place with much affection.'"

Two new customers entered the room, and the waiter approached them. One of the customers pulled a pipe from a leather case.

Wen asked through his nephew, "'Would you like to try a pipe?'"

"I'm trying to cut back," I replied.

When I introduced Anne, she asked, "I'm glad to meet you, but I'm not clear why I was invited here today."

After translation, Wen replied via his nephew, "'I have never before met an American woman. I was curious. This seemed like a good opportunity.'"

"Really? I'm the first?"

"'I've read a lot about American women, though. My granddaughter subscribes to *Cosmopolitan* and leaves the magazine at my home once in a while, and I glance at them. You are'"—here the nephew paused to grope for a word—"'more subtle in appearance than I was expecting.'"

Through shifting clouds of smoke appeared one of the largest men I have ever seen, perhaps six feet seven, and weighing maybe 350 pounds. He took a position at the dragon head's elbow. His gaze switched back and forth between my hands and the doorway. Wen didn't introduce him. Much of the fellow's weight was muscle, which was packed onto his arms and thighs and chest, but some of it was fat, which padded the back of his neck and his belly and his chin. The fabric of his pants and shirt sleeves was strained almost to ripping. His head was as perfectly round as the moon. His ears were the size of coat buttons, so small as to look useless. He wore a buzz cut, and his scalp showed through short black hair. His eyes were close together, and were alert with malice. I took him to be a bodyguard.

"'I wanted to show you my business here,'" Zhu Jintau translated. "'I use your McDonald's as a business model. I offer a clean place with a good product and fast service. I have maintained the original wall paintings and the original furnishings down through the years. Sometimes I come here to sit for an hour and reflect on my good fortune. This is my first store, but I have six others in Kowloon, and thirteen more in Shenzhen and the other cities across the border. I am considering franchising them. A person could do well with a business like this in, say, San Francisco. It is something for you to consider.'"

He might have been joking. I said, "I limit my investments to blue-chip stocks, Mr. Wen. DuPont, Boeing, those sorts of companies. But I appreciate the offer."

Anne asked, "Do you use opium yourself, Mr. Wen?"

"'I am not a fool, madam,'" came the translated reply. "'Nor does anyone who reports directly to me. I won't have it.'" He turned back to me. "'I have information for you. We have found the second kidnapper in the town of Badan, at the mouth of the Pearl River.'"

I looked around the room for a television set and a VCR. "I'm not going to watch another snuff film, if that's what you have in mind."

After the translation, Wen said through Zhu, " 'Your face turned a terrible white the first time, and you swayed on your chair. I would not threaten your health again with another video.' "

The old guy was grinning at me, which pulled taut the scar along his jaw. I don't know why I was sensing this, or how it might have occurred, but I had begun to think this old gangster liked me. There apparently was no reason for my invitation to this address, other than for him to show me how he got his start, in this opium den. And he smiled at me more than a feared triad leader would normally smile. He was in no hurry, taking the time to solicit questions and comments. He frequently glanced at Anne. His bodyguard—if that's what he was, the burr-cut fellow looming behind Wen—scowled at me, his lips pressed to a thin line. He was looking for an excuse to kung fu me out a window, was my guess.

Zhu translated, " 'This second kidnapper's name is Yan Luo-han.' "

Wen was using the present tense, so perhaps the kidnapper was still alive, or maybe his nephew didn't know his English tenses well.

Zhu went on with his uncle's words, " 'He told us the name of his superior, and we were able to determine that the superior is employed by the Shenzhen office of the People's Republic of China's Data Center.' "

I said, "I've never heard of that office."

After switching my words to Cantonese, Zhu replied for his uncle, " 'It collects census information.' "

"A census bureau would kidnap your nephew?"

" 'Yan Luo-han told us that he does whatever he is ordered to do. That is all we've been able to learn from him despite' "—Zhu paused in the translation to find a phrase—" ' "intense questioning." ' "

I looked around again at the opium-smokers. A few nodded their heads. One moved an arm back and forth for no apparent reason. Another smiled crazily.

" 'Come with me,' " Zhu said for his uncle. " 'I will introduce you to the murderer of your father, the man who threw him over the rail. You will see the last face your father ever saw.' "

The dragon head led us from the opium den, then down the stairs. At the door to the street, the giant stepped in front of him, and Wen walked in his large shadow four steps to a Lodestone armored truck that had pulled up while we were upstairs. The truck normally traveled between banks and businesses carrying money and negotiable instruments, but Wen had it at his service. Maybe Lodestone was one of his legitimate businesses. Gun ports were in the cab door and the cargo bay. The windows were bulletproof. The Lodestone emblem—a bar of gold emitting rays like the sun—was painted on the sides of the cargo bay.

The big bodyguard opened the rear door, and gave his arm to Wen, who climbed up and into the bay with surprising agility. Apparently delighted to be away from her desk and seeing the real Hong Kong—for she, like many *gweilos*, perhaps suspected that much of Hong Kong's modernity is a veneer, and that ancient China lies close beneath—Anne grinned at the bodyguard. She climbed up and in, then so did Wen's nephew.

Then, just before I stepped up to enter the armored truck's bay, the giant bodyguard, holding the door open, smiled at me. Or perhaps it was a grimace. Emeralds glittered from his teeth.

* * *

We drove north, I thought. The armored truck's cargo bay was lit by a single overhead bulb and was air-conditioned, which made me think Wen used the truck frequently as his personal transport. Padded wood benches were along the bay's sides. The driver was separated from us by a steel grate.

After a few minutes, Wen spoke, and the young man translated, " 'I lost my father, just like you did, Mr. Williams. It was an act of violence that might have been prevented. I came home one day—I was seventeen years old—and found my father's hands in the washbasin.' "

Anne asked, "What was your father doing? Washing clothes?"

After translation, Zhu gave his uncle's reply, " 'Only his hands were in the basin. I never found the rest of him. It taught me the need for precautions.' " He gestured, indicating the armored truck.

Anne was silent for a moment, then she asked, "Did you ever find out who did it?"

Zhu gave his uncle's answer. " 'Fifteen years later I finally did. It was the red pole of Beneficent Harmony, a group that was a rival to 88K.' "

Anne asked, "Did you alert the police?"

Zhu paused before translating the question, and Wen also paused before answering. He glanced at me, puzzlement on his face. Then he looked at Anne like she might be a moron.

" 'No,' " came the answer.

"Well, how did you—?"

She only stopped when I tapped her ankle with my shoe.

Zhu translated a few more words. " 'Justice was done, I assure you.' "

We rode in silence for a while. The enforcer, the red pole, filled the back end of the cargo bay, where the light was weakest. He must have had a quarter-million dollars in gems imbedded in his teeth. I tried not to stare at him. His hands were on his knees, and he was still.

Wen spoke and Zhu turned it into English. " 'I have let it be known in Hong Kong and the border towns that I will pay a million Hong Kong dollars for the return of my grandson. And I offered amnesty to whoever is involved in the kidnapping if the boy is returned unharmed.' "

"Do you think it will work?" I asked.

" 'Perhaps, unless they figure out that I am lying about the amnesty.' "

The armored truck slowed, and I could see the driver roll down the side window and swipe a card against a reader. The vehicle moved forward again and began to turn right and left repeatedly, winding its way along narrow corridors.

When the vehicle stopped again, the giant opened the rear door and we followed him out. We were in a valley of cargo containers. This was the Kwai Chung Container Terminal in the New Territories, which is alongside Rambler Channel near Stonecutter's Island. Acre after acre of stacked, oceangoing steel containers were set out in perfect grids. Kwai Chung handles fourteen million containers a year. By comparison, the Port of Seattle loads or offloads a million a year. At one end of the terminal a long line of trucks waited to take on containers. Ten-story rail-mounted jib cranes lifted the containers from moored ships and placed them on the truck trailers. Front loaders and toplifters moved among the container rows. Cosco and Evergreen and Inter-Ocean ships were moored at the quays. A dozen other vessels waited in the bay for slots to open.

We were in a line of refrigerated containers, each with a humming cooling unit attached. Shao Long—the fabled red pole, the enforcer with the gems in his teeth—stepped up to a red container and removed a padlock, then threw the bolt. Wen gestured us to gather around. Shao pulled open the metal hatch. A cloud of frosted air rolled from the box. Then out came a man.

He stumbled into the heat, then fell to the pavement. His arms were tied behind his back. Shao Long gripped the man's head in two hands like a melon and lifted him to standing. Anne inhaled sharply. Shao grinned, and the emeralds flashed in the sun.

"'This is Yan Luo-han,'" Zhu translated.

"What are you doing to him?" Anne asked.

"'We are shipping him to Oakland, California, USA, in a container that is also carrying pork bellies.'"

"He is going to die in there," she said.

And soon. Yan's stare was glassy. The skin of his face suffered a blue pallor. He may have shivered for a while, but now he was beyond that. He stood there, disoriented and taking only shallow breaths, still in the enforcer's grip. Ice particles on his skivvy shirt quickly melted in the heat. He was barefoot. Its diesel engine clattering, a toplifter carrying a Cosco container passed in front of our row of containers.

Wen spoke and Zhu followed, "'He doesn't look like much now, does he? Just like the rest of the pork bellies in the container. Someone in Oakland is going to have a surprise when this container is opened.'"

"You can't just murder him," Anne protested.

The old man was silent.

"I want to take him to the Hong Kong police," I said.

After my words were changed to Cantonese, Wen's face became pinched with disapproval. The jade charm the kidnapped boy's mother had given me was in my pants pocket. I rubbed it. Maybe it would give me the courage to negotiate with the old man. "I won't be party to a murder."

Zhu translated my words, then his uncle's reply. " 'This man threw your father over a deck rail, and your father fell twenty stories to his death. And you want to hand him over to the Hong Kong courts?' "

"Yes."

" 'That's not our way here in Hong Kong.' "

"But it's my way," I replied. "This man told you he worked for a Shenzhen census office, which is probably a front for something else. You've hit a dead end in your investigation, yet your grandson is still missing. I have contacts, and I will continue to be your partner, but only if we take this man to the Hong Kong police."

My reputation among my FBI peers was as a vigilante. They thought I had thrown Bill Adamson's killer down a flight of stairs. It was a false reputation. I believed fervently in the process of justice, even for the murderer of my father.

The old man looked at me as he might a fish at a street vendor's stall. Finally he barked several words, and Shao Long lifted Yan by his pants and shirt collar, then tossed him into the back of the armored truck, where Yan landed heavily. The old gangster climbed back into the truck, and we all prepared to follow him.

But before we did, Anne squeezed my arm and said, "*Now* you're my big hero."

10

Tingsia was a village on the Hochou River, a tributary of the Pearl, inland from Hong Kong sixty miles. Tingsia was built on steep bluffs over the Hochou, and was believed to be a farming village, before all the villagers disappeared and the village ceased to exist many centuries ago.

Tingsia's fate is a fairy tale, some say. Others insist it is historical fact, and those facts are these: six hundred years ago, in the early years of the Ming Dynasty, and during the second Ming emperor's rule—this would-be Emperor Chien-wen—the village of Tingsia produced a young lady so fair that tales of her beauty reached the emperor's palace in Beijing. The young woman, whose name was Morning Flower, was the village cobbler's daughter, but all of Tingsia lay claim to her as their own, and it was said that she was so lovely that flowers turned their blossoms toward her as they would the sun. An imperial edict arrived in Tingsia, demanding that Morning Flower be sent to the palace in Beijing. The cobbler and the other citizens of Tingsia refused, and when the emperor next sent a saddlebag of silver, they still refused.

So next the emperor sent a thousand soldiers to Tingsia, and the villagers—every last one of them—were driven off a cliff onto the rocks of the Hochou River's shoreline. Four hundred people fell to their deaths, including Morning Flower, whom the villagers had disguised as an old woman. The emperor's soldiers then burned the village and filled in the well and tore out the steps down to the river and ripped apart the village's fishing nets. Even the fog crows left the village because there was nothing left to eat. It is also said that the earth was so hateful of the emperor that it refused to issue forth crops or trees or even weeds, and those acres where Tingsia once stood have been barren down through the centuries and are still barren.

It sure looked barren when I arrived there—dusty, wind-blown acres with nothing growing in the cracked yellow ground. I could see a place where the village might have been, over near the cliffs, and true to the legend, not a living thing was in sight. White boulders marked the dirt here and there, and a tumbledown stone fence separated what might have once been fields but which were now hard-packed dirt. The canyon was a narrow, winding gap in the ground half a mile away. Visible through a dun-colored haze, a small village was on the canyon's far side, maybe three dozen huts and two grain storage buildings. Trees grew on the far sides, and carefully tended vegetable farms were divided by fences. But on this side, nothing. The sun was a flat disk overhead, and it coppered the land, making every feature of the landscape a weak yellow. Flies the size of quarters circled me.

I wasn't on the spot where the town of Tingsia had been, but nearby, maybe a quarter-mile away, on the road between Lochan and Changto, a two-lane asphalt road that had been neglected for so long that the asphalt lay loosely in fist-sized chunks on the road. Twelve or so buildings were inside a hurricane fence. A sheet-metal garage held two dump trucks and a front loader. Another building appeared to be a repair shop, and yet another was a foreman's shop. A sign hung on the fence identified the installation, but it was in Cantonese, so I couldn't read it. I had been told that it was a provincial road-repair yard.

The gate was closed but unlocked, and I pushed it open. Behind me was a blue Mercedes sedan I had driven out from Kowloon, one of the dragon head's cars. He had said I would have no trouble getting it through the border, and he had been right. I was wearing a striped Polo sleeveless sports shirt and a pair of jeans. A camera bag hung from my belt. I looked like a tourist. I carried a map in my hand and was glancing at it, then turning my head to look at the road, then returning my gaze to the map. A lost tourist.

I walked across the gravel yard. Steel barrels were along one side of the vehicle shed. A thousand-gallon gasoline tank was elevated on a wood frame. A pile of discarded truck parts was near the back fence. I caught the scent of grease. A road grader sat on wood blocks, all its wheels and its blade missing, and rust eating away at the turntable and engine housing. Behind the yard, on the other side of the back fence, was a gravel yard with a dozen cones of gravel.

Darrel Reese had found this place. I had asked him how, and he was vague but had mentioned that the Kuomintang still had many followers in China, who in their defiance of the regime could do nothing effective except report certain things to certain people. I had passed the location on to the dragon head.

I walked toward the crew quarters. The building was made of concrete blocks. A telephone line was rigged to the building, and two chimneys rose from the roof. Six windows were on the side of the building facing me, though one had been covered with a wood slat. Reflections hid my view of anyone who might have been watching me from the windows.

I tapped on the door, hesitantly, the lost tourist, loath to intrude but desperate to find my way. Then I tapped again, louder, my head down at the map. I resisted the urge to scratch my head as I stared at the map, thinking it might be too melodramatic. Just as I was about to knock yet again, the door opened.

A man stood there, wearing a white shirt, jeans, and sandals. He barked something I'm sure was rude, and was about to close the door when the air above my shoulder was rent by Shao Long's enormous arm, which wasn't there one instant but was the next, as Shao reached over my shoulder, grabbed the man by the face, and yanked him out into the sun, so slick that the man hardly brushed me. I turned to see the man already senseless on the ground—I had no idea what the red pole did to him—and Shao Long rushing passed me into the building, pushing me aside like a gate.

I heard a yelp, then a hollow blow and then another, then a rattling sigh, then something heavy falling to the floor, and then plates shattering, and then something else hitting the deck, and all this was before my eyes had adjusted to the dimness.

When I sheepishly stepped into the room, it was over, and only the results of Shao's invasion were evident. On the floor were three men in various depths of unconsciousness. One's nose was shattered, and I mean it was pushed sideways on his head so that it pointed to the left. He lay there, splayed out, his arms and legs akimbo. Another man was draped over a chair, belly down on the seat, his head to one side and his legs to the other. Blood from his nose was pooling on the concrete floor. A third man was facedown on the floor, and I couldn't see any damage to him. He was breathing but was motionless. A cabinet containing dishes and pots had been knocked over. A pistol was on the floor, a semi-automatic of some sort. A folding chair had been overturned. Eight bunk beds were in the room, along with a television set and a VCR. Taiwanese comic books were stacked on a wood bench. Thirty-pound sacks of rice were on one of the bunks.

Shao Long had a young man in a bear hug, and the lad was whooping and hollering and laughing, his arms around Shao's thick neck. Shao's huge grin displayed the emeralds in his teeth. The boy was Wen's kidnapped grandson, Hsu Shui-ban, the other member of the 20th Floor Physics Club. Still in the big man's arms, Hsu patted Shao's burr-cut head again and again, a playful tattoo. Both laughed, and Hsu squeezed the enforcer's neck again.

Shao said something to Wen's grandson, and the boy said in English, "He says we must go quickly. There are more of them, but I don't know where they are."

The giant released the boy from his hug, and they stepped toward the door, both still grinning at their reunion. At that moment another man—a fifth person who had been guarding the boy—rose from behind a bunk and stepped toward Shao and the boy. The man held a pistol and was bringing it up, and his mouth was turned down with purpose, and in that instant I could see his finger start to pull back. Shao didn't see the man, and the gunman was so focused on the giant Shao that he didn't notice me.

I dove at the man. My hand knocked aside the pistol and my shoulder hit him in the side of his chest. The pistol fired, but the bullet ripped through a window instead of into Shao's back. The window instantly shattered. The gunman was a slight man, and my weight knocked him hard against a bunk bed, and then he bounced to the floor.

Shao spun around, rushed across the room, and sent a sap into the man's temple. It was the first I'd seen the sap, which had the dimensions of my forearm and was black. The gunman stayed on the floor. Shao put a hand under my arm and lifted me to my feet as easily as I would lift an empty sack.

I had banged my knee on the floor. I tried not to wince, and I wouldn't let myself rub it, not in front of the giant. Shao looked at me intently, as if through a clouded window. I had just saved his life, pure and simple. He stepped up to me and put his ham-hock arms around me and crushed me to him. He surrounded me, lifting me off the floor in his embrace, and I'm no flyweight. He smelled of ginger. Then he released me, and my feet found the floor again.

He stared at me, and nodded, sending me some message that I didn't get.

The boy said, "Come on. Let's go," then repeated it in Cantonese.

Hsu fled the road-crew barracks that had been his prison, and I followed him out the door. Shao came after me, out onto the gravel, and when I glanced at him again, he was still staring at me and nodding, and then I saw those emerald-imbedded teeth again.

* * *

"Do you go out with anyone?" Anne asked, clasping a shrimp between her chopsticks.

"You mean, dating?"

She grinned. "Your expression is as if I'd asked you how much money is in your savings account. Don't be so private."

"I'm young—relatively young—and single. Of course I do."

"Like who?" she asked.

"You wouldn't know her." I hastily corrected, "Wouldn't know them."

"Maybe I do. Hong Kong is a smaller place than its skyline suggests."

This was going to require considerable skill at evasion, I could tell. I sipped tea, giving me a moment. We were having lunch at Chop Fo, a tiny Sichuan restaurant on Queen's Road East. Anne had offered to buy lunch, laughing and saying, "Don't read anything into it." I dabbed at my mouth with a paper napkin.

"You are stalling." Anne was wearing olive-green slacks and a white shirt. A silver bracelet was around her left wrist.

"Well, there's Chrissy Fleming."

"You go out with a girl named *Chrissy?*" She adopted a look of astonishment. "What is she, an eighteen-year-old cheerleader?"

I hadn't seen Chrissy in two years. "She's a ceramics curator at the art museum at the Chinese University of Hong Kong."

"Where did you meet her?"

"Why am I being grilled?" I asked.

"I'm keeping you sharp, Clay. At your age, you need it."

"I'm being killed every minute here."

"So where did you meet this Chrissy?"

I tried lifting rice with my chopsticks. You'd think that a culture that invented the abacus could've invented the fork. "I met her at the Metropolitan."

"In New York City? The art museum?"

"Well . . ."

"I'm impressed, you going to a museum. Who would have thought?"

Anne sure enjoyed sticking me.

I had to say, "At the Metropolitan Bar and Grill on Lan Fong Road at Causeway Bay. She was playing pinball when I first saw her."

Anne stared at me. Hung over the door to the kitchen, a bug zapper hummed.

I hurried on. "It was Gottlieb's Four Aces. Her beer was on the glass top of the pinball machine, and she was bumping the game with her hips, getting just the right English on the ball."

"A museum curator playing pinball? First time in history."

"Her blond hair was down to the middle of her back, and she was studying the game intensely, oblivious to everything else. It was quite a sight."

"Chrissy sounds like the perfect tramp."

"You would've liked her. You both ask a lot of questions."

"Are you still dating her?"

"Not for a while, actually."

She smiled. "Which one of you sobered up?"

"Can we talk about something else?"

"Sure." She lifted a slice of pepper with her chopsticks. "So who are you going out with these days?"

I didn't say anything.

"You are obligated to answer me, Clay. I'm buying lunch, after all."

I sighed loudly. "Nobody of interest, really."

"Like who?"

"Well . . ." I scratched my jaw. "Several young ladies."

She waited.

"One or two, really."

She lowered her chin, studying with amused surmise. "Come on. Fess up. Anybody?"

After a moment I said, "Not really."

"Why not?" She lifted her teacup.

"I've been busy."

She offered a gentle smile, free of irony. "That's not really it, is it?"

"Sure it is."

"You don't date at all, do you?"

"Lot's of dates." I made a swift noise in my throat. "You can check my address book."

"You still love your wife, and so you don't go out."

"That's preposterous."

"You told me you had factored her ditching you into your assessment of her—you sounded like an actuary—and that you no longer love her, but you do."

"You're talking nonsense."

"Admit it."

"No." I reached for my glass of water.

"I feel sorry for you."

I laughed, trying to make it sound sincere. "Don't feel sorry for me. I'm doing fine."

"You need to find someone else, Clay. Not a woman you meet at a pinball machine. Someone of substance."

I tried lifting a piece of pork. It slipped through the chopsticks.

"You need to find a person who is devoted to you, a person who loves the institution of marriage, which you clearly do."

"Not many of those women around."

"There's more than you think. If you search diligently, you'll find her."

"Sounds like a lot of work and trouble." I returned my chopsticks to the plate.

She paid the bill and left a tip. We rose from our chairs.

"Maybe I should help you search." She stepped toward the door. "I have some nice friends."

"Spare me."

"You should move forward, Clay." Her voice had gained a warm tone. "You need the stability you had early in your marriage with Olivia."

I smiled. "What I need is less amateur analysis."

"You need someone who is smart and funny."

"I need to carry a fork with me when I eat Chinese food. I can't work chopsticks, so I'm still hungry."

We stepped out onto the street.

Anne added, "And you need to find someone who has a nice laugh."

She laughed, nicely.

* * *

My father also taught me about sorrow. I haven't mentioned my older brother Mike yet, as he was there and gone in my life, and now I have trouble bringing his face to mind, and when I can, it's always Mike's face at sixteen, the last time I saw him, a blast of red hair and a mouth full of shiny orthodontic braces. He had a crazy laugh, I remember, a laugh that always sounded like he was up to something.

On the last day of my brother's life, my dad had taken me with him to his foreman's office, not having anywhere else to send me and promising we would drive into Medford for lunch, which meant a milkshake and fries, plus a hamburger I never ate. I was fourteen years old.

Dad was in the foreman's office, and I was outside fiddling with a sprinkler, pointing it out over the road, hoping a car would drive by so I could douse it. Pear trees were in all directions, lined up in even rows. This was in the early summer, when the fruit had just begun to grow and was still hard and green. I remember that bees and butterflies were thick in the air, and dust spurted from under my shoes with each step. The sun was close and heavy.

I heard Mike's friends when they were still a hundred yards away, up the county road. They were shouting, and one might have been crying, I couldn't tell. They were on their bicycles, three kids, all in high school, kids Mike had known all his life. They pulled off the country road, and tore down the dirt road toward the foreman's office, still hollering. All three of them were wearing jeans, and they were wet, dripping water onto the dirt. Dad came out from the shed, and the boys spoke all at once, gesturing wildly, and one of them was crying.

Dad ran to his pickup, and the boys climbed into the back, and they took off, dirt spinning from the rear wheels. The foreman emerged from his shed to watch them go. He looked at me for an explanation, but I had to shake my head. He waved me into his truck, and we took off in chase. The foreman's name was Antonio Ramirez, who had worked for Dad for twenty years, and who often had Sunday dinner with our family.

A half-mile away the county road crossed over an irrigation canal. Antonio and I found Dad's truck there, and Dad and the boys were running along the canal bank a hundred yards downstream. I saw Dad wade into the water, which was up to his chest. Canals wind around the valley, and everybody lives within a couple hundred yards of a canal, and children are taught never to go near them. Antonio used his truck's CB radio to call for help.

Dad waded frantically back and forth along that stretch of the canal, often bending over to feel the muddy bottom. After a few minutes, sheriff's deputies began arriving, then the fire station crews. Their rigs were parked on both sides of the county road at the bridge. I walked alongside the canal toward my father. He was moving downstream, his arms out in front of him, hands under the surface, searching the black water. A low keening of agony was coming from him.

Mike's friends said they had been riding their bikes along the road, and suddenly one of them had the good idea of going for a swim. They had chucked their shirts and shoes, and soon were splashing and laughing in the canal. The sides of the canal were muddy and slippery, and the boys couldn't agree on their story, whether Mike might have fallen and hit his head and then gone under, or whether he just disappeared beneath the surface when no one was looking. Mike's friends looked for him for fifteen minutes before jumping on their bikes and riding toward our house. The foreman's shed was on the way, and they had seen Dad's pickup.

Search-and-rescue squads looked for Mike all that day. I stayed with Dad, sometimes entering the water to help him feel his way along. As evening came, the parents of Mike's friends came to get their boys, and the sheriff's deputies and the firemen and the volunteer crews packed up their equipment and left the area. My father stayed in the canal, walking mile after mile, back and forth. I waded along with him, but the water was cold and I would begin to shake uncontrollably and would have to retreat to the banks to warm up, and then I'd go back in after a while.

As night fell, my father called out Mike's name, as if Mike might be just sitting in some nearby orchard, lost. "Mike, it's Dad," and "Hey, Mike, come on out, son. Dinner is on." And then Dad began yelling Mike's name again and again, just his name, and at times he sounded angry and at other times he was pleading. The moon rose, and the pear tree leaves turned to silver, and Dad still walked the canal, and he was still there when the sun rose, but by then his calling of Mike's name had turned to barely audible moans. Finally, I walked into the water to guide him out. He followed me like a blind man. I couldn't drive Dad's truck, and I didn't think he could either just then, so I walked him a half mile back to our house and put him in his chair by the fireplace. I took off his boots.

In the days that followed, my father shut down. He sat in that chair, and he didn't eat and he didn't sleep, and when the sheriff came to tell him that Mike's body had been found up against a diversion gate, Dad nodded and didn't say a word. I found him unconscious on that chair six or seven days after the drowning and called our family doctor. Dad was taken to the hospital in an ambulance. He had not been eating or drinking and had passed out from dehydration.

He had lost his wife and now he had lost his oldest son, all within two years. When he returned from the hospital two days later, I made him eat, opening up a can of Hormel chili and warming it on the stove and shoving it under his nose and keeping it there until he ate. I served him chili ten days in a row, as we had a case of it in the pantry and it was all I knew how to cook. I made him eat it, wouldn't go away until he did. I did the same with glasses of water.

Then two weeks after Mike died, my father rose from that chair and he shaved and took a shower, and then he came to me as I sat out on the porch.

He said, "I'm done, Clay."

"What do you mean?"

"I'm all done." He patted my knee. "Let's you and me go into town. Antonio is going to meet us at the irrigation supply store, and we need to look at some new sprinkler heads."

From then on Dad seemed fine. I thought for the next week or so that he had excised Mike from his mind. He didn't go into Mike's room, and he didn't mention him, not once. I missed Mike, too. I wanted to talk to Dad about him. I didn't want to forget him.

Then the next Sunday, he and I went rafting on the Rogue River. He knew a long, calm stretch. We both were drifting along, and it was cool in the canyon. A green heron pecked at the water near the shore. Dad said to me, "Mike would've liked this."

So he could talk about Mike, after all, and from then on we did, whenever we were particularly missing him or when we wanted to share a good memory. So Dad's lesson was that you needed to put grief in a corner of your mind and visit it when you needed to. Otherwise, leave it there.

It was a good lesson, I suppose, but I didn't learn it too well. I found myself grieving over my father there in Hong Kong, unable to put it aside. Sometimes, I would run through my favorite memories of him, and my spirits would lift, and then I'd realize again with another sickening jolt that he was gone, that he had been murdered. Taken away, cheated out of the last decades of his life.

So my father taught me about sorrow, and he taught me there were better ways to handle it than it turns out I could. I was spending a lot of time, in my chair up there on the twentieth floor, staring out the window, thinking about my old man.

*   *   *

Anne Iverson and I walked along Mai Tau Road on the Kowloon side. At the corner was St. Paul's Orphanage, an old four-story sandstone building that was in need of repair. Behind a wrought-iron gate a dozen children were playing in a cobblestone courtyard. Two nuns in black-and-white habits supervised the children, who were jumping rope and playing hopscotch. Two six-year-olds sat on the steps to the front door, both with red-haired Madeleine dolls. An ancient cast-iron box with a slot in the top was attached to the gate, with a sign above it asking for donations. Anne put in several HK dollars, then we followed the orphanage's iron picket fence around the corner to the next building, which belonged to the 88K, I had been told.

This building was designed by the same expatriate Englishman, Ronald Combs, who had constructed the Helena May Club on Garden Road, and was a Belgravia-style town house. Planters filled with red geraniums were in front of the building. A doorman greeted Anne and me with a broad grin and opened the massive oak door for us.

We entered a hallway decorated with a red and green Persian carpet. Leather club chairs were arranged around a mother-of-pearl-inlaid table. A wide, carpeted stairway with a brass banister led to the upper floors. Wen Quichin, the dragon head, must have been told we had arrived, because he hurried out into the hallway, then took Anne's elbow to lead us into the back room.

This was the 88K's gambling house, known as the Always Luck. Wen's nephew, Zhu Jintau, was at the door to the gaming room, ready as the interpreter. The room was thick with cigarette smoke. Fifteen tables were up and running, and I could see the games of blackjack, roulette, fan-tan, and big-and-small. A hundred slot machines—called *hungry tigers* in Hong Kong—were in a bank along one wall. The place was crowded, with every seat taken at the gaming tables. An ornately carved oak bar was along another wall, manned by three bartenders. Waitresses rushed drinks to the gamblers. To one side were tables filled with domino players. In Hong Kong the game of dominoes is called *connecting dragons*. Security cameras inside glass domes were above every gaming table. The room was not as noisy as a Hong Kong restaurant, which has the decibel level of a riot, because the gamblers were bent over the tables, concentrating. Gambling is serious business in Hong Kong. Other than the Happy Valley and Sha Tin racetracks and the lottery, it is also illegal. None of the gamblers glanced at Anne and me, even though we were the only *gweilos* in the room. They were too busy losing their money to the 88K.

The old gangster guided us toward a corner of the casino where three leather couches were arranged. Six men sat there, all of them somber and none of them drinking anything, obviously waiting. They all stood smartly, as if given an order from a drill instructor. Wen introduced me to each one of the men, and I had read about several of them in the OCTB file on the 88K. Guo Cheuk-fai was a white paper fan, an administrator of the 88K's loan-sharking operations, which fielded more than three hundred lenders in the city. Wu Hop-ha was the chief of 88K's opium-smuggling efforts. Zeng Kwan was Wen's second-in-command. I didn't catch the names of the other three. I don't doubt they were also 88K senior executives. A waitress delivered champagne flutes, one to each of the men and to Wen, and then to Anne and me.

Wen raised his glass and spoke, and his nephew translated, "'To the friendship between our club and Mr. Clay Williams.'"

All the men raised their glasses to salute me, then sipped their champagne. A few ventured small smiles of approval. After a few moments and another round of handshakes, Wen led Anne and me away.

Through his nephew, Wen asked, "'Do you play cards, Mr. Williams?'"

"Pinochle with my old man when I was a kid," I replied. Zhu struggled with the word *pinochle*, I could tell.

"'How about twenty-one?'" Wen asked through the translator.

I had been assigned to the Las Vegas FBI office for a while. I had tried blackjack a few times. I always lost my small stake, and quickly.

I said, "Never had much luck with twenty-one, I'm afraid."

"'I enjoy the game. Here, sit next to me.'"

I found myself in front of a blackjack table. All seven stools were taken, but on seeing Wen, two of the gamblers immediately took their chips and left the table. I sat next to him, in the sixth stool from the dealer's left.

"What's the minimum wager?" I felt like a rube.

The dealer spoke in English. "One hundred Hong Kong dollars, or twenty U.S. dollars."

I pulled out a hundred U.S. dollars, figuring with my luck at cards that it would last me five hands. My meager offering was changed into five chips, a tiny stack in front of me. Wen removed several bills from his pants pockets and purchased ten chips. My chips were U.S. dollar chips and were blue clay. Wen played with Hong Kong money, and so received rust-red chips. The dealer had a professionally complacent face, with a slight, encouraging smile over a small chin. His hair was greased back over the knobs of his temples. His passed his palm over the table, side to side, calling for bets.

I shoved one chip out. I dislike gambling; I work too hard for my money to hand it over at the whim of playing cards. And I didn't understand the ethos of the gambler, the let-it-ride mentality.

Wen laughed, then spoke, and Zhu, standing at his shoulder, rendered it into English. "'You'll never get rich, betting only twenty U.S. dollars per deal.'"

The old gangster placed five chips in the betting square in front of him. I followed his example, adding four more chips to my wager, my entire stack. A hundred dollars, a breathtaking amount for someone not inured to gambling.

The dealer issued cards. I peeked at mine. A nine and a six. I didn't know a lot about blackjack, but I knew this to be a terrible hand. The dealer's up card was a ten. He checked his hole card but didn't have a blackjack, so he squared his two cards. The fellows to my right stayed or called for cards, and when it was my turn, I nodded, wanting another card. I was dealt a six, a lucky draw. I had twenty-one.

Wen called for a card and busted out, flipping his cards over. Then the dealer issued himself a card, and he also went over twenty-one. The dealer put my winnings in front of me, five chips worth a hundred U.S. dollars.

The other three gamblers picked up their chips and cigarette packs and left the table, so there were only two of us. Anne was at my shoulder. I was about to put a two-chip wager out, but Wen said something, and Zhu translated. "'You must learn our Hong Kong ways, Mr. Williams. The meek remain behind.'"

So I put out my entire stack, ten chips worth two hundred U.S. dollars. I figured I'd let the house get its money back, along with my original five chips, and I'd get this over with. Wen bet another five chips. The cards came around. I was dealt a queen and an ace, a blackjack. I flipped my cards over, and the dealer paid me. Now I had twenty chips worth four hundred dollars.

Wen reached into his wallet to bring out several more bills, smiling and clucking at himself. He said through his nephew, "'This must not be my day.'"

I pulled my chips to my chest, and returned only five of them to the wagering square. Wen shook his head happily and said through his nephew, "'Has Hong Kong taught you nothing, Mr. Williams? When good fortune is offering a ride, do not prefer to walk.'"

Anne helped: "He is telling you not to fight a run of good cards."

Well, it was mostly house money now, anyway. I put out my entire stack, four hundred dollars' worth. The cards came around. I had a six and a seven, a losing hand almost always. The dealer's up card was a nine. I called for a card. Amazingly, it was an eight. My total was twenty-one. The dealer busted out, then matched my pile of chips with chips from the house. I now had eight hundred U.S. dollars.

Wen received a blackjack. He said through his nephew, "'Maybe my luck will follow your luck for a while.'"

"I simply can't wager eight hundred dollars," I said.

After translation, Wen replied, "'And you are the people who won the Second World War?'"

The old fellow was beaming, having a wonderful time even though he was losing more than winning. He seemed to enjoy my modest run of good luck. I left the entire pile of chips out there. What the hell. Only a hundred of it was mine, really.

The cards came around, and I received the ace of diamonds and the jack of clubs. The dealer exchanged my chips for higher-denomination chips. Now I had sixteen one-hundred-dollar chips in front of me. Wen busted out, losing several chips.

"I think you ought to take your winnings and run," Anne said.

"Not the people who won World War Two." I wagered my entire pile. "We don't run from anything."

I held on eighteen, and the dealer hit on his fifteen, and busted. He pushed stacks of chips across the felt to me. Wen lost his hand.

I looked over at Wen and said, "I dislike admitting this, but I am constitutionally incapable of betting this much money on the turn of a card. I'd like to quit."

"'Of course,'" Zhu translated the old man's reply. Smiling, Wen pocketed his few chips and rose from the table.

I'd never heard of such a run of luck as I had just had. I hadn't lost a hand. I gave a chip to the dealer, who bowed graciously, tapped the table loudly with it for the security camera overhead, then put it to one side. The minute we left, other gamblers stepped up to fill the spots.

Wen walked next to me for a few steps, but he stopped in front of a roulette table. His head only reached my shoulders. He spoke, and Zhu translated, "'My club owns this establishment, as you know, Mr. Williams. I find it difficult, as one of the proprietors, to let you walk out with my thirty-two hundred United States dollars.'"

"It's only thirty-one hundred dollars. I tipped the dealer.'"

"'Thirty-one hundred, then.'" He stepped up to the roulette wheel. Several gamblers immediately moved aside for him. "'What do you say? Give me a chance to win it back.'"

"What do you mean?"

He renewed his grin. His nephew translated, "'Put it all on a number on the roulette wheel.'"

"The entire thirty-one hundred dollars?" It was a ton of money. Maybe not to the old man, but certainly to me.

He lifted an eyebrow and spoke softly. It was a challenge, surely. His nephew translated, "'There comes a time when we all need to ask ourselves the question.'"

Yes, a challenge that called on my more base instincts. A schoolyard dare. This grizzled old murderer and thief and smuggler was sticking it to me, staring right at me.

I dislike reporting that I am susceptible to such things. I leaned over the green felt and put my thirty-one chips on number five. The dealer, a woman in her sixties who wore her hair tied in a bun at the nape of her neck, glanced at me, then at Wen.

Anne exclaimed, "Clay? What are you doing?"

"'Five is an unlucky number in Hong Kong, Mr. Williams,'" Zhu said, translating his uncle's words.

I quickly lifted my tall stack of chips from the table. At times like this, I believe in luck.

The old fellow spoke, and Zhu translated, "'I have always favored the number eleven.'"

Why not? Wen had been lucky in his life, having survived a dangerous occupation. I put my stack down on eleven. I was a tad dizzy—thirty-one hundred dollars on a long-shot, and me not even a gambler.

The dealer spun the wheel, and sent the ball in motion the opposite direction along the rim. Roulette pays thirty-five to one when betting on a single number, as I was. There are thirty-seven individual numbers to place a wager on. The discrepancy between those two figures—thirty-five and thirty-seven—is the house's advantage.

The ball lost speed, dropped onto the spinning wheel, clattered between several numbers and settled in the slot labeled number 11.

I blinked. With robotic calmness, the dealer issued me my winnings, 108 one-thousand-dollar chips and a five-hundred-dollar chip. I had just won $108,500. Plus, I had my original $3,100 from the blackjack table. I blinked again.

Wen was still smiling. Anne helped me scoop up the chips. The dragon head walked us over to the cashier's cage. I was given a manila envelope stuffed with U.S. hundred-dollar bills.

"'I should have known not to fight a man's luck,'" Zhu translated. "'I learned a lesson today, so your winnings are not entirely a loss for me.'" Wen clucked at himself.

I was still dazed, carrying a fortune in a manila envelope. Wen guided us out of the room and along the hallway to the door.

"'I will see you again, Mr. Williams'" were Wen's parting words. "'Invest your winnings wisely.'"

Anne and I stepped out into the rush of sunlight.

She said, "That was a pure payoff."

I pulled at an earlobe. "Yeah. I know."

"Mr. Wen just decided to give you a big wad of money to thank you for getting his grandson back, and he didn't think you would accept an envelope of cash unless he laundered it through his casino."

"I know."

Anne said, "You can't take money from gangsters."

"Who appointed you my conscience?" I felt my money slipping away from me.

We turned the corner onto Mai Tau Road. The orphans were still outside, running around. Two of them had climbed an oak tree near the fence. The two nuns were still chatting near the front steps.

"What are you going to do with the money?" Anne asked.

"Buy a Harley-Davidson, for starters."

"No, you aren't. That's blood money in that envelope, Clay. Those are criminals, no matter how charming old Mr. Wen is."

I stared lovingly at all my cash. The envelope was thick with U.S. greenbacks.

"Give me that envelope," she demanded.

When I handed it over, Anne pushed open the gate to the orphanage. It squeaked loudly. She walked briskly up to the two nuns and gave them the envelope. She said a few words. The nuns leaned forward to peer into the envelope. Their faces whitened, both of them. Anne smiled at them, then turned on her heels to return to the sidewalk, stepping around a boy dribbling a soccer ball with his feet. She closed the gate.

"There." She dusted her hands together. "Do you feel better?"

"No. I feel sick."

"Yes, you feel better."

"I can't believe you just did that. There was—what?—over a hundred and eleven thousand dollars of my money in that envelope."

"Mr. Wen said to invest the money wisely, and you just did." Anne took my arm, gripping me tightly to lead me along, as if I might bolt back into the courtyard and snatch back the envelope.

I glanced back at the orphanage. The nuns hadn't regained any of their color, though one of them had begun pulling out hundred-dollar bills to count them.

Anne laughed, tugging me along. "I should have told you I was an expensive date."

11

I despise little scenes, those sudden blow-ups that embarrass onlookers and participants in equal measure. One of the reasons I stayed with the FBI so long was its professionalism, which touched all aspects of the organization, from investigations to personnel relations. Not once in those twenty years did I witness anything like what I did that morning at the base of the Fifth Millennium China Tower, when John Llewellyn went off his nut.

I had been told by Lien Yang-sun, director of the tower's security, that I was not to concern myself with the island's new construction, that all the boats and barges that had suddenly appeared on the west end were not within my jurisdiction. Still, I found myself near the construction site at the west end that morning, watching the work, puzzled by the size of the effort.

The sun was high overhead, and its light was clear and strong. Rain had fallen heavily that night, and now the morning had a scrubbed feel. The air was so clear I could see the green Rolls-Royces in front of the Peninsula Hotel on the Kowloon side, and the workmen—tiny at this distance—installing neon signs on the convention center's glass front over at Wan Chai on the Hong Kong side. At this spot, a few feet above sea level, Victoria Harbor was the bottom of a canyon, with skyscrapers rising on both sides of the water.

A flotilla was moored near Heroes of the Revolution Island's west end. There were barges and dredges, but there were also several vessels whose purpose I couldn't identify. I stepped nearer the chain-link fence that cordoned off the new construction area. A few days ago this had been a flat expanse of concrete, almost in its final form, waiting for tourists. Now dozens of workers labored behind the fence, using jackhammers and Bobcats. I signaled someone I knew, an engineering supervisor who was on the other side of the fence. His name was Don McKibbon. He didn't grin like he usually did when we met, and I thought for a minute he was going to ignore me, but after a moment of hesitation, he walked over.

"Can you answer a couple of questions, Don?"

McKibbon was as bald as a cue ball under his hard hat. He had an easy grin, and grinned most of the time, as if smiling were his face's default setting. His eyes were faded and tired under the rim of the hard hat.

"You've got questions, and I can't answer them." McKibbon was from Pine Mountain, Georgia, and he spoke with long vowels.

"You are working on a ferry terminal, and you can't talk about it?" I asked. "Ferry terminals aren't classified projects anywhere in the world that I know of."

"Clay, I've got a huge bonus coming to me—and I mean huge—if this project goes well and it is done in secrecy, and I don't want to blow it by talking to you. I might be jeopardizing everything now, just chatting with you through the fence."

"You are being watched?"

"We've been watched all along," McKibbon replied. "You know that. You did most of the watching yourself."

"I've been frozen out of this new project here at the west end. Do you know why?"

He shook his head. A cell phone hung from his belt. I first thought he had been carrying a clipboard, but it was a flat-panel organizer the size of a book.

"Well . . ." I thought for a moment. "What's that vessel right there? The one with the long tubes?"

"It's a barge."

"Come on, Don. Don't be a hardballer."

He hesitated. McKibbon was always the first to laugh at a joke, and he seldom met you without patting you on the back as if you were a long-lost friend. But just then he was nervous, glancing over his shoulder.

I said, "I'll find out some other way, Don. *Jane's Construction Vessels*, maybe."

"It's a floating compaction grouter."

The barge had an enormous rolling mixer, like a concrete truck but much larger. Pumps and generators were also on the barge's deck. A derrick held aloft metal tubes that went from the barge to the westerly-most tip of the island, where the tube was stuck into the island's surface. The tube had the diameter of my waist, when I was younger. Five workmen were stationed around the tube where it broached the island's concrete surface. Perhaps half a dozen men worked on the barge, one in an elevated cab, from which he controlled the derrick that positioned the tube. A tug was tied to the barge. On the tug's green smokestack was an orange profile of an echidna, Australia's spiny anteater. The tug and barge belonged to Ferguson Construction of Sydney. Three of these identical vessels were at work at the west tip of the island. Beyond these barges, dredges were removing mud from the bottom of the bay.

I asked, "What's a compaction grouter?"

"It densifies."

" 'Densifies'? Is that a word?"

"It shoots grout into the soil to improve the soil's bearing capacity."

"So how is it done?"

"We drilled through the concrete cap, and then drove injection pipes into the subsurface," McKibbon explained. "That big yellow machine over on the barge is a specially-designed low-volume, high-pressure compaction driver. The bulb of slump grout expands as it leaves the injection pipe, and the radial force of the expansion compacts the surrounding material, makes it more dense."

I said, "You've got three of these compaction grouter barges here, and they are all working today, and they've been working around the clock for two days. How long is this going to take?"

"Compaction grouting is slow—the sump grout is sent in at a measured rate—because we don't want the soil to fracture, and we want to drive off any water that's under there, and we want to avoid a buckling on the surface."

The engines on the barges were producing a constant background hum.

McKibbon added, "We're pumping the grout in deep right now, but we'll place injection pipes at shallower and shallower levels when we're done at this depth, working our way up."

"So how long will it take?"

"We'll keep going at each depth until refusal pressure forces us to stop."

I asked, "That means until you can't push any more grout under the surface?"

He nodded. "Those green boxes you see—four of them—along the shore of this end of the island are laser-readers. We can keep filling the subsurface with grout until surface heaving begins. Those lasers will detect any surface movement to the smallest of tolerances. Once surface heaving begins, we have to stop with the injections because the subsurface can't be compacted any further."

"But why are you doing this, Don?"

"To densify the soil," he answered with vast patience. "We've been told this end of the island needs more compaction."

"For a new ferry terminal? What kind of a ferry terminal requires secrecy, and all this equipment? You've got almost as many earth moving vessels here as when the island was under construction."

"I can't say anything more, Clay."

"That must be some bonus you are getting."

He said, "There's more at stake than just a big cash-out when this project is completed."

"More at stake?"

"We've been talked to by some people who know how to do it, people from China's Ministry of State Security."

"From Beijing?"

He nodded.

"Did they threaten you?"

"Not in so many words. Their intent was clear, though. Keep my mouth shut about the project or there would be repercussions beyond losing this job."

"So why are you staying around?" I asked. "Life is too short to put up with thugs from Beijing."

"The bonus is big enough to put up with it. A month from now I might be able to retire." He glanced over his shoulder again. "I've said too much. I'll catch you in the cafeteria sometime."

He walked toward a grouter pipe, leaving me at the fence. I turned back toward my trailer. The tower surprised me again as it came into my line of sight. It was too large for my mind ever to accommodate. The scale—2,500 feet high, taller than eight redwood trees stacked on top of another—was beyond my ability to understand. I likened John Llewellyn's tower to Albert Einstein's theory of relativity. As long as Einstein's theory was being explained to me, I understood it. But the moment the explanation stopped, my understanding fled. Each time I heard the theory again, I marveled at it anew. The same with the tower. When looking upon it, whether from its base at Heroes of the Revolution Island or from the Peak or from anywhere else in Hong Kong, I could comprehend its height and massiveness. It was there to see, after all. Unavoidable and demanding attention. But when I turned away from the tower, the comprehension vanished. I could not retain my understanding of it. So each time I looked at the tower, it seemed new to me again, and shocking. It never failed to give me a start.

After a moment I could bring my eyes back down from the restaurant overhead, letting my gaze slide down the Swan's golden neck. At that moment John Llewellyn was coming out of the tower's base, leading a group of men and women, perhaps twenty people. He was gesturing widely, pointing out feature after feature. Everyone was wearing business suits, the men in blue and gray with bright ties and the women in slacks or knee-length dresses. Llewellyn was wearing an iron-gray suit. Anne Iverson was walking with him. They paused under the restaurant, Llewellyn pointing straight over his head.

I began walking back toward my trailer, which was on the other side of Llewellyn. I would learn later that the group with Llewellyn included Dennis Dermody, designer of the new Oilers' stadium in Edmonton; Khalid Shukri, architect of the new mosque in Cairo that featured the world's tallest minaret; and Suzanne Jennings, chief project manager of the Salisbury Cathedral restoration. I neared the group, intent on skirting them toward my office. I could hear Llewellyn's silky voice, intense and persuasive and condescending all at once, even though I couldn't yet make out individual words, not over the construction noise at the west end of the island.

I was surprised at the change in Llewellyn. The great architect appeared to have aged twenty years in a week. The skin of his face no longer looked taut, but rather had gained webs of wrinkles around his eyes, and his cheeks and jaw were a pallid gray, without the usual flush of excitement and conviction that made him seem so young. Purple-yellow pouches had developed below his eyes. His silver hair—his signature feature—seemed sparse and dingy. The ramrod in his spine had been removed, and his shoulders were slightly hunched. His step was missing its confident spring. Even his gestures seemed tired. Llewellyn had somehow been made old in a few days. Anne had told me that Llewellyn had appeared to flee Hong Kong four days ago. I wondered where he had been and what had happened to him to cause this transformation.

Workmen streamed passed Llewellyn and his group. A truck carrying a compressor rattled by, and about twenty electricians from Hong Kong's Yau Mai Tei Electrical Corporation—known for their robin's egg–blue hard hats—walked toward the cafeteria trailers. Another truck, this one carrying cable spools, dodged the group on its way toward the new ferry terminal's site.

The tile contractor, Xiao Chai-son, who had forty employees onsite that afternoon, was supervising installation of decorative work on the slab. It was said that Xiao viewed himself as an artist, not a tile installer. He liked to carry around a large leather portfolio. His crew was working on a design that would cover a portion of the island, a subtle pattern that would visually break up the expanse of the slab without competing with the grandeur of the tower. Xiao had submitted twelve designs before Llewellyn agreed to one. Wearing a white linen business suit and white shoes—the artiste, I suppose—Xiao was holding a sheaf of computer printouts, conferring with his foremen, who had gathered around him. His portfolio was on the slab, leaning against his leg. Half a dozen table tile saws were in the area.

At that moment a woman in Llewellyn's group bent over and pointed at the concrete slab on which they were all standing. Then, unexpectedly for someone in a skirt and jacket, she got down on her knees to peer more closely at the deck. This, it turned out, was Suzanne Jennings, the Englishwoman working on the Salisbury Cathedral. Several of the other visiting architects and engineers followed her example and went down on their knees to look more closely at whatever it was. Others were satisfied just bending over for a look.

John Llewellyn stared down toward his feet, his fists on his hips. He laughed sharply, but then his mouth turned down in a ferocious scowl, and he stepped toward the crowd of architects and engineers. They looked like children studying an anthill, all with their heads lowered, some squatting, staring down, others on their knees, pointing and earnestly talking with one another. One of the architects laughed brightly, and others joined in.

At this distance—Llewellyn was maybe forty yards from me, and I was still walking toward my trailer—it appeared as if a bicycle-tire pump were being applied to him, inflating him: he grew taller and became rigid, and his head rose up on his neck, and his mouth pulled back in a terrible grimace as if the skin of his face were suddenly too tight. Anne Iverson must have seen this change and appeared to be startled. She took a step away from Llewellyn, staring at him without speaking. He marched over to Xiao Chai-son, the tile artist. Xiao's assistants scattered like pigeons.

John Llewellyn was known for his entertaining conversations, for his wit and his storytelling ability and his total recall. He would inject little-known anecdotes into a story to make his point, something from the Napoleonic Wars or from Egyptian prehistory or from Newtonian theory, anything. With a wink and a nod, he could tell a story on himself, making himself the butt of the anecdote, or he could recall the last time he met anyone he was speaking with and remember to ask after that person's spouse and children by name. Llewellyn was an irresistible conversationalist. He owed much of his rise in architecture to it, most people thought.

Yet all this skill fled him at that moment, standing in front of the tile contractor. Llewellyn puffed himself up like a grouse and emitted a shriek of primal rage, high and thin and clear in the air. Llewellyn's hands shot out from his sides, and then he gestured up and down, pounding the air like Mussolini. Xiao backstepped, but Llewellyn followed him. When Xiao's portfolio fell to the ground, Llewellyn kicked it aside, and then he grabbed Xiao's collar and shook him.

Xiao's eyes were wide with fright and he tried to pull away, but Llewellyn held him there, all the while yelling, his face three inches from Xiao's. Llewellyn released one collar to stab a finger at the concrete slab, then seized the shirt again. His yelling was so strident and loud that I couldn't make out a word, as if Llewellyn in his rage had lost the ability to form consonants. Sounds poured out. The man was ranting. Xiao's crew stopped with their tasks, and a few gathered around, but not one moved to help his boss.

Then Llewellyn tried to pull Xiao down toward the ground, an inept hip roll that failed, Xiao having some weight to him. Xiao tried to swat away Llewellyn's hands, but that only further enraged Llewellyn, who did what I thought must be impossible, and that was to increase the volume of his screeching. Anne tried to shove herself between them like a boxing referee, but Llewellyn held the contractor in a vice's grip, and Anne was pushed aside by their struggle.

The group Llewellyn had been escorting stood back, aghast and indecisive, not one of them moving to intercede. I started toward the two men. I could make out a few of Llewellyn's words now, though they were still rendered in a tenor bellow. "You're through! You've ruined me! You're through!" Llewellyn was shrieking.

Then Xiao figured he had had enough, and he popped the architect on his forehead, not much of a hit, but it staggered Llewellyn and loosened his grip. Xiao turned to run from the madman. Llewellyn found his footing and charged, tackling Xiao like a linebacker. Both men fell onto the new tile work.

I reached them, and stripped Llewellyn's hands away from Xiao, then pulled Xiao away.

"Take it easy, John," I said. "Take a breath, will you?"

It didn't work. Llewellyn tried to crawl after Xiao but I stepped between the two men. I nudged Xiao farther away, and Xiao now let loose with a long stream of Cantonese, all of it invective, I presumed. He shook a fist at Llewellyn. Xiao's face was red, as if all the capillaries were trying to surface.

Llewellyn had apparently run out of words, and he gasped for air and rose to his knees, panting. Then he collapsed back to a sitting position, his legs out in front of him. He was breathing like a runner. His shoes were scuffed, something I never thought I'd see.

He barked out, "Get off the site. You're through."

Xiao was also breathing heavily. He wiped his mouth and glared down at Llewellyn. Xiao switched to English. "You . . . you cannot terminate me."

"I can fire anybody I choose, and that includes an incompetent contractor. Get your men and equipment off my island."

Anne Iverson tried to help Llewellyn to his feet, lifting him by an arm, but he sat there pointing at Xiao, and his voice was rising again. "There's always a weak link. Always somebody who can't do the work."

Xiao brushed his coat, then he gripped his belt to straighten his pants. He stepped to his leather portfolio and lifted it with as much dignity as he could muster. Llewellyn's face was red in splotches. He glanced at his guests, then firmed his jaw and rose to his feet. His left palm was bleeding from a scrape. The lining of his jacket had been torn and was hanging down. Anne tried to brush him up, to get the dust and concrete flecks off his coat, but he moved away from her, toward his guests. He rolled his head on his neck, perhaps a quick physical inventory. A red mark was on his forehead where Xiao's fist had connected.

The touring architects and engineers were rooted to the spot and had nothing to say. They couldn't even look at Llewellyn, who rejoined them, squaring his tie and dabbing a handkerchief at his palm.

Llewellyn said loudly: "These things happen in any project of this size. It is a slight thing, and will be easily repaired. Now I want to show you the bronze siding. We'll get up close so you can see the workmanship."

Nothing more was said to Xiao, who walked—now with a slight limp—toward several of his workers. Anne Iverson caught my eye and shook her head slightly. She didn't know what had just happened to Llewellyn. The great sophisticate had just engaged in a schoolyard shoving match with one of the contractors. I doubt she had ever seen anything like it before, could hardly have imagined that the icon of architecture, the silken designer of the Fifth Millennium China Tower, would act like a soccer hooligan. Llewellyn—normally as imperturbable as he was smooth—had just acted entirely unlike his carefully constructed self. She hurried to catch up to him.

Glancing at each other, raising their eyebrows and pursing their lips in wonderment and embarrassment, the group slowly followed Llewellyn toward the base of the tower. As he walked, his stride gained some of its old confidence, and he began pointing out features and speaking loudly, acting as if nothing had just happened.

I had spoken to Anne earlier in the day about Llewellyn. When he had returned from Brisbane that morning, he had offered no explanation to her, she had told me. It wasn't like him, this four days away with nothing to show for it.

His travels were always accompanied by high-profile meetings and press conferences, always a full itinerary. Not this time, to Brisbane. He had just flown there, and as far as Anne could tell, he had not met with the mayor or the city's leading architects or given a talk at the university or had been on the local TV or had been feted by the city's luminaries at a gala dinner. These were the staples of John Llewellyn's life ever since the tower had begun construction, but not this time. He had apparently checked into the Brisbane Sheraton and had holed up there for those three days. He wouldn't tell her why. He was acting like an escapee from a nuthouse, abruptly flying off to Brisbane, and now with this absurd and childish demonstration in front of his guests. Something was wrong with the man.

I walked over to where they had been standing and looked down at the concrete. The tile work here was incomplete. Some of this section of the platform had been smoothed with circular grinders in preparation for the tiles. I couldn't see anything unusual, not at first, staring down toward my shoes.

Then I saw it. A long—twelve feet—crack in the concrete. I bent down for a closer look. It was narrow, not more than a quarter of an inch wide, and would pass unnoticed on any sidewalk, but here it was on Heroes of the Revolution Island, in the shadow of the grand tower, a tiny breach in the otherwise perfect project.

I studied it for a moment. I couldn't tell if it was deep, probably not. I ran my finger along it, as if that might reveal the problem. Llewellyn must've thought the tile contractor had caused the crack. I looked over at the barges and dredges, and wondered if maybe the compaction grouting had created this little crack. Perhaps the base was heaving. No, the lasers would have caught it, McKibbon had said. That's why they were there, and they were precise.

I straightened up. All projects like this had small things go wrong. It was the nature of the construction business. I wondered, though, about Llewellyn's crazed reaction to this trifling crack.

I turned back toward my trailer. I was sure that Llewellyn, the minute he ditched the visiting architects and engineers, would order the concrete contractor to fill the crack, and it wouldn't take the contractor fifteen minutes.

*   *   *

I always had the notion in Hong Kong I was being watched. Two oc-currences within two days proved me right. I suspected it was Beijing's Ministry of State Security, which I thought would monitor me as a matter of course. I couldn't have been more wrong about who was watching me.

The first instance happened when I borrowed Darrel Reese's car to drive over to Aberdeen to have dinner with one of my father's friends, another Medford pear-grower who was in Hong Kong on a holiday. The fellow had heard of Jumbo, the enormous floating restaurant, and I was happy to meet him there. Evening had come, and the moon slipped in and out of the clouds. I had been careful on my drive across the island. No one was following me.

I found a car park about two hundred yards from the restaurant. It was a small lot, attended by an elderly gentleman wearing a conical straw hat. I locked Reese's car and then paid the old guy the required ten HK dollars. Just as I reached the edge of the dirt lot, headed to-ward Jumbo, two young men—maybe in their late teens—stepped out from behind a Dumpster.

"We'll guard your car," one of them said in English. He was wear-ing a red leather jacket with a dragon sewn onto the left breast.

The other fellow stepped to one side so the two of them bracketed me. Sometimes I wished I still carried a weapon.

"I don't need a guard for my car, do I? There's an old fellow over there who'll take care of it. I already paid him."

The first teenager sneered, an exaggerated pull of his mouth he had learned in a movie theater. "Your car needs guarding, believe me."

This was the Comiskey Park shakedown. If you don't pay the guy who approaches you as you leave your car for the ballpark, he'll run a car key back and forth along your new paint job.

I wasn't going to tussle with these two. They were filled with testos-terone and thought themselves big-time gangsters. Just as I reached for my wallet, a giant stepped out of the night and appeared right next to me, and his pylon arms snapped out, and his bowling-ball–sized hands grabbed the leather-wearing teen and lifted him fully off the ground. Then one hand grabbed a fistful of the kid's hair, and the giant spun to the second extortionist and smashed the first one's head into the second one. Then he let the first kid drop to the dirt on top of the second one.

Shao Long, the 88K's red pole, bent down to the boys and uttered a few Cantonese words. I couldn't tell whether the boys were sensate, but Shao seemed to think a sentence or two was appropriate. Shao then rose again and walked away without looking at me. All of this took seven seconds.

I had no doubt that the car would be just fine when I returned from Jumbo. I put my wallet back into my pocket.

Then the second incident that led me to believe I was being watched was this: My aunt—my father's older sister—had sent me a five-dollar bill for my first birthday, another five-dollar bill for my second birthday, and she has sent me five dollars every year since, even on my forty-fifth birthday. My father held her dear, and whenever we visited her in Eugene—every single time through the years—she would serve liver and onions, which my dad would eat with great gusto and loud admiration, but which I couldn't get past my gag reflex, so I would sneak bits of it under the table to my aunt's golden retriever. With Dad dead, she was my only kin, and liver and onions or no, she was a fine old lady. She was about to turn eighty years old, and I had decided to buy her a gift. She had been sending me five dollars each of those many years, and I had never given her anything.

Hong Kong is known for jade, of course, but unless you know something about jade or purchase it at a well-known shop, it is easy to be taken. In fact, it is likely you'll be taken. Jade is almost impossible to tell from lesser stones and from some plastics. I wasn't looking for an ornate sculpted piece of jade for my aunt, just a small, colorful piece of green stone that would nevertheless thrill her.

I found myself at Harry Chow's House of Jade on Hollywood Road in the Mid-Levels, not too far from my apartment. Camel bells on the door rang as I entered. It was a small shop, maybe twelve by twelve feet. On three walls were glassed-in shelves filled with jade of all colors from cream to lima bean to forest to orange and purple. The pieces were in human and animal forms, and there were also carved trees and blossoms and village tableaux. Under a glass countertop were jade jewelry, paperweights, snuff boxes, and charms.

Harry was ready for a *gweilo* shopper. "May I help you, sir?"

"I'm looking for a small gift for someone in the States."

"Jewelry, perhaps?"

"Well, I'm looking for something sort of modest." I had refrained from adding up my age, multiplying it by my aunt's five-dollar gifts, and setting that as my limit. I was going to be generous but within the bounds of my salary and the bounds of her having fed me liver and onions during all those visits. "Maybe a bracelet."

"Ahhh," Harry Chow said, and he made it sound like a check being torn from a checkbook. "I have many to choose from."

He lifted a tray of bracelets from under the glass. "This will delight your . . . woman friend, is it?"

"My aunt. She's old."

"Can you tell me anything about her?" Harry said.

I thought for a moment. "She always smells like talcum powder."

"I have just the bracelet." He removed one from the display rack. "Look at this one, sir. Handcrafted in China. It is jadeite, the finest of stones. Feel how cool it is to the touch."

The bracelet did feel cool. A crosshatch pattern was carved into its curved surface. I supposed it was a good piece. How would I know? Harry Chow had a good reputation, is what I was counting on. I looked at the price, hanging from a tiny tag attached to the silver clasp. I swallowed. Well, she was my only aunt, and my father loved her, and she once had a good dog. I passed the bracelet back to him and reached for my wallet. "I'll take it."

The camel bells rang, and damned if Shao Long didn't appear beside me. He filled the little shop, throwing shadow on the floor corner to corner. His belly touched the counter. He smiled his green smile at Harry Chow but didn't say a word. He put his meaty hand on my shoulder, just for a second. He was wearing brown slacks and a sports coat with an open collar.

Harry Chow inhaled slowly, his eyes darting about. Then he

whisked away the tray of bracelets, including the one I was about to purchase, and said, "Your aunt, you say, sir? This calls for something truly special, something worthy of such a lady, something one-of-a-kind."

From a drawer under the counter he removed a small tan flannel bag tied with a red ribbon. He pulled out a jade bracelet carved to resemble two snakes wound together. It was highly detailed, with scales and fangs. It must have taken weeks and weeks for the jade carver to bring those reptiles out of the living stone.

"It's beautiful," I said.

"It is at least two hundred years old, carved during the middle of the Ch'ing Dynasty." He glanced at Shao Long, and I'm sure he was searching for signs of approval. "I purchased it from a museum in Canton twelve years ago. I have been saving it for a special customer."

When I made to look at the price, Harry Chow quickly pinched the tag, hiding the numbers. He said, "You have come all this way to find a gift for a beloved lady. I insist on giving you a special price, one for my good customer on this important occasion."

He whispered the price, just loud enough for me to hear. And for Shao Long to hear. It was less than the first bracelet I had looked at.

"I'll take it, and thank you."

Harry Chow took only a moment to wrap the bracelet, and then he shook my hand and kept on shaking it as he said, "This was an excellent bargain for you. And for me."

Somehow during the wrapping of the gift, the red pole had left the store without my noticing. I turned a full circle, as if he might be hiding. The place seemed much larger with Shao gone.

As I went back out onto the street, my purchase in my pocket, I automatically looked around for Anne Iverson, thinking that if she were anywhere nearby, she would snatch the bracelet from me and mention shakedowns or extortion or blackmail or some other unpleasant concept. She wasn't there, of course, so I turned uphill toward my apartment.

So as you see, I was being watched by my own personal giant.

* * *

"Is joining complicated?" I asked.

"If you can sign your name, it's not hard," replied Hsu Shui-ban.

We were standing on the Hsu balcony. The range finder was on its tripod. Hsu's parents had invited me to dinner to thank me for my part in finding their son. Dinner had been eight courses, prepared by Mrs. Hsu and two cooks she had hired for the evening. I didn't know the names of most of the dishes, but they had been elegantly prepared and were the best food I'd had in my ten years in Hong Kong. As I've mentioned, people there seldom entertain at home, and I was honored.

Mr. Hsu collected scotch. He must have had two hundred bottles, with many brands I'd never heard of before. He pressed a dozen samples on me. He and his wife smiled all through the meal.

During dinner I had asked Hsu again about his kidnappers. They had knocked, and when he had opened the door, they had seized him. They were spiriting him toward the elevators when my father happened out into the hall. One of the kidnappers punched my father, and while Dad was dazed and in pain, the kidnapper shoved him back into the apartment toward the balcony. Hsu didn't see what happened next. Nor did he see his friend Soong Chan, who had just gotten off the elevator, and who hurried back into it.

During those days he was a prisoner—first at the net storage building in Sha Tin, then at the road construction site near Tingsia—the kidnappers seldom spoke to him. They had been kind to him, other than keeping him a prisoner. Hsu had not been told and had not figured out why he had been kidnapped.

After dinner at the Hsus, Soong Chan asked if I wanted to join the 20th Floor Physics Club as an honorary member. He assured me there were no dues. We were now out on the balcony.

"But you have to sign the oath of allegiance." Soong lifted a white mailer from the deck table and pulled out a handcrafted document filled with Chinese words in several colors and sizes. At the top of the document was a meticulously drawn compass rose, and at the bottom were thirty lines for signatures. Only two lines had names on them, and they were the names of the two boys on the deck with me, Hsu Shui-ban and Soong Chan. They once had had grand ambitions for the club, but it had stalled at two members. Also on the table was a three-ring binder.

"I can't read these words," I said. "They are in Cantonese. How do I know what I'm pledging allegiance to?"

"To pure science and perpetual enlightenment," Soong explained with the earnestness of youth.

"All these words just for that? How do I know you're not tricking me into signing up for an RV park time-share?"

Hsu said, "You'll be the club's third member, with important responsibilities, even if they are honorary responsibilities."

I signed my name. The pen had green ink.

Hsu nodded solemnly, then inserted the membership roll back into the envelope. He asked, "Chan showed you the range finder?"

"An impressive piece of equipment," I said.

Both boys grinned at the compliment.

"Did Chan show you how accurate it is?" Hsu asked, aiming the laser at the Fifth Millennium China Tower.

"He did."

"I found out something weird about the tower," Hsu said. "I sent the architect John Llewellyn an email about it. I found his email address at the tower's Web site."

"You sent Llewellyn an email?" I asked. "About what?"

Hsu replied, "About some measurements I took."

"I didn't know you did that," Soong Chan said. "Did you tell him how we measure the distance from here to the top of the tower?"

"You don't know the half of it, Chan, because I didn't have the chance to tell you before I was captured by those men."

"Tell me what?" Soong Chan asked.

"His tower is moving."

Soong laughed. "What?"

"Remember our last measurement of the tower?" Hsu opened the three-ring binder. His gaze followed his finger down the page. "When we first took a measurement of the tower—this would be two weeks ago—the top was 3,622.5 meters away, from this deck to our target point on the tower's restaurant level."

He showed me the entry in the binder. The boys were using graph paper to chart their measurements, and were writing in tiny letters, filling the page.

"So a week later I was out here by myself, playing around with the range finder, and I measured the tower again, and the distance was 3,622.47 meters."

"How much difference is that, between your first and second measurements?" I asked. "I don't know the metric system."

"Almost exactly an inch," Hsu said.

Soong Chan added, "And when I showed Mr. Williams the range finder, the tower was 3,622.44 meters away. Remember, Mr. Williams? I didn't have the three-ring binder, but I made a note of it."

"That's almost another inch?" I said.

Hsu returned the notebook to the table, and aimed the range finder at the tower. He bent to the spotting scope and carefully aimed the laser, making small adjustments to the tripod.

"Fire," Hsu said, as if commanding a battery. Then he bent down to the readout. "It's 3,622.41 meters. Hey, it's another inch closer, from this deck to the top of the tower."

"Another inch?" I pulled at my earlobe. "Your range finder is broken."

"Not a chance," Hsu said.

"How do you break a laser beam?" Soong backed up his friend. "You can't break basic physics."

"Well, if it's as accurate as you say, what accounts for the four different readings? I mean, according to your range finder, the top of the tower is four inches closer to this deck than it was two weeks ago."

"Maybe the tower has hidden wheels," Soong suggested. I couldn't tell if he was serious.

"Maybe it's the wind," I offered. "All tall structures are designed to bend a little in the wind."

Hsu pointed across the street, where a red Chinese flag hung from a pole atop an apartment building. "That flag is limp. There's no wind today. There wasn't any wind on the other days I took measurements."

Then I remembered the crack in the slab, the one that had triggered John Llewellyn's fit. I said, "If your range finder is accurate—"

Hsu cut me off. "It *is* accurate, Mr. Williams."

I formed the words, scarcely crediting them as I spoke: "Then the Fifth Millennium China Tower has begun to lean."

12

The gangster Wen Quichin must have thought Anne and I were a couple, because his next invitation was again for both of us. Wen's nephew had telephoned, saying Wen had information for me, and please bring the American woman. I informed the FBI.

The address was in Kwai Chung near the container terminal in Kowloon. Anne and I had gotten off at the Kwai Fong station and then had walked along Container Port Road. The streets were filled with semitractors that produced a constant diesel roar. Taxis can be found nearly everywhere in Hong Kong but not here in the factory district and the container port area. Buildings were one and two stories high, and most were electronics, plastics, and apparel factories employing hundreds of thousands of people. Shipping boxes were piled in every space not allotted to road or building. I had heard that wild monkeys still lived in the neighborhood, though I couldn't see a tree anywhere.

We found the address, a block from the gate to the Sea-Land Services Terminal, and walked into a reception room of sorts. The only person there was a Sikh guard, wearing a turban and beard. I didn't doubt he was armed. The guard's scowl seemed set in stone, as if he had never smiled, not once in his life. The room had one chair and no desk or phone. Not many folks were received here, it looked like. The guard turned a key in a heavy metal door to a back room and pushed it open for us.

The old gangster was inside, his smile in place, and he shook Anne's and my hands as if he hadn't seen us in months, when it had only been a day. His nephew was standing at his left shoulder as always. The room was filled with the whine of small electrical drills.

"'Mr. Williams, I have some news for you,'" Wen said through his nephew Zhu. "'I would have telephoned, but I am not allowed to use the telephone.'"

"Who prevents you from using the phone?" Anne asked.

"'The Hong Kong Police, Interpol, Scotland Yard, your FBI, the Ministry of State Security. Many people.'"

I said, "Mr. Wen means, he can use the phone, but he doesn't dare to."

After translation Wen nodded. "'Yes. That's it.'" He raised a hand to direct our attention around the room. "'This is another of my businesses. I heard from an associate that you were interested in jade, so I wanted to show my operation here.'"

"What news do you have, Mr. Wen?"

He stepped toward a barrel that contained rough stones. Most of the rocks were dark green with white streaks across them. Zhu translated in a loud voice, above the whine of the drills and lathes, "'These come from Burma. It is uncut jade. Nephrite. I produce pieces of art here.'"

More accurately, the fifteen gem-cutters sitting at small desks lining the room produced the art. Their desks were the size of old treadle sewing machines. On each desk was mounted a gooseneck lamp. Some of the artisans held small pieces of jade in their hands and were grinding them into shape with electric hand drills. Others used small lathes mounted to their benches.

Wen said through his nephew, "'My great uncle was a jade-carver, and his lathe was powered by his own feet. And he used diamond dust as the abrasive. Today electricity powers the drills and lathes, and emery and crushed garnets are the abrasives. And those are diamond-pointed drills. It is highly efficient.'"

The artisans worked on small pieces destined for the tourist shops. Around the room frogs, blossoms, dragons, fish, whales, and incense burners were emerging from the stones. None of the workers wore eye protectors or earplugs. The air was gritty with jade and abrasive dust. The floor was bare wood, and the only window in the room looked out on the flat side of a steel container a foot away from the window. Above a metal hook was a sign saying in English FIRE EXTIN-GUISHER—USE ONLY IN EMERGENCY, but the extinguisher was missing. The carvers were careful not to even glance at Wen Quichin.

Zhu translated his uncle's words, "'I am considering moving some of my jade business to Mexico.'"

"Why Mexico?" Anne asked. She was wearing a white cotton boat-neck shirt and khaki pants. "It looks like you've got it set up nicely here."

After translation, the gangster said, "'The cost of labor here in Hong Kong has quickly risen. And the jade-carvers' union is a problem.'"

I wanted to ask, what sort of a gangster has problems with a union? I kept my mouth shut, of course.

"'I was thinking of placing a plant in Ciudad Juárez, across from El Paso in your state of Texas.'"

I wondered if Wen was making a joke. The Chinese are inscrutable, we all know. Maybe their sense of humor is inscrutable, too.

"'I understand that you are familiar with Mexico,'" Wen said through his nephew.

"I like Mexican food, if that's what you mean."

"'I could use a good manager in Ciudad Juárez, once the plant is open.'"

"Me?"

"'It would be a good career opportunity,'" Zhu said. "'The salary would be commensurate with the skill you have displayed to your friends in the 88K, and that has been a high level of skill indeed.'"

"Live in Ciudad Juárez and manage a jade-carving factory?" I asked. "That scenario has never crossed my mind, I can honestly say."

He patted my arm, and Zhu translated: "'Give it some thought. I don't need an answer today.'"

Wen walked us toward the door.

Anne asked, "You had some news, Mr. Wen?"

After the question was rendered into Cantonese, Wen spoke and Zhu translated, "'The second kidnapper—the one you so valiantly rescued from the refrigerated container, Yan Luo-han—who you turned over to the Hong Kong police? You remember him, of course.'"

I nodded.

Zhu translated, "'He was detained at the Mong Kok jail, but now he has been released.'"

"Released?" I exclaimed. "That's impossible. He's in jail awaiting trial for murder. The judge didn't set bail, saying he was a flight risk."

Wen's smile was knowing. "'He is across the Special Administrative District border, and is no longer in Hong Kong.'"

I sputtered, "But that's . . ."

Zhu translated, "'Certain of my friends saw him leave the Mong Kok jail. Yan Luo-han stepped through the jail's front door, smiling, and he entered a car—an American Buick—laughing and talking to his friends, who drove him away.'"

"Well . . ."

Wen said, "'You trusted the wrong people for justice, Mr. Williams.'"

I scratched the back of my hand. I dislike being made to appear the fool. We left the building through the reception room. Several feet away, the Lodestone armored truck was parked on the street.

"Clay, I still think you did the right thing, turning him over to the police," Anne said, entirely unhelpfully.

"'I'm not done with those criminals,'" Zhu translated for Wen. "'They didn't come up with the idea to kidnap my grandson on their own. I am still working on the case, as you policemen say.'"

"Your grandson has been returned," I said. "Why continue?"

"'If this account is not fully settled, my enemies will think I am weak, and then Hong Kong would become a dangerous place for me.'"

I nodded.

"'And your account is not settled either, not with the second kidnapper, this Yan Luo-han, still alive. So we must continue our search.'" Wen turned toward the armored truck, but then hesitated and turned back. "'We will continue to work together, and I must say I look forward to the prospect.'"

With that he boarded the armored truck. I looked around the street. I didn't see my personal giant anywhere, the one with the emerald teeth. I wondered what he did with his time when he wasn't watching over me or the old gangster. With a roar the truck pulled away.

"Did you notice?" I asked as we walked along Container Port Road back toward the station.

"Notice what?"

"Wen didn't offer us a ride."

She shrugged. "He probably has someone to go kill."

* * *

Sitting on my sofa, Anne Iverson spread her arms, resting them on the back of it, an expansive gesture, and she was smiling, but then she saw my grim expression, and she placed her hands on her lap. She said, "You look as if you want a serious talk, Clay."

"I have Tiger beer, a chardonnay I've never heard of, Diet Coke, or tap water. Take your pick."

She asked for the wine, then ran her hand along the top of the lamp table behind the couch. She looked at her fingers. "You should try dusting your apartment once in a while."

I checked to make sure the glass was clean, then poured the wine.

"You aren't going to try to talk me out of my relationship with John Llewellyn, are you?"

"Well . . ."

She looked over at the small stereo. "What kind of music do you have?"

"Lots of zydeco."

"What's that?"

"Louisiana dance music, with a squeezebox and a fiddle. Real jump stuff."

Carrying a Tiger beer, I stepped across the rug and sat next to her. Her pale blue eyes were on me.

"I have something important I want to talk to you about. Something really important."

She twisted a bit on the sofa so that she was facing me. "Well, I'm ready to hear it."

"I'm not sure you are, actually." Not sure at all.

The tower had dispensed fame and fortune, and John Llewellyn had garnered most of it, but there was still much left over for others who worked on the project, and Anne Iverson had been collecting her shares. She had been on the cover of *Project Manager Today* magazine, which, as she had said, was not exactly *Time* but was still noteworthy in her profession. And while *Time* hadn't put her on the cover, it had listed her in its article "100 to Watch," a catalogue of up-and-comers in the arts and the professions. She had told me she was receiving three or four invitations every week to speak, and she had accepted several, including being the keynote speaker at the International Federation of Civil Engineers' annual conference in Mexico City the following September. The American Society of Structural Engineers had awarded her the Roebling Prize for "project management involving new systems." The prize was named after the father and son engineers of the Brooklyn Bridge. Even I—a layman—knew it was a prestigious award. And best of all, Anne had told me, was that her services were in high demand. Her work on the tower was ending within a few weeks, and she was being seriously courted by BC Hydro to manage construction of the Site C dam on the Peace River in British Columbia, and by the Osaka Prefectural Government to manage building of a new light-rail line. "It's a bidding war," she had told me, delighted, "and I'm playing hard to get."

Anne Iverson had worked hard for the recognition that was coming her way, had worked seventy-hour weeks for four years. Her labor on the tower was now paying off handsomely. I was not going to mention my meeting with the boys of the 20th Floor Physics Club, their fooling around with a laser range finder, and our conclusion that the Fifth Millennium China Tower was four inches out of vertical alignment.

At least, I wasn't going to mention it lightly. What would I tell her? That two teens—neither of whom was shaving with any regularity—had built a range finder from scrounged equipment, soldered it together themselves, and were measuring the distance to most every building in Hong Kong from a balcony because they didn't have anything better to do, and that they had discovered that the grandest engineering project in a hundred years had—how would I put it?—a small flaw? Anne's future—her career ambitions, her place in engineering history, even the location of where she would live for the next several years—was inseparably connected to the success of the tower.

My first instinct had been to dismiss Hsu and Soong's homemade range-finder readings. The boys were just a few years removed from Legos and Erector sets or whatever Hong Kong kids play with. What they were suggesting—that the top of the tower was four inches closer to their balcony than two weeks ago—was surely the product of faulty equipment or faulty readings produced by youthful exuberance. Still, as I reviewed the peculiar things that had happened to those involved in the tower—the deaths of Yao Bok-kee and Little Harold Lethbridge being the most peculiar—I believed it best to bring it up with Anne. Keeping her from bursting out laughing would be a principal concern.

Her gaze roamed my small place, and she asked, "What's that, the long gray thing hanging on your kitchen wall?" She was postponing whatever I had to say.

"It's a bayonet in a leather scabbard."

"A bayonet? You mean, like you put on the end of a rifle?"

"I bought it at an army-navy store for three dollars when I was ten years old."

"Is it a lucky charm?"

"It's an old bayonet. It goes wherever I go, is all. It's a tradition."

"John Llewellyn has a three-hundred-year-old Flemish tapestry on his wall. And you have an army surplus bayonet." She laughed. "The tapestry suits him and the bayonet suits you." She leaned forward to examine the magazines on the coffee table. "What's this?"

"What's it look like? It's a magazine."

"It's *Car and Driver* magazine. I've never been out with anybody who reads *Car and Driver* magazine."

She was having a fine old time, teasing me.

Still, I was on the defensive. "I'm shopping around for a car, maybe a BMW."

"Will this be before or after your Harley-Davidson?" She pointed a finger. "And what's that? That glass cage."

"It's a terrarium."

"For what?"

"When I first moved to Hong Kong, my friend Jay Lee told me that all Hong Kong citizens keep geckos in their apartments to eat the bugs."

"Lizards are in there? How many?"

"He said you take them out at night and put them on the floor, and any bugs that come in, bang, they get eaten. He said those blue bug lights were illegal, so everybody had geckos."

"You fell for it?"

"It only took me three or four weeks to figure it out. Jay apologized, sort of, and said the joke was his small effort to compensate for all the wrongs done by western powers to China over the centuries."

"You still have the lizards?"

"They are easy to grow fond of, for reptiles."

Anne elegantly crossed her legs. She had long legs. "I can tell a lot about a person based on his living quarters."

"You are a trained architect, after all."

"Precisely. And from your apartment I can tell that you are fifteen years old."

I laughed.

Anne said, "A bayonet. A terrarium. A car magazine. Weird music. Dust."

She had an inexhaustible supply of expressions, accenting her words with a turn of her mouth or a tuck of her eyebrows or a lift of her chin. Her voice would be cool and low one instant, then light and dry the next, and then crackling like electric sparks the next.

"I'm comfortable here," I said. "What did your architecture classes say about a person's living space? Doesn't comfort have something to do with it?"

She raised her wineglass to take a sip, and then grimaced. "Where is this wine from? North Korea?"

I scratched a bug bite on the back of my neck. "I want to talk about the Gold Swan. I've got to ask you a couple of questions. One big question, actually. About the tower."

"You brought me here to talk about work?" She was wearing a slightly pained expression, as if her shoes were too tight.

"I need to set out something for you, some facts that I have, and I don't want you to laugh or, worse, run for my bayonet."

She leaned forward to place her glass on the coffee table. I needed to marshal my facts, to build a case, and to be careful about it. "The tower team has suffered two deaths in the past week. One of them, Yao Bok-kee, was the project's chief geotechnical engineer. Yao and his firm did the site investigation and feasibility studies and much of the detailed design work."

She said pensively, "He was a terrific guy, so courtly and proper, but when you got to know him, he loosened up and was fun to work with."

"Yao's firm did the stability and compaction studies, all the stuff big geotech firms do."

"I worked on the studies with him."

"He was the go/no-go guy on whether the site in Victoria Harbor was suitable, and on whether the fill design for the island and the tower's foundation would work."

She nodded.

"He was arrested on graft charges," I said. "Why, do you think? Well, absolutely no one working on the tower believes Yao was engaged in graft. The Deloitte and Touche auditors can't find any evidence of him stealing money, of bribery or skimming, nothing. His arrest was ordered in Beijing and was done by mainland police. No one in the Hong Kong police force took part or even knew anything about it before it occurred, Jay Lee tells me. Yao was then executed in a summary manner."

"I know all this."

"And Little Harold Lethbridge was the chief of EMU, the principal fill contractor. He was in charge of dredging the dirt from the bay bottom, down to where it was stable, and then he was in charge of moving all the fill—the dirt and gravel and rocks and whatever—into position for the island. He was the main guy for this work."

"Sure."

I hoped Anne was paying attention. A small smile had returned to her face, and I was afraid she would go off in another direction before I had given her the bad news.

I hurried on, "Yu Chi-yin, who heads the Singapore police's Criminal Investigation Department, has told me he doubts Lethbridge was killed during a mugging, as was his department's first guess. For one thing, Lethbridge's wallet was still in his pocket, filled with cash. Yu and his department have concluded that Lethbridge was murdered because someone wanted him dead, not because someone was trying to mug him."

"Those are dreadful events, two good men gone in terrible ways. But what's your point, Clay?"

"Both Yao and Lethbridge were involved in the tower's base, which is Heroes of the Revolution Island. More than just being involved, they were the main people—the top decision-makers—in the tower's base, the thing that keeps the tower upright."

Anne asked, "Where are you going with this?"

"Yao and Lethbridge were punished for something they had done, and I'm not talking about the charge of graft against Yao. It's something else."

"Punished? For what?"

"Let me bring up a couple of other things first. A fleet of dredging, earth-moving, and compaction equipment has suddenly shown up, when everyone thought all that work was long completed."

"Everyone is wondering about that."

"I have a friend in the CIA who says a lot more of this equipment is on the way, coming down from the Three Gorges project and from a highway project in Kwangtung. The gravel yards across the border at Shatou are suddenly humming with all this highway equipment. More fill is being dug."

Anne reached for her wineglass, considered it, then left it on the table.

I asked, "Why do you think all this equipment has arrived so suddenly and secretly?"

Her voice was crabbed. "I'm not in that decision loop, apparently. I wasn't told anything about it. It's because of the stupid new ferry terminal."

"You believe that?"

"I shouldn't believe that?" she asked.

"And then there's the matter of John Llewellyn's precipitous decline."

"He's been working hard. He deserves to look tired."

I shook my head. "It's much more than that. He is deathly afraid. Fear is working on him like a worm. It is changing him physically—he has suddenly aged by a decade or two—and it's changing him mentally. He flew off to Brisbane for no stated reason, but he had just heard Yao had been executed, and I think that was the reason."

She pursed her lips, her eyes on me.

"And you saw him fly off the handle, humiliating the tile contractor, wrestling him to the ground like a six-year-old, shouting and tussling."

"I was embarrassed for everybody involved."

"It's not the pressure of work that has abruptly changed Llewellyn. He has endured that pressure all his life. He obviously prospers in that kind of pressure."

"Then what is it?"

"It's the pressure of fear."

"Fear?" She shook her head, a small movement. "Why would he be fearful?"

I rubbed my hands together. They were cold. I was afraid of this information, and was apprehensive of imparting it to Anne. I said, "He's afraid because he has learned something."

I briefly summarized the two events that had occurred in this build-ing, the kidnapping of Hsu Shui-ban and the murder of my father, telling Anne how they were connected, my father accidentally coming across the kidnappers as they pulled Hsu down the hall, and paying for it with his life. Then I spoke of the 20th Floor Physics Club, telling her of their equipment and the fun they had with it.

"So this 20th Floor Physics Club shoots distances with their home-made range finder?" Anne asked. "I'm impressed."

"But then the boy, Hsu Shui-ban, discovered something—found out something truly strange—using his range finder, and he sent an email to John Llewellyn about it. I think the information contained in the email is the reason Hsu was kidnapped. A huge effort is under way to keep the information from getting out."

She ran her hand through her hair. "What did he send John?"

"Some range-finder measurements."

"Come on, Clay," she said. "Out with it."

"Well, the tower has a problem."

"A problem?" She laughed lightly. "I'd be aware of any problem, wouldn't I?"

"I don't think you are. Very few people are."

She asked, "What sort of problem?"

I inhaled through my teeth. "It's a big problem, Anne."

* * *

"This is a fool's errand," Anne said. "And I'm up here with a fool."

She was referring to me.

She added, "How did my life come to this?"

We had just soared up in an elevator to the top of the Gold Swan, and were walking from the lobby out onto the viewing platform, ele-vation 2,500 feet above sea level. It was ten o'clock in the evening.

She wasn't done. "I could be jet-setting somewhere with John Llewellyn, enjoying the good life, being pampered and cared for, but I'm stuck with a crank who has an addled brain."

She was referring to me again. I was tiring of her theme, which she had been elucidating in some detail for the entire ninety minutes it had taken us to telephone a surveyor and to get from my apartment to the tower. I suppose it was her defense against my bad news, which was to dismiss it as impossible and to call the deliverer of the news a crank.

The platform hung out over the restaurant below, and in certain places the platform's deck was thick glass, so viewers could look down through their feet, and enjoy—or suffer—the sensation of being suspended in the air half a mile high. John Llewellyn had at first resisted this feature, claiming that the tower wasn't a Six Flags thrill ride, but he eventually had been convinced that teenagers needed an extra reason to visit the tower. And it indeed was thrilling—*frightening* is a better word—to step onto the glass, and have Hong Kong visible between your feet. I don't mind normal heights, say, looking down a flight of stairs, but this was different. I felt as if I were hung halfway between the clouds and the sea, with nothing in any direction but air. I had been up here several times, and always caught myself daintily tiptoeing across the glass deck, my breath in my throat, and the last time I did so, Anne was with me and she laughed mightily, but she wasn't laughing this time. We walked across the glass toward the surveyor, who was already at the rail.

"Thanks for coming, Ming-an," Anne said. "I know it's late." Anne introduced me to Xing Ming-an, Xing pronounced *Kzheeng*. Anne said he was the chief of the project's Department of Surveys.

He shook my hand, and said in English, "It is all set up."

An aluminum box was attached to the safety rail at the edge of the platform. Xing had a doughy face with a large, blank forehead and dark eyes set deeply in his head. He was wearing jeans and a short-sleeved shirt.

Anne tapped the box, which was an eighteen-inch square adorned with readouts and lenses and buttons. She said, "This is a laser transit. Ming-an is going to settle this."

Anne walked back toward the elevator lobby, just a few steps, then turned toward me again, then back again.

"You're pacing," I said.

"I have a right to pace, after your little performance in your apartment," she said. "I didn't know whether to laugh or throw my wine-glass at you."

"I just tried to lay out the facts as I know them."

She glared at me. "You've been caught up in a web of coincidences and faulty science and your wild imagination."

At this time of night it was noticeably colder up here than at sea level. Or maybe I was too near Anne Iverson. I wished I had a jacket.

She said, "You've built a case on coincidences and a science project. If those two kids had studied volcanoes, you'd be telling me that the Peak is about to blow." She laughed harshly.

Xing Ming-an glanced at me and said, "This is an Optilaser L10, a laser level, a modern theodolite. We shoot transits with it, both horizontal and vertical. It's got a red rotating beam and a plumb spot. I've manually plumbed it in its vertical mode. It's got a working radius of one thousand meters when using the laser receiver, which I'm doing."

Anne had stopped her pacing. She gripped her hands in front of her.

The surveyor said, "The L10 has built-in global positioning capability, receiving coordinates from satellites, but I'm not using it for this."

The aluminum case of the Optilaser transit was a bright yellow. It was affixed to the rail with rubber grips that were an accessory, maybe brought in the empty nylon bag at his feet.

"I'm going to use our bench mark near the base of the tower," Ming said. "That'll give us our reference datum. That's where the laser receiver is."

He peered into a scope along the side of the transit, peering to the ground. "This is a visible beam laser, so you'll see the ray." He looked up at me and smiled. "Lasers are cool."

I laughed, despite my anxiety and Anne's continuing glower. Ming sounded just like the members of the 20th Floor Physics Club.

He checked his machine for a moment more, then bent over the rail to put his eye to the lens again. Below us, Hong Kong and Kowloon were vast tracts of brilliant light, separated by the black harbor. The

lights were in all patterns, from the rigid geometry of white light coming from office windows to the splashes of color on the enormous
neon signs hanging from some buildings. Lights from dozens of vessels were visible against the dark background of the water. Near the
shores the water shimmered with reflected light.

Xing said, "Anne, I've used this very spot on this deck as a bench
mark, as you know. There's hardly ever been a more located reference
point in the history of surveying."

"Get on with it, will you, Ming-an. You are killing me with all this
chatter."

He laughed, then bent over his instrument again.

"I just want your reading so I can go home and soak my feet."

"No wind tonight," the surveyor said. "So no wiggle in the tower."

I tightly gripped the rail and peered down just as he flicked on the
laser. The luminous green ray was as thick as a pencil, and it disappeared from my sight not too far below, the beam eerily hanging
there. I presumed the light was reaching the base but I couldn't see it.

The dredging and compacting work continued around the clock,
and two dozen vessels were arrayed around the island's west end.
Portable lamps threw cones of light on workmen. Three grout chutes
ran from barges to the island.

Ming said something to himself in Cantonese, stood upright,
frowned, examined the readout, then leaned over the scope again. He
said in English, "Let me check this again."

I was still looking down the shaft of the laser beam, but I could feel
the weight of Anne's stare on me.

Ming stood again. He regarded the laser transit narrowly, then
damned if he didn't flick its aluminum case with a finger three times,
like I'd tap a balky radio.

"What is it?" Anne asked, her voice the ghost of a whisper.

Ming shook his head slightly, as if trying to clear it of an errant notion. Then he bent down to the scope again. "This spot on the tower,
this rail right here, is five inches to the west of where it should be."

"What's that mean?" Anne asked, though I suspect she well knew.

The surveyor said, "The tower isn't . . . isn't where it is supposed to be."

Last I had heard, it was only four inches off. Now it was five.

Her words tumbled over each other. "That can't be right. I mean, the foundation . . . The supports . . . We've got the plans that show . . ."

Ming's voice was like an undertaker's. "The Gold Swan is tipping."

"That can't be," Anne shouted.

"You know transits," he said. "You can check it yourself right now if you don't believe me. Here." He gestured toward the laser level. "See for yourself."

Both of Anne's hands were on the rail. She stared out at the city, and I don't think she was seeing anything. She repeated, but softly, "That can't be."

Ming worked quickly to unbolt and pack the laser level. He nodded at me and headed back to the elevators, the laser slung over his shoulder.

I said, "I'm sorry, Anne." It sounded dreadfully inadequate.

"I have to talk to John," she said in an old woman's voice. "I'd better talk to him."

"He knows the Gold Swan is leaning," I said. "That's why he is afraid, and why he is acting strangely."

I didn't know if she had heard me. She stood there for a long moment, blind to the world. Then she said, "Please. Go."

I turned toward the elevators and left her there at the rail.

13

I had made a mistake up in my apartment talking with Anne Iverson, though I didn't know it at the time. An amateurish mistake, and I would chide myself later. I should have been more cautious. But I wasn't, and both Anne and I almost came to grief because of my error.

I had received another call from Zhu Jintau, the dragon head's nephew, inviting me to meet with Wen again. Wen's not trusting the telephones had become a nuisance, and he seemed to think I would respond instantly to a call from him at any time, day or night. This call came at nine in the evening. I returned my shoes to my feet and left the apartment, heading uphill. I turned from May Road and started up Tregunter Path. Frogs chirruped from all directions. The path wasn't lighted, and passing clouds obscured the moon, so I could see little ahead of me. A sweet-gum branch brushed my sleeve. To my right was a dark bank of foliage, and below to my left, seen through branches and vines, were the lights of Hong Kong. The low rumble of Hong Kong at night came from below.

I was still a hundred yards from the dragon head's steps when I noticed a smudge on the path ahead of me. A dark figure on a black background was all I could see. It wasn't too late in the evening, and perhaps this was just someone out for an evening stroll. Yet the figure stood there motionless. I couldn't much make him out, so he must have been dressed in black. I think one of the benches was behind him, though I couldn't see it clearly. I took a few more steps, then stopped. The distant sound of a siren came from below.

I was about to turn on my heels and retreat when a voice I didn't recognize said, "Mr. Williams?"

I was silent.

"It is me, Shao Long."

The 88K's enforcer, the red pole, waiting for me on a dark path? I hesitated.

He walked toward me. He was smiling, and in the darkness the emeralds made his teeth resemble black pegs. He drew near, filling the pathway and looming over me.

"You speak English?" I asked.

"Only when I need to."

Relief made me say stupid things. "Then I'm glad I didn't say anything in English about your green teeth or your weird haircut."

"I'm glad you didn't, too," he replied.

I wondered if he ever laughed. "Where did you learn English?"

"In school here." He voice was surprisingly high, almost a tenor. "And then I studied for two years at the International Culinary Academy in Pittsburgh."

"You were going to be a cook?"

"I started out as a chef, but then Wen found me and recruited me, and now I work for him. Still, I own three restaurants in Hong Kong now. It is a sideline."

Shao was wearing black pants and a dark sweatshirt.

"Why are you out at night on this path?" I asked.

"I was lending you a hand," the red pole said.

"Well, I'm probably grateful. How were you helping me?"

"You should be more careful when you speak on the telephone. We all should."

"What do you mean?" I asked.

"And Wen's nephew should have delivered Wen's invitation himself, rather than using the telephone. Zhu was busy, and so he thought he would save himself the trouble of coming to your apartment with a message. He telephoned you instead."

"And what happened?"

"Your telephone is tapped and your apartment is bugged."

"How do you know?"

He smiled. "The 88K does it, for one."

"You do? I should be affronted."

"But others do, as well."

He moved aside, allowing me a view of the park bench alongside the path. I stepped closer. A man was sitting on the bench, his hands on his knees, staring out at the night lights. He was wearing jogging shoes, sweat pants, and a work-out jacket, and was motionless, peering through the foliage toward the downhill side.

Shao Long said, "This fellow was waiting for you on the path." He walked over to him. The man didn't turn toward Shao and me. His long hair was pulled back in a ponytail, unusual for Hong Kong. His eyes were open, and his lips were slightly parted.

The red pole held out a piece of paper. "This was in his pocket."

I held up the paper to my eyes. It was a photograph of me, a head shot, the one that was on the Fifth Millennium China Tower's staff Web site. Even though I was a security consultant, there had been no reason for me to remain anonymous because I didn't do clandestine work. The Web site listed brief bios of managers working on the site, along with photographs. This photo had probably been downloaded from the site.

Shao held out his other hand. "And this was in his other pocket."

It was an automatic pistol, a tiny one.

"It is a Colt Junior Pocket Model," he said. "It fires a .22-caliber bullet. I like this model myself." He slipped the pistol into one of his own pockets.

I asked, "He was waiting for me on the path?"

"He no longer waits for anybody."

Shao leaned forward and gripped the man's hair, then slowly turned the man's head around so that it faced backward, accompanied by a soft grating. The man's dead stare was now at the brush behind him. The bones in his neck had lost all their connections.

Hong Kong had suddenly become much chillier, and I found myself breathing shallowly. I was frightened.

"You should be more careful," Shao said.

"With you around, why do I need to be careful?"

"Sometimes I'm around, and sometimes I'm not."

"Is he from China? A security agent from their ministry?"

"He is from the same people who took Mr. Wen's grandson, I am sure."

"So, why are they after me?"

He shook his big head. "I don't know."

But then I abruptly did know. It came together for me in that instant. I said quickly, "Tell Wen I can't meet him tonight."

"I will."

"I've got to do something right away."

"The dragon head will understand."

I turned to hurry back down the path.

"Do you want help?" Shao Long called after me.

I broke into a trot, hoping I didn't collide with a tree or run off the trail into space. "No. I won't need it."

But Anne Iverson would need help, and within a matter of moments.

* * *

I was just at the base of Tregunter Path, only a few moments after leaving Shao Long, when my cell phone rang. I lifted it to my ear.

"Clay, this is Anne." She was out of breath. "I'm in some trouble, I think."

"What kind of trouble?"

"Someone is following me, and I don't know who it is, and I have turned a couple of corners and he still keeps up with me . . ."

"Where are you?" I cut in.

"Near North Point, but I don't know exactly."

"Are there people around? You need to find a crowd, and they'll keep you safe."

"Clay, I think he's getting closer." Her voice was rising. "It's dark here and I can't see, but I think I see him, and I don't know what to do."

"Where are you?" I demanded. "Look at a street sign and tell me."

"There aren't any signs here, just a bunch of barrels and trash alongside the buildings." She was breathing in gulps between words.

More loudly than I had intended, I said, "You need to tell me where you are, Anne. I can't get the police to you, or come to help unless you tell me where you are."

There was no response, only the rush of her breathing.

I shouted into the phone, "Anne?"

Nothing.

I added pointlessly, "Anne, put the phone to your ear, damn it."

Sounds coming through the phone were of brushing and scraping, and maybe footfalls. I could call the police and have them contact the telephone company to locate her signal, but that would take a few moments, and I would have to break the connection with Anne.

I grimaced. I was making one mistake after another. The first was having a conversation of any substance—mine with Anne discussing the tower—in my apartment, and the second was not instantly telephoning Anne when Shao Long showed me the body of the assassin who had been waiting for me. It had only been a few minutes ago, meeting up with the 88K's enforcer on the Tregunter trail, but perhaps had I reached for my phone at that moment, rather than chat away with Shao, Anne wouldn't be in trouble.

"Anne?" I said into the phone.

More breathing. She sounded like she was running, holding the phone. She was being stalked, and I couldn't do anything about it. I was standing there in the dark on a Hong Kong hill, and all I could do was knot my fist with the rage of helplessness and sudden knowledge.

I now understood that not one but two massive efforts were under way regarding the Gold Swan. The first involved the influx of half the world's dredging and compaction fleets into Victoria Harbor and the huge amount of land-side earth-moving equipment that had been sent to the New Territories. This effort was the attempt to right the tower.

The second effort was to stop information about the tower leaning from becoming public. A public relations disaster was imminent. China is obsessed with appearances. Beijing would go to extreme lengths to prevent word of this difficulty from leaking.

The world was taught this lesson after the Tiananmen Square massacre. Beijing denied much of anything had happened, and while thousands of witnesses and hundreds of still cameras and video cameras must have been at the square on the night of June 4, 1989, little evidence of the massacre has ever come to light. Few witnesses, few photographs, few written statements. Whether fifty people or two thousand people were killed is not reliably known. The military units involved are not known to the public. Where the order to end the demonstration by force originated is not known. It was a forcible, quick, and almost completely successful suppression of evidence. Tiananmen Square was not the first time nor the last time prodemocracy demonstrators have been dealt with that way in China, Darrel Reese told me.

I had suddenly realized that such an effort was under way regarding the Fifth Millennium China Tower. The tower had been heralded by Beijing for years and had become the symbol of the new China. Everyone in the country, from the president in Beijing to the peasant in the rice field, was proud of the thing. The tower was China's statement to the world. It had become closely associated with China's ambitions and with the current government.

News of a flaw in the tower—any flaw, much less one as substantial as a crumbling foundation—would result in an immense loss of face for the country. Word of such a failure simply could not get out. I had no doubt that a mammoth effort was under way to prevent spread of the news. Anyone with knowledge that the tower had begun to lean was in grave danger, and that's why a murderer had been waiting for me on Tregunter Path, and why Anne was being hunted.

"I'm in a corner," Anne gasped. "Walls on three sides."

"Can you see anybody there, anybody at all? Run up to them and ask for help."

"Nobody is here." Her words were serrated with fright. "There's a door in the side of the building and I tried it, but it's locked."

"Anne, I can't get to you in time. I've got to hang up and call the police."

"No," she shouted into the phone. "Don't leave me here."

I started running down the hill, looking for a pay phone box. A dog barked to my left. I was too high on the hill for a pay phone, I knew. "Anne, keep moving. Can you run?"

She croaked piteously, "I'm in an alley, and I can see a guy coming, Clay. What am I going to do? He's coming right for me."

"Do you have a knife or pepper spray?"

"Clay . . ."

I found a pay phone, a small box attached to a pole near an intersection. I fumbled for my wallet, intent on swiping a credit card at it. I felt powerless.

"Oh God, he's here," she said. "He's got a knife and he's got it in his hand and he's coming for me and he's right here."

"Anne, please." I ran the card through the slot. "Scream. Make noise. People will look out their windows, anything."

From my phone came, "I . . . What . . .? What's happening? Clay, something has happened."

I had a phone at each ear, and I said into the pay phone receiver, "Dispatcher, this is an emergency."

"Clay, the man is now on the ground. He's at my feet. His knife is on the pavement next to him. He's not moving."

"Anne, are you hurt?"

The police dispatcher said into my right ear. "Please give me your location."

"I'm okay," Anne said into my left ear. "I'm fine. My lord, the man is bleeding from his ear. A puddle of blood is on the ground under him, and he's . . . he's not moving." Her words spilled out. "He's been shot through his ears. And I didn't hear anything. He had me in a corner and his knife was coming up, and then down he went. My lord, what . . .? Who could have shot him? I didn't see anybody."

I hung up the pay phone and said, "Anne, you need to get out of there. You aren't safe there. There may be more of them."

"I don't see anybody. Who saved me?"

"The 88K saved you, just like they did me a couple minutes ago. Just leave wherever you are, right now."

I could hear her footsteps.

I said, "Find somewhere safe, a café or a tearoom, and call me, and I'll come and get you. I'll be there as quickly as I can."

"I'm shaking so much I can hardly walk. I just want to get to my apartment."

"They'll be waiting for you there, Anne." I rubbed my forehead. "You can't go home. Neither of us can."

*   *   *

For an architect, designing a structure so that it stays erect would seem to be a minimum requirement for the job. The aesthetic sense, the grandeur, and the symbolism would be secondary to keeping the structure upright. Regarding architecture, I am a layman, but it seems to me that preventing an edifice from falling over would be rather high on the designer's priority list.

History is filled with spectacular failures, instances where the architect didn't meet the most basic of requirements, that the structure remain upright. Perhaps the earliest known case is the Bent Pyramid at Dashur near Memphis, Egypt, built by Sesostris III four thousand years ago, where a side of the pyramid starts off at fifty-two degrees, but then suddenly changes to the less steep angle of forty-three degrees, giving the pyramid a hunched look. It is believed that as the pyramid was being built it began to fall in on itself when the weight of the upper stones crushed and displaced lower blocks that lined the interior passageways and chambers, so the side's angle was changed to lessen the pyramid's height and weight.

On the middle peak of Tianma Mountain in Songjian County, a suburb of Shanghai, is the octagonal Huzhu Pagoda, known as the Leaning Pagoda, which was built in the second year of the Yuan Fen period of the Northern Song Dynasty, which is 1079 A.D. It is difficult to blame the pagoda's designer for the tilting. In 1788 part of the pagoda was destroyed by fire, and piles of money were found between the bricks of the foundation. When fortune-hunters dug up much of the rest of the foundation, the tower began to lean to the west, and to this day it leans a threatening twelve degrees off vertical.

Another early failure was Wells Cathedral in Somersetshire in southwest England. The cathedral was built in the twelfth century, and then in 1338 the central tower was heightened. Under this extra load, cracks began appearing in the cathedral as it sank into the marshy ground. Beginning that year and taking the next ten years, the master mason William Joy built the unique, inverted scissor arches on three sides under the tower. The arches have prevented further cracking over the centuries and are now looked upon as striking and lovely parts of the structure.

Even back then architects knew that a structure sinking, say, an average of a foot wasn't so bad. It's just that usually a part would sink three feet, and another part not at all, for an average sinking of that hypothetical foot. This would lead to leaning.

All the world knows of the Leaning Tower of Pisa. The leaning started during its construction, which began in 1173, and to correct the impression of the tilt, the builders curved the building's axis north, erecting new stories straight up, even though the tower's lower portion was no longer vertical. So, for example, the base of the belfry, which was at one time horizontal to the ground, has six steps on the south side but only four on the north. The tower has the shape of a banana.

In Montreal, Christ Church Cathedral, built in the 1850s, began to sink on its foundation, and the first attempted remedy was to replace the stone steeple with a lighter aluminum one. When this failed to prevent further sinking, a shopping center was built under the cathedral in 1987, and now the cathedral is supported by the shopping center's roof. The sinking has stopped.

The oldest and largest cathedral in Latin America, the National Cathedral on the Zócala Plaza in Mexico City, has been surrounded by scaffolding to prevent further cracking as the earth under its foundation sinks. The National Palace, also on the Zócala Plaza, is tilting dangerously. Hundreds of other buildings in Mexico City are in danger of ruin because over the past century underground aquifers have been drained of their water, and the city has sunk a remarkable thirty feet.

Venice has sunk nine inches in the past century, modest by Mexico City standards. Even so, many buildings, such as the tower of the Church of St. George the Greek, lean out over Venice's canals, their foundations slowly giving way.

And in Hong Kong, Jardine House, the city's first skyscraper, owned by the venerable trading company, sank on its reclaimed harbor foundation. Nets were strung over the surrounding streets because thousands of tiles began popping off the building. Jardine House had to be reclad with new tiles.

So history is filled with buildings that failed for one reason or another at their principal function, which was to remain upright and in place. It appeared that John Llewellyn's Fifth Millennium China Tower was joining their ranks.

* * *

I needed a place to stay where no one could find me, so I asked a taxi driver for the name of a cheap hotel, by which I meant a place where the clerk doesn't ask for your passport and where the clientele list isn't emailed to the police every day. I needed time to collect myself, and to think. It was late at night. The driver suggested the Chrysanthemum Hotel. I telephoned Anne on her cell phone—this was only five or six minutes after the fellow who had been stalking her had become a dead body at her feet—and told her I would meet her there. By then she had found her way back to a lighted street and said she could see a taxi stand from her location.

Most of the girlie bars in Wan Chai—the home of Suzie Wong, where in the old days visitors could find a girl, a tattoo, a dinner, and a fistfight, all within an hour—have been replaced with trendy discos and pubs and restaurants. Even the legendary Pussycat Club is gone and is now Big Mamma's, a jazz and blues venue. The edges of the district remain seedy, though, and I began to regret accepting the cabdriver's advice when he pulled up to a decrepit eight-story building with a neon sign in Cantonese hanging out over the sidewalk that presumably said CHRYSANTHEMUM HOTEL.

In front of the hotel was a table where a doctor was tending to a bare-shirted man lying on his back. The doctor had placed a moxa cone—a one-inch circle of moxa wool—on the man's stomach, and had placed several pinches of grated garlic on the cone. With a lighter he set the cone on fire. I could smell the garlic. The patient grimaced with the heat. The doctor removed the moxa cone after it had burned the man's skin red. The patient was being treated for tuberculosis, I think.

The hotel apparently rented out the space on the sidewalk in front of its lobby window. A second doctor was treating a fellow sitting on a fruit crate. Next to the crate was a propane burner where the doctor heated glass cups. He applied the warm cups to the skin, then yanked them off, producing a loud *wup*. It was late in the evening, yet the street flowed with people. A bamboo pole–seller walked by, a hundred 12-foot laundry poles over his shoulder. Another vendor was carrying a cardboard box filled with knockoff GameBoys. Strips of cooked pork hung from a wire in a small stall. An outdoor barber clipped hair, his customer on a folding metal chair.

A cab pulled up to the curb, and Anne stepped out onto the sidewalk. She paid the cabdriver, handing him the bills through the window. Her mouth was set with tension, and in just those few seconds I could tell that her normally fluid confidence had left her. She saw me, and the relief was evident in her expression. Her face seemed more delicate than I had remembered. She was wearing black slacks and a black blouse. A purse hung from her shoulder. She put her arms around me and hung on to me as if I were a life ring. She was trembling.

After a moment she broke away. She attempted a smile. "Where have you brought me now?" She turned to survey the street. "It doesn't look promising."

"I don't think we can trust our cell phones," I said. "I gave you the name of the Chrysanthemum Hotel over the phone, but maybe people are listening in on us."

Her brows furrowed. "Who is listening?"

"The same people who don't want news of your tippy tower getting out."

"But who?"

"All the powers in China, is my guess." I looked around. "There's another hotel across the street."

She followed my gaze. "I don't see a sign. Not one in English, anyway." The street was festooned with hundreds upon hundreds of signs pasted to the buildings and hanging out over the sidewalk.

We crossed the street. This time of night, cars and trucks had been largely replaced by pedestrians.

"How can you tell a hotel is over there?" she asked.

"Indian and Nepalese and Pakistani vendors are returning for the night, carrying their sample cases. They are traveling salesmen, and are going into that door over there. I can't read the sign overhead, but it must be a cheap hotel."

Near the entrance to the hotel an eight-person ensemble was singing a piece from a Chinese opera. Their ululating falsetto and their banging on percussion instruments added to the street's cacophony.

We entered a small lobby, and I asked the clerk for two rooms. He didn't say a word as I handed him money and he passed us the keys. Behind the clerk a round wall clock had stopped at four-thirty, maybe that afternoon, maybe years ago. Room keys hung from a pegboard. The lobby had fifteen chairs arranged against the wall opposite the check-in counter, and all the chairs were filled with men, none of whom was reading or working or checking his wristwatch or doing anything but passing the time. Anne had given them something to concentrate on. The lobby smelled of mildew. I still didn't know the name of the establishment.

Anne and I stepped toward the elevator. Ten others were waiting for the lift. The floor-number dial above the door was missing. Cracked green linoleum was curled up at the edges of the lobby. Three men waiting for the elevator where shirtless, and another wore a yellow singlet. Several vendors wore turbans and carried large cloth bags over their shoulders. One of the vendors was apparently dealing in mechanical toy cats. From his bag came tinny meows. An Indian salesman was carrying umbrella samples in a golf bag. "Brace yourself," I said as I heard the approaching elevator clunk and groan.

"What do you mean?" Anne asked.

"When the door opens, stay with me."

Hong Kong is a place of a thousand irritants, and I have at times made mental lists of them, ranking them from the most irritating to the least in descending order, sitting in front of my computer screen pretending to work. Top of the list is the Hong Kong predilection for picking noses. The habit is endemic, and cuts across all classes and professions and occupations. It's not so much the picking I mind, it's the studying whatever is found. The second most irritating thing about Hong Kong is elevator protocol, or lack thereof. When the elevator door opens, it's Katie-bar-the-door, and you'd better move or you'll be trampled by dozens of size seven shoes.

The door slid open, and I grabbed Anne's hand and dove forward, and everybody else did the same thing. We rushed in and turned to face the door, and just when I thought the elevator was at capacity, five more fellows pushed their way in. Anne was squeezed up against me, and so was a Cantonese fellow who was coughing raggedly.

The elevator jerked several times before beginning its ascent. One of the riders had apparently poured Old Spice over himself, and someone else smelled of cabbage. Cigarettes hung from the mouths of four of our fellow riders, and the elevator cage filled with gray smoke.

Anne asked, "Are you doing this on purpose?"

"What?"

"Bringing me to these places? I'm an orthodontist's daughter from San Diego. I don't think I can take any more of this."

At each stop the crowd lessened. I could only hold my breath until we reached the fourth floor, and now I had to inhale, and was treated to a rich stink, almost making me light-headed. Finally we were delivered to the seventh floor.

The hallway was narrow, and ill lit by overhanging bulbs. When I found my room, I unlocked it and stepped inside. Anne stood in the doorway, perhaps not wanting to venture into her room without an escort.

I don't think cockroaches make a noise when they run—surely the *tappity-tappity* of its little feet was in my head—but a cockroach the size of my thumb scuttled across the floor to safety under the bed.

There was no point in hunting him down and squishing him because he was only the advance scout. His troops would be waiting for lights-out. The room contained two beds and one dresser and one table on which was a small lamp with a tattered green shade. A yellow fly strip covered with dead insects hung from the ceiling. The window to the street had iron bars over it. The room's walls were institutional green. There was no bathroom. I supposed it was down the hall, and I hoped it was more than a bucket. I began to itch.

Anne announced, "I'm not staying in this place one more second."

"Where else can we go?" I pulled back the thin blanket to look at the sheet. It appeared clean. "I need time to think. I have friends and contacts in Hong Kong." I could count on Darrel Reese at the CIA and Fred Allison of the FBI. "Attempts have just been made on our lives. We need to sort things out."

"'Our' lives?"

I told her of the fellow with the pistol waiting for me on Tregunter Path, and my rescue by Shao Long, the 88K's enforcer.

"So the attacks were coordinated?" she asked.

"I'm sure of it."

"But why are people after us?"

"Because we know too much about the Fifth Millennium China Tower," I said. "Beijing simply can't stand such a loss of face. They'll do anything to prevent the news from getting out."

"So you think it was the Chinese government that sent that man after me?"

"I don't have any better conclusion."

"And then you said the 88K rescued me?" She was leaning against the doorframe, half in and half out of the room.

"Pardon me, madam," came from behind her in a clipped Indian accent.

Anne looked over her shoulder, then stepped aside to admit into the room a small man wearing an olive-green suit so worn that it reflected light. He was carrying two large plastic suitcases.

He said, "You would not believe the day that I have had."

His hair was the color of a crow's wing, and the skin on his face was so dark it was blue. On his nose were wire-framed glasses. His features were tiny, except for his coffee-black eyes, which were round and expressive.

He carefully placed the suitcases on one of the beds. "May I introduce myself? I am Baldev Vajpayee from Bombay. *Baldev* means *godlike in power,* which is God's little joke on me in that I am a manufacturer of emery boards."

I said, "You may have the wrong room, Mr. Vajpayee."

"No, I do not think so." He glanced at his key. "Number seventy-four, it says right here on my key, and it says the same thing on the door."

I looked at my key. It also said *seventy-four.*

"I have just arrived from Bombay," he said. "My company has come up with a new design for the emery board, and I am in Hong Kong to negotiate production with several factories here."

He sat on the bed next to his suitcases. "This could be a very big product for my company, the first new design in emery boards in two centuries. All Bombay is excited about it."

"Mr. Vajpayee, I think there has been a mistake here," I said.

"If we can find a plant to manufacture them for less than eighteen U.S. cents each, we will undoubtedly become the emery board market leader in eastern India. Would you like a sample of the new product?"

"No," I said.

"Yes," Anne said.

Delighted, Baldev Vajpayee opened a suitcase. Inside were covered plastic trays. He flipped a tray open, and with a flourish he pulled out one of his prototype emery boards.

"Have you ever seen anything like it?" he asked with excitement. "This will do more than sell. It will conquer." He spoke with the accent of the Raj, precisely yet liltingly, and with—to my American ears—the accent on the wrong syllable in every word.

Anne stepped farther into the room to accept the emery board. She immediately put it to work on one of her fingernails.

I said, "Mr. Vajpayee, we need to go down to the front desk to straighten out this misunderstanding. I'm quite certain the clerk has assigned you the wrong room."

"Room?" he asked, closing the suitcase and throwing the clasps. "I did not rent an entire room. I rented a bed."

"A bed?"

"Maharashtra Emery Board Limited cannot make a profit if its executives are indulging in costly excesses such as occupying an entire room while traveling."

"This is clearly an advance in emery boards," Anne said, examining her newly filed nail.

"No animals are used in the testing or manufacture of our boards." He opened his other suitcase to remove a small bolt of red cloth, then leaned forward to unroll it on the narrow space between his bed and mine. He took out a one-foot-tall plastic statue of Vishnu reclining on the coils of a serpent, and reverentially placed it on the lamp table between the beds. Next from his suitcase he removed a string of small lights such as might be put on a tree in other parts of the world, and he artfully arranged them around the base of the plastic statue, and then plugged them into the socket near the lamp table. The lights glittered feebly.

"Are you looking for investors?" Anne asked.

"I have a prospectus with me," the Indian said. "Maharashtra Emery Board Limited is trading at three hundred seventy-six rupees per share, its fifty-two-week high."

Next from his suitcase he removed a Tupperware container and a small stainless-steel bowl. He poured a clotting reddish liquid from the container into the bowl. The room instantly filled with the scent of curry. Then from the suitcase he brought out a Bunsen burner.

"How many employees does the company have making emery boards?" Anne asked.

"Three thousand." He got down on his knees to examine the electric socket.

"Have you risen from the ranks of those employees?"

"Not at all." He unplugged the table lamp. The room was suddenly dark, except for the tiny lights around Vishnu. "I have a Ph.D. from Georgia Tech, which readily allowed me to enter the corporate offices."

The lamp came on again. I saw that he had produced—undoubtedly from his suitcase—a three-way plug. Now the tiny lights, the lamp, and the Bunsen burner could all be plugged into the same socket. From the suitcase came a linen napkin and a spoon. The Bunsen burner's coil began to glow red.

He asked, "Do you mind if I dine?"

Just then the red pole appeared at the door, filling the frame side to side and top to bottom. Alarmed, the Indian dropped his spoon into the bowl.

Shao said, "Mr. Wen has learned that you may need a place to stay. He offers his guest rooms."

I thought about it for a fifth of a second. "So long, Mr. Vajpayee."

"Do not forget your prospectus." The Indian quickly found one in his suitcase and passed it to Anne.

She smiled her thanks at him, then followed me out the door into the hallway. I said to the giant, "That's the second time you've rescued me in one night."

14

"How is it possible that you have a videotape of a Central Committee meeting?" I asked.

Darrel Reese smiled. "Cao Ah-kin is China's minister of state security. He is a veteran of the General Office of China's Central Investigation Department, which was transformed into the Ministry of State Security in the 1980s. Cao learned how to protect his fiefdom, and one of the ways was to collect and store as much information as you can on your friends, not just your enemies."

We were once again in the bugproof conference room at the U.S. consulate in Hong Kong. Darrel Reese's remote control was on the table in front of him. He was wearing an olive-colored sport shirt that was open at the neck, tan cotton pants, and deck shoes. His red-gray hair was thick, as if there were too much hair for the size of his head. His blue eyes flashed with amusement and satisfaction, as they always did when he was about to dispense knowledge. It made him jolly and loquacious.

"Cao Ah-kin is in the intelligence business, and he takes it seriously." Reese laughed. "He gathers as much intelligence on his peers on the Central Committee as he does on foreigners."

Ross Shepherd was also in the room, sitting across the table from me. His thin frame was bent over the table, studying a sheaf of documents. He looked up. "Cao Ah-kin makes videos of the Central Committee meetings. We believe the other Central Committee members are unaware of them."

"Then how do you get the videos?" I asked.

Reese smiled in that officious and patronizing manner that FBI agents believe is taught in a class at Langley. "That would take too long to detail." Meaning I wasn't allowed to know.

"You'll be able to hear the committee members as they speak, and you'll also hear a voice-over translation we've added," Shepherd said.

A few minutes ago, at the beginning of this meeting, Ross Shepherd had been reintroduced to me with more specificity. I had been impressed and also been made curious. He was the CIA's deputy director for operations, whose only superiors at the CIA were the director and the deputy director. The Directorate of Operations, which Shepherd ran, had responsibility for collecting foreign intelligence. Under Shepherd were the Counterintelligence Center, the Counterterrorist Center, and the National HUMINT Requirements Tasking Center. Shepherd was very senior. What was he doing in Hong Kong meeting with me? I wondered.

Shepherd said, "The first speaker—you can see him there in the middle: here, I'll put an arrow on him—is Duan Cho-li, China's minister of construction. He is an engineer, with a degree in missile engineering from Harbin Military Engineering College, and before he joined the Ministry of Construction he was mayor of Qingdao City. Duan now oversees all of China's public works, including the Three Gorges Dam, the Kwangtung highway project, the Fifth Millennium China Tower, and all the rest."

The Central Committee tableau on the white wall, which was acting as the screen, was frozen. A white arrow was pointing at Duan Cho-li, who wore a black business suit with a red tie, and whose few strands of hair were combed back over a head that shone under the lights. His eyebrows were hidden behind tortoiseshell glasses. His lips were pulled back in a combination of a grimace and a grin, and there was a small gap between his two front teeth.

"Compacting of soils is designed to improve the load-bearing capacity," Duan said, glancing down at his notes as he spoke. Although I could hear Duan's voice, it was in the background, and the interpreter's voice was louder. "We are looking at soil modulus, also called soil stiffness."

Reese froze the scene. "This meeting occurred yesterday in the People's Conference Center, across the street from Jingshan Park in Beijing. You can see Chen Langing, China's president, to the left, at the head of the table. Next to him, on his left, is the vice president, Bai Mu-tsu. With his back to us is Fan Bao-tian, president of the state council. Seven ministers are also around the table."

On the conference table in Beijing were pitchers of water, glasses, cigarette packs, and ashtrays. In a corner of the room was a potted palm tree.

Reese pressed a button on the remote control. The minister of construction, Duan Cho-li, again spoke, his mouth moving only slightly. "The foundation's designer was instructed to overspecify compaction to insure the soil met compaction standards and to avoid rework."

President Chen raised a hand, palm down over the table. "It would be viewed favorably, Minister, if you would be brief. It is not necessary to educate us in the engineering of soil compaction."

The minister nodded. The person doing the voice-over changed his pitch when translating for another speaker.

Duan continued, "When I say that the compaction on the project was overspecified, I mean that the site was built to support the tower plus much additional weight. No chances were taken in specifying soil density."

"Was density tested?" asked someone with his back to my view.

The minister of construction said, "On an hourly basis during the filling process."

"With accurate equipment?" that same person asked.

"Several years ago, American engineers reworked a device that incorporated seismic and acoustic detectors to locate land mines, and came up with a soil stiffness gauge. I have brought one with me."

The minister leaned to one side to reach to the floor, then brought up a yellow foot-high canister that had a yellow handle on top. The device resembled a bucket with a closed top.

He said, "This soil stiffness gauge was manufactured by Tower Industries of Houston, Texas, in the United States. You place it on the top of the soil, and it produces vibrations that are measured by its sensors."

"What is it measuring?" Vice President Bai asked.

"It records force and displacement time. Not only were surface samples taken as the fill was dumped into place, but core samples were also taken, sending the gauge down into bored holes to take measurements."

"How frequently were these measurements taken?" Chen asked.

"Stiffness measurements were always being taken, every hour of every day during the fill procedure, and then later when the concrete cap was added to the island." The minister of construction cleared his throat, which the voice-over didn't bother to translate. "The stiffness of soil is defined as the ratio of force to displacement—"

"Enough," interrupted the president.

Duan pushed ahead: "Soil stiffness relates to density, shear modulus, and void ratio. These can all be measured. To eliminate undercompaction on the project, statistical quality control was implemented, and—"

The president slapped the table. "Enough, enough, enough, Mr. Minister."

Duan stared down at his notepaper.

"Have you taken recent stiffness tests?" Bai asked.

"The tower commission has hired an independent testing company, Taegu Geotechnical from South Korea, and they have been testing the site for two days now."

"What do they report?" Chen asked.

"Of the samples taken, the mean modulus was seventy megapascals, and the standard deviation is—"

"Put it in Mandarin," Chen demanded.

I could see beads of sweat on the construction minister's forehead. He said, "Discrepancies exist between the compaction reports submitted by All-Asia Geotech during the filling of the island, and the results found by Taegu Geotechnical."

Reese stopped the video. "All-Asia Geotech was founded and run by Yao Bok-kee, who was arrested on Heroes of the Revolution Island and then executed."

"Why was he arrested on the island, using all the policemen?" I asked.

"Yao knew he was being hunted by the Ministry of Security. He hadn't left the island for days and was sleeping in his trailer. He thought he would be safer there than at his home at North Point. Turns out he underestimated the ministry."

Reese began the video again.

"What sort of discrepancies?" The translator added a new pitch as he asked the question.

Reese once again froze the scene, and Ross Shepherd said, "That voice belongs to Cao Ah-kin, the minister of state security. He is off-camera to the right. Cao is the president's nemesis. He and Chen have struggled for years for control of the Central Committee, and Cao looks for any opportunity to undermine Chen. President Chen suspects this is so, but doesn't know the extent of it. Cao is seeking to replace Chen as prime minister."

The video rolled again. Construction Minister Duan said, "The All-Asia Geotech samples taken during construction showed the earth fill to be more dense than the samples taken this week by Taegu Geotechnical."

"How much more dense?" someone asked.

Duan bowed his head to his notes. "We have a hypothetical design modulus—"

Chen cut him off again. "I don't want hypothetical. I want it made plain, and I want it now."

"Samples taken during construction showed that the mean soil modulus was 4,092 kilograms per square centimeter. This number directly relates to weight-bearing capacity."

"And the samples taken after construction of the Fifth Millennium China Tower?" asked the president.

"They show a mean soil modulus of 2,728 kilograms per square centimeter."

The president pushed his seat back several inches. His palms were flat on the table. Behind him on the wall was an enlarged photograph of Deng Xiaoping. Chen asked, "So you thought that the tower was being built on a foundation that had a soil modulus of 4,000 kilograms per square centimeter, but it now appears that it is only 2,728?"

"That is correct, President Chen."

"I am not a builder. Is that difference architecturally significant?"

"It is highly significant, Mr. President."

The Minister of Security asked, "Could the earth under the tower have somehow changed densities between the tests?"

"No, not significantly," came Duan's reply.

"So it is the measurements that have changed?" the president asked. "Is that correct?"

"That must be the case, President Chen."

The committee's room was silent for a moment as the members absorbed this news.

Then the president asked, "How did that happen?"

"We do not know," Construction Minister Duan replied.

"Could the soil stiffness gauges that did the testing during construction have been malfunctioning?" asked Fan Bao-tian, who was president of the State Council.

"Over forty different gauges were employed," Duan said. "It is unlikely they all were uniformly in error."

Bai asked, "Then the fault was in reporting the measurements, would you say, Mr. Construction Minister?"

"Esteemed colleagues, I cannot tell you how the discrepancy came to exist between the soil tests taken during construction and those taken a few days ago. My ministry is looking into it, but we have not reached any conclusions as yet."

Darrel Reese stopped the video. "This fellow—the construction minister, Duan Cho-li—doesn't know if he'll leave this meeting still as construction minister. He is in the witness chair, and he is trying not to incriminate himself." Reese pressed the button again.

The minister of state security, Cao Ah-kin, said, "My ministry is also looking into it."

President Chen's voice on the tape became quieter, and so did the translator's. "We must find who is responsible for this."

Cao said, "Our investigation is well under way."

The president's eyes closed for a moment, and his face was a study of perturbation, with his brows low and his teeth showing sourly. Such a display was weakness, and he quickly caught himself. He rubbed his palm on the table, as if polishing it, and asked, "What will be the result if the man-made island's earthen fill is too soft, Minister Duan?"

"We are doing absolutely everything in our power to compact the fill."

When Darrel Reese paused the tape again, Shepherd said: "Notice that the construction minister dodges the president's question. And you'll notice that the president allows the dodge. He doesn't pursue the answer. No one in that room wants to face what might happen to the tower."

The video began moving again. President Chen said: "The People's Republic of China cannot tolerate information regarding this problem to be released to our citizens or to the world community. The loss of prestige to China, and to those of us around this table, would be incalculable."

Minister of State Security Cao said, "Measures to insure silence on the matter are well under way."

"What about the Hong Kong press?" Chen asked.

"They will not publish rumors. As long as this story is viewed as nothing but rumors, we are safe. The newspapers and broadcast stations have been warned. Also, those criminals in Hong Kong and the rest of China who promote anti-Chinese rumors on the Internet are being arrested."

"Perhaps the opening ceremonies should be postponed until the problem is resolved," Fan suggested.

"Absolutely not." President Chen's voice was compelling. "Planning for the opening ceremonies has been under way almost as long as the tower has been under construction. Seventy heads of state will be arriving in Hong Kong. Six thousand media representatives will be there. All of the State Council and three-fourths of the National People's Congress are scheduled to be in Hong Kong. We are anticipating the largest international gathering ever. The entire world is turning to Hong Kong—and to us—on that day. It simply cannot be postponed. The very notion is unthinkable."

Chen poured himself water. The room in Beijing was quiet for a moment.

Then Chen said: "We must not fool ourselves regarding what is at stake here. Our system of government is not as secure as it was twenty, even ten, years ago. Forces are loose in our country that mean to sweep us away. The Falun Gong is only the best-known insurgency movement. Minister Cao assures me there are many others, waiting for an opportunity to deny us our mandate to rule. And many, many of our countrymen would join such a movement once it is under way, you have told me, Minister Cao. A blow such as this—such as the Fifth Millennium China Tower leaning—would embolden them. It would be viewed as a symbol of our fallibility, and would be disastrous."

Vice President Bai Mu-tsu said, "The commission to design the tower should never have gone to this John Llewellyn. One of our own architects should have designed the tower."

Chen turned to him. "Beijing is filled with the products of our own architects. Not a single memorable structure has been built by a Chinese architect in China in fifty years. Not one, not in Beijing, not in anyplace in China."

"Well . . ."

"Name one, Mr. Vice President. Name a structure in our country designed by a Chinese architect in the past fifty years that will be studied after our time."

Bai said nothing.

"My friend John Llewellyn has given China a masterpiece. It will be the most celebrated structure on this earth for as long as such things matter."

Duan said petulantly, "Llewellyn might have arranged for it to remain upright."

"That is your job now, Mr. Construction Minister." Chen pushed his chair back. "We are adjourned." The video ended.

I said, "I'd better leave Hong Kong. I don't like people coming after me with guns."

Reese brought up the remote control again. On the wall appeared a street scene. "This photo was taken twenty minutes ago by a camera on our roof as you arrived outside the building. You can see yourself down there. You are crossing the street, headed for our doorway."

The sidewalks were jammed with people, as they are in the city between noon and two o'clock every day. The white arrow appeared on the screen. It pointed at a pedestrian's head.

Reese said, "This fellow on the sidewalk fifteen feet behind you is Will Jeffers, one of us. Jeffers won a silver medal in judo in Sydney." He moved the arrow. "And this is Dennis Tan, one of us. Dennis spent eight years in the Marine Corps before joining the CIA." The arrow slid to another part of the photograph. "And this is Jennifer Cho, also one of us. She came to us from the Secret Service. You've had three of us on you since last night. Same with your friend Anne Iverson. You both are extremely well protected."

Shepherd said, "Your contract with the tower commission runs until the tower is completed. It isn't completed yet. You should stay in Hong Kong."

"We'd like you to stay," Reese said. "Let's see what happens if we keep the mix the same."

I looked at him, then at Shepherd. That they knew more than I knew was clear.

"We aren't often presented opportunities like this," Shepherd said.

"Like what?" I asked.

"When a group is agitated and afraid, they often give chances to their enemies," Shepherd said.

"They make mistakes," Reese added. "They desert their long-laid plans when they are afraid."

Shepherd said, "You just saw the video of the Central Committee meeting."

I nodded.

Shepherd added, "That was a roomful of frightened old men."

* * *

My apartment building was guarded by two teams. The first was made up of CIA personnel. Several were posted near the building's entrance, and others were at the elevators and stairwell, and still several more were on my floor.

The second team consisted of 88K members who guarded the dragon head's grandson, Hsu Shui-ban. They were less evident, preferring to remain on the streets near the building, but the 88K was based on neighborhood cells, and their knowledge of the neighborhood was vast, and so its soldiers knew who should be coming and going, and they intercepted anyone they didn't recognize. The two teams were aware of each other, of course, and ignored each other. I had never felt safer.

I arrived at my apartment on the twentieth floor that night to find a note that had been slipped under my door. It was from the dragon head's grandson, Hsu Shui-ban, down the hall.

The note said in carefully printed English: "The next meeting of the 20th Floor Physics Club is Tuesday at 7:00 at my place. The newest member—which is you—always brings the refreshments. I can't eat anything sticky because of my braces. Hsu Shui-ban. P.S. I just took a new measurement of the distance to the top of the Gold Swan from my balcony. It is now eight inches closer than our first reading."

* * *

We found John Llewellyn in the tower lobby, the large hallway that was carefully not so immense as to diminish the humans who entered it, nothing *fascismo* to it. Most of the interior had been completed, and the lobby seemed sculpted out of marble and granite. Installation of the lighting was finished, and the hall's tones were both muted and striking. Enormous Chinese flags celebrating the imminent opening had been hung in the lobby, though Llewellyn had argued against them, saying the interior spoke for itself and needed no dressing, but on this issue he was overruled.

The granite and tile floor was comprised of complicated forms that could not be taken in from any one position. The tiles' patterns led the viewers from spot to spot. Stylized chrysanthemums and dragons were arrayed on the floor. They were subtle, and it was possible to walk from the door to the elevator bank without noticing them. But if you looked, they were there, and could command your attention for many minutes as the patterns guided you along. This, too, was on purpose. Llewellyn said that the ground-floor lobby mustn't challenge the vertical sweep of the tower, but he had wanted a space with more interest than an aircraft hangar.

The floor's designer, Pu Ji-yong, who was principal instructor at Martyrs of the Revolution School of Design in Beijing, had said his inspiration for the floor had been ancient Chinese Kossu scrolls. His tile design for the tower had been reproduced as a print, and had been a fast-seller in Hong Kong for months.

Anne and I walked across the lobby toward Llewellyn, who was surrounded by photographic equipment near the lobby's north wall. An electronic flash and power pack and several lighting soft boxes were on the floor, connected by cables. Two cameras were on tripods. Llewellyn was sitting on a bench, turned to his right, with his chin raised in an artificial way, as if he were looking down his nose. The photographer put a finger to the point of Llewellyn's chin to lower it a fraction, then stepped back. A light meter was around the photographer's neck, and she was wearing camouflage pants and a striped T-shirt. Her auburn hair was pulled back into a ponytail. The Frank Lloyd Wright Prize was on another bench, perhaps used as a prop for several shots and now put aside. Also nearby were American and Chinese flags mounted on a wood frame so that they crisscrossed, and an enormous bouquet of flowers, mostly lilies and birds-of-paradise, and these were also props. Llewellyn was wearing a crisp light blue suit. His red and blue tie was kept in place by a silver tie clasp.

"John, you are sweating again," the photographer said. Her name was Jillian Franks, I learned later. Her subjects ranged from presidents of the United States to *Sports Illustrated* swimsuit models. She had come from New York for this session.

One of her assistants was a makeup artist, and she rushed forward to mend the damage. The skin of Llewellyn's face had been dulled by makeup, and his lips appeared to be colored. His eyebrows had been darkened, and his silver hair was perfectly in place. The makeup had restored his healthful appearance, yet had also made his face artificial, a little too much color and drama.

The photographer said, "You have a narrow face, John. We'll try flattening the lighting a little."

The lighting assistant opened the louvers on a light box. Llewellyn squinted against the new makeup being applied to his face. Only a few tradesmen were in the lobby. One was up a ladder, working on a balky light fixture. Two others were installing computers at the information desk.

"May we have a couple minutes, John?" Anne asked.

He turned slightly. "Can it wait?" His voice was testy. "You can see I'm busy."

The photographer said, "Why don't we take a break? Fifteen minutes. John, don't go out into the sun where your face will melt, okay?"

Llewellyn rose stiffly from the bench. He adjusted his pants, shot his cuffs, and asked brusquely, "What is it?"

"Can we sit down for a minute?" Anne asked.

He led us to a grouping of wood and leather chairs he had designed for this lobby. "I need to be careful. If I nod my head, the pancake makeup on my neck will get on my white collar."

He placed himself cautiously on a chair. Anne sat next to him. She was wearing an apricot yellow sateen jacket and white cotton pants. Her hair was loose to her shoulders.

"Clay, I did you a favor yesterday," Llewellyn said with delight, his mood changing instantly.

I smiled.

"A recruiter at Lloyds of London—no less than a vice president there—called to inquire about you. They apparently are considering making you a job offer."

I hadn't heard anything about this.

He said, "I raved about you over the telephone, then sent a follow-up letter of recommendation. You would blush to read it."

"I'm grateful," I said.

"Anne, you should see the proposal I'm working up. It's marvelous, it really is." He leaned forward to frame the air with his hands. His cheeks had been highlighted with makeup, and his lips were an unnatural pink. "A grand bridge. You can picture it. Across the western harbor from Tsim Sha Tsui on Kowloon to Sheun Wan on Hong Kong."

"There's already a tunnel there," I said. "Why would a bridge be needed?"

"A suspension bridge unlike anything the world has seen." The architect raised his hands as if bracing the ceiling. "Magnificent spires rising from the sea. Glittering, stainless-steel–encased cables. A soaring bridge deck that sweeps across the horizon."

"Have you discussed this with anyone?" Anne asked. "With the powers-that-be in Hong Kong and Beijing?"

"The bridge would introduce the Fifth Millennium China Tower as you arrive in Hong Kong from the west. And from the east it would act as an enchanting backdrop."

"We need to talk about something," Anne said.

Llewellyn's enthusiasm spilled out. "The bridge—call it the Asia Gate—would give context to the entire city, and especially to the tower. It wouldn't challenge the tower for primacy in the harbor but would wrap it in a glittering setting."

I glanced at Anne. Her face was as bright as paint. She was embarrassed for Llewellyn, who appeared to be separated from reality, setting out some grand new plan for Hong Kong and blind to his tower's plight.

"The bridge will bring together many different levels of symbolism, and will be graphically powerful, a tour de force," Llewellyn said. "It will display Hong Kong's limitless future, but it will also stand in stark contrast to the modern urban condition."

He was out of breath and winding down, so Anne cut in, "You knew what that crack was, didn't you, John?"

He was not accustomed to interruptions, but more than this, John Llewellyn was not used to listeners resisting his charm and enthusiasm when he described a project. He sat upright. "Pardon?"

"The other day when the crack on the island's concrete cap was discovered, you blamed the tiling contractor, Xiao Chai-son, and you fired him on the spot in that disgraceful performance . . ."

"Yes, yes, yes." Llewellyn waved away the complaint. "I telephoned Xiao two hours later and begged his forgiveness, and asked him to stay on the project, and he agreed. It was terrible of me, I know." He put his hands to the sides of his head, cupping it, as if to contain his thoughts. "I just don't know what happened to me."

"The crack wasn't due to anything the tile contractor had done, but was created when the tower's massive weight shifted."

"Well, it's not exactly shifting," Llewellyn said.

"What, then?"

He glanced at the photographer's setup. His eyes had a dry glitter. "Anything that is occurring to the tower is well within design parameters. The structural integrity is not an issue."

"Design parameters?" Her tone was mawkish. "I'm an architect on the project. I know all about the design parameters. Leaning is not in any of the tower's design parameters."

He said: "What I am saying is that nothing has occurred that cannot be corrected. The situation—it is hardly a problem, but rather a situation—is well in hand. The most experienced foundation contractors on the planet are here now."

"What's their prognosis?" I asked.

He laughed in a brittle way. "They are like medical doctors, and are afraid of giving precise forecasts, but I'm confident that all will be well."

"Why didn't you talk to me about this?" Anne asked.

"I know how much you invested in the tower project, professionally and personally, and I didn't want to worry you. Plus"—he hesitated, his mouth moving as he searched for words—"this has all been a bit embarrassing, if you know what I mean."

I said, "Anne was almost murdered last night."

His eyes opened, showing all of his irises, and his lips parted. His alarm seemed genuine. I briefly told him what we knew about Anne's close call on that unknown North Point street. Then I mentioned my own run-in on Tregunter Path.

"Who do you suppose is doing this?" Llewellyn asked.

"Someone who doesn't want information about the problem with the tower getting out."

"It's not really a problem, Clay." He gestured quickly toward the ceiling. "There's nothing that can't be reengineered. You aren't an architect, and so you wouldn't know that things like this always come up. Building something, whether it's a tool shed or a skyscraper, always involves taking two steps forward and one step back."

I felt sorry for the fellow, sitting there, explaining away a massive problem, trying to portray it as routine. I didn't know whether, being the good general, he was simply trying to rally his troops through his optimism or whether he was delusional.

He went on, "You should have seen the problems with my first major project, the Stamford house in Braintree, Massachusetts." He laughed, and there was a shrill note to it. "I went out to the site, where the framers were on the second floor, and—"

He stopped mid-sentence when the loud growl of a diesel engine came from the lobby's west entrance. A Caterpillar wheel loader was there, and had stopped just outside the lobby's high glass entryway. On one end of the loader was a bucket, and on the other was a pneumatic hammer mounted on a back-hoe arm.

"What's going on?" Llewellyn asked. "Why the equipment?"

Out in the sun behind the loader was a second loader, also equipped with a pneumatic hammer, and behind that was a yellow dump truck. Workmen began walking into the lobby.

"I don't know anything about this," Llewellyn exclaimed. "I'm supposed to know everything that goes on around here, right? What is this?" He rose from his chair to cross the lobby.

Ann and I followed him. The crew's foreman was carrying a roll of blueprints, and his eyes were on the doorframes. He was wearing a hardhat and a tie. Glass plates made up the lobby entrance on that end of the tower. The glass plates were framed in bronze so that they matched the tower's exterior and were tinted green to reduce glare.

Llewellyn quick-stepped towards the workers. He held up his hand and called out over the sound of the diesel engines, "I'm John Llewellyn. Tell me what's going on."

The fellow with the tie replied in English, "I'm the new foundation contractor, Lin Boon-min, of Pan-Pacific Construction."

"I don't know anything about a new foundation contractor." Llewellyn's voice had gained an octave. "Who sent you here? What's all this equipment?"

"Mr. Llewellyn, I've been told to begin digging by four o'clock this afternoon or I lose my contract."

"Digging?" Llewellyn's voice was now as high as a bird's. "Nobody is going to dig around here. What are you talking about?"

Another workman approached Lin Boon-min, and they spoke briefly in Cantonese, ignoring Llewellyn who rose and fell on his toes. His hands were clenched. The workman turned away, heading back to the loader.

"Mr. Llewellyn, I apologize, but I do not have the time to argue with you. I have a job, and it must be done, and it must be done now."

"But who—?"

"And I regret to tell you that my equipment won't fit through the entryway, and we don't have time to do anything about it."

"What are you saying?" Llewellyn's voice wavered.

The loader's engine wound up, and machine lurched forward. The enormous front doors were open, but were not wide enough to accommodate a piece of road-construction equipment. The steel bucket ripped out a door frame, and three panels of glass exploded into shards that rained down onto the floor. The glass doors fell, and the glass fractured. The loader rolled into the lobby, pulverizing the glass.

Lin Boon-min walked in front of the loader, alternately glancing at the document in his hand and at the floor. The second loader followed. He pointed to a spot on the floor, right on the stem of a tile chrysanthemum. The loader spun around so that the pneumatic hammer was over the spot; then the driver turned his seat so that he faced the hammer.

The boom and arm lowered the steel tip to the tile. The hammer pounded. Tile shattered and pieces of it spun away. The operator raised the boom and lowered it to another spot, this one a tile that was part of the chrysanthemum's petal. The hammer roared, and the tile disintegrated. Dust rose in a cloud.

Lin Boon-min studied his prints, then waved at the second loader, directing him to another spot in the lobby. The dump truck waited outside.

I looked over at Anne. She was gripping Llewellyn's hand. She was weeping, and so was he.

15

Nothing is free in Hong Kong, not even a small act of kindness. No favor is forgotten. No good deed can remain unpaid. *Maijiang* is Cantonese for the trading of credit. When face is given, it is understood that it will be returned. Performing a service or rendering a favor is smiled upon and received with gratitude, and it is not forgotten either by the giver or the recipient. Giving a favor is like opening a bank account. The credit will be there when it is called upon.

Sikdjo means knowing what must be done. The debtor always knows, and if he is unable to pay, or is not called upon to pay, then his children must do so when the time comes. Whether the credit is as small as a token gift or as large as the saving of a life, it must be repaid.

"'This is my great-grandfather,'" Wen Quichin said through his nephew Zhu Jintau. "'He was a fine gentleman. I have only a few memories of him, but his name is still spoken with respect in Hong Kong.'"

We were in Wen's study in his home on the Peak. A screen was set up in front of the bookcase, and we were viewing an ancient photo that had been made into a slide. Wen's great-grandfather was dressed as a mandarin prince: a hat with a peacock feather tassel, a court-robe collar from which hung a *p'u fang*, which is a square showing a coat of arms, and a dragon robe with horse-hoof cuffs. He was sitting on a small stool, and his legs were crossed in front of him. His black eyes were so far back in his head they appeared to be drilled holes. I didn't know why Wen's great-grandfather would wear the robes of a mandarin when he was Cantonese.

"Was he . . . in your business?" I asked.

"'He was a dynamic leader who first brought 88K from Canton to Hong Kong. He died in his fifty-sixth year, a tragic though not unanticipated end.'"

"How did he die?"

"'The British hung him.'"

Also in the room was Shao Long, the red pole, whom I had seen less and less of now that I was being guarded by Americans. He was sitting in a leather chair, eating a two-gallon bowl of fried shrimp, using chopsticks, his hand working methodically between his mouth and the bowl. His legs were up on a stool, a relaxed pose I took to be an indication of the respect and affection between Wen and Shao. Other 88K soldiers would keep their feet solidly on the floor.

Wen thumbed the remote control. "'And this is my grandfather. He was a considerate old gentleman who taught me many things.'"

This slide showed Wen's grandfather standing in front of a 1940s Buick. He was wearing slacks and a shirt with an open neck, and was smiling at the camera. His bottom teeth were stainless steel.

Zhu translated for his uncle, "'Grandfather expanded 88K. There were five times as many members when he died as when he became the dragon head. He loved that Buick. I used to wash it for him, and he would give me a few coins. He was the first to put Tsim Sha Tsui in our hands.'"

Tsim Sha Tsui is the main business district of Kowloon. A bowl of shrimp, a much smaller one, was on a TV table next to Wen's chair. I had already eaten my shrimp and had declined more from a waiter who wore a holster on his hip under his shirt.

Zhu translated, "'My grandfather was the first to engage in regular business. He purchased a newspaper, the *Hong Kong Post*, that put out editions in both Cantonese and English.'"

"Did he live long and prosper?" I asked.

"'He would have lived longer had he not also been hung by the British.'"

Shao Long shook his head. "Very bad," he said in English around a mouthful of shrimp. "Should not have happened to that good man."

The invitation to this slide show had come through Zhu Jintau. I was not sufficiently acute to know the status of the *maijiang* between Wen and me. We had done services for each other. There may have been a method to weigh the respective values of those services, but I was unaware of it. I was certain, though, that I had been invited to his home so that he could ask a service of me.

Wen worked the remote control. A new slide came up, and Wen and Shao laughed at it.

Zhu said for his uncle, "'This is me as a young rooster.'"

The photograph showed Wen standing in the door of a building. He wore a belt from which hung two holsters. The grips of the pistols were visible. Resting in his arms was a bolt-action rifle. Arranged along the wall outside the door were five other rifles and a submachine gun. Wen's hair was full and dark in the photograph. He was snarling at the camera, none too convincingly.

Wen laughed again. "'This was when I was red pole. I took the job seriously. I read a Karl May western that had been translated into Cantonese.'"

On a table in the den was that day's edition of *Ming Pao*, a leading Hong Kong newspaper published in Cantonese. On the front page was a photograph of a dump truck entering the Gold Swan's lobby. The photo was taken at a good distance, perhaps as far as from a building on the Hong Kong side. The Chinese characters above the photograph were large, and although I couldn't read them, I knew they announced the same thing as had all other Hong Kong papers that morning: a shopping arcade was going to be built under the tower.

That morning I had read an interview with Kao Lai-tai, the tower commission chairman, in the *South China Morning Post*. Kao had said that new studies indicated souvenir shops at the ferry terminals on both sides of the harbor and the small one at the tower's restaurant level would be inadequate to meet demand, so new construction below the tower had been authorized. He did not believe the addition of a basement complex would delay the opening of the tower, though he did not discuss how a delay was possible to avoid. The newspaper story was glaringly inadequate, rife with internal inconsistencies and unanswered questions.

Taming of the Hong Kong media had begun even before the Handover. The press's freedom was taken away in small increments, with particular restrictions on news and opinion regarding Beijing. But in the past two days the restrictions had become severe. Jay Lee had told me that newspapers and broadcast outlets had been visited by representatives of China's Ministry of State Security. CEOs and station managers and publishers had been taken into their offices, and the message given to them had been simple: any newspaper stories or broadcast reports regarding difficulties on construction of the Fifth Millennium China Tower would be considered as a breach of state security, a capital offense. The messengers had not specified what that difficulty with the tower might be, or why such a warning was being delivered to Hong Kong's media, but the messengers were blunt. Nothing negative was to be reported about the Fifth Millennium China Tower.

Lest anyone in the media miss the message, the manager of radio station RTHK7 was taken from his office in handcuffs, and not a word had been heard from him since. The *South China Morning Post*'s lead editorial writer was dragged from his home by plainclothes policemen at two this morning. No charges had been filed, and his family and employer had not been told where he was. A reporter for the *Asian Wall Street Journal* simply disappeared. Sixteen foreign correspondents—those considered too independent—were summarily expelled from Hong Kong, given sixty minutes to gather their belongings, but not given a reason for their ejection. Cao Ah-kin, China's minister of state security, had intended to frighten Hong Kong's press, and he had succeeded.

To prevent Internet rumors, four Hong Kong service portals were closed, and much of Hong Kong was left without Internet service. Further, anti-Beijing Internet rumormongers—who had thought themselves immune from identification and punishment due to their witty electronic names such as BeijingRevealed and DragonTattler, had been identified long before, and were swept up by the Hong Kong police on orders from the ministry. Internet bulletin boards in Hong Kong—those ready sources of rumor and fact—were no longer operating.

Changes also occurred in the tower's media department. The manager, the official spokesman, and all twelve other employees of the commission's public relations office were fired, and were replaced by one man, Su Chee-yoong, the new official spokesman, a retired Red Army colonel with no previous press or public relations experience. Tower management was warned to say nothing to the press. All information regarding the Fifth Millennium China Tower would come from Su Chee-yoong. Further, the Ministry of the Interior issued an edict directing all reporters to submit their work to Su before it was printed or broadcast. Censorship of tower news would be absolute.

" 'Now this is me at age twelve,' " Wen said through his nephew.

In the photo Wen is sitting in a punt about thirty yards from shore, waving his hand at the camera. Dead fish float all around his boat.

" 'One of my uncles was a trader. He never owned a shop, but rather he used a goat cart, and then later a three-wheeled bicycle cart. He bought low and sold high, anything he laid his hands on, from discarded dentures to oyster shells to pencils. I never knew what he would have on his cart. One day I asked him what was in the wooden box on his cart, and he showed me twenty-four Japanese hand grenades. They were early grenades, and when you pulled the pin, you had to strike the cap. I bought all twenty-four from my uncle. Used up all my savings. In this photo I have pulled the pin and dropped a grenade into the water, and it exploded, and all those fish came up. I took home two baskets of fish. My mother was proud of me.' "

Shao chuckled, and said something in Cantonese. Wen laughed, his small frame shaking and his eyes narrowed with mirth. Zhu didn't translate.

Up came another slide. " 'And this is me when I was sixteen. I was quite proud on this day.' "

In the photo Wen was grinning fiercely and holding a Japanese officer's *tachi* sword across his chest. On Wen's head was a khaki cork sun helmet. Brown leather boots rose to his knees. The shirt collar was outside the tunic collar, and the badges of rank were pinned to the tunic's lapels. A belt was around his midriff, and narrow belts were over each shoulder.

I asked, "You served in the Japanese army?"

After the translation, Wen laughed so hard I thought he would topple out of his chair. Shao Long chuckled along, his eyes closed and his chopsticks arrested in mid-journey. His emerald teeth glittered.

"'No, no, no,'" Zhu translated. "'The fellow I took this uniform from was in the Japanese army.'"

Then I noticed that dark stains were under several small tears in the uniform blouse.

"'I rationed myself those hand grenades over the years,'" Zhu said for his uncle. "'When the Japanese were here in Hong Kong, I walked into the Sun Garden restaurant in Wan Chai, went upstairs to the private dining room, and tossed two grenades into the room. Six Japanese officers were quite surprised, and quickly quite dead.'"

Shao undoubtedly had heard the story many times, but he nodded and laughed along.

"'Those hand grenades have served me well,'" Zhu said for his uncle. Zhu sat in a straight-back chair and did not help himself to the refreshments. He was wearing khaki pants, an Abercrombie & Fitch sport shirt, and boat shoes. He continued, "'Now here is a photograph taken two days ago.'"

On the screen appeared a photograph of a man wearing cotton trousers and a red short-sleeved sport shirt. He was pulling open the door of a dark blue Chrysler sedan, and he was grinning. On the other side of the car was a young woman wearing a black sheath dress with spaghetti straps. She held a beaded purse in one hand, which was resting on top of the car as she opened the passenger door. It was night, and a neon sign was in a building's window behind the couple.

"'Do you recognize the man?'" Zhu asked for his uncle.

I shook my head.

"'Look more closely. He is Yan Luo-han, the fellow you last saw in the container at Kwai Chung. When the Hong Kong police released him, he traveled to his home in Shenzhen, just across the Special Administrative District's border, where, as you can see, he is having a fine time. He apparently made a lot of money, kidnapping my grandson and murdering your father. That woman is a prostitute he has hired for the evening.'"

The waiter came into the den and pointed at my glass. I didn't want another one, so I shook my head. I was drinking a Beck's beer.

"'At least, Yan thinks she is a prostitute,'" Zhu translated.

This passed as high humor in the room, because Wen and Shao laughed mightily, Shao patting the arm of his chair.

Another slide came up. "'Now here is Yan's nice new Chrysler ten minutes later.'"

The automobile was shredded. Glass had been blown out of all the windows and lay around the car in fragments on the street. The Chrysler's roof was ripped open, and strips of tortured metal curled toward the sky. The rearview mirror lay on the street. The trunk lid was open.

Zhu translated, "'At an intersection the woman climbed out of the car, reached into her purse, pulled the pin and struck the cap on one of my grenades, then tossed it onto the car's floor. That lump on the front seat is Yan.'"

All I could see through the Chrysler's open door was a dark smudge on the front seat, leaning forward over the steering wheel. I couldn't make out the body in greater detail.

Zhu translated, "'Here's a better look.'"

The next slide was a close-up of the car's interior. Yan's head was attached to his neck only by a few threads of tissue. One of his hands was missing entirely. Instead of eyes and a nose, he had only black holes in his skull. The blast had scalped him, leaving a knot of red tissue where his hair had been. He was blackened and curled, and resembled a large pork rind.

"He looks remarkably dead," I said.

"'Yan entered death too quickly,'" Wen said via his nephew. "'But we had to take what we could get.'"

The waiter came into the den carrying a circular gong on a frame. He struck the gong with a mallet, and the red pole stood quickly and brushed shrimp crumbs from his pants. He put his hand under Wen's arm to gently help the old man to his feet. Wen led us into the dining room.

A massive circular mahogany table under a crystal chandelier dominated the room. An elm sideboard with brass fixtures was against a wall. The wallpaper was a deep red that had a subtle pattern on it in silver, a pagoda scene. I was given the guest of honor's spot at the table, which is always the chair farthest from the door. Wen signaled for his nephew to seat himself at the table. The young man smiled at the pleasure of the unexpected invitation. Teacups, glasses, chopsticks, and plates were on the table. A waiter arrived with a plate on which was a reddish-brown oval of something unrecognizable.

I glanced at Zhu, and he said, "Preserved abalone."

Shao said in English, "To be born in Suzhou / To live in Hangzhou / To eat in Guangzhou / and to die in Liuzhou."

Guangzhou is Canton. Though he spoke no English, Wen recognized the poem, and nodded vigorously. A larger tray arrived, and on it was a roasted piglet, including its head and tail. Then came a third tray, which held a stewed shark's fin in brown sauce. The last tray to the table contained chicken with ginger and shallots, rice starch noodles, and beef fillets with broccoli. Wen loudly smacked his lips, then turned his chopsticks around to use the blunt ends, moving food from the trays onto my plate. Then he served Shao and Zhu. The red pole asked if he could carve the piglet, and Wen nodded happily. I helped myself to a small portion of the rubbery abalone. I was undoubtedly an honored guest, as this single abalone would have cost Wen the equivalent of three hundred U.S. dollars. The waiter arrived with the final item, soup served with chrysanthemum petals, which meant it was snake soup. The waiter filled our glasses with brandy rather than wine.

The Cantonese associate silence with sadness and solitude, and will have none of it during a meal. Wen spoke while eating, a monologue that caused Shao to laugh frequently. Zhu translated as best he could while still trying to feed himself. Wen told a story of how he received a scar on his back, and it involved a blood enemy beating him with a tuna gaff, and the story caused Shao to laugh uproariously while at the same time cramming food into his mouth at a piston's pace.

When Wen turned to his abalone, the tenor of the conversation changed. He asked through his nephew, " 'Mr. Williams, do you know why I am never arrested by the police?' "

"I have asked myself that, but have no answer," I replied. I might have asked Jay Lee, but such a question implied Jay and his department were derelict in their duty. I peered down into the bowl of snake soup. I wondered what part of a snake was edible. I hoped I didn't see an eyeball staring back at me.

" 'The police know who I am and what I do, and they know where I live. They could pick me up at any time, and in my youth they arrested me frequently. Now they like to portray me as a myth or as no longer important, and sometimes they even claim I am dead, which saves them from explaining why I am not in prison.' "

Wen was purposely directing the conversation. We would get to his destination in his own time. There was *xinyong* between us, trust that was tied to our brief history together and the services we had done for each other. He was about to propose something, I was sure.

Zhu translated, " 'I am not arrested because I am a source of stability in Hong Kong. Whenever a dragon head dies or is arrested, much trouble results in the neighborhoods. There is death and destruction.' "

Wen sampled the shark fin. Then he said through his nephew, " 'Hong Kong cannot have instability, and such instability also occurs when a fool will not accept what he has inherited.' "

He produced a photograph from his wallet. It showed a young man in front of an electronics store.

Wen spoke, and Zhu interpreted, " 'This is Pen Kai-ge. For twenty-five years Pen's father was the dragon head of Peach Blossom, a rival society from the San Po Kong neighborhood.'"

San Po Kong is next to Kai Tak, the old airport, and is bounded on three sides by the Choi Hung Road.

"'Peach Blossom's main business was selling insurance to restaurants and jewelry shops and the like.'"

By which Wen meant the triad was a gang of extortionists.

Zhu continued with his translation, "'Pen's father was an honorable man who knew his limitations, and when he died, his son, Pen Kai-ge, this fellow here'"—Wen waved the photograph—"'became dragon head. He is young and full of energy, and I understand that a gem is not polished without friction, but there has been too much friction, and Pen does not appear to be gaining a polish.'"

Shao Long pointed to my portion of the abalone, which was missing only the smallest bite allowed by protocol. I slid my plate over to him. He dug into it.

"'Pen has caused unneeded deaths and the loss of a great deal of goodwill that our brotherhoods have patiently built over the years. My attempts to give advice to Pen have been arrogantly turned aside. He struts around San Po Kong, preening and showing off, acting the fool, bringing discredit on all our societies, and causing the police to look more closely at all of us.'"

The red pole said, "Pen is causing much instability."

Wen took several bites of rice. "'I had hoped for better from Pen.'"

Shao grunted, then said in Cantonese, followed by his own English translation, "You cannot find ivory in a dog's mouth."

"Is there something I can do?" I asked.

"'There is,'" Zhu translated. "'A small thing that will cause you only the slightest of inconveniences.'"

"What is it?"

Zhu translated my question, then rendered his uncle's answer into English, "'You can help me kill him.'"

*   *   *

One problem we folks of Anglo-Saxon stock suffer in Hong Kong is maintaining a grip on reality. The place was once called *the white man's graveyard* because of smallpox, cholera, malaria, dysentery, and dengue fever. Now the drinking water is safe, but pigment-challenged people like me still suffer.

I have not habituated to Hong Kong, not in the ten years I've been here. I tell this to Jay Lee, and he replies that the answer is easy: I'm a wimp. I'll be walking along a street in Wan Chai, and see some fellow carrying a pig in a conical wire basket, and it'll still bring me to a dead stop. Same with coming upon a woman skinning a snake. Same with watching a dentist pull a tooth from his patient who sits on a folding chair on the sidewalk. The senses are bombarded in Hong Kong. The neon canyons, the sharp clack of mah-jongg tiles, the constant stream of pedestrian traffic, the steamy heat alternating with the meat-locker cold inside the offices and department stores, the incessant loud chattering of the citizens, it is all endless and draining. Jay says that he is sure he would feel the same way—utterly foreign and overwhelmed by stimulus—were he to stand in a pear orchard in Medford.

Places of magical serenity exist in Hong Kong, but they must be searched out. As a matter of self-defense against the city, I needed to visit one of them every four or five days, and this time I invited Anne along. We took the MTR to the Sham Shui Po station, then caught a taxi to the Kowloon reservoirs. We left the taxi and began walking, the road soon narrowing to a shoulder-width track. Monkeys—long-tailed macaques, I think—screeched in the trees. I had insisted to Darrel Reese that our phalanx of guards drop off at the trail head, and he had agreed, providing I was armed, so I carried a pistol on my ankle. It was a Beretta Minx, a .22 semiautomatic, the classic assassin's weapon, and worthless in most other situations. Still, it was light and easy to conceal.

As Anne and I walked along, I asked, "Do you hear the dragon roaring?"

The noise was a low, gurgling rumble coming from a canyon. Nothing was visible but woods, mostly red pine and slash pine.

She cocked an ear. "I only hear the monkeys."

"Listen more closely."

"I hear it now, sort of a growl. I wish it were a real dragon. What is it?"

"Parents tell their kids it's a dragon, and it's the highlight of their stroll. But it's a water-pumping station over in those trees."

Anne walked with her arms crossed in front of her as if she were chilled. A butterfly called an orange-red shirt flew alongside us for a few seconds, and a crested mynah with a shrill whoop was perched in a tree above us.

"You don't look so good," I said.

She laughed bitterly. "I look better than I feel."

Pouches under her eyes were new, and were a light shade of purple-green. Her cheekbones were more pronounced, and tendons on the back of her hands stood out. She had lost weight.

"Not holding up too well?" I asked.

"I dropped a bottle of water this morning, my hands were shaking so badly. I'm thinking of seeing a doctor. Maybe he could prescribe something, a pill or something."

We walked along the dirt path. Elephant ears and horsetails grew on the sides of the trail. A flying squirrel the size of a cat peered down at us from a camphor tree.

Anne ran her hands along her temples as if trying to contain her thoughts. "Yesterday, I booked a flight home to San Diego. I was going to march into John Llewellyn's office and quit, and leave him and his tower to their fates, and then take the train out to Chek Lap Kok and fly out of here. Back to Mom and Dad and my room."

"Did you quit?"

She shook her head. "I decided it would be cowardly to run away like that, tail between my legs. So I canceled the reservation."

We walked between rows of lacy ferns. On the dusty path were claw prints of a bird, maybe a moorhen.

Anne said, "I haven't had any sleep in three days, and I can't keep food down. I have such a bellyache all the time, I'm thinking of going to that barefoot doctor and have him treat me with moxa cones." She tried a little laugh, but it died in her throat.

"How're you tolerating the guards?" I asked.

"The fellows outside my door, I've gotten so I hardly see them. But the lady who sits in my living room with an automatic shotgun is harder to ignore. She is pleasant, and smiles, and will chat a moment or two, but mostly she stares at the door and frowns whenever she hears something on her two-way radio, which is plugged into her ear."

"I kicked my guard out of my apartment," I said. "I told him he can do his sitting and watching somewhere else. These folks who are watching over us? I'm under the impression they are plenty tough."

Ahead of us were several small tunnels in the steep mountainside. The tunnels are named after British railway stations, King's Cross and Charing Cross and others. They were dug into the hill by the British army as it prepared to meet the Japanese invasion. The Japanese took all of two days to roust the defenders from the tunnels.

"Your friend Darrel Reese visited me, did he tell you?" Anne asked.

"I figured he would."

"He told me he wanted me to 'keep it under my hat,' that's the term he used. He doesn't want me talking about the Gold Swan's tilt to anyone. Why, do you think?"

"I'm not sure. The CIA is up to something, but that's in their job description, being up to something. We might never know what it is."

"Are you following this Darrel Reese's orders, not telling anyone about it?"

"It's not just him. When I met with him, the CIA's deputy director of operations was in the room. So the tower is being looked at by some serious and high-ranking people. Yeah, I'm going to be quiet about it. The Ministry of State Security doesn't know that, though, and that's why they came for me."

We walked along. Anne rubbed her hands together to warm them. The air was almost viscous, like in a hothouse, yet she was cold.

She asked, "You know what I lay awake thinking about last night?"

I shook my head.

"I was curled up in a protective ball, the blanket pulled up to my chin, wondering how I was going to finesse this on my résumé. I mean, I can't just put down 'Anne Iverson, project manager of the millennium's greatest architectural disaster.' How would that look? How many doors will that open?"

"The tower isn't a disaster yet. It's got a tiny bit of a lean to it, is all." I had heard that the work being done in the tower's elevator lobby was an attempt to underpin the foundation. I hadn't been able to learn any more than that one word, *underpin*.

She said, "I suppose I could just leave the last four years blank on my résumé. And if an employer asks about them, I'll make up something, maybe that I was in prison, which would look better than what I actually did."

"Anne, you are making assumptions about the tower's future that aren't warranted yet."

"Maybe I'll teach, find a small college somewhere. They won't hire me to teach anything about architecture or engineering or project management, but maybe something more simple. I'll teach needlepoint at a community college."

I laughed. "This is an amazing skein of self-pity."

"What if my name becomes a noun? What if in future years, buildings that sink and tilt on their foundations are called *iversons*. 'I paid good money for this house, but it turns out I bought an iverson.'"

"Lack of sleep has addled you, Anne."

"Two hundred years from now, lists will be made of the ten women who caused the most damage to society in history. Sort of a top-ten list. Let's see,"—she held up her fingers to count them off—"there'll be Typhoid Mary and Mao's widow and Ma Barker and Anne Iverson. Who else, do you think?"

I couldn't help but laugh again.

"They'll make rhymes of my name, like they did with Lizzie Borden, who took an ax and gave her mother forty whacks."

"For Pete's sake . . ."

"I lay there last night trying to think of what rhymes with Iverson.

Tilt doesn't. *Collapse* doesn't. *A disaster unprecedented in the annals of architecture* doesn't. *A billion dollars down the toilet* doesn't."

"*Worsen* rhymes with *Iverson*, sort of."

She looked at me with a measure of disgust. We followed a sign toward Smuggler's Ridge, climbing a steep hill, and winding around in the trees. We were both breathing deeply. The back of my shirt was wet.

Anne said, "John and I got together last night."

"How's he doing?"

"It's strange. He has two personalities. While I was there, over at his place, he was interviewed over the phone by the BBC, and he chatted away, laughing and being his usual witty self. He was charming and delightful, even charismatic, a real salesman for the tower. Then when he hung up the phone, the life went out of him. He sat there on the davenport, his eyes on the far wall, and he didn't say anything for an hour."

"Sounds like it was a fun date," I said.

"He didn't move a muscle. He might not have even blinked. Just sat there in a stupor. I had gone over to his home to get some moral support and ended up mostly trying to give it to him instead."

We topped the ridge, and the view opened to us. Below was Kwai Chung, the terminal and industrial area. Across Rambler Channel was Tsing Yi Island, connected to the mainland by the railway to the new airport. In the distance Lantau Island was partly obscured by haze. We found a rocky knoll where we could watch the freighters pass by below. I leaned back against a clump of grass and Anne joined me, her arms and legs not quite touching mine.

"I just wish I could sleep," she said, yawning. "Maybe this exercise—tramping around these hills with you—will do it."

We sat there awhile, not saying anything, me wanting to ask her where she was going after she left the tower and Hong Kong but not knowing how to bring it up in a disinterested way.

She folded her arms across her lap. "This is nice up here. I never knew about this place."

I let the sun warm my face.

"I can't see the Gold Swan from here," Anne said. "It seems far away, farther away than it's been in four years. Thank you for bringing me here."

"Did you ever get John to talk last night?"

She sounded drowsy. I glanced sideways. Her eyes were closed.

She said, "Yes, but only a few words."

"What'd you and he talk about?" I asked. "The tower? I mean, what's his latest spin?"

"He asked me to marry him."

My stomach suddenly soured, and my breath stopped in my throat. I was about to protest, but cut it off without a word. This reaction was absurd. I had no claim on Anne Iverson, never meant anything to her other than someone she could spend an hour or two with, a diversion. We enjoyed each other's company once in a while, is all. I might've wanted more from the relationship—I daydreamed a little about it, in fact—but me stepping forward to challenge her affection for the great John Llewellyn had seemed ridiculous. Why court that humiliation? So I took what I could get, lunches now and then, and things like taking her to an opium den and on this mountain hike.

My eyes on the distant sea, I asked in a voice that was carefully indifferent, "So what was your answer when he asked you to marry him?"

She said nothing. A nearby bush warbler made its odd ticking. After a moment I turned to look at her. She was asleep.

Part Three

All architects want to live beyond their deaths.

PHILIP JOHNSON

16

Now a word about the dragon head's invitation to commit a murder. That evening I only nodded when Wen Quichin solicited my help to eliminate Peach Blossom's new leader. I had known a request of some sort was coming, the method of gangsters the world around being predictable. That I didn't indignantly refuse and then march from Wen's home was perhaps a mark of how much I had already been co-opted by the 88K. Crime scene investigators know that you can't touch an object without picking up or depositing evidence of the contact, and so it is with gangsters: you can't contact them without picking up a trace or leaving behind a trace. Perhaps it was more than a trace. I had told Wen that I needed to think about his proposal.

That same day I contacted Fred Allison, the FBI chief in Hong Kong, telling him of Wen's proposal. He consulted with Washington, D.C., while I waited, and then said, "The FBI has no position on the idea."

"What does that mean?" I asked.

I could somehow hear his smile over the telephone as he replied, "It's between you and God."

I wasn't about to murder anyone, of course, but I spoke with Jay Lee about Pen Kai-ge, Peach Blossom's dragon head, and he told me what he knew about Pen. Were I homicidally inclined, Pen Kai-ge would be a fine target.

"He's a slaver," Jay had said.

"There are slaves in Hong Kong?"

"In all but the name," he replied. "Peach Blossom has an arrangement with a Bangkok gang called Tak Fang, whereby Tak Fang collects young women from the slums of Bangkok—not women, really, but young teens—and promises them jobs and a place to stay in Hong Kong."

I grimaced.

"Yes, you know the routine. Tak Fang supplies the girls, and Peach Blossom places them in houses of prostitution, some in Hong Kong, but most in Shenzhen and the other boomtowns across the New Territories border. The girls are no more than slaves. This is a new venture for Peach Blossom, and Pen Kai-ge is the force behind it. His father would have had nothing to do with such a business."

We were having a beer in the Original Chicago Eatery on Hollywood Street, down the hill from our apartments, and so were two CIA agents who were looking after me. Another one was out on the sidewalk somewhere. Our beer mugs had been chilled in the freezer and were leaving circles of condensation on the bar. Darrel Reese hadn't asked for his Beretta back, and I was still wearing it around my ankle.

I said, "Wen Quichin told me that the Hong Kong police don't arrest him because he is an element of stability in the city."

Jay was wearing a blue blazer and a red tie. He sipped his beer. "There's some truth to that."

"How much truth?"

"If we were to put Wen into prison, another 88K member would rise to dragon head, and we don't know who that would be."

I said, "So the enemy you know is better than the enemy you don't know."

Jay nodded. "Wen is a ruthless killer, but he's a benign ruthless killer."

I reached for salted peanuts in a bowl on the bar.

Jay Lee continued, "But this Pen Kai-ge doesn't add anything to the city. We would take him out of the action—is that how you Americans say it?—if we could find him. He spends a lot of time in Shenzhen. He fashions himself a dragon head, but he's nothing but a pimp."

I ordered us another round. I don't think Jay Lee liked beer much, but he enjoyed the faux American ambience of the bar.

He added, "Anyone who would percolate up in Peach Blossom to replace Pen would be better than Pen."

We sat there for a moment, chewing peanuts. The stereo system was playing the Dave Mathews Band. A print of Marilyn Monroe standing over the sidewalk grate was on a wall. Rows of glasses hung from a wood fixture over the bar. We were the only customers in the place, not counting my guards, so the bartender occupied himself by wiping the bar again and again.

Jay said, "So if you are inquiring whether the Hong Kong police would object to Pen Kai-ge's demise, the unofficial answer is no."

"You are suggesting I help Wen kill the guy?" I asked.

He laughed. "Nothing of the sort. That would make you a murderer. Don't your churches and synagogues over in America teach you about that? And I would be obliged to arrest you." He purposely added a wistful tone to his words. "But it still doesn't prevent me from daydreaming about Pen Kai-ge's body being found in a car trunk someday."

Well, as I say, I leave justice to the proper authorities. I'm no vigilante. It didn't cross my mind to assist Wen Quichin. The old man hadn't told me what he had in mind, how he would use me in his plan. He just brought forth the idea and had given me time to ponder it, not that I was.

Jay said, "My sources say that a number of the younger soldiers in Peach Blossom would turn the triad's energies to other, more seemly, endeavors were Pen Kai-ge no longer the dragon head."

"You are saying that removing Pen would eliminate the trade in those young Thai women?"

"It would significantly reduce it. Nothing will eliminate it."

"You are encouraging me to help Wen."

He laughed. "I already said I wasn't."

"Sure you are."

"You are finding things in my words that aren't there," Jay said, sipping his beer. "The policy of my Organized Crime and Triad Bureau is that we bring criminals to justice, and we discourage citizens from taking the law into their own hands." He sounded sincere, reaching for another handful of peanuts. Then he added, "That's our stated policy, and no amount of interrogation would ever get me to admit there might be exceptions to the policy."

"There you go again," I exclaimed.

"What did I say?" he asked, all innocence.

"Pushing me on, inveigling me toward a life of crime."

"Where's your head been?" He smiled enigmatically. "I said nothing of the sort."

"I would never consider such a thing," I said righteously.

"Of course not. You are a law-abiding citizen of the first rank. America and all mankind can be proud of you."

Jay paid the tab and left a tip. It was his turn. We rose from our stools and made our way toward the door, the guards making ready to follow me. I was tired of them, always around and underfoot.

Jay pushed the door open. "Do you know anything about Confucius?"

"Wasn't he the Chinese Ping-Pong champ?"

He ignored my comment. "Confucius dreamed of a pure and just society."

"Yes?"

"And your Dr. Martin Luther King dreamed about a society of equality for everyone."

I followed him out onto the street. "He did, yes."

He said, "But my ambitions are more humble, and I only have one dream, and it is indeed modest."

"Yeah?"

"And that would be to find Pen Kai-ge's body in a car trunk someday."

* * *

The New Century Building on Lockhart Road, just inland from the Wan Chai Sports Ground, is a forty-story cube, undistinguished in all architectural aspects, and lost amid Hong Kong's other skyscrapers. It cannot be seen from the Peak or from the harbor, or from any other direction unless the viewer is standing on the streets just below it. The New Century is clad in sandstone-colored siding, and its windows are small circles, resembling a ship's portholes. I had passed the building hundreds of times during my stay in Hong Kong and still couldn't recall it when Anne Iverson informed me that it was our destination.

Over the years, fewer and fewer people worked in the New Century, replaced by more and more computers. The building had become Hong Kong's leading location for service farms, where floor after floor was rented by Internet service providers. Where real estate developers and shipping executives once worked, rows of computers sat in overly air-conditioned rooms, attended by a few technicians who, rather than white coats and hair nets, wore Nike workout jackets and baggy cargo pants.

A small rain had come and gone that evening, leaving the streets glistening, and now a thin moon was overhead as we walked into the New Century Building's lobby. A security agent at a desk looked up from his newspaper. Anne nodded at him, which was enough to return his attention to the paper. I had a flashlight in my pocket.

We had gotten rid of the bodyguards. At first the Ministry of State Security—though I can only guess who was behind it—suspected we knew about the problems with the Gold Swan and tried to stamp out the information by stamping us out. But now several days had passed, and the world still didn't know about the tower's lean, so perhaps they figured we didn't know anything about it, or for some reason weren't spreading the information around. I believed the ministry had called off any action against Anne and me. None of the guards had spotted anything untoward, and I was tired of having the guards around all the time, and so was Anne. Darrel said, "Suit yourself," but insisted on keeping guards at our apartments.

That night in the New Century's lobby, Anne said, "We'll see if this works," as she held a card in front of an electronic reader set on the wall between two elevators. "I've been to this place a couple of times for meetings about our intranet provider."

When the elevator button light came on, she nodded. "My access card hasn't been blocked. I'm surprised."

We rode the elevator to the fifteenth floor, then walked along a hallway that was darkened for the evening. We stopped in front of a glass door that looked in on a reception room. In the past this office hosted clients, as I could see a desk, several chairs, and a wicker basket that might have once held magazines. The reception room was lit only by light coming through the door from the hallway.

Anne ran her card across the lock's reader. Nothing happened.

"I've been blocked from entry," she said.

"I don't know how to pick locks, if that's what you're wondering," I said.

She pulled another card from her wallet. "I took John's card last night. Maybe he still has access. Let's see if this works."

She passed the card across the face of the reader, and the lock clicked open. We hurried inside, closing the door behind us. This was the location of the tower commission's service provider for its intranet, where architectural and engineering information was stored and exchanged. For security reasons the intranet was cut off from the Internet. This service farm was a stand-alone system that could not be hacked into by someone not connected to the tower's intranet.

We passed through the reception room into the back office, where two IBM AS400s were in the center of the room, each the size of a file cabinet. Along the sides of the room were three PCs. Cables and wires crossed the floor, making us place our feet carefully. Anne sat behind a monitor. She brought out a Zip drive disk from her purse and inserted it into a CPU. I rolled a chair over to sit next to her. The windows looked out onto the side of a higher building across the street. We left the lights off, so I pulled out the flashlight and aimed it at her keyboard.

"Tell me again who talked about the discrepancy," Anne said as she turned on the monitor.

"China's minister of construction, Duan Cho-li, testifying—that's the word because he was really being grilled—to President Chen and other Central Committee members. Duan said that discrepancies existed between compaction measurements submitted by the geotech during construction and those taken this past week, after the tower began to tilt."

"Well, the measurements are all in the AS400." She rubbed her forehead with several fingers, her eyes closed. "I'm rummy, Clay. I need some sleep."

"How long will this take?"

"Couple of minutes." She stared at the screen. "Here's the data. I'll copy it to the Zip drive." She entered several commands. The drive clicked.

I said, "Tell me how the island was filled."

Anne leaned back in the chair while the data was copied to the Zip drive. "An underwater wall was made of huge stones, the island's perimeter. Then split barges were used to bring in the fill. Split barges can open up their hulls on the bottom, releasing the entire load."

"And does the fill fall to the bottom of the bay . . . how, intact?"

She replied, "There's only a little separation of fine and coarse material. When the fill is dumped from a split barge, it lands in a fairly compacted form. But then when the fill gets to within ten feet of the surface, split barges don't work anymore, so fill is pumped in."

"How does that work?"

"A water-and-sand slurry mix is pushed through pipes from dredgers. You remember them, shooting big arcs of dredged-up mud onto the site."

"And does this fill—the slurry that is pumped from the dredge—land in a dense form? How could it?"

She rubbed her cheeks with both hands. "It doesn't. It's usually loose when it lands in place. It can't support a heavy structure until it is compacted."

"So the fill is compacted, right?" I asked. "It's pressed together to make it stronger."

"Compaction increases soil strength, which increases bearing capacity. It does some other stuff, too, such as reduce chances of liquefaction during an earthquake." She leaned forward to look at the screen. "This is a huge file, all those years of readings."

"And the fill is constantly tested for strength?"

She pulled out a tin of Altoids from her purse and put one into her mouth. I took one, too.

She said, "The geotechs on the island used several kinds of tests, such as a pressure meter, where a measuring cell inside a slotted tube is inserted into the ground. It's a self-boring device."

"What else is used?"

"A dilatometer is a flexible steel membrane that is placed along a blade. Inside the membrane is a pressure chamber and a distance gauge that measures movements of the membrane when pressure inside is altered. Hollow rods are used to press it into the soil. Seismic tests, using wave refraction, were also performed."

"And all of that data is gathered electronically . . ."

"All the equipment is computerized. The information is downloaded into the database as it is gathered, with no lag time."

I glanced over my shoulder. I could see through the interior doorway into the reception area, and then beyond that through the glass door into the hallway. I held the flashlight for her as she pressed several keys. Then she leaned back to wait for more of the download.

"And the soil stiffness and density tests are taken throughout the compaction, aren't they?"

"I didn't sleep at all last night for the third night in a row." She was wearing a striped hooded jacket over a red and yellow striped T-shirt, and white shorts. "I just tossed and turned. I got up this morning and took a shower and then put on my shoes without realizing I hadn't put on my slacks."

"How was the fill compacted?" I asked.

She squeezed the bridge of her nose. "Well, at first explosives were used, where the blast liquefies the soil, which reconsolidates because of the pressure."

"But that wasn't the only way. I remember the big tampers."

"Explosives are by far the cheapest way to compact soil. But the tower commission and John wanted favorable press, so as the fill got higher and higher, and more visible to Hong Kong citizens, explosives were deemed too worrisome. So the tampers were used."

Tamping is where a crane lifts a twenty-five-ton concrete block and drops it onto the fill from a height of seventy-five feet. The block is called a *pounder* or a *tamper*. The cranes travel across the fill in a predetermined grid pattern, lifting and dropping, lifting and dropping.

I asked, "The tampers had sensors on them, didn't they?"

"The sensors recorded the applied energy and the soil's dynamic response." She pointed to the computer monitor. "Those readings are all in here, too."

I glanced again at the hallway. We had not obtained clearance to be in this room. Off-site access to this data had been blocked, at least from any computer Anne and I could find. She had told me that normally this compaction data was freely available to engineers working on the island. Now it had been locked up.

"It's cold in here," she said as she replaced the full Zip disk with an empty one in the drive.

"And then the fill was given its final compaction with another method," I said. "The vibrators, I remember. Is that what they were?"

"The final compaction phase—called *ironing passes*—was done with lower compaction energy because the upper soil layers needed to be densified without remolding the already-compacted deeper layers. So vibration was used."

"They looked like pile drivers, as I recall."

"Caterpillar tractors carried vibrators on top of probes. The probes were pushed into the ground, and the vibration frequencies were tuned to the resonance frequencies of the dirt. Vibration energy was sent into the soil, and the dirt oscillated, causing compaction."

"And the vibrators had sensors, didn't they?"

She nodded. "They recorded probe depth, vibrator frequency, fill vibration velocities, and other parameters." She tapped the keyboard. "All those measurements are in here, too."

"We need more than the raw measurements," I said. "We need the application software, too, the program that turned all the readings into graphs and charts and whatever."

"I've already got it on the first Zip disk. It's called GeoPlace 3.1."

At that instant the beam of a powerful flashlight caught me right in the face. A voice barked, "You are under arrest. Put your hands in the air where I can see them." The guard was pointing a pistol at us.

We rose from our chairs. Anne grimaced, and glanced at me. The guard brought up his two-way radio, about to call down to the lobby for assistance.

I said, "Let me reach for my identification. It's in my wallet."

The guard's eyes narrowed. The business end of his pistol was pointed at my nose. He nodded.

I lifted my wallet from my back pocket. "There's more than one way to resolve a problem."

His flashlight beam was squarely on my face.

I pulled out a wad of U.S. hundred-dollar bills, five thousand dollars in all. The flashlight beam settled on the currency. I said, "My friend and I need another thirty minutes in this room. We won't take anything with us when we leave. No one else will ever know we were here." I held out the money.

Perhaps the guard was accustomed to such deals, because he didn't hesitate for an instant. Without a word, he took the money and left the office, returning down the hall to the elevator and slipping his flashlight into his belt.

Anne and I worked for another twenty minutes and then left the room as we found it, returning to the elevators. I wasn't quite accurate when I had told the guard we wouldn't take anything. We were taking data. When Anne and I left the building, we were carrying several Zip discs, the ones we had brought with us. The information on those discs would answer many questions.

* * *

Hong Kong is frenetic even on normal days. The city is a narcotic buzz, a mad dash of activity from morning to night, and then all through the night. It never subsides, this relentless bustle and commotion. I would have thought that Hong Kong's dial was set to maximum, that not one more human endeavor or ambition or plan could be fit into the city. It was spilling over with energy and effort. But that's not how the Fifth Millennium China Tower Inaugural Planning Commission viewed it.

The opening ceremony had been conceived as a gala six-hour event, but as the tower's inauguration drew near, the ceremony had evolved into a seven-day blowout, an extravaganza that was to be unrivaled in opulence, enormity, and, some said, tackiness.

The Inaugural Planning Commission viewed it as their civic duty to outshine the upcoming Beijing Olympics ceremonies. They were in a duel, they knew: Hong Kong versus Beijing. The Hong Kong planners wanted to put together an event that Beijing simply could not top. The inauguration planners were gripped by a passion—increasing in fervor by the day, it seemed—to set a mark for extravaganzas that could never be bested, and certainly not by their backward cousins in Beijing. On the wall in their office in the Bank of China Tower was a six-by-eight print of the one hundred white grand pianos of the Los Angeles Olympics's opening ceremony. Now *that* was an extravaganza.

One event after another was announced, each more grand—and some said bizarre—than the last. Preparation and rehearsals for these events intensified as opening day drew near, and were making the always-hectic city bubble and churn with activity.

Every day five thousand synchronized swimmers rehearsed in Victoria Harbor, their movements precisely timed to Gershwin's *Rhapsody in Blue* played over loudspeakers on a nearby tender. On the morning of the swimmers' performance the song would be simultaneously played on every radio and television station in the city.

In a surprising move, given the reminder of the city's colonial past, the four hundred pipers and drummers of the Edinburgh Military Tattoo had arrived in the city, and were practicing at the Happy Valley Sports Ground. They would be the lead unit in the Grand Tower Parade. Forty professional float designers—all with Rose Bowl Parade credentials—had been flown to Hong Kong, and with two thousand assistants hired from Hong Kong's florist industry, were rapidly constructing the nine floats that would anchor the parade. Louisiana State University's Golden Band from Tiger Land was headed for the city, as were the six hundred members of the Beijing Ribbon Marchers, the two-hundred-member Harlem High-Steppers, the four-hundred-member Canton Drill Team, and fifty other units from around the world. PLA General Phan Gap had wanted to have a Red Army division in the parade—nine thousand soldiers marching in columns, followed by mobile rocket batteries, howitzers, and tanks—but his request had been turned down.

Orrefors Crystal had been commissioned to design and construct the Tower Ball, a crystal globe, twenty-five feet in diameter, lit from within, that would slowly ascend the exterior of the Hong Kong Convention and Exhibition Center, where as it reached the roof, the globe's interior lights would blaze, marking the official moment the tower was open. Ceremony officials had first wanted the ball to rise the entire 2,500-foot height of the tower, on a line between the base and the viewing platform, but John Llewellyn had successfully argued that such a sight would detract from the tower's architectural integrity at the very instant it was being officially presented to the world.

Temporary grandstands were being constructed along the Hong Kong and Kowloon shores, and an ingenious and massive card display would send colors and patterns and words scrolling along both shorelines, thousands and thousands of Hong Kong citizens holding up colored cards with precise choreography.

The Central Committee had declared that the tower's opening day would be a holiday, not just for Hong Kong but for all of China, an unprecedented gesture not seen since Mao's death. A new national order had also been announced, the Order of the Tower, and it was to be awarded to the twenty most senior tower executives—both Chinese and foreign—to Hong Kong's chief executive, and to the president and other members of the Central Committee, and thirty others involved in the tower, both in Beijing and Hong Kong. The order's medal was a brass circle on which was stamped a tiny replica of the tower, and which would be hung from a red ribbon. For everyone else one million commemorative coins had been produced with the tower stamped on them. The coins were numbered and would be handed out only on opening day. Already an unofficial futures market in these coins had begun, with prices rising, even though the coins were still in storage.

Five million tiny red flags had been ordered, so every citizen could wave the emblem of Hong Kong's new sovereign, the People's Republic of China. Flower baskets had been hung from every lamppost within three blocks of the Hong Kong and Kowloon shorelines. A Jackie Chan film festival would run the week prior to the opening. Ice-making machines had been brought in from Australia and the United States, and two hundred shaved-ice stands would dot the city, offering free flavored cones.

Two days before the opening, the Grand Aviary Assembly would take place in Victoria Park, and anyone with a caged bird could attend. An estimated hundred thousand birds were expected. The Red Messengers—the Chinese air force's aerobatic team, was in Hong Kong, rattling the buildings with jet engine noise as they swooped across the harbor and soared into the sky, practicing their barrel rolls and maple leafs.

The largest balloon launch in history was planned, with two million red balloons to be sent skyward. Four hundred people would spend ten hours the prior day inflating the balloons, four a minute; it was all worked out. Five hundred parachutists would drop into Victoria Park. A new song had been commissioned, *Bend Me to the Socialist Future*, which was being learned by the Hong Kong orchestra, though the concert master and the percussion section had quit in protest. The Fifty-Year Candy Company of Canton was instructed to create a new Tower Chocolate Bar, and they promptly copied the Baby Ruth, even calling it the Baby Tower. The Asian Tai Chi Federation approved the first new position in forty years, the Gold Swan, where the arms reached skyward in a graceful arc, and the legs were elegantly bent to continue the arc down to the ground. Carlos Santana was booked to play China's national anthem, *March of the Volunteers.*

Tower-watching had become a citywide mania, particularly watching the sun's first morning rays reflect off the tower's giant curve. The mania grew and grew, and as inauguration week drew near, hundreds of thousands of Hong Kong citizens woke up early each morning to walk to the shoreline or to a favored viewing point to observe the sun first touch the Gold Swan.

Not everything planned for the festivities was celebratory. I've mentioned the arrests that were occurring. There wouldn't be a pickpocket or mugger in the entire city by the time the police were done. And as the inauguration neared, police action was increased even more. Over six hundred members of Falun Gong were arrested in a massive midnight operation. They were not allowed to communicate with anyone, and no one but the police knew their fate. Residences of a two-block area in the Sham Shui neighborhood, notorious for open drug trafficking, were given five days to clean up their neighborhood, and when they failed, wrecking balls and bulldozers went to work, leveling the fourteen buildings on those blocks.

The Ministry of State Security reinforced its message to the press that utterly no negative or even questioning comments about the tower would be tolerated. A news broadcaster for television station HKJ mentioned the "curious" construction at the base of the Fifth Millennium China Tower during a dinnertime broadcast. He said nothing critical, and only used that one word, "curious," but it was enough. Within two hours HKJ was off the air. The station's news set was dismantled and its studio cameras seized. The announcer, the station manager, and the news director were arrested. The lesson was learned quickly. Not another inquiring word was heard from any media outlet.

Most Hong Kong citizens viewed these police matters as inconsequential. The tower's inauguration was going to be a joyous celebration that hundreds of thousands of residents would take part in. It would be a mammoth, historic, giddy event, and the people of Hong

Kong were in a fever of anticipation. The recent, unplanned construction activity on the tower's island and a few arrests hadn't dampened their enthusiasm in the slightest. Not yet, anyway.

* * *

I had begun to feel safe again, what with the CIA and my own personal giant following me around. But I had overestimated their ability to protect me.

Anne and I had left the New Century Building—Anne carrying the discs of compaction data—and I had dropped her off at her apartment and had returned to my building. As I inserted my key into my door lock, I didn't notice the drops of blood that had soaked into the hallway rug.

I pushed open the door, stepped into the living room, and found a body on the living room floor, splayed out in a position unattainable by the living. The body had two bullet holes in the chest. The carpet had wicked away blood from exit wounds. I gulped air. In the FBI, I had seen plenty of corpses, but I never got used to it. Holding my hand in front of my mouth, I hastily looked around my apartment but found nothing else out of line, so I returned to the living room.

I didn't recognize the dead person, who wore an expression of astonishment, with his eyes and mouth wide open. He was an Anglo, and had been wearing a baseball cap, which was on the floor next to the pool of blood. His jacket was open, and I could see a shoulder holster, the pistol still in the leather. I would learn later that this was the CIA's Will Jeffers, the fellow who had won the silver medal in judo at the Sydney Olympics. He had been guarding me, and now he was dead. He had probably been shot outside my door in the hallway—there were drops of blood out there—then dragged into my room. I would also learn later that the killer's weapon had been silenced, as none of my neighbors had heard anything. My CIA guards had had keys to my apartment, an arrangement I had agreed to.

I picked up the phone to call Darrel Reese. He wouldn't like my news at all.

17

Not all of Hong Kong's triads were equal in power and wealth, which was obvious to me upon stepping into Peach Blossom's grand triangle, as they called their clubhouse. The first story of the concrete building was a metal stamping plant, and half of the second floor was occupied by a rattan furniture manufacturer. Jay Lee had told me that Peach Blossom moved into the other half of the second floor several years ago, and no one had dared to ask them to leave. The triad didn't pay rent.

I had walked here from the ferry terminal. If I'm working at it, I can detect when someone is following me, a skill learned in the FBI. It takes three times as long to go anywhere, but it's almost foolproof, with all the stopping, changing directions, and looking back. No one had followed me, I was sure, but I was still nervous.

I was escorted from the street up the stairs, and before entering the clubroom I had been roughly frisked by my escorts, two men in their early twenties who apparently thought sneers were part of the Peach Blossom uniform, along with their T-shirts, jeans, and sandals.

My escorts led me along a hallway, passing two doors, then into a backroom. Peach Blossom's dragon head, Pen Kai-ge, was sitting at a small desk, studying several photographs, a cigarette between his fingers. He didn't look up for a moment, studying the snapshots and exhaling gray smoke. The escorts remained by the door, watching me. Pen's hair was parted in the middle of his head and combed to the sides, and it gleamed with pomade. His eyes were small and belligerent. He had an undershot jaw and ears that stood out like flaps. He stared intently at the photos, arranging them on his desk.

Pen finally deigned to look up. He spoke in English. "The last 88K emissary sent to me, I cut with a razor blade. Cut him all up. You can see the bloodstains over there on the floor."

Wen hadn't mentioned this. This situation demanded that I not glance at the spot on the floor, but I couldn't help it. I didn't see any dark stain. Wen had told me Pen Kai-ge was a boastful liar, and I earnestly hoped he was lying about the razor blade.

The dragon head leaned back in his chair. "Why has the old man sent a *gweilo?*"

"Wen and I have built a relationship of trust," I replied. "And Wen does not want his soldiers knowing of this approach to you, so he has sent me, an outsider. He wants to come to an agreement with you before word of it spreads to the 88K."

I could lie as well as Pen. Wen had told me this response would be adequate to the inevitable question of why a round-eye would represent the 88K. The true reason that I was being sent to the Peach Blossom leader—one I tried not to take offense at—was that Pen would lower his guard around me. "*Gweilos* aren't as cunning," Wen had explained.

Pen motioned toward a metal folding chair near his desk. The room hadn't been swept in months. An air conditioner rattled in the window frame. A blanket had been hammered over the other window, and the room was lit by an overhead bulb and a lamp on Pen's desk. An empty coatrack was in a corner. Cardboard boxes were along one wall. I couldn't see what was in them. A laugh came from the next room. Flies circled the room, and the place smelled of malt. A small brewery was down the block. Nothing in the room identified it as Peach Blossom's meeting place.

"You are here to try to push me away from my new business," Pen announced.

I shook my head slightly.

"Old Man Wen would do better to think about his own affairs, and not mine."

"I'm only here to extend an invitation to you."

"And all he will talk about are my young ladies. He doesn't like my business and cannot understand that it is just that: my business, not his. That old man does not realize that times are changing for our societies, and that we must adapt."

"I am here only to relay his invitation to meet with him. I'm not here to argue with you, or to relay anything you say back to him. You can save yourself the trouble of trying to convince me of anything."

The gangster's eyebrows lowered. "The old man is senile, I've heard."

"Nor am I here to listen to you insult my friend Wen. The invitation is to his granddaughter's wedding, where your safety will be assured."

Pen's cigarette had burned down to his fingers, and now he stabbed it out on the desk, then brushed the butt aside, and it landed on the floor. He leaned back in his chair, staring at me.

He said, "Let me show you what is troubling Wen Quichin." He switched to Cantonese, giving my two escorts an order, I presumed. He went back to English. "The last time I spoke with Wen, he called me an overripe melon." Pen laughed disagreeably.

Wen had told me that Pen Kai-ge had inherited the title dragon head when his father had died, but that the secret societies were not dynasties, where authority was automatically passed to the oldest offspring upon the death of the father, but this often occurred temporarily until new lines of authority could be established, which is what happened when Pen's father had died. Pen had assumed control, but his soldiers were restive with his leadership, both Wen Quichin and Jay Lee had told me. Pen did not have his father's experience or charisma and did not possess the web of obligations upon which triad loyalties were built. Pen was impetuous and arrogant. His confidence in his own ability was pronounced but misplaced, and he had no appreciation of his own manifest limitations. He appeared unwilling to learn. Wen had said that Pen's fall was inevitable, that Peach Blossom's members would not long tolerate inept leadership. "But we cannot wait," Wen had said. "The young fool is tempting the dragon."

One of my escorts pushed a young lady into the room, right up to

Pen's desk. She stood there meekly, her eyes on the floor and her hands knotted in front of her. She was wearing a shabby print wraparound and a yellow blouse that was missing its two top buttons. Her feet were bare. She was without ornaments of any kind, no rings or bracelets, no necklace, though I could see small punctures in her earlobes where she had once worn earrings. Her hair hung to her shoulders and was filthy and matted. Despite her disheveled appearance, she was an attractive girl, with large brown eyes, pronounced cheekbones, and full lips. The skin under one eye had been blackened.

Pen gestured expansively. "What do you think? She is fourteen years old, and is first-grade prime. We will turn her into a working girl."

"Where did she come from?" I asked.

"Bangkok, just yesterday. She has a few things to learn, obedience for one. But she will be a quick study."

The girl braved a look at me. Perhaps the word *Bangkok* had prompted it. She probably spoke neither English nor Cantonese. Her expression was of bafflement and meekness, but also in the quick flash of her glance, defiance. She was a young Thai, an innocent, hardly yet a teenager. She had been kidnapped, undoubtedly on a street near her home, then smuggled into Hong Kong, and within a few days she would be a Hong Kong prostitute. This was the Peach Blossom's new business that so rankled Wen Quichin.

"What's her name?" I asked.

"We never have a reason to ask. She will be called Full Cup, a name that suits her."

"How much for the girl?" I asked abruptly.

Pen Kai-ge stared at me, then laughed loudly, slapping the desk, rudely pointing at me, then hitting the desk again. "You Yankees live up to your reputation." His laugh trailed off, then he stroked his chin, apparently deep in thought, his eyes glittering. He lit a new cigarette. "I must charge a premium, as it will be her first time."

I stood up. "I'm talking about . . . her entire service contract."

"Her service contract?"

"I want to purchase her from you. I'll take her with me right now."

He grinned meanly, the cigarette hanging from his lips. "You have been struck by this girl's freshness and beauty, those same qualities that will make me a fortune."

"I'm taking her with me," I insisted. "Name the price."

"She is not for sale. We went to too much trouble to find her and bring her here."

"Of course she is for sale," I said. "That's the nature of your business, you being a pimp. Whether I purchase her in thirty-minute installments or all at once should be of no concern to you."

Pen stared at me, the abacus working in his head. Then he eyed her again, still calculating. "Look at her. She has many curves, wouldn't you say? Many tempting curves."

The girl was as thin as a bed slat.

"And I would of course have to charge extra because she is pure and fresh," he said.

"How much?"

He hesitated, his eyes back on me, trying to measure my wallet. Then he announced, "For fifty thousand U.S. dollars, you can take her with you."

I pulled my checkbook from my back pocket and filled in the numbers, hesitating only a fraction at all the zeros after the five. Let me say that when my father sold his pear orchards—seven thousand acres around Medford, as I mentioned—he became a wealthy man, and when my father died, I became a wealthy man. I would telephone my bank later in the day to transfer funds to cover this check. I slid the check onto Pen's desk.

I stood and held my hand out to the girl. She stared at the floor, not seeing it. She came up only to my shoulders. I gently touched her arm, and only then did she look up, her eyes fearful. I tried a smile, but she flinched as if I were about to strike her.

I said, "Come with me. I'll get you home."

She didn't understand a word of it, but perhaps something in my tone offered a glimpse of hope. Moving silently, she followed me to the door.

I turned back. "Wen Quichin will meet you at his granddaughter's wedding at his home at ten o'clock Saturday morning. There will be a large crowd there, and you will be safe. Don't bring any of your soldiers with you. Do you understand?"

He didn't like my imperious tone, I could tell by his scowl, but I wasn't feeling civil, not toward a pimp and a slaver. When Wen had asked me to help kill Pen Kai-ge, I had listened to his proposal, knowing I would never do such a thing, as I've said, but after meeting Pen the Pimp, and seeing his victim, this girl from Bangkok, my resolve against vigilantism was weakening. The world would be well rid of Pen Kai-ge.

This wasn't assisting in a murder. I was simply setting up a meeting. I didn't mind negotiating on Wen's behalf. I felt like I owed the old guy, felt like I was in his debt, though I'm not sure how that sentiment had come to be. He was in my debt, if anything. He was a likable old guy. Maybe that had something to do with it.

I reached again for the Thai girl's hand. Pen had lifted my fifty-thousand-dollar check to study it. He was clucking to himself with pleasure.

The girl let me lead her out of the room, along the hallway, down the stairs and then out onto the sidewalk. I headed for the Star Ferry, and for the American consulate. They would have an interpreter who would find out this girl's name and Bangkok address. Then I would contact Darrel Reese, and as a service to me he would obtain a temporary passport and visa for the girl, and would do so within a few hours.

And then I would take her out to Chek Lap Kok airport, buy her a ticket, and give her cab fare for when she arrived in Bangkok. She would be home with her parents before nightfall.

*   *   *

The 20th Floor Physics Club was working on a new scientific device, Soong Chan had told me, and he and Hsu Shui-ban wanted to show it off, so they appeared at my apartment, both grinning with excitement. Hsu carried a cardboard box. A bodyguard had followed Hsu the few steps from his apartment to mine. He was never without them, all of them 88K soldiers. His grandfather wasn't about to lose him again. The guard was posted outside my door.

Soong Chan was also carrying a cardboard box. Loose wires were visible at the top of it.

"What's in the boxes?" I asked, handing the boys bowls of microwave popcorn.

"You won't believe it," Hsu exulted. "Grandfather Wen bought it for me. He has suddenly become a softie."

But first they had to scope out my place. They both admired my bayonet, asking permission before removing the blade from the leather scabbard. Hsu asked if I had ever used it on anyone, and I had to admit I hadn't. They only glanced at the terrarium, a common item in Hong Kong homes. Will Jeffers's blood could not be adequately cleaned from the carpet, so I had had it replaced.

"My orthodontist says I shouldn't eat popcorn, but he doesn't know everything," Soong Chan said, still looking around. "Someday I'm going to get an apartment like this. You should see my room at my parents'. It doesn't even have a TV."

I took out cans of Coke from the refrigerator, then we gathered around the coffee table in front of the sofa. I could tell that my apartment—as plain and as functional as it was—was leaving a deep impression. This was how a man lived. Television set, stereo, couple of chairs, bookcase. Microwave popcorn anytime he wanted it. Stay up late. No parents. No worries.

Hsu was wearing black baggy workout pants with ADIDAS printed in huge red letters along a leg. He announced, "The 20th Floor Physics Club is building a seismograph."

"No kidding?" I caught myself rubbing my hands together. "I built one when I was your age. I don't know anything about laser rangefinders, but seismographs are my specialty."

"You know about seismographs?" Soong Chan voice was filled with doubt. "The device that measures earthquakes?"

I admit to being delighted at the prospect of helping them build a seismograph. By comparison to these high-tech teens' lives, my teen years—with my balloon-tired Schwinn and my two-knob radio—

were primitive. These two lads were the cutting edge of the species. They could speak English in scientific jargon so thick that I might as well have been listening to Cantonese. But with seismographs, I could contribute. I was, after all, an honorary member of the 20th Floor Physics Club, and a contribution was called for.

I said, "Back when I was in high school, I took some two-by-fours and a couple of dowels, and made a base and stand, and then I used two bricks for weight. This was my frame."

The boys looked skeptically at each other.

"A pencil was taped to a rod that hung from the frame over the tin can, and the rod wiggled side to side when the ground moved. A tin can with adding-machine paper wrapped around it was the recorder. I'd rotate the can with a wood handle made out of Popsicle sticks." I laughed. "We never had an earthquake in Medford, but I would take my seismograph to the road near the house. Passing trucks made the rod tremble."

Hsu said, "Well, we aren't really . . ."

"There's a craft room on the second floor," I said. "We can go down there and get a start on it. I'm pretty fair with a hammer and drill, I don't mind saying."

"That's not exactly what we had in mind, Mr. Williams." Hsu reached into the box to pull out a green plastic electronic thingy. He held it up.

"What's that?" I asked.

"It's a CMG-3T sensor with a USNSN circular electronic board, and a sixty-four–bit dynamic range digitalizer module."

"His grandfather Wen got it for us," Soong Chan added, then laughed. "Shui-ban told me not to ask his grandfather where he got it."

"Now we need to obtain a Guralp sensor and a couple of other components, and the seismograph will be complete," Hsu said. "Grandfather said he'd help."

"It'll all be compatible with our PCs," Soong said. "We'll be able to download our information from the seismograph to our computers."

Feeling as useful as a slide rule, I stood up. "You fellows want more popcorn?"

"We were wondering if we could use your TV set," Hsu said.

"Sure. Feel free. I'm going to do some paperwork at the dining table."

Soong Chan pulled out a Nintendo from the box he had brought with him. He was wearing a Hooters T-shirt. Hsu reached for the two control pads.

"You guys are welcome here," I said, "but don't you both have TVs at home that you can play Nintendo on?"

"We've got a new game, and we want to play it," Hsu said.

"Your folks won't let you play the game?"

They looked at each other and apparently decided that honesty was the best route. They shook their heads.

Hsu said, "My mom took one look at the game's cover and tossed it out into the hallway and told me not to bring it back."

"What's the game called?" I asked.

"Slasher Madness," Soong answered around a mouthful of popcorn.

Hsu said, "It's about this guy who walks around this city, and he's carrying this four-foot-long blade, and he—"

"Guys, don't you have a game you can play, where your parents won't come over here and personally kill me dead if they find out I let you play it on my TV set?"

Disappointment was writ profoundly on their faces. Finally, Hsu pulled out another cartridge from the cardboard box. "We can play this." He held it up in two fingers, as if it were tissue about to be discarded.

"Might as well play Bambi Meets Barbie," Soong complained.

They made their way over to my TV and VCR to plug in the Nintendo and the control pads. The TV came on, and they bent over their control pads. The boys had apparently decided that my apartment was the 20th Floor Physics Club's new clubhouse.

Since my wife left me, I have slipped into a few bachelor ways, most of them small things, such as wiping my hands on my socks rather than getting up and crossing the room for a napkin. I wear new socks every day, so what's the problem? Another is that I make a huge pot of chili every Saturday, and eat it as the urge strikes me throughout the week. I make real chili, with boneless pork steak, jalapeño peppers, onions, garlic, tomatoes, and a dozen spices, and then I cook it long and slow. I got the recipe from Hubie Delmonica, owner of Delmonica's on Scott Street in Wichita Falls, Texas, and he told me the recipe was the most valuable thing he owned, and I've treated it with due respect since. The pot had been cooking most of the day, and I had stepped to the kitchen to sample it when the doorbell rang.

I crossed the living room to look through the peephole. Anne Iverson was standing there. I opened the door. Also in the hallway were two of Hsu Shui-ban's bodyguards, who nodded at me. Anne smiled shyly and stepped into my apartment. I closed and locked the door.

The boys were playing their game, and the living room was filled with shrieks of doom and massive explosions, so Anne and I went into my tiny kitchen, where we could still hear the game but at least couldn't see the television. Concentrating, Hsu and Soong didn't look up from the television. She pulled up a stool and leaned against the refrigerator while I hung over the stove, stirring the mix with a wood spoon.

Anne was wearing a charcoal Irish linen jacket with tiny checks woven into it, and matching pants. A white T-shirt with a squared neck was under the jacket. Her hair was pulled back into a French braid. Her face was clouded, with her mouth turned down and her eyes remote.

I bent over to smell the chili. "Almost done simmering. Are you hungry?"

"I haven't been hungry for two weeks." She shifted on the stool. "Clay, I need to apologize for something."

"Giving my gambling winnings to the orphanage?"

"I didn't really mean to lead you on these past few weeks."

I looked at her. "You haven't led me on."

"Well, I've been acting sort of flirty, and I didn't mean to. It was just . . . just so much fun to banter along with you. I'm comfortable with you, is maybe the reason. With the tower's troubles, you were a needed tonic."

I walked over to Hsu and Soong. "You fellows want some chili?"

"Sure," Hsu said.

"What's chili?" Soong asked.

They were ferociously tapping their control pads. Neither looked up from the screen. I returned to the kitchen and found several bowls in a cupboard. I spooned chili into them. Purists usually don't eat saltine crackers with chili, but I can't eat one without the other. I placed crackers on a plate, and then two spoons, and took it all into the living room.

When I returned, Anne said, "I mean, I didn't mean to sort of imply by my attentions that . . ."

"Nothing was implied. Don't worry about it." This came out convincingly.

"Clay, for a week I haven't been able to see beyond the tower's inauguration, and whatever else is going to happen to it. The future is a blank wall for me. With the tower . . . acting up, I can't plan anything. I can't even imagine a future. It's as if the last pages of my calendar have been ripped out and tossed away."

I sprinkled some grated onions on our chili, then handed her a bowl.

"I need to tell you something," she said.

I stared down into the chili. Seldom is good news preceded by "I need to tell you something."

"I'm going to marry John Llewellyn," she said in a low voice.

I absorbed this news. For some reason it made my breath shallow, and I could feel the blood rise to my face. I suppose I knew it was coming. I tried to be clinical. "What does marrying John Llewellyn have to do with you seeing your future as blank?"

"It accounts for the days following the tower's inauguration. It gives me something to write on the calendar."

"That sounds so romantic."

"You've already laid out your case regarding the romance of John's and my relationship. Spare me a rerun."

"All I'm saying is that—"

"John loves me, I think. And he needs me, that's pretty clear. I've become an anchor for him. He opens up to me, when he can't to anyone else. He seems so frail now. His mood elevates when he is around me. I see some of his old self."

I passed her a spoon. I didn't see any point in arguing. There's seldom any profit in trying to make a case against someone's fiancé.

"He even gave me a ring." She held out her hand. A large diamond—it must have been two carats—was mounted on a simple setting. I hadn't seen it until that moment. Maybe she had been hiding it, wanting to tell me before she showed me.

"Nice ring," I said. "Do you have any trouble lifting it?"

She said, "And I need him. I need . . . I need . . ." She sighed, a long, rattling breath. Scowling, she stabbed the chili with the spoon.

I tasted the chili. One of my better batches.

She said under her breath, "It's in my best interests to marry him."

"It probably is."

"What's my alternative?" she asked, as if I were arguing. "Run home to Mommy and Daddy in San Diego, and go into my room and hide under my blanket? Honest to God, until I decided to accept John's proposal, that was the best I could dream up for my future, retreating to my childhood bedroom."

She brought the spoon to her mouth and tested the chili by quickly touching it with her tongue, a fetching motion. She tried half a spoonful.

"This is good," she said finally. "I didn't know you could cook."

We ate in silence for a moment. That is, we didn't speak. Loud explosions were coming from the television set.

She said abruptly, "John and I have been together a long time. I sort of owe it to him."

I nodded, then passed her a tray of crackers.

"I'm sorry, Clay," she said, looking at me.

"Sorry for what?"

"You know."

Well, I did know, and there wasn't any use pretending otherwise. Our relationship—such as it was—had had potential. With her apology Anne was admitting she had seen it.

I was about to say something—and may have been generating the courage to make a pitch for myself—when Hsu walked into the room with an empty bowl.

"This is good," he said. "I've never had anything like it."

I ladled more chili into his bowl.

"You should see our new equipment, Miss Iverson," Hsu said. "We're building a seismograph. My grandfather is helping us."

"Your laser range finder no longer interests you?" Anne asked.

"It's not so much fun now that it doesn't work on the Gold Swan anymore."

Soong called from the living room. "Hurry, Shui-ban. I just got into the seventh level."

I looked at Hsu. "Why doesn't the range finder work on the tower?"

"The angle of the laser light reflected from the tower has changed." Carrying his chili, he turned back toward the Nintendo game, and then said over his shoulder, "The laser doesn't bounce back to me anymore."

"It doesn't bounce back?" Anne asked. "Why?"

He called from the living room, "Because the tower has tilted too much."

* * *

"Most Chinese still do not know that men have landed on the moon," Darrel Reese told me. "Did you know that?"

"How can that be?" I asked.

"Suppressing news is an art form, really. We're going to see the master of it in a few minutes, I think. The man is a genius. I'm a fan, not of what he does, but of his ability to do it. I just want a glimpse of him. That's why we came out here."

Lau Fau Shan was a village in the New Territories, on the western border with China, only a mile from the enormous township Tin Shui Wai, with its rows of gray apartment buildings, a town startlingly new and fully formed. Lau Fau Shan, though, was an old oyster-harvesting village, and its small homes were built on islands of discarded oyster shells. Hills of white oyster shells were in every direction, and seawater lapped against the oyster-shell shoreline. Men and women in conical straw hats knelt on the shell beds, plucking new oysters and dropping them into red plastic buckets. Sampans and oyster barges were anchored offshore. A swollen yellow sun was overhead, and a pale blue sky was above a gauzy horizon. Not a breath of air stirred, and the water of Shenzhen Bay was utterly calm, as if the heavy sun were pressing it flat.

Darrel Reese and I were sitting on an overturned oyster crate, next to the town's herbal medicine shop. He was wearing a Panama hat with a black ribbon around the brim, and shorts and sandals. He had a redhead's pale complexion, and the skin on his cheeks and neck was flaking from too much sun. Binoculars were on his lap.

Reese said, "My boss, Ross Shepherd, cluster-bombed me when he learned Will Jeffers died."

"I don't doubt it."

"He said that from now on you and Anne Iverson can take care of yourselves. So we aren't guarding you anymore. I'm sorry about that."

"I can handle things." This was said with as much bravado as I could generate, which wasn't much. "Maybe she can, too."

"Will Jeffers was plenty tough and smart, but somebody caught him by surprise and took him out. So watch yourself, Clay."

I nodded.

Reese looked toward a small house in the distance and changed the subject. "The fellow's name is Xu Chao, and he's here from Beijing, just arrived this morning. Right now he's over in that house, visiting his son who he hasn't seen in almost thirty years."

"Thirty years?" I asked.

"The son escaped China way back then, sneaking in under the wires on the New Territory border. Xu is very senior in Beijing's Ministry of State Security, and before today he didn't view it as ideologically acceptable to visit his son, who had deserted socialism's glorious future."

"Why is Xu Chao here in Hong Kong?" I asked.

"On business." Reese pulled several five-by-seven photographs from his pocket. "These were taken over the past three days, the photographer standing on the Peak, using a telephoto lens."

The first photo showed a portion of Heroes of the Revolution Island's concrete pad. The base of the great bronze spire was just visible at the right of the photo.

Reese pointed. "You see here a crack in the concrete, about eighty feet west of the tower. The crack is thirty feet long and three inches wide. This photo of the crack was taken yesterday morning. Now here's a photo of the same crack later in the afternoon, with laborers all around."

The second photo showed workmen on their knees, using spreaders. Portable cement mixers were nearby, as were wheelbarrows.

"They are patching the fissure, looks like," I said. "Concrete is being dumped into the crack, then it's being smoothed out."

"Our engineers have examined these photos. They tell me that the repairs we see being made to the pad in this photo are entirely cosmetic."

I passed the photo back to him.

Reese said: "And here's another photo, taken just this morning. You'll see that yesterday's crack—the one in the first photo—has been filled in, but a new fracture has appeared eight feet farther west. And this new crack is being hastily filled in. You can see all the workmen."

"So what's your conclusion?" I asked.

"Beijing is rapidly working to correct the tower's tilt—with all the compacting equipment and the barges and dredges—but just as important to them is the suppression of information about any tower fallibility. And that's why Xu Chao is here."

Two men passed us, carrying a pole on their shoulders, with a wicker basket of oysters suspended from the pole. Normally this spot would have offered a view of the Shekou Peninsula across Shenzhen

Bay, eight miles away, but the haze was too thick. On the peninsula is a fishing village with the formidable name of Baoanhaishuiyang-zhichang. A junk with battened red sails was slowly crossing the bay, heading toward the mouth of the Pearl River. It would soon disappear in the haze.

Darrel Reese said, "China is a nation peculiarly susceptible to the suppression of information. Xu Chao, the fellow visiting his son in that house over there, is a legend among China's Central Committee, and is highly rewarded for his work, with a large apartment in central Peking near Tiananmen Square and a weekend home on Kunming Lake near the Summer Palace."

"So what does Xu Chao do?"

"Xu engineered the containment—perhaps *disappearance* is a better word—of facts regarding the Cultural Revolution. The old saying is that facts are stubborn things, but Xu has no difficulty with them at all, stubborn or not. He is a master engineer of facts."

A skinny dog walked passed us, its nose on the ground. Two children, maybe four and six years old, dressed only in T-shirts, had emerged from a house to study Reese and me.

"Here's an example," Reese said. "In all the years since the Cultural Revolution, the Chinese government has admitted that seventy people were killed by the Red Guards, and that's what almost all Chinese now believe. In truth, the number exceeds a million. Information regarding the torture and murder of thousands of teachers by their students—when teachers were drowned in fountains, beaten with nail-spiked clubs, forced to swallow chemicals—has simply never been allowed to spread."

A gull sailed in from the west, landing on the oyster shells thirty feet away. It, too, began to study us.

"The Chinese people have no knowledge of the widespread horrors," Reese said. "Those Chinese who actually witnessed the brutality have been told that what they saw were isolated incidents. China has almost no memory of the Cultural Revolution. Xu's job has been to deny the Chinese their history, and he has been superb at it."

I could smell oyster sauce being cooked. Most oysters from this village were rendered into sauce and then bottled. The oysters were in decline because of pollution in the bay, and so the village was also in decline.

"The last official job Xu did before his retirement was Tiananmen Square, and it was done brilliantly. Now he's been brought out of retirement to handle the Fifth Millennium China Tower."

"He's going to be challenged," I said. "The tower is a big thing to wish away."

Reese laughed. He was in a good mood, an expansive mood. "There he is."

Two men had emerged from a squat cement home. An older white-haired gentleman was holding the younger man's arm. They leaned toward each other to speak, and walked slowly along a gravel path toward a blue Mercedes-Benz, where a driver in a black sport coat waited near a rear passenger door.

"He doesn't look like much, does he?" Reese said. I detected a touch of awe in the CIA agent's voice.

Xu Chao could not have been five feet three. He walked with an agreeable stoop and was so thin he was lost in his clothes. His son was a full head taller and was wearing the knee-high black rubber boots of the oysterman. He was smiling broadly and nodding at his father's words.

Reese asked, more to himself, "I wonder what Xu's plan of action is?"

"What do you mean?" I asked.

"Until now Beijing's attempts to suppress information about the Gold Swan's tilting have been crude and scattershot. Too many hands have been involved; the Ministry of State Security, the Red Army, the Ministry of Construction, and others."

"The attempts on Anne Iverson's and my lives weren't so crude. They were almost successful."

He nodded. "Some people who knew about the tower's troubles have disappeared, and you are being pursued, but it's all been disjointed, and I think it's because Beijing at first reacted hastily to the news and didn't have a concerted plan. Their efforts were reflexive, and as a result, they were confused. They're still looking for you, but now they have a plan."

"And they've brought in the master?"

"Exactly," Reese replied. "Xu Chao is here, and you can bet that all information suppression is in his hands now."

The old man and his son slowly approached us on the walkway, heading for the car. Now Xu was holding his son's hand in one small hand, and tapping it with the other. Both men were dipping their heads and smiling.

Reese said in a quiet voice, "I wonder how that old man will try to make history disappear this time."

The two men continued up the path toward us and the Mercedes. Xu Chao had a seamed face and a piratical grin, as he was missing a front tooth.

The father and son passed near our oyster crate, and when Xu Chao looked up, he caught Darrel Reese's eye for a moment, and hesitated an instant before breaking the gaze and moving on toward the car.

I glanced at Reese. He was smiling.

"It's going to be between me and him," Reese said in a soft voice, more to himself.

"It is?"

He nodded. "Me against him. It'll be a duel."

18

In Chinese history the era is known as the Time of the Warring States, twenty-four hundred years ago. Feudal lords fought each other for land and primacy. Tradition and culture demanded that all China be unified, and many warlords tried to be the grand unifier, and many failed. Kingdoms—for the feudal lords chose to call themselves *kings* —rose and disappeared. It was a time of treachery and turmoil.

Qu Yuan was born to a wealthy family in the state of Chu, which is present-day Hubei Province. His intelligence and discernment allowed Qu Yuan to rise quickly at court, and he served as *fa ling guan*, the minister of laws and ordinances in the regime of King Mei Huai. When he was not busy at court, Qu wrote poetry. His *Elegies of Chu* are among the earliest recorded Chinese poems.

The king treated Qu with respect and rewarded him for his prescience. A man of such talent, and a man who stands in such favor with the king, always generates heated jealousy at court, and so it was that the chief eunuch began to plot Qu Yuan's downfall. A campaign of lies—in which the chief eunuch painted Qu Yuan as vain and boastful—succeeded, and Qu was banished from the kingdom.

Such was Qu Yuan's shame that he tied a stone around himself and jumped into the Mei Lan River. Villagers set out in fishing boats to rescue the poet, but they could not find him, nor could they find his body. They began to slap the water with their paddles and to beat drums to keep the spirits away, and they tossed rice dumplings into the river so the fish would eat dumplings rather than Qu's body. The ghost of Qu Yuan is still occasionally seen, all these centuries later, hovering over the river and moaning that water monsters have devoured him.

Qu disappeared on the fifth day of the fifth lunar month, and the event is still celebrated in China every year when boats take to the waters, beating their oars against the water to scare fish away from Qu's body.

In Hong Kong the celebration takes the form of dragon boat races that are held in the Shing Mun River in the New Territories, but this year the races coincided with the opening day of the Fifth Millennium China Tower inauguration week, so the event was held on Victoria Bay in the shadow of the tower. The races marked the beginning of the tower's weeklong inaugural festival.

I thought I might be able to watch the dragon boat ceremonies from Heroes of the Revolution Island, maybe even from the top of the tower, but that morning all tower personnel—all the construction workers, the management teams, the adjunct staffs such as security, catering, and public relations, and anyone else who had worked on the tower's construction—were shipped off the island. Only those working on the so-called new ferry terminal and the so-called subgrade shopping arcade were permitted on Heroes of the Revolution Island.

It had been an eviction. A brigade of the People's Armed Police, subordinate to China's Ministry of State Security, had been ferried to the island, and all workers there—except those laboring on the new projects—were rousted from their desks and work sites. Nobody was given time to clean out a desk or retrieve tools or pack up a computer or get an umbrella. We were all herded together at the ferry terminal building, made to stand in long lines while our names were taken down on clipboards by PAP lieutenants. Our work-site identification cards were confiscated. The policemen were not carrying weapons but looked stern and businesslike, and accepted no excuses for delay.

Anne Iverson was incensed and shouted something at a lieutenant, who pretended not to hear her. None of us knew whether we were still employees of the Fifth Millennium China Tower commission. I tried calling my superior, Lien Yang-sun, the tower's director of security, but was told that he no longer worked for the commission and that he had not been replaced. I asked the person on the other end of the phone what city she was in, and she replied, "Beijing." The same thing happened to staff who worked in other departments. Nobody could get through. Nobody could find answers. Everyone who had worked on the tower—some for the entire six years of design and construction—was suddenly cut off.

An entire week of festivities was planned, beginning with this ceremony to launch dragon boat races and ending seven days later with the tower's inauguration. A barge had been moored just offshore from the convention center on the Hong Kong side, and a dais had been constructed on it. A hundred officials and perhaps another hundred representatives of the press were on the barge.

Hong Kong's chief executive, the police commissioner Kwok Kan-yan, and John Llewellyn were the only people I recognized on the barge, all sitting in chairs facing the shoreline. Anne Iverson hadn't been invited, nor were any of the other senior tower officials, except Llewellyn.

Central Committee members were due to arrive from Beijing later in the week. Loudspeakers had been set up for half a mile in both directions along the shore. Many food stalls had appeared on the streets facing the barge, and were selling *zhongzi*, glutinous rice and meat dumplings wrapped in bamboo leaves, the traditional dragon boat-day snack. Newspapers would later estimate that a half-million people crowded the shoreline. The tower rose behind the barge, the top of it hidden in clouds, so it's just as well I wasn't trying to watch from that viewpoint. At one end of the island the barges and dredges and compaction vessels continued their work.

Jay Lee and I were among the crowd, standing on the walkway that circled the convention center, maybe eighty yards from the barge. Bobbing in the small chop, more than a hundred dragon boats were arrayed around the barge. Each held twenty paddlers, a coxswain, and a drummer. The majority of boats were painted red because red is the color of the number 5, which represents heat and fire. The vessels were more than thirty feet long, and narrow, ten paddlers long and two wide. Elaborate dragons' heads were mounted on the bows, and the dragons were flashing fangs and rolling tongues and glaring with sinister eyes. Hulls were painted to resemble dragon scales, and carved, twisting wood tails were mounted on the boats' sterns. The crews wore matching T-shirts and caps. Chinese words were painted on their paddle blades. In the front of the boats the drummers leaned over their drums, their short sticks in hand. The races would begin once this opening ceremony ended, and the fidgeting paddlers were hoping for short speeches.

"I used to be on a dragon boat crew," Jay Lee said. "The Hong Kong police enter a boat every year." He was wearing a Gore-Tex jacket, jeans, and basketball shoes. "It's fun, being out there."

"You no longer do it?"

"I can't make the team. I'm too old. Some of the teams train year-round."

I asked abruptly, "Does the tower look crooked to you, Jay?"

His gaze rose to the tower, then it came back to me. "What do you mean?"

"Does it look out of alignment to you?"

I hadn't mentioned the tower's tilt to anyone not involved with its construction, and very few of them, for two reasons. First, knowing of the Gold Swan's lean would put a person at risk—witness Hsu Shui-ban's kidnapping, and my life lately dodging whoever was hunting me. And, second, I was earnestly rooting for the tower. I was part of the team, after all, and while I hadn't worked the CAD programs or the cranes' controls, I still felt as though my role had been important to the project. I had a pride of authorship. I didn't want to see the tower fail, not in the public imagination or in its structural integrity. And, as I say, I had a romance with the tower, just like everyone else in Hong Kong.

Jay tilted his head, staring at the tower. "It's not out of alignment. You are seeing things because of the great curve, the swan's neck."

"Yeah, I suppose so."

The speeches were in Cantonese, and John Llewellyn was standing at the podium before I knew he had been introduced. He received wild applause from those standing around me and all along the shoreline. An interpreter stood next to him with his own microphone. The distance was too great for me to make out Llewellyn's face clearly. Near Jay and me was a preschool class and their teachers. About twenty children were clinging to a rope that kept them together. They were eating rice cakes and probably couldn't see anything through the crowd.

Llewellyn began, his voice bouncing off the convention center: "Ladies and gentlemen, thank you for your warm welcome. I approach the Fifth Millennium China Tower's inauguration and opening to the public this weekend with great pride and greater humility."

His voice was robust, though made metallic by the speakers.

As Llewellyn paused for the translator, Jay said, "I'm thinking of taking a vacation."

"You deserve one."

"I want to see the Grand Canyon," he said.

Llewellyn continued, his voice booming over the speakers, "And now, as I look upon our creation . . ."

The architect dramatically looked over his shoulder at the Fifth Millennium China Tower, which rose and curved toward the passing clouds, and I'm sure everyone in the crowd followed his gaze. But then when Llewellyn turned back to the podium and the audience, he was silent.

The translator waited, nodding his head in encouragement. The crowd was quiet, waiting.

Llewellyn said nothing. His hands were gripping the edges of the podium, and his eyes were on the small expanse of water between the barge and the convention center. The dragon boats drifted idly in the bay.

A moment passed, and then the translator leaned toward Llewellyn to say a few words. Llewellyn didn't react, not that I could tell from my distance. He was silent and still, as if lost in a reverie. Another moment passed.

Then Hong Kong's chief executive rose from his chair and put a hand on Llewellyn's arm, maybe saying something to the architect. Llewellyn was motionless. The chief executive signaled for another official to approach, who placed a hand around Llewellyn wrist, taking a pulse.

The chief executive barked something at the translator, who then said a few words in Cantonese to the crowd. He switched to English, "There will be a short delay in today's ceremony."

The chief executive peeled Llewellyn's hands from the podium, and then helped escort him toward the back of the barge. Llewellyn could walk, but apparently needed guidance from the helping hands on his arms. He was taken to the aft end of the barge, out of sight of the onlookers, who buzzed with speculation.

The translator said in Cantonese and then in English, "The chief executive will offer some remarks in just a moment."

I had come to hear John Llewellyn, and if he was through, so was I. I began making my way through the crowd, Jay Lee following me.

"What's wrong with Llewellyn, do you think?" he asked. "I mean, he stopped right in the middle of his speech and sort of went into a trance."

"I've no idea what the problem is," I said, though I did have a pretty good idea.

Jay laughed. "Maybe I'm not the only one who needs a vacation."

* * *

"You should get a tattoo, Miss Iverson," the young man said. "Perhaps a dragon on your arm."

"My arm is a little thin for a dragon," she replied.

"How about an eel, then?"

The young fellow, Henry Tong, appreciated tattoos, that was clear. On his right arm was a scaled green and red serpent that was breathing fire, and on his left arm was James Dean on a motorcycle. On the back of his right hand was a spider's web. He was wearing Bermuda shorts, so we could also see his legs, and on his right leg was an orange and blue pattern of some sort, perhaps Celtic. His other leg was still free of the artwork.

Tong saw me examining the Celtic design, and he said, "It's my newest. Just two months old."

Anne said, "In America tattoos are becoming passé."

This brought up the young man. "Really?"

"Cher had hers removed."

"Really?" He was clearly troubled, glancing down at his dragon. "Does it hurt, getting them removed?"

"I don't know," she said. "I'll call her and ask."

Tong rubbed the dragon, perhaps testing its indelibility.

Anne offered, "Piercing may still be cool in America, though."

He grinned with relief. One of his ears had four brads through it, and a silver ring was punched through the skin of his eyebrow. The hair on top of his head had been spiked with gel, while the sides of his head had been shaved, giving him the look of a paintbrush. He wore a black leather vest. Tong had a rounded face and looked to be sixteen years old, though I knew him to be twenty-two.

We had been careful, making our way to this meeting, constantly insuring we weren't being followed, and now we were on his parents' boat, a 122-foot Broward motor yacht moored at the Royal Hong Kong Yacht Club facility at Kellett Island in Causeway Bay. Henry Tong's father, Long Fu "Bob" Tong, was a clothing manufacturer with plants in Hong Kong, Shenzhen, and Canton. Tong Industries manufactured 8 percent of the world's output of blue jeans, contracting from Levi and others, and 10 percent of the world's athletic shoes, manufacturing under contract with Nike, Brooks, and others. Bob Tong's father had begun his working career at age fourteen, when he was apprenticed to a tailor on Nathan Road in Kowloon and was paid three Hong Kong dollars a day. But that had been forty years, a home on the Peak, and a 122-foot Broward ago. The boat was named the *Pearl*.

One of Bob Tong's offices was on the *Pearl*, a cabin aft of the wheelhouse. Several oak file cabinets and a massive mahogany desk were in the office, as was a Chuchou rug in reds and purples. Two computers with flat-screen monitors were in the office. On the bulkhead behind the desk was a photographic portrait of the Tong family, showing Bob and his wife and their four children, including Henry. In the photo, Henry was younger, with no tattoos or ear studs.

Henry Tong was behind one of the computer monitors, his hands over the keyboard. He could wish us and the world away, apparently, and several moments elapsed without a word from him, his eyes on the screen and his fingers tapping at the keyboard.

"How'd you get into this business?" Anne finally asked.

He looked up from the screen. "A series of mistakes. My father calls it my downhill trajectory. I started out at Berkeley. I was there three quarters."

"What happened?" I asked.

"I hacked into the mainframe in the registrar's office and raised my Philosophy 101 grade from a C to an A."

"You were caught?" Anne asked.

He nodded. "And booted out of the school. So I enrolled at the University of Hong Kong. But I hacked into the dean of admission's computer and directed the computer to admit four of my friends. So I was kicked out of UHK, too."

"And then?" I asked.

He rubbed his jaw. "Let's see. Next was Oregon State in Corvallis."

"And?"

"I hacked into the student food service's central computer and altered the recipe of something called the farmer's meat loaf, and a couple of other recipes, adding several pounds of salt here and there."

"Oregon State kicked you out, too?"

"Yes, and a couple of more schools, until I found myself at Kowloon Voc-Tech, and I was trying to hack into the American embassy's computer, and that's when the FBI came to talk to me."

"They put the scare into you?" Anne asked.

He laughed. "Not at all. They recruited me. I've been working for them on and off now for two years. Sort of on a contract basis."

Fred Allison of the FBI's Hong Kong office had put me in contact with Henry Tong. I had told Allison I needed a computer wizard, someone who knew how software programs might be deliberately corrupted.

"But I'm not being paid enough," Tong said. "I might have to join my father's company."

"The agony," Anne said.

She was wearing a blue cotton polo shirt and double-pleated khaki pants. Her straw-and-honey-colored hair was loose to her shoulders and tucked toward her neck. She was also wearing her engagement ring. She had visited John Llewellyn at Queen Mary Hospital on Pokfulam Road, where he was on the seventh floor of Block J, part of the psychiatric ward. His room was guarded by the Hong Kong police, but when Anne explained that she was his fiancée, they let her visit him for a few minutes. He had been under a thin cotton blanket on a bed, his hands resting by his sides, and he was staring at the clock on the wall opposite the bed. On a table next to him was a tray of untouched food. Behind Llewellyn was a head wall with outlets for oxygen, nitrous oxide, and medical air, along with an examination light. An IV bottle was feeding something into one of his veins. Anne had said hello, then had gripped his hand, and there had been no response from Llewellyn. He blinked several times, and nothing more. She asked the physician at the nurses' station whether Llewellyn was on medication, or whether he was just blank like that, and the doctor replied that he was not allowed to say anything to anyone. Who, Anne asked, was not allowing you? He had shaken his head and turned away. Then when she had demanded that Llewellyn be released into her care, the doctor signaled the two policemen, who had escorted her out of the building.

The tower commission's press release on John Llewellyn's speech had been laughable: his microphone had malfunctioned so he could not continue. The Hong Kong media reported it as told to report it.

Henry Tong said, "I've found something in the program and data you gave me. Something weird."

I had asked Henry Tong to examine the application software, called GeoPlace 3.1, that had been used by the geotechs when gathering compaction data to design and implement Heroes of the Revolution Island's fill. GeoPlace was manufactured by Geotechnic, Inc. in Denver, and they had sent me a copy of the program when I explained I was with the tower's security office. So Tong had been studying two GeoPlace 3.1 programs: the one Anne and I had downloaded from the tower's central server, which we had told Tong was the red program, and the new copy provided by the company, the green program.

Tong pointed at his screen. "The first clue is that the red program has a hundred fifty thousand more lines of code in it."

"What do you mean?" I asked.

"Just that. The red program is longer."

"Well, the green program has just been taken out of the manufacturer's wrap. It's the stock model."

Anne asked, "So the red program has been altered?"

Tong nodded. "By someone who went to great lengths. A hundred fifty thousand lines of code is a lot of work."

"What does the added code do?" I asked.

"It manipulates data," he replied.

Anne said: "The instruments used during construction of the island measured density of the fill, and the information was fed to this program every day. And you are saying that the program can shade those numbers?" She glanced at me, then back to the hacker.

"I don't know how it alters them yet," Tong said. "That's going to take more work, and I'm not an engineer or mathematician. But, yes, those extra lines of code were put into the program to change the values of the data from the field. Good data in, garbage out."

Anne looked at me again. "So the geotechs engineering the island's fill were working with inaccurate compaction figures."

"Who altered the GeoPlace program?" I asked.

"I can't tell." Tong smiled. "They didn't leave a signature."

*   *   *

"'I demand to know who ordered two divisions of Peoples' Liberation Army soldiers out of their barracks and into the city,'" President Chen said, the interpreter's voice rendering it into English.

Even though the camera's point of view was several yards from the table, I could see that Chen's face was grim, his eyes glacial. He sat at the head of the conference table, a poker down his spine. His palms were flat on the folder in front of him.

A voice off-camera replied, and the interpreter rendered it into English, "'General Gu and I thought it best if the masses were reminded of the state's central authority.'"

Watching the screen with me, Darrel Reese said, "That voice is Cao Ah-kin, minister of state security. He never puts himself on camera, and he set up this camera. As I mentioned, he unfailingly works to undermine the president."

"'Where do you find your authority to bring troops into the city?'" President Chen asked.

"'I am a general of the army.'" General Gu was in full uniform, and was facing the camera. "'And that is sufficient authority.'"

"'You report to me,'" Chen said. The voice-over interpreter increased the pitch of his voice to match the president's. "'I approve divisional-level movements.'"

"'With the difficulty in Hong Kong, you have other responsibilities that are more pressing than overseeing the placement of troops,'" the general said. "'The units—the Fourth Division and the Deng Division—are adequately guided under my care.'"

Even before the translator did his work, I could detect the challenge in the general's voice.

Reese was leaning back in his chair, his legs outstretched and his head back as if in the first row of a movie theater. A glass of lemonade was on the table next to him. The remote control was in his hand. He was relaxed and enjoying himself.

Chen's voice rose. "'The Summer Palace garrison is directly under my control, General.'"

"'As you are aware, the Fourth and the Deng Divisions are not of that garrison,'" the general said smoothly. "'The Summer Palace troops are still in their barracks near the palace.'"

Chen slapped his hand on the table. "'And I tell you this has a whiff of a coup.'"

"'Nothing of the sort,'" the Minister of State Security said.

"'You have posted soldiers at Tiananmen Square, and at four broadcast stations, and more units have been moved around the Memorial Hall and the government buildings.'"

"'It is merely precautionary, Mr. President,'" Minister Cao said.

"'And will you tell me why?'" Chen asked.

"'We believe that a show of the army's solidarity with the people is appropriate at this time.'"

Darrel Reese paused the video. "This meeting occurred last night. It's the first midnight gathering of the Central Committee since Mao's death." He pressed the remote again.

The interpreter's voice resumed, translating Cao's words, "'Much of what I am charged with accomplishing, as minister of security, is detecting and extinguishing sparks. History is filled with examples of governments that were swept away because of a tide of emotion caused by an event—often some small, seemingly insignificant act— that was unseen or overlooked by the government.'"

Reese interjected, "Cao is smooth, isn't he? He is also formidable, and President Chen knows it."

Also at the conference table in Beijing were Vice President Bai Mu-tsu, President of the State Council Fan Bao-tian, Minister of Construction Duan Cho-li, and others.

"'Look at our former allies in Marxism, the East Germans,'" Cao said. "'One day they were there, and the next day they had been swept into history, all due to a simple error. I have intensely studied their demise, and have concluded that one man's will exerted at the proper time would have saved the German Democratic Republic. It was the weakness of a single moment that led to the disaster.'"

The president was silent as he studied the minister.

Cao went on: "'Even within our country, the Taiping Rebellion and the Nien Rebellion could have been quashed quickly, had weakness not taken hold of our rulers. Weakness and delay, only for a short time, proved fatal.'"

"'And you are saying that you have that will?'" Even before the translation of Chen's Mandarin, I could detect the sarcasm.

"'I am saying, Mr. President, that my ministry has the ability to detect such sparks, and it is my responsibility to pinch them out as quickly as I can.'"

Chen said, "'I have read nothing from you to indicate such troop movements are required. There is no spark in Beijing.'"

"'I believe that if the Fifth Millennium China Tower fails in its purpose . . .'"

Reese stopped the video. "Get that, Clay? If it 'fails in its purpose.' Talk about an understated way to say it." He laughed brightly. Once again, Reese was in a fine mood. Of course, with his red hair, and eyes set at a merry angle, he always appeared to be in good spirits.

The video rolled, and the minister of security continued mid-sentence, "'. . . then unrest may occur. Such things have happened in the past, here and elsewhere.'"

"'And to prevent such an event, I am repositioning certain units,'" General Gu said. "'In addition to the Beijing deployments, I have moved the Eighth Division from the Shan Bu barracks to the outskirts of Shenzhen near the Special Administrative District border.'"

Cao continued, "'General Gu and I have made certain contingency plans for pacifying the masses that I am prepared to share with you now, Mr. President.'"

The general added, "'They are all well within our respective jurisdictions, and we are confident that you will approve them, Mr. President.'"

Bai and Duan said nothing, their heads moving back and forth as they followed the conversation.

The president rubbed the table, a small left-right movement, as if polishing it. He said nothing for a moment, the interpreter pausing also. Then he continued in a low voice, and when I leaned forward to hear, Reese tapped his remote control to turn up the volume. "'I must tell you, comrades, that I too have examined history. I have studied the demise of Liu Shaoqi and Deng Xiaoping, and Khrushchev and Brezhnev and many others, and they have one thing in common.'" Chen paused, eyeing each of the committee members in the room one at a time. "'The leader was first cut out of the lines of communication. He was made blind to the plotting around him.'"

"'That is not what has happened here,'" General Gu protested. "'I am simply doing the job you assigned me to do.'"

"'I fully understand what you are about.'" Chen lifted his hand and slid it under the table.

One second later the conference door opened—visible in the background, behind Bai's head—and four policemen entered the room. They rounded the table and placed themselves next to the general.

"'What is this?'" General Gu demanded. "'Who are these policemen?'" He glanced at Minister Cao.

Cao said, "'They aren't mine. I don't know who they are.'"

The president said, "'These policemen are from a special force that I created several months ago, and they report directly to my office, rather than the People's Liberation Army or the Ministry of State Security.'"

The policemen were wearing green uniforms, black berets, and holsters. Not one of them appeared to be older than twenty.

Cao blustered, "'They should be under—'"

Chen cut him off. "'General Gu, you are relieved of your command and placed under house arrest. Any attempts by you to communicate with your commanders or units will lead to dire consequences for you. Take him away.'"

The general sat there until one of the policemen reached for his arm. He rose unsteadily from the table. Without another word from Gu, the policemen led him from the room and closed the door.

Reese said, "The general can call it a career."

The president continued, "'Minister Cao, I find that I cannot replace you as readily as a general, but I am moving six people from my office into your ministry where they will monitor you. Whether you will continue as minister of state security beyond one week from now has not been decided.'"

With that the president rose from the table and walked to the door. The other Central Committee members didn't move until he had left the room, and then they rose from the table, a bunch of old men moving slowly. The conference room vanished, leaving only a white wall.

Darrel Reese said, "President Chen is correct, I think."

"How so?" I asked.

"That little scene at the Central Committee—a PLA general and the minister of state security taking it upon themselves to move troops without the president's knowledge and consent—had the scent of a beer hall putsch."

I nodded. "They've been talking together behind the president's back."

Reese placed the remote control on the table, and he smiled widely. "Clay, you know the Gold Swan is tall, at twenty-five hundred feet."

"Sure."

"But I'll bet you didn't think it would have this long of a reach."

19

Weddings in Hong Kong take place in the morning, and most of them are more western than eastern. The bride and groom had said their vows and had been pronounced man and wife. Chan Juan, whose name means *graceful*, was wearing the flowing gown I had seen being fitted in her grandfather's living room. The groom was in a tuxedo. The newlyweds were out on the lawn, their backs against the foliage-covered cliff that rose to the Peak. A photographer and his assistant were placing them in one pose after another. Chan Juan had a bouquet in her arms, and her smile was radiant.

There must have been four hundred guests. Tents had been set up on the lawn, where caterers hovered over roasted pigs, salmon, and dozens of other dishes, all served on glittering silver platters. No eggplant would be served, because it was believed that eggplant caused sterility in young women. And pig's brains were not on the menu because they might induce impotence in the groom. Just as well, because pig brains aren't my favorite.

Tables and chairs were on the lawn, with enormous flower arrangements on each table. A portable dance floor had been laid down at the west end of the lawn, and a DJ wearing a headset was preparing his first set. Speakers the size of refrigerators were on both sides of him, and on top of the speakers was revolving lighting equipment that would throw colored beams onto the dancers. Until the DJ began his work, a string quartet on a raised platform near the house was entertaining the guests.

I recognized several people there. Guo Cheuk-fai, the triad's white paper fan and Zeng Kwan, who was Wen's second-in-command, were sitting at a table covered with dishes, and they were sampling each serving of food, chopsticks going from one plate to another. A small woman in a saffron-colored dress sat between them, sipping from a champagne flute, Guo's wife, I think. Wu Hop-ha, who directed 88K's opium-smuggling operations, gently bounced a toddler wearing a pink bonnet on his lap. Zeng Kwan was speaking with a younger man, Zeng's hand hiding his mouth while he ate. The young man nodded earnestly.

I was among friends, I believed—well-armed friends—and could relax. For the first time in days, I didn't have to look over my shoulder every thirty seconds.

"Is everybody here a gangster?" Anne asked.

"Some, but there are also many businesspeople and a few politicians."

"Did we bring a wedding gift?" When she sipped her glass of champagne, her engagement ring flashed in the sunlight.

"It's in my pocket. I had to consult with Hsu Shui-ban's mother on the protocol. She said I needed to put money into a red packet called a *laisee*. And because the word for *eight* is *bat*, which also means *prosperity* and *fat*, the amount should have an eight in it. She said eighty-eight U.S. dollars would be appropriate."

The old gangster Wen Quichin was receiving congratulations from triad members, one after another, who made their way to his table to shake his hand and bow. His half-grin was in place, and his small eyes flashed with pleasure at each greeting. Guards wearing tuxedos were posted at several places on the edge of the lawn, their weapons lumpy under their formal jackets. Many children ran about, the boys wearing ties and shorts, the girls in frilly dresses. One boy had brought a Frisbee, and his mother waved him toward the edge of the lawn, away from the knots of people.

Six girls—all of them thirteen and fourteen, and wobbly in their high heels—chatted together near the DJ's speakers, glancing surreptitiously at the teenage boys who were loitering about, hands in pockets, laughing and joshing back and forth, and ignoring the girls. Some of the girls were eating from small plates, careful to hold their chopsticks near the top, because where a young woman held her chopsticks was the distance she would have to travel to find a husband. Grasping them near their base meant she would marry the boy next door. Holding them at the top indicated she would have to travel to find him, and these young women wanted to travel. It was cooler here than down on the waterfront, but still the brassy sun threw a flat, heated midday light on the festivities, and my back was damp.

Anne had called me up that morning and said John Llewellyn had been released from the hospital, but that she couldn't find him—maybe Llewellyn was away on business somewhere, and you'd think he'd keep her apprised of his whereabouts, she had complained—and asked what I was doing, and whatever it was, could she join me. When I said I was attending a wedding, she said she owned just the dress. She was wearing a gas-blue sheath dress with bare arms. Around her neck was a string of pearls. She was the only blond at the wedding.

Anne asked, "How is it that you've become so close to a gangster that you are invited to his granddaughter's wedding?"

"I'm not sure."

"He's using you."

"Maybe Wen just likes me."

"That old gangster liking an American cop, even if he's an ex-cop?" She shook her head. "He's using you, and you just don't know how yet."

"Yeah, I suppose so."

Holding silver platters of hors d'oeuvres, waiters in white waistcoats drifted among the guests. The photographer summoned Wen and other family members, and they gathered in front of the cliff, the dragon head only as tall as the bride's shoulders. Wen shoved his spectacles up his nose. The photographer moved his subjects here and there—Wen with much deference—as he composed the photographs. The assistant adjusted the angle of silver reflecting umbrellas.

Below us the sun bounced off countless windows of the skyscrapers in Central and Wan Chai. The water of the harbor was deep blue and still, a Star ferry crossing toward the island, leaving an expanding white wake behind it.

When the photo session was over, the family dispersed. The bride and groom received good wishes from one guest after another. Wen made his way toward his home, bent and looking tired.

Zhu Jintau appeared next to me. The translator was wearing a black suit and a red silk tie. He said, "My uncle would like to see you in his study, if it is convenient."

"How about my friend Anne?" I asked.

"Just you, Mr. Williams, if you please."

"Maybe I'll go and get some advice from the bride." Anne laughed lightly as she stepped away.

I followed Zhu through the crowd. He walked slowly, as if not to draw attention to himself. The DJ said several short words over his speakers, testing his system. Propane lamps and Chinese lanterns had been set up at a number of places in the yard, indicating the party would continue after nightfall. Chan Juan and her new husband were going to honeymoon at Dunk Island, off the coast of Queensland, just inside the Great Barrier Reef.

Zhu and I entered the mansion, the chilled air enveloping us. Zhu led me along the hallway toward the dragon head's study, where we found Wen sitting on his burgundy leather chair. He smiled narrowly at me, waved me toward another chair, and spoke in Cantonese, which Zhu translated.

"'Pen Kai-ge will be here in a moment, and Pen wanted you in the room as a mediator. You must have impressed him.'" Zhu smiled. "'He apparently feels safer with you about.'" The old man spread his hands to encompass the room. "'You would think he would feel entirely safe at my granddaughter's wedding.'"

"You haven't told me why you invited the Peach Blossom's leader to the wedding," I said.

After translation Zhu said for his uncle: "'So Pen would feel comfortable. I want to talk business with him, and I would not get much done were he anxious and guarded. This is as good a place and time as any.'"

Behind Wen, through the windows, were the vines and leaves covering the bank that rose to the Peak. A tea service was on the mother-of-pearl–inlaid table. Sunlight glittered off the gold trim on the leather-bound volumes on the bookshelf. On the carpet were three large matching red leather trunks that hadn't been there during my last visit, each with circular, incised brass hardware. The trunks were open, their lids leaning back and held up by small chains secured to the chests' corners. One chest was filled with wedding gifts, which were wrapped in paper that was mostly yellow and white, with ribbons of all colors. The smallest chest contained the red pockets, as Cantonese call the packets containing money. Many more people had sent the red pockets than had been invited to the wedding, as the chest was half-filled with them. The largest red chest was open but entirely empty.

"'I have decided to end the animosity between 88K and Peach Blossom,'" Wen said through his nephew. "'I'm sure that Pen Kai-ge will listen to my proposal, and agree to it.'"

A few words in Cantonese came from the hallway, a guard alerting us to Pen's arrival. Then Pen entered the den, escorted by the guard, who quickly left the room. Pen was wearing an olive-green sport coat instead of a black suit, intended to insult the host, I was sure. His greased hair glistened in the light. His ears stood out like handles. He said nothing, just rising and falling on his toes, perhaps nervous. He glanced at me and nodded. I suppose he did feel safer with a *gweilo* in the room.

Wen did not rise from his chair, an insult for an insult. He spoke to Pen, and Zhu translated for my benefit, "'I'm glad you came today. Much can be resolved at a quick meeting. And I am in favor of resolving difficulties.'"

At that instant Shao Long, the 88K's enforcer, the giant with the emeralds imbedded in his teeth, stepped through the door from the hallway. Pen didn't see or hear him. Shao seized Pen's head in both his meaty hands and viciously yanked Pen's head around on his neck. Shao Long's massive arms bulged under his jacket. Pen dropped to the carpet, and Shao followed him down, yanking his head around. Bones loudly snapped and grated. Shao twisted the head until it was backward on the shoulders, and only then did Pen's gaze find Shao, but by then Pen was dead.

The giant lifted the body by the hair and belt buckle, then dropped him into the empty chest. He stuffed the legs and arms in, then slammed shut the lid.

Wen said through his translator, " 'Well, that difficulty has been resolved.' "

* * *

A visitor to Hong Kong will tell you that the city vibrates with energy and that by comparison most other cities are somnolent. The visitor would also say that Hong Kong's dial is all the way to ten, that the city simply couldn't be busier or louder or more crowded. It had hit the maximum on all those scales.

The visitor would have been wrong, because during the tower's inaugural week, Hong Kong became even more frenetic. In its determination to out-Beijing Beijing, the tower commission added event after event and piled invitation upon invitation.

Hong Kong and Kowloon streets, never easy to negotiate in an automobile, became almost impassable as the motorcades sped heads of state and other dignitaries to meetings and dinners. Tinhorn presidents and premiers and generals compensated for their countries' puniness by ordering up six-car motorcades, escorted by siren-blaring motorcycles. Whenever one of them entered or exited the car, bodyguards would temporarily freeze the street, closing intersections and blocking traffic.

Neighborhoods sponsored lion dances, which drew large crowds into the streets. The dances date back to the early Ch'in and Han dynasties, twenty-three hundred years ago. The lions signify happiness and joy, are usually manned by *kung fu* students, and are accompanied by drums, gongs, and cymbals. The dancers under the lion perform the three-star movement and the seven-star movement and the high dance. Firecrackers are thrown at the dancers' feet. At any given time that week, night and day, three dozen lion dances were under way in Hong Kong.

The new Chek Lap Kok airport, built to meet Hong Kong's travel requirements to the twenty-second century, was operating at peak capacity, with every seat on every incoming flight filled, and with an airplane—including hundreds of corporate and private jets—landing every forty-five seconds round the clock. Cruise lines had offered Gold Swan Inaugural cruises, and twelve of the vessels—seven-hundred-foot behemoths with white and blue hulls—crowded the harbor.

Hotels were booked solid, some of the dignitaries taking up entire floors. Ever industrious, Hong Kong citizens were renting out rooms at U.S.$200 and more per night. One home on the Peak was rented for U.S.$10,000 per day. Restaurants were filled from morning to night, and Hong Kong businessmen—who understand the laws of supply and demand as well as any group on earth—were charging three times preinauguration prices for meals. Several newspapers called for restaurant price controls, but the owners of the thirty thousand restaurants in Hong Kong were too influential, and the idea came to nothing.

The tower commission was intent on layering one event over another. The Miss Fifth Millennium China Tower Pageant drew comely representatives from 130 countries, most declaring that they would work for world peace once the contest was over. The world's most inflated men—shiny, tanned bodybuilders—came to Hong Kong to compete for the title of Mr. Fifth Millennium China Tower. The tower commission announced that the Happy Valley Race Course would host a HK$1,000,000-added horse race, the Tower Cup. Causing outrage among Happy Valley regulars, portable grandstands were erected on the course's grassy midfield in anticipation of huge crowds.

The tower sponsored a convocation of fengshui divines—more than two hundred geomancers from Hong Kong and mainland China, all masters of classical cosmology—who unanimously issued a procla-

mation stating that the tower's design was propitious and that it was
without malignant or demonic influences. The gathering was well attended by Chinese Ministry of State Security agents, who stood over
each fengshui master as he signed the document, some of the geomancers clearly distressed at the agents' proximity.

Adding to Hong Kong's giddiness that week, the Hong Kong Football Club defeated visiting Manchester United, one of Great Britain's
premier soccer teams, an unprecedented achievement that sent rabid
fans running into Hong Kong streets to celebrate.

The Hong Kong Lepidopterists' Society announced that a newly
discovered butterfly species, found along the shores of Clear Water
Bay, had been named *Leopidoptera toweri*. Researchers at the St. John
Hospital named a new influenza virus the Hong Kong Millennium
Tower flu, until they were visited by the Ministry of State Security,
and the name was quickly changed to the 63R virus. The elevated
highway that lined the North Point shore, the Island Eastern Corri-
dor, was renamed the Tower Causeway. Jardine's Lookout, in the hills
above Causeway Bay, was renamed Tower Lookout. China issued a series of six postage stamps, each with a different view of the tower. Two
thousand nonviolent offenders were pardoned in honor of the tower,
and many of the city's jails were emptied. The pardoned convicts were
bused out of the city to Shenzhen.

Hong Kong clothing designer Fen An, known the world around as
Fragrance An, presented her Gold Swan line of designer clothes for
women, and the gala runway event at the trade center attracted fifteen
thousand guests. The new Fifth Millennium Tower Lottery Jackpot
with a guaranteed return of not 50 percent but rather 75 percent
broke records for purchases of tickets. The city's chief executive announced that to commemorate the tower's inauguration, five acres of
landfill at the site of the former airport would be set aside for a park,
and would be named the John Llewellyn Park. The University of
Hong Kong announced that John Llewellyn had funded a new chair,
to be called the Llewellyn–Fifth Millennium China Tower Chair of
Architecture.

Ran-Ning Novelty Company, with a plant in Shenzhen just across the Special Administrative District (SAD) border, distributed a hundred thousand free Gold Swan squirt guns to Hong Kong children. On the menu at the Peninsula Hotel's Spring Moon restaurant was a new dish, the Tower Entrée, where the noodles mysteriously remained in a long curve, resembling the tower, on the plate. The owner of the Queen's Road Bakery won a citywide contest, his seven-foot-high cake most closely resembling the tower. The Clock Tower next to the Star Ferry Pier was repaired so that for the first time in living memory all four clocks displayed the same time. That week Coca-Cola issued its product in cans that had a slight curve, a chunky imitation of the tower. Seiko issued a limited-edition wristwatch on which both hands resembled tiny towers. The city suspended relicensing fees for any business that changed its name to include the word *Tower*, and more than five hundred establishments, from dry cleaners to topless bars, made the change. Demand for dragons and skulls declined precipitously at the tattoo parlors in Wan Chai, customers preferring Gold Swans.

China's president, Chen Langing, and other Central Committee members arrived in Hong Kong, as did hundreds of other senior Chinese leaders, including many from the Ministry of Construction. All large hotels hosted media centers. Broadcasting networks from around the world had sent their senior anchors. Hong Kong citizens were becoming accustomed to being stopped on the street by TV reporters and asked about their feelings regarding the tower's impending inauguration.

A weeklong holiday had been declared in Hong Kong. The citizens continued to work, of course—a weeklong holiday is as foreign to the industrious Cantonese as would be a rodeo—but the pace of work slowed. People spent a little more time celebrating and a little less time working that week. Schools were canceled for the final three days of inaugural week. Streets and promontories with views of the harbor were crowded night and day, as citizens gazed in wonderment at the tower.

Speculation about the dredges and barges and cranes still working round the clock was constant, but almost all citizens believed the reports that a new ferry terminal and an underground arcade were being added to the island.

John Llewellyn had returned to inaugural week duties in full force and was now seen everywhere, at speeches, at lunches, at awards ceremonies, at parades. He looked haggard, his eyes deeply bagged and his hands noticeably trembling, but he was never far from a camera and the crowds, and he spent his days smiling, accepting congratulations, shaking hands, and making speeches. He possessed manic energy, appearing at fifteen events a day during inaugural week. His voice became hoarse, and occasionally his hair was unkempt, but he kept going, rushing from one venue to the next.

The great architect acted as if nothing were wrong with his tower, nothing at all. Hong Kong was crazed with anticipation and delight, and John Llewellyn gave inauguration week his very best.

*   *   *

I travel light. I had been in Hong Kong many years, but my clothes and personal items filled only two suitcases, and those suitcases were open and on the bed in my apartment, and I was tossing clothes into them, not bothering to fold the pants and shirts and jackets. I was thickheaded with fury and guilt, and my movements were constricted by anger.

I tossed my shaving kit into a suitcase, then a framed photo of my father, and older photos of my mother and brother, my old bayonet, my jogging shoes. I tossed in my sweat socks with more force than required.

The doorbell rang, and I ignored it, chucking my running shorts into a suitcase. Next went my sunglasses. I had thought of tossing out Mrs. Hsu's good-luck jade—I had been carrying it since she gave it to me—but I left it in my pocket. It hadn't done me much good. I ripped off my tie and dropped it into a suitcase. I was still in the suit that I had worn to the wedding.

The doorbell rang again, and I heard Anne Iverson call from the hallway, "Clay, it's me. I want to talk. Open up, will you?"

So I crossed into the living room to let her in. She was still in her blue sheath dress. She demanded, "Where did you go?"

I inhaled loudly. "I'm sorry. It was sort of childish."

In Wen's study I had watched as Shao Long snapped Pen's neck and tossed the body into a trunk—the red pole ruthlessly efficient and the old man smiling benignly, as if this were some everyday event, a common occurrence at a wedding—and I had bolted the house, sped across the lawn, and hurried down the long flight of steps toward Tregunter Path. A few minutes later I was in my apartment, packing my belongings, and sick of myself.

"What happened?" she asked.

I went into my bedroom to continue placing my belongings into suitcases. "I saw a man being murdered. Wen's rival, the Peach Blossom's leader, I saw him killed, right there in the old man's house while his granddaughter was celebrating her marriage outside the window."

My words carried more feeling than I had intended. I told her all that I had seen, and all that I had heard, the crunching of neck bones, the smile on Wen's face.

I added, "And I shouldn't have bolted and left you there. Sorry."

She lowered herself to a chair in the corner of the room. "You are packing up all your things. Where are you going?"

"Home. Medford."

"You have a home there now? I thought you said the family home was sold."

"It has, but I'm just going to stand out in a pear orchard for a while."

"You were suckered, and that's why you are angry." She crossed her legs. "Is that it?"

Her remark was breathtakingly on the mark, as if my roiling thoughts were printed on my forehead. I threw my jogging T-shirts into a suitcase and didn't say anything.

"Am I right?" she asked.

"Anne, you know what an FBI agent is? A federal bureaucrat who pushes paper around most of his days." My voice rose. "Same with my security job at the tower. I'm a lifelong mid-level nothing . . ."

"Take it easy, Clay."

" . . . and the thing that has kept me going . . ." My words trailed off. I despise sounding pathetic. I grabbed my alarm clock, yanked the plug from the wall, and dropped it into a suitcase. With my jaws clamped together so tightly my face ached, I said, "All his life, all the time I knew him, my father had a framed print in his bedroom. It was a small thing, maybe ten inches by four inches, and he told me once that his father had given it to him. In Old English red letters, it said DO RIGHT AND FEAR NO MAN. He lived his life by that credo."

"I'm sure he did," she said softly.

"It seems a simple notion: do right and fear no man. But I flunked the test."

She leaned forward to pull a crumpled polo shirt from my suitcase. She folded it expertly, then returned it.

"Criminal gangs are alike the world around," I said, my words choppy with anger. "If you get involved with them—doesn't matter how, doesn't matter at what level—you will always lose. They will draw you in, take what they want from you, and leave you the worse for it. And that's exactly what happened to me. I was suckered, just as you say."

She reached for the alarm clock, wound the cord around the clock, then put it back into the suitcase.

I said, "I was captivated by the old guy, and it overcame my better judgment. He was polite, sincere, funny, and very powerful. He liked being around me, it seemed. He bragged to me about his operations, showing me his businesses, inviting me to his granddaughter's wedding. I was flattered and pleased. And it was all a setup."

"How do you mean?"

"He used me to get to his enemy, the Peach Blossom's leader, Pen, whom I just witnessed being murdered. I was used to put Pen off his guard. I saw myself as an intermediary, but instead I was being used as bait."

I had thrown my several pairs of street shoes into a suitcase, and now Anne placed rolled socks into the shoes to save space. Mostly, though, she was looking thoughtfully at me.

"Even the giant—Shao Long, with the green emeralds so cleverly inlaid in his teeth—was using me, following me around, doing me services, but he was in on it with his master, Wen. They were setting me up, intent on using me to kill an enemy dragon head. I should have seen it all along. I was foolish and careless and gullible."

"It's not as if you saw a saint being killed," she said. "The world is a better place without that slaver."

"That has nothing to do with it," I replied with heat. "This was a murder because it was extrajudicial. And you know as well as I do that someone who is complicit in a murder is as guilty as the guy who does the actual killing. My foolishness has made me a murderer."

"You didn't know Shao Long was going to kill Pen."

"Only criminal stupidity kept me from knowing."

"Well . . ."

"I have broken a covenant with myself, Anne: the covenant to do right."

"You're leaving Hong Kong?"

"I'm sick of Hong Kong and I'm disgusted with myself. And I'm sick of skulking around, knowing I'm being hunted. So I'm going home to regroup."

The furniture and kitchen utensils belonged to the landlord. Everything I owned in Hong Kong except the clothes on my back was now in my suitcases.

"You are running away," she said.

"Yes." I closed my suitcases and threw the clasps. "I'm running away, and I'm happy to do so." I walked toward my apartment door.

I was being testy and inane, but Hong Kong had finally done me in. I was revolted with the city, the Gold Swan, and myself. And I was angry with Anne, unfairly, I knew, but I couldn't help it. She had somehow addled me. My attraction to her and my taking her with me to the opium den and the container port—showing off in front of her, there was no better phrase for it—had dulled my wits, and now I felt silly and juvenile. I would buy my ticket at the airport. There weren't any empty seats coming into Hong Kong, but there were plenty on flights going out. With luck I'd be on a flight in less than an hour.

She followed me toward the door. "You are leaving me here?"

I had to lower a suitcase to open the door. I lifted it again, and as I passed through the door and headed toward the elevator, I said, "I'm leaving John Llewellyn's fiancée here, yes."

*   *   *

It was said later that a young boy noticed it first, that—with no school during the last days of inauguration week—he was just leaving the swimming pool at Victoria Park, just inland from the Causeway Bay typhoon shelter. He had his swim bag over his shoulder, and he was walking with friends, and he suddenly came up short, pointed at the Gold Swan, and yelled out in Cantonese, "Hey, the tower is leaning."

His friends gaped and pointed and speculated for a moment, then loudly agreed that the restaurant, which was 2,500 feet above the base, was no longer directly over the base, but hung out a little toward the west. Entering and leaving the park, passersby stopped to look at the tower and listen to the boys, and they, too, saw the lean. It was plainly evident that the tower was out of alignment. It wasn't like this yesterday or the day before, they all agreed. Something must be wrong.

More and more pedestrians gathered. Soccer players in the park paused in their game to look where the boys were pointing. Then students from nearby Queen's College came from their buildings to peer at the tower, as did guests at the Park Lane Radisson, which was across from Victoria Park. The great scimitar curve of the tower was not quite right, was a bit tilted, it was easy to see. Onlookers held up pens and pencils in front of their eyes to use as visual references, as plumb bobs. Then people walked out into the park from Windsor House and the Regal Hong Kong, staring up at the tower.

Word spread outward in a concentric circle from Victoria Park, to pedestrians on Causeway Road and Hing Fat Street, to the Police Officers' Club and the Tin Hau Temple, and still farther outward. People pointed and stared and whispered.

Drivers stood outside their cars for better looks. Faces appeared at office building windows overlooking the tower. Street repair crews put down their jackhammers and sledgehammers to stare. Customers left shops. Street vendors put aside their wares. Within moments, hundreds of thousands of Hong Kong citizens were staring at the tower, whispering among themselves and daring to mention such words as "tilting" and "leaning" and "slanting." Many people could not say anything. Many wept.

Beijing had been working assiduously to keep information about the tower's leaning away from the public, but now it was there for all to see. For those few moments of awful revelation, the city came to a halt. Hong Kong was as silent and as still as it had ever been.

* * *

The arrests began that day. Behind the veneer of modernization, China is at bottom a police state, and police states know how to make arrests in great sweeps, and this is precisely what happened in Hong Kong the day the tower's problem could no longer be suppressed.

Everyone who had worked on the tower in the past two years was picked up by agents from the Ministry of State Security and officers of the People's Armed Police. The craftsmen and journeymen, the civil and electrical and mechanical and geotech engineers, public relations specialists, materials testers, failure analysts, architects, project managers, truck drivers and machinery operators, ferry operators, interior decorators, caterers, guards, and many others were caught up in a well-planned operation that took only a few hours. When an arrestee's door was slow to open, it was kicked in. When a spouse objected, he or she was roughly shoved aside. Anyone who resisted was beaten. No calls to family or lawyers or consulates were allowed.

Nationality made no difference. Most were Hong Kong citizens, but Australians, Americans, Canadians, Britons, Malays, Singaporeans, and dozens of other countries' citizens were arrested. Consulates and embassies began issuing protests, which were ignored.

The police vans made up a long procession, heading from Hong Kong Island across the bay on ferries, then from Kowloon into the New Territories, then across the SAD border. Perhaps fifteen thousand people found themselves in jails and camps. Rumors circulated of arrests in Beijing.

The oddly named People's Liberation Army Navy (PLAN) sent into Victoria Harbor two *Luhu*-class destroyers and three *Jiangwei*-

class frigates, and it was reported that a Chinese submarine was seen in the Sulphur Channel just east of Hong Kong Island. After the Handover the Chinese had been careful not to post too many PLA soldiers in Hong Kong, but that same day more than thirty thousand PLA troops crossed the SAD border. In troop transports and scout cars, they rolled into Kowloon along the Route Twisk and Castle Peak Road and the Tai Po Road.

Soon PLA troops were in every public park, at every intersection, in every hotel lobby, at the convention center, at the exits to the Western Harbor Tunnel and the Cross Harbor Tunnel, at every station of the Mass Transit Railway and the Kowloon-Canton Railway, at all ferry terminals, at Chek Lap Kok airport and every port facility, at the Peak and every other scenic outlook, in the lobbies of all skyscrapers, at every temple and church, at every university and secondary school, at the Hong Kong Stock Exchange, and at offices of the Hong Kong Telephone Company.

Major roads were lined with troops: Nathan Road, Queen's Road Central, Robinson Road, and many others. The Central Market and the Stanley Market were occupied by troops, as were Happy Valley and Sha Tin racecourses. PLA troops took over all government buildings, including police headquarters in Caine House and all division headquarters. Three Type 85 main battle tanks were stationed at the Noon Day Gun on Causeway Bay.

Television and radio stations were taken over by soldiers and were allowed to broadcast, but could make no reference to the tower, the mass arrests, or the PLAN and PLA's activities. Internet service providers were shut down throughout Hong Kong. Foreign correspondents were detained, their cell phones and computers confiscated. Reporters were allowed no contact with their news bureaus.

The thousands of visitors who had come to Hong Kong for the Fifth Millennium China Tower's inauguration were ordered to remain in their hotel rooms. The heads of state and other dignitaries were told the same.

Through it all, not one official word regarding the leaning tower came from Beijing. The Xinua News Agency, China's official news bureau, announced that a vast conspiracy had been discovered in Hong Kong, and that decisive measures were being taken to quash it. No mention was made of what the conspiracy might involve, or who might be the conspirators, other than "the traditional enemies of the socialist state."

*   *   *

All of this occurred in the hours of Wen's granddaughter's wedding and during my packing my suitcases. I missed being arrested by a few moments, I believe. I saw the People's Armed Police flood my neighborhood just as I left my apartment building, my two suitcases in hand. I turned around to reenter the building, intent on getting Anne out of there, but she had followed me on the next elevator and was crossing the lobby toward me.

"What's going on?" she asked as she joined me under the building's portico.

"The Chinese have moved in force. We need to get out of here."

"Where?"

A line of ten armored cars roared down the street. Several clipped off fenders and bumpers of parked cars, and one rolled over a crosswalk sign.

She asked again, "Where is it safe?"

"Come with me," I said as I turned down the hill. "The American consulate. We'll be okay there."

I grabbed her hand and we hurried along the sidewalk. The consulate was only a few blocks away. But we never made it.

20

Hong Kong streets had become eerily quiet. The throngs that had emerged to view the leaning Gold Swan had vanished, caution trumping curiosity, as Chinese police and soldiers rushed through the streets, making thousands of arrests and occupying the streets and all other public spaces.

Anne and I hurried toward the American consulate on Garden Road, me gripping her hand, and she standing out like a beacon, with her blond hair and the sultry blue dress she had worn to the wedding. PLA troops marched through the streets, their rifles over their shoulders. A truck pulling a howitzer rolled by, a red star on the truck's door. We walked passed a flower stand that its proprietor had abandoned. Same with an espresso stand, the cups and napkins ready but no one behind the counter. A metal antitheft grate was in place in front of the door to the Gucci shop. A jewelry store owner was hammering plywood over his display windows. People ran by in many directions, many holding hands, the young pulling the old, many looking back over their shoulders. Bicycles streamed past. A young man pushed an elderly woman in a wheelbarrow. A PLA helicopter gunship, called a Gazelle, came into view overhead, just above the skyscrapers, filling the street with the pounding of its blades, the quiet gone.

It was then that the hunters found me. In my haste and self-disgust, I hadn't been checking over my shoulder, hadn't been evading potential followers since leaving my apartment, but just then, maybe out of habit from the last several days, I glanced over my shoulder and saw

two men—both Asians, both wearing sport coats with no ties—walking quickly after us, staring at us, and picking up their paces to close
with us. One of them reached into his jacket.

I dropped the suitcases and grabbed Anne and pulled her along,
breaking into a run. She kept up with me, even though she was on
heels, the shoes she had worn at the wedding. I pushed through the
crowd, plowing into people's shoulders, rushing by them. I looked
over my shoulder. The two men were running after us. One of them
had a pistol in his hand. They were closing.

We rounded a corner, and there was the consulate, with the American flag on a pole next to the building. On Garden Street was a PLA
single-barrel antiaircraft gun, towed there behind a truck in camouflage colors. A crowd was at the consulate's gate, several calling
through the fence demanding attention. Guards let some of them in,
one at a time after checking identification papers. Marines and foreign service officers patrolled the grounds.

Rifle-carrying PLA troops ringed the embassy, standing at ease.
Three troop carriers were parked in front of St. John's Cathedral.
Anne and I rushed forward, intent on passing through the loose ring
of Chinese soldiers.

A hand abruptly gripped my shoulder, and I feared it was one of the
two men who had been chasing us. I was spun around. A People's
Armed Police lieutenant had gripped my shoulder and was carrying in
his other hand a sheet of paper with my photograph on it. He said
something in Cantonese or maybe Mandarin. He released me to gesture to several of his men, who closed in on me.

I glimpsed the two men who had chased us. They were slipping
away in the crowd, apparently thwarted by the PAP. In a few seconds I
could no longer see them.

Maybe I should have taken my chances with those two men. I re-
gripped Anne's hand and tried to bolt toward the consulate's gate. One
of the PAP policemen swung the butt of his handgun at me, and down
I went.

The blow had glanced off my forehead and knocked me to my

knees. Anne called out, a sound that ended with a yelp of pain. I tried to rise, but was struck again, this time on the back of my neck, so painfully that I collapsed to the concrete and I was instantly nauseated. Then several hands yanked me to standing and propped me up when my knees buckled. I was searched. My cell phone was removed from a pocket, as was the small handgun I had been carrying, and my wallet and keys, and Mrs. Hsu's jade good-luck piece.

Anne was on the street, on her back, her arm across her head. Drops of blood formed on her temple. PAP officers grabbed her arms and lifted her to her feet. She tried to bend over to clutch her head—the bruise was already purpling—but the policemen held her up. Her mouth sagged open. Her eyes were closed. A few passersby glanced at us but quickly moved on.

The PAP lieutenant called out an order, and we were pulled toward an olive-green truck. Anne couldn't walk and was dragged along by two policemen, her feet scraping the street. I tried to step toward her but was roughly shoved forward, almost falling. Four policemen had me in their grips. They brought me to a PAP van.

I struggled to make my voice level. "I am entitled to speak to officials at the U.S. consulate."

One of the policemen growled something in Cantonese. My stomach was rolling over, and my head was throbbing. I began to sag, but a hand gripped my hair to tug me upright. My arms were pulled behind my back, and handcuffs were secured around my wrists. I heard tape being peeled from a roll, and then duct tape was roughly wound around my head, covering my eyes. Hands lifted me, then threw me forward into the cargo bay of the truck.

I gasped out, "Anne," but heard no reply.

The van's doors closed. I lay there for a moment, trying to summon the will to rise. My head was pounding.

"Someone else here?" a voice asked in English.

I rolled over—hard to do with my hands cuffed behind me—and struggled to sit up. "Who is here?"

"Jack Rainey. Is that you, Clay?"

Rainey was the Australian security consultant who shared my

trailer on the island. I coughed raggedly, trying to keep bile down in my throat.

"You okay?" he asked. "I've got tape over my eyes. Can you get up? There's benches along the sides here."

I asked, "Anne, you here?"

I was answered only by the truck's engine starting. I managed to put one leg under me, and I carefully stepped to the side of the truck, until the edge of the bench pressed against my legs. My back against the panel, I slid down to the bench.

"Anybody else in here?" I asked.

"Just you and me," Rainey said. "They picked me up at my apartment a while ago."

"Why were we arrested?"

"All I can figure out is that we worked on the tower," Rainey answered, his Australian accent pronounced. "Just before these cops beat on my apartment door, I received a telephone call from Don McKibbon's wife. She was frantic, saying her husband had just been taken away by police. I told her I'd try to figure it out and call her back as soon as I could, and just as I put the phone down, cops appeared outside my door."

I could hear the van's door open again. Several people entered the bay, and then the doors slammed shut.

I asked, "Someone else here?"

I was answered by being kicked in the belly, a solid blow with a boot. I doubled over and groaned, then slid to the metal floor. Then the top of my head was slammed with a sap or a club, and out I went.

*   *   *

Peach Blossom was being extinguished during those hours. The old gangster began with its dragon head, Pen Kai-ge, and once Pen was dead, a signal went out to 88K soldiers, who already had their orders and were in place. Peach Blossom was nowhere near as large or as powerful as 88K, and Jay Lee would tell me later that his Organized Crime and Triad Bureau learned that senior Peach Blossom members were being killed the very hour I was arrested.

The murders were accomplished with Wen's typical whimsy. The body of Peach Blossom's enforcer, Ni Man-leung, was found when it slid out a concrete truck's chute during the laying of an apartment building's foundation, concrete being Wen Quichin's signature. Gong To-wai, the recruiter, was found dead at the Lei Chenk Uk grave, a two-thousand-year-old burial vault, now a tourist attraction. Gong's body was discovered there the next morning. Dai Zhi-weng, a senior Peach Blossom soldier, was found later that day hanging upside down on a rope from a telephone pole, his neck cut open. There might have been others, but Jay Lee could only account for these three. Jay told me he was distressed by the killings, then he burst out laughing.

With its leadership dead, Peach Blossom disbanded in the next few days. Some of the society's members joined other triads, others satisfied themselves with jobs and families. Then 88K moved into its territory in the San Po Kong neighborhood. Wen had won.

*   *   *

I don't know how long I was unconscious. I learned later that when Jack Rainey had made a move to help me, he was kicked in the face, and he could do nothing but slump in the truck's corner in much pain. Eventually, I came around and could climb back to the bench, the tape and handcuffs still in place. I didn't say another word during the drive, which I'd guess lasted about two hours.

The truck finally stopped, and the doors were opened. I was gripped by the arms and pulled out of the cargo bay. Trying to climb down, I missed the fender, and fell to the gravel, where I was kicked in the back, then jerked to my feet by rough hands. Commands were issued.

"Anne?" I called out.

I was slapped in the face, and a guard snarled something at me. Guards pushed me across gravel, and then I entered a building, I could tell by the change in the air. A guard shoved me down into a chair. When he pulled off the tape, chunks of my hair were pulled out.

I squinted against the light. A man was backlit against windows, but I couldn't make him out, not for a full minute as my eyes adjusted. Then I saw he was wearing the uniform of a PLA soldier. He was sitting on the front of a desk.

"You were handled carelessly. I apologize for that, and I will speak to the commander of the guards who brought you here." His English was accented but readily understandable. "I am Colonel Shan Bi-jun of the People's Liberation Army. I have been assigned an urgent matter."

"Since when is a conversation with me urgent?"

"I also apologize for the handcuffs, but it's in the manual."

He took a moment to light a cigarette. He had a bored, haughty face, with a small mouth set in a permanent smirk. His eyelashes were long and feminine. His uniform was drab olive and showed no indications of rank or unit. He rose from the desk to slowly walk along the window. White daylight was so bright it washed out whatever was outside the window, and it backlit the colonel, casting his features in dark shadow.

"I am a medical doctor," he said. "An anesthesiologist. I find myself in the army." He smiled. "I've tried to resign my commission, but have not been allowed to do so. My skills are needed in the modern army, I'm told."

I heard the truck pull away from the building.

Colonel Shan said, "I want to discuss with you the conspiracy surrounding the construction of the Fifth Millennium China Tower."

"I am unaware of a conspiracy."

"You were a security consultant for the tower. If anyone would know, you would."

"Then nobody knows," I said.

With my hands tight against my back, my shoulders and arms had begun to ache. My eyes crossed and uncrossed uncontrollably several times due to the blows to my head and neck.

The colonel removed the cigarette from his mouth to study the fired tip of it, turning it around, giving it all of his attention. He returned it to his mouth. "I must tell you that very senior people in Beijing are interested in what you have to say, and I have been ordered to relay the contents of our discussion to them as quickly as possible."

I shook my head, then looked around the small room. The desk and a chair behind it were the only furniture in the place, with unfinished walls and a floor made of planks. A telephone and a gooseneck lamp were on the desk, as were my cell phone, wallet, keys, and the piece of jade. My handgun was missing. The building might have been put up that day.

I looked over my shoulder. At the edge of my vision was a hospital gurney and an IV stand. Two clear bottles of fluid hung from the stand.

The colonel said, "I have been told that I cannot be concerned with your comfort."

"You going to torture every single person who worked on the tower?"

He shrugged. "My concern at this moment is with you. And no, there will be no torture involved. Chemicals are all I ever need."

I shifted on the seat, trying to ease the pain in my shoulders.

"The earth compaction data was altered, was it not?"

I cleared my throat. Why not tell this fellow everything I knew? What had I to hide? I had nobody to implicate, nobody to protect. I hadn't been entrusted with state secrets regarding the tower. I had never before been tortured—chemically or otherwise—but I didn't doubt I'd crack in three seconds. Why even tolerate three seconds of it? But for some reason I was silent. I dislike being bullied. Maybe that was it.

Colonel Shan said, "The tower was built upon earthen fill that could not support the structure."

I coughed again. My head was sending bolts of pain into my neck. The cuffs had begun to scrape skin from my wrists.

The colonel stood in front of the window, the cigarette held over his palm in the manner of a Frenchman. "And the reason the fill could not support the tower is that the fill was less dense and less strong than was indicated by tests. The software insured that the island would fail. I am right in this, am I not?"

"I'm an American citizen, and . . ." My voice trailed off.

He put the cigarette in his mouth and leaned back against the window. "I have been charged with determining the extent of the conspiracy that has damaged the tower. I have been told that my country must know who its enemies are, and that I am not to spare any efforts or waste any sympathy on those who have this information and won't reveal it."

I tried coming up with something brave, but the aching in my arms and shoulders and head had given way to deadening fear. My mouth had dried up, and I suspected the nausea was no longer from the blow to my head but from fright.

Still leaning against the windows, his features hidden by bright light pouring into the room, the colonel said, "I'm in a hurry, Mr. Williams. Tell me who altered the program that gathered and analyzed the island's compaction data."

I shook my head, as much defiance as I could muster.

"Well, then, you force me to use certain medications that will lower your discretion." I think he smiled, but it was washed out by the harsh light behind him. Smoke veiled his face, and he spoke around the cigarette in his mouth. "Don't worry. You won't remember anything."

Just as he began to take a step toward me, the window behind him shattered inward, and glass fell in a shower of shards and chips. An enormous arm—seemingly covered with sparkling glass scales—shot through the window and seized the colonel by the neck. The falling glass sounded like a harsh laugh.

The colonel's hands went to his throat in an attempt to resist, but he was yanked back toward the window. Glass fragments still hung from the window frame, resembling teeth. The huge arm pulled the kicking colonel back and through the window, where he disappeared into the hard white light. Glass fragments skittered across the floor toward me.

A moment later the door opened. Shao Long, 88K's red pole, stood there, a few beads of blood on his arm where glass had pierced his skin. He stepped across the room, glass cracking under his feet. He had keys to the handcuffs—perhaps taken from the colonel's pocket—and he freed my hands. The cuffs fell to the floor. He didn't say anything, but there was a slight smile on his face. He helped me to my feet. I rubbed my wrists, then lifted my belongings from the desk, putting them into my pocket. Then I followed him through the door.

A long black Mercedes sedan was parked just outside the building. The car's engine was running. I looked around. We were at a makeshift camp, which included three buildings and dozens of tents. Several trucks were parked near the tents. A grove of trees was at one end of the camp, and barren hills rose behind them.

The colonel's body was on the gravel below the shattered window. His head was cocked unnaturally to one side, and his dead eyes were open. The cigarette was still in his mouth and still trailing gray smoke.

Shao opened the car's rear door for me. I climbed in. Wen Quichin was in the backseat, leaning against the other door, smiling. In the middle of the seat was Jack Rainey, who had a red bruise on his forehead. Anne was in the front seat, her hair ruffled and a piece of duct tape still clinging to her shirt. She looked at me but didn't say anything. Shao Long got in behind the steering wheel.

The car pulled away from the building. We slowly drove fifty yards along the gravel road to a gate that was open. Four PLA soldiers were standing there, their rifles over their shoulders as they chatted to themselves. Not one of them looked at the Mercedes as it passed through the gate. They studiously ignored us. When the car cleared the gate, two of the soldiers lowered the barricade. Wen's triad had a long, long reach, I realized then.

Still on a gravel road, the car turned away from the sun, back toward the New Territories. We drove alongside two hundred yards of fence that had been newly installed, I could tell by the fresh dirt around the poles. The hurricane fencing was topped with razor wire. Behind the fence were dozens of trucks, some just arriving, the occupants stepping down from the cargo bays, guards yelling at them. Rows of tents filled the area. Several armored scout cars were parked just outside the fence, the gunners standing in the open hatches behind mounted machine guns.

Many of those arrested in Hong Kong were being brought here. A convoy of trucks passed our car and then stopped at the gate behind us. Hundreds of prisoners milled about inside the fence. Soldiers and policemen were spaced along the fence. A guard tower was being constructed at the corner of the compound. Workers used wheelbarrows to bring concrete to postholes that had just been dug, as the compound was being expanded. Clouds of dust rose from the compound.

Shao Long turned the Mercedes onto an asphalt road, and the car picked up speed. The old man reached across Jack Rainey and patted my hand. I looked over at him. He wore his half-smile, like he always did.

From the driver's seat, Shao Long spoke in English: "That colonel's body back there, Mr. Williams?"

"Yes?"

He turned to grin at me with his sparkling green teeth. "You owe me an emerald."

*   *   *

Wen commanded twenty thousand eyes, and they found Darrel Reese quickly. All American government employees in Hong Kong had been rounded up, but the police had missed Reese, who had fled his apartment, probably heading to the American consulate, but apparently discovered he couldn't get through the ring of policemen and soldiers, so he had holed up at the Queen's Hotel near the Central Market in the Central District.

I knocked on the door. "Darrel, it's me, Clay Williams."

After a moment he opened it a crack. "You haven't been caught in the sweep, looks like." He pulled the door open to let me in. "How'd you find me?"

"I've got lots of friends in Hong Kong," I replied blandly, not adding that they were mostly gangsters.

He locked the door after I entered the room. I lowered myself to the only chair in the room, which was next to a tiny desk. A framed photograph of the Ten Thousand Buddhas Temple was on a wall. The faded bedspread had an orange and green pattern. The red carpet had cigarette burns on it. The room did not have air conditioning, and the place was fetid.

"What brings you here, Clay?" He smiled narrowly. CIA agents don't like surprises, and my showing up at his hotel door was a surprise. Curtains covered the window, and Reese's red hair was auburn in the weak light in the room. "Seeking a refuge, maybe?"

"It was a CIA operation, wasn't it, Darrel?"

He sat on the edge of the bed. He looked at me, his face professionally impassive.

I said, "The software that determined fill loads, GeoPlace 3.1, supposedly manufactured by Geotechnic, Inc., in Denver, is owned by the Central Intelligence Agency, or else the CIA obtained the software somewhere along the line, and made alterations to it."

"I'm sworn to secrecy on all this stuff, Clay. You know that. I can't tell you my middle name, much less anything about the tower."

I rubbed the side of my nose. "Darrel, I know you're a patriot, and acting in the best interests of our country. But I still would like to know what's going on."

He shook his head in a small way. "Can't tell you. Sorry."

I shrugged. "I figured as much. I'm curious, is all." I turned to the door and said in a loud voice, "Shao Long."

Instantly the giant's fist shot through the door just above the lock, fragmenting the wood and sending splinters flying. The big hand reached down to unlock the door, which was then flung open so that it cracked loudly against the wall. Shao stood in the doorway, filling it, his arms like hawsers, and his smile revealing the emeralds.

Reese involuntarily pushed himself back on the bed so that he was against the headboard. His eyes were wide, and his mouth was pulled back in a grimace of fear. The red pole stepped into the room and stood in front of the bed, his hands at his sides.

I said, "My friend Shao here is also curious. He and I have different temperaments. He is less patient than I am."

Reese gasped out, "You're threatening me."

"Not at all." I waved my hand airily. "We can continue our conversation about the Gold Swan, or I'll leave the room and go somewhere else."

"And leave this . . . this fellow here?" Reese pointed as if Shao were a statue.

"He'll stay if he wants," I said. "He likes to chat. I must warn you, though. Shao Long is extremely fast, and he would take offense were you to, say, reach for a hidden pistol somewhere."

Reese found his dignity and scooted to the edge of the bed to place his feet on the floor. His eyes never left Shao. He said, "The government of the United States of America has had nothing to do with the tower's failure, with the dredging and filling of the island, none of it."

"What about folks acting on the U.S.'s behalf?"

He managed to block-and-tackle his gaze from the giant over to me. "Nobody representing the U.S. or on behalf of the U.S. had anything to do with it, either."

"What about Geotechnic, Inc., of Denver?"

"It is owned by GeoWorld International, based in Los Angeles."

"And who owns GeoWorld International?" I asked.

"A holding company, a shell, that has a Singapore address." Reese's eyes ticked between Shao and me. "It's called South Sea Limited, which is incorporated in the Cayman Islands."

"Is there an end to this ownership chain, Darrel?"

"There is." He smiled in the CIA's patented way that FBI agents find so galling. "South Sea Limited is owned by the Canton Trading Company, based in Guangzhou." Guangzhou is the other name for Canton.

"It's a Chinese company?" I exclaimed.

"It is," he said with satisfaction. "The Canton Trading Company sounds like a vegetable wholesaler, but it is a software firm employing about ten programmers, and I've heard they are the most skilled and experienced programmers in China."

Shao Long took another step into the room, positioning himself near the dresser so that he was not quite as threatening.

"My agency had nothing to do with altering that software, with making the GeoPlace program fudge the compaction numbers, or anything to do with the tower."

"But you've known about it?"

"For quite some time." He held out his hands in a gesture of peace and understanding. "Our policy is not to interfere."

"I'm sure."

"We didn't interfere," he said. "We only watched. We've had nothing to do with it."

"Nothing?"

He grinned. "Except to make sure that news of the tower's leaning reached the people in Beijing, which we've been able to do. The old man I pointed out to you, Xu Chao—the master propagandist, the fellow who can make history disappear—couldn't contain this one. It's an age of satellites and the Internet and cell phones, technologies beyond Xu's power to control. Most of China knows about the tower. We've seen to it."

"So you've won your duel with Xu Chao?"

"Won it decisively. He has returned to Beijing with his tail between his legs."

I asked, "So who owns the Canton Trading Company, the people who altered the software?"

He eyed me carefully, intending to savor my reaction. "Cao Ah-kin, China's minister of state security."

* * *

Anne and I stepped onto Heroes of the Revolution Island, the boatman helping us onto the dock.

I pulled out eight hundred Hong Kong dollars and passed it to the boatman, who had one foot on his sampan's rail and another on the dock. "You'll get another eight hundred if you wait here thirty minutes to give us a ride back."

The boatman nodded his head. The Gold Swan rose above us. Reflected from the water, waving lines of light made the tower's curved shaft resemble molten gold. Anne had called me on my cell phone, telling me that John Llewellyn had gone out to the island, and that with the tower leaning more and more, he was in mortal danger. Entirely against my better judgment, I offered to try to retrieve Llewellyn, and she said she would go with me.

The frantic work on the island had been abandoned. Much equipment—trucks, concrete mixers, cranes—remained on the work site but looked as if it had been ditched quickly, with doors left open, dumps in the upright position, and portable generators still running, black smoke coming from their exhaust pipes. In the workers' haste to get off the island, tool belts and lunch tins had been left on the concrete. Office paper blew across the platform, including blue architects' drawings.

Anne ran toward the tower's west entrance, and I followed. A deep rumble came from the concrete beneath my feet, which shivered side to side, and I stumbled, catching myself before I fell. I ran around a bank of portable lights, and then around rolls of coiled wire rope.

The concrete pad in front of the tower's lobby door had been ripped open, exposing the foundation below. I entered the lobby on a wood catwalk over the construction hole. Much of the lobby had been dug up, the granite tiles strewn everywhere. Trying to keep up with Anne, I picked my way among the excavation debris. The air conditioning had been turned off, and the air in the lobby was dank, smelling of concrete dust. The construction crater in the lobby was forty feet deep, exposing I-beams and blocks of concrete. Four backhoes were in the lobby. Anne stepped over loose cables, and I followed in her footsteps. Lights were on overhead. The lobby's furniture was carelessly piled against the walls.

We found John Llewellyn sitting in a metal folding chair near an open elevator. His hands were clasped together on his lap, and he was staring at the far wall. He didn't turn his head as we approached.

Anne didn't waste any words. "Come with us, John. It's dangerous here. We've got a boat outside."

The building rumbled, a bass groan that came from all directions. I could see a metal girder shift down in the hole. Llewellyn's cheek twitched, then again and again, an uncontrollable tic. He smiled down at his hands, his lips twisted by the tic. His hands were covered with dirt and grease. He was wearing a gray suit that had smears of concrete dust along one side and a tear on the left sleeve. His red tie was loose and coated with dirt. His tasseled black shoes had grime on them. He appeared to have been single-handedly trying to save the tower, working among the construction debris. The skin of Llewellyn's face had an ochre hue and was puffy and slack. His silver hair was stuck messily to his scalp.

Anne gripped his shoulder. "Let's go, John."

He laughed, a mirthless rattle that sounded like a stick dragged along a picket fence. "I've tried my hardest, but I can't come to grips with it."

"Now is not the time for self-analysis," she said. "I want to get out of here. Are you coming?"

"It was so lovely, all of it, not just the tower, but these past few years." He clapped his small hands together once. "Don't you think? Just lovely. We lived in the world as I made it. Every construct was my own. Everywhere I looked, I saw myself and my work. Now"—he held out his hands to encompass the tortured lobby—"look at it."

Her voice was sharp. "John, you can reminisce and grieve after we get out of here. Stand up and let's go."

Something cracked deep inside the building, a noise so loud that I jumped.

"Now I sit amidst rubble," he intoned, his cheek twitching. "It's all come down on top of me."

"Not yet, it hasn't," I said. The tower loosed another moan, things all around shifting and grating. "I don't have time for this prattle, John. Come on." I gripped his arm and made to lift him off the chair.

He exploded off the chair like a lineman, and with ferocious energy pushed me backward. I tripped over a coil of wire and fell onto the floor.

"No," he cried out, "I'm not going anywhere!"

Anne had stepped back, startled. She looked at me as I rose to my feet, then she tried again, reaching for Llewellyn's arm. "John, you aren't thinking right. You're acting nutty. Let's go. We need to get out from under here."

When she tried to pull him along, he jerked his arm free.

Her voice was tremulous. "John, what's going on?"

He looked at her as if she were a stranger, nothing in his expression admitting to the slightest recognition. "The great always fall. It's just a matter of time, I suppose."

"John, please." Tears welled in her eyes. "You're not making sense. You're scaring me."

Llewellyn stepped to the open elevator, calling out in a voice fogged with self-pity. "I want to be by myself. My tower and me."

Anne cried out, "John, come back." She hurried after him.

"There's a unity between the tower and me, you see." Llewellyn's tone was of a lecturer. "I can be alone up there, just me and my tower."

She reached for him again, placing her hands on his shoulders. He grabbed her arms, spun her around, and pushed her away. She tripped over a pile of tiles and fell, skinning an elbow. I hurried over to her and helped her to her feet.

He entered the elevator and pressed a button. I thought for a moment that Anne might run after him, but she dabbed her bleeding elbow with her fingers and didn't make a move toward the elevator. She had been baffled and fearful, but her face transformed in that moment, and her countenance hardened as she stared at her fiancé, who pressed the elevator button.

She shook her head with disgust, and didn't make a move toward the elevator. "So long, John."

The elevator door closed, and John Llewellyn began his journey to the top of his masterpiece.

She touched her elbow again, then examined the blood. "My fiancé is an idiot, and I've been a fool to ever think—"

The tower growled again, down in the foundation, a deep rumble that seemed to come from the center of the earth.

She began walking toward the lobby door. Her expression was one of pale fury. The sound of metal scraping together came from above us.

We began to run, but just as she came to the lobby's door, walking across the catwalk, she stopped, yanked the diamond ring off her finger, and tossed it into the construction crater.

As we hurried across the island toward the sampan, she said, and now there was an unmistakable note of amusement in her voice, "Why did you ever let me get engaged to an idiot?"

*   *   *

The Gold Swan fell thirty minutes later, just as the Noon Day Gun sounded. The PLA and police sweeps were largely over, and while soldiers were still everywhere, they were no longer making massive arrests. A degree of calm had returned, and shock at the sight of the leaning tower had given way to resignation and mourning.

The citizenry had returned to the streets to stare at the tower, hundreds of thousands of men, women, and children, ringing the shoreline and filling the streets. Early that morning several thunderous cracks had come from the island that could be heard throughout Hong Kong. The lines of dredges and other vessels that had been attempting to repair the tower were quickly cast off, and the crafts had pulled away.

More cracks from the foundation echoed between the hills, and the tower was seen to shiver and shift, and then the restaurant at the end of the giant curve lurched out over the island, way off-center, dangling there. Great chasms opened in the island's concrete cap east of the tower. From where I was standing—the Wan Chai Sports Ground, between Causeway Bay and the convention center—the tower appeared to sway, then right itself a bit, then lean even more. Each motion was met with gasps and cries from the enormous crowd at the sports ground.

Shao Long was standing next to me. He said in a low voice, "I love that tower."

"I do, too," I replied, a catch in my throat.

I had gotten off the sampan fifteen minutes ago. Anne was holding my hand. She brushed a tear from her cheek.

The Noon Day Gun was fired, and as if in answer a metallic shriek came from the island, a grinding tear that rang out across the harbor. The tower staggered, caught itself, then staggered again, the restaurant and viewing area swaying at the end of the long arc.

Then the western base of the tower sank into the concrete pad, and the structure began to fall. Slowly at first, the great arc began moving through the sky, and the restaurant swung out, and then down. The curved tower swept through space, out and down, a vast scythe aimed at the harbor, the tower's foundation rumbling and wailing as it tore loose, as if it were pitiably calling out to us across the bay. Down the tower came, whistling through the air, plummeting toward the bay. John Llewellyn rode it all the way down.

The restaurant hit the water first, sounding like another shot from the Noon Day Gun. A spout of water leapt hundreds of feet into the air. At that instant the tower was horizontal, its base and its top at sea level, with the huge arc in between, soaring up and over and down. But only for an instant.

The restaurant level was driven into the bay, and the Swan's neck fractured and crumpled all along its half-mile length. Bronze panels plummeted into the water. Girders bent and gave way. Steel twisted, reinforced concrete disintegrated. The Swan's neck crashed into the island and into the bay, sending up dust and water, and making a sound that was strangely like a human groan.

So the tower was down and shattered, and the air above the bay was empty again, and all Hong Kong hearts were broken, including mine.

21

The bartender slid a beer mug to me, and another to Jay Lee. We were at the Original Chicago Eatery again, bellied up to the bar. Jay was chewing peanuts from the bowl. The giant-screen television was showing an Australian Rules football game, which, as far as I could tell, was comprised of about twenty muscular felons intent on killing each other, with no rules whatsoever. A copy of the *South China Morning Post* was on the bar in front of me. The three-column photo was of China's new president, Cao Ah-kin, promoted from his position of minister of state security. He was flanked by smiling and applauding Central Committee members as he was being presented to the National People's Congress at the Great Hall of the People in Beijing.

"So it was Cao, all along?" Jay asked.

I nodded. "He had been working against President Chen for years, making secret alliances, doing favors, putting people in his debt. But he needed a shocker, something that would rattle the Central Committee, and threaten them, and something that suggested that President Chen was incompetent. The tower was it."

"It was President Chen's agents who were chasing you?"

I said: "Chen feared news of the calamity getting out, so he tried to silence those who knew about it. His people were chasing Anne and me and some other people who knew that the Gold Swan was leaning. They almost got me on the path to Wen Quichin's house, and they almost got Ann over near North Point. And, looking for me, they killed the CIA bodyguard in my apartment."

Jay sipped his beer and nodded.

"Chen hoped the tower's leaning would stop," I went on, "and that news of it would never get out, and that all would be well. When the tower began to lean visibly, and when all Hong Kong could see it plainly, he panicked and sent troops into the city. All the arrests followed. Pure, reflexive out-of-control panic."

"Chen had much prestige tied up in the tower," Jay said.

"And when it fell, so did Chen."

A below-the-fold headline in the *Post* announced an amnesty for all persons arrested in the past five days in Hong Kong and Beijing. The tower workers caught up in the sweep were all being released from the jails and camps. No explanations were being offered for the arrests or the amnesty. PLA and PAP troops had been removed from Hong Kong as quickly as they had come. Speculation was that Cao, as minister of state security, knew that sending divisions of soldiers into the city would fan the crisis, insuring that the president would be toppled. Inaugural week celebrations had been canceled, of course. Decorations were being taken down in Kowloon and Hong Kong. The cruise ships had left the harbor. The heads of state and other visitors were leaving the city as fast as possible. Salvage ships had been called in, and the process of clearing the tower's wreckage from the harbor had begun, and it might take two years, salvors had said. Normalcy had returned to the streets, which is to say, Hong Kong was back to business.

"Did Cao have high-level help in his conspiracy?" Jay asked after a swallow of beer.

"He had several coconspirators on the Central Committee. My CIA contact Darrel Reese doesn't know who, but thinks the vice president might've been in on it. The disgraced President Chen has been removed from the Central Committee, and removed from Peking. Reese says the U.S. government doesn't know where he is."

Jay asked, "Why did my boss, Police Commissioner Kwok, plant false evidence indicating your father committed suicide? Do you have a theory on that?"

"Darrel Reese does. Ex-President Chen and Commissioner Kwok go a long way back, Reese says."

"Really? I didn't know that."

"Not many people do. Chen helped Kwok's career many times along the way, and Kwok owed Chen. When Chen asked Kwok to do everything in his power to stop news of the tower's problem from spreading, Kwok was glad to help, and that included minimizing the boy's—Hsu's—disappearance and my father's death."

Jay said, "Well, Kwok has been fired—probably on orders from the new president—so I don't have to worry about working for him."

I glanced down at my suitcases, which were parked next to my barstool. My suitcases had been turned in to the police, and Jay had delivered them to me. I felt an abrupt tug of sadness. I was leaving Hong Kong after ten years, with no plans to return. Maybe I liked the city more than I knew, aggravating as the place was.

"You know, you've found justice for your father's death, sort of," Jay said.

"How do you figure?"

"Chen—or someone reporting to him—must've ordered that news of the Gold Swan's problems be quashed, and that order led to your dad's death. And now Chen is gone. And Commissioner Kwok helped in the scheme, and he's gone, too. So there's some justice there."

"Then how come I don't feel better about it?"

"The trouble with you round-eyes is that you don't realize that some things never balance out," Jay replied. "We Cantonese know that some things just hang there, never to be remedied."

I stared at the foam on my beer. "Yeah, maybe you're right."

Jay looked down at my suitcases. "When does your flight leave?"

I glanced at my wristwatch. "Two hours from now."

"I'll walk you to the Airport Express Railway terminal when it's time."

I sipped the beer. "Come and visit me when I get settled. I'll email you my address as soon as I get set up."

"I want to see the Grand Canyon, not Medford, Oregon."

"I'll take you there. We call it The Big Ditch."

"Really?" I could see Jay tuck this away for future use. Then he asked, "Can we get to the Grand Canyon on Route 66? I've always wanted to drive down Route 66. You know, Flagstaff, Arizona, don't forget Winona. Kingman, Barstow, San Bernardino."

"I'll check it out and let you know. Plan on coming over in a month."

Jay abruptly twisted on the stool, and he blurted out something in Cantonese, a syllable of astonishment. I looked over my shoulder. The red pole, Shao Long, stood there, hovering over us, his smile revealing the emeralds.

Jay moved to stand up, but I put a hand on his arm. "Take it easy, Jay."

"I've been trying to find and arrest this man for ten years," he said in English. "You are under arrest, Shao."

Shao said in English. "Maybe, maybe not." He sat on the stool on the other side of me. "I don't like beer."

"It's a developed taste," I said. "Give it another try."

A mug of beer was produced by the bartender who, glancing nervously at Shao, quickly removed our check from the bar. I don't think Shao ever paid for anything.

"Where are you going?" Shao asked.

"To Medford, Oregon, where I was raised."

"You're under arrest, Shao." Jay sipped his beer. "I mean it."

"What are you going to do in Medford?" Shao asked.

I said, "I've been thinking about buying a small pear orchard."

Jay looked at me. "You, a farmer?"

"I won't make much money at it, but I don't need to make much money. A hundred acres of pears, with a house in the middle of it. In sunny Medford. It's sounding better and better."

"What about the woman?" Shao asked, grimacing at the taste of the beer. "I like her."

"Anne is going back to San Diego. Flying out today, too. She's going to look for a job there. Our planes leave about the same time, so I'm meeting her at the airport to say goodbye."

Shao shifted on the stool to look at me. "She must be grieving, losing her . . . what's the word?"

"Fiancé," Jay helped.

"Yeah, she's probably grieving," I said. I didn't want to talk about Anne.

Shao leaned forward so he could address Jay. "I was going to be a chef before I was led into a life of crime."

"What kind of chef?" Jay asked.

"Pastries, maybe."

I looked at my watch again. "I've got to go. Jay, you stay here and finish your beer. No need to walk me to the station."

I shook Jay's hand, and he said, "Route 66, remember. I'll come over in a month."

Then I shook Shao's huge hand.

The red pole said, "Maybe I'll come, too. What is Route 66?"

I lifted my two suitcases. "Jay will explain it to you."

So I left them there. At the door I looked back, and Jay and Shao had returned to their beers, and were leaning toward each other, chatting about Route 66, probably in Cantonese.

*   *   *

I walked under the airport's barrel vaults toward the check-in counters, wishing I had rollers on my suitcases. I was taking a Singapore Airlines flight to San Francisco, then a United flight to Portland, then a Horizon flight to Medford.

After a short wait in line, I checked my bags, then found Anne, who was waiting in a chair between a Singapore counter and a yogurt stand. Her flight to Los Angeles was scheduled to leave twenty minutes after mine. Only a carry-on bag was next to her, so she had already checked her luggage. She had been staring off at nothing when I approached, lost in her thoughts, and she started when I said hello. She grinned feebly and tapped the chair next to her, and I sat down.

"You know what's been bothering me, Clay, more than anything?"

"What?"

"I was angry at John Llewellyn after he pushed me around in the tower lobby, but now I'm terribly sad for him. He died not knowing that the tower had been sabotaged, that the failure was not due to his faulty design."

"Well, he knows now."

"You think so?" She glanced sideways at me. "You go to church or something?"

"I'm planning to."

She was wearing a peach-colored cotton sweater that had green and blue embroidery along the cuffs and neck, and white jeans and sandals. Her hair was loose to her shoulders, and in the harsh light in the terminal it was a mix of colors, gold and yellow and cream. The light also made the freckles across the bridge of her nose stand out. Her boarding pass was on her lap.

I looked at my boarding pass, then glanced at a clock on the wall. I wasn't looking forward to saying goodbye to Anne. Since my father had died, seeing her had been the one damned thing I looked forward to every day.

Boarding had begun for my flight, and a line had formed at the gate. I would be sitting near the front of the coach section, and so would board last. When I turned back to Anne, her peculiar blue-gray eyes were studying me.

"Clay, I need to ask you something."

I nodded.

"And I don't want you to equivocate or dodge or go off into one of your tangents about bayonets or something."

"Sure." Where was this going? I wondered.

"And I don't want you to bring up some story about your father—may his memory be a blessing—or of your childhood in the orchards or your stint in the FBI at Wichita Falls."

"Okay."

"Because big things depend on you being absolutely candid." Her eyes shone with some secret amusement and maybe a little agitation, and then, for reasons unknown to me, tears welled in her eyes. A tear spilled over, and she dabbed it away with her fingers. "Big things. Do you understand, Clay?"

"Not at all."

She laughed lightly as she wiped away another tear.

"How can you laugh and cry at the same time?" I asked. "What's going on, Anne?"

The gate attendant called passengers in the middle rows. Travelers rose from their seats to head to the gate. My row would be called next. The flight to San Francisco would take ten hours. I wanted to say something to Anne about keeping in touch after we both returned to the States, but she was talking on and on about something.

"I took a risk a few minutes ago," she said, sniffing. "A huge risk. And I'm about to discover if I was right."

"How about getting to the point sometime before my flight leaves."

She reached over to touch my hand. She hesitated a long moment, and then she asked, "You love me, don't you, Clay?"

I looked away and inhaled swiftly, and then I glanced at the wall clock for something to do. I could feel the heat of her stare on the side of my face. My thoughts spun around, amounting to little.

She pressed my hand. "Tell me the truth, Clay."

My row was called by the gate attendant.

Again she pressed my hand. "Tell me."

"Yes," I whispered. Then a little more strongly, "Yes, I love you."

She laughed triumphantly and held up her boarding pass. "I changed my ticket a few minutes ago. I'm on your flight to San Francisco, and then to Portland and Medford. I'm even in the seats next to yours."

I finally managed to look at her again. Her hang-and-rattle grin was in place, but there was more than humor there, a lot more.

Anne said, "Come on, sweetie. It's time to go."

So I lifted her carry-on bag for her, and we walked down the boarding ramp together, and then found our seats, and she held my hand all the while. I still had Mrs. Hsu's good-luck jade piece in my pocket. The thing worked, that's for sure.

About the Author

James Thayer is the author of eleven previous books, including the gripping suspense novels *White Star*, *Five Past Midnight*, *Terminal Event*, and *Force 12*. An attorney, he lives in Seattle, Washington, with his wife and two daughters. He can be reached through his Web site, jamesthayer.com.